THE FOLK OF THE FRINGE

THE FOLK OF THE FRINGE

Orson Scott Card

A Legend Book
Published by Arrow Books Limited
20 Vauxhall Bridge Road, London SW1V 2SA

An imprint of Random Century Group

London Melbourne Sydney Auckland
Johannesburg and agencies throughout
the world

First published in the UK in 1990
by Legend an imprint of
Random Century
20 Vauxhall Bridge Road,
London SW1V 2SA

Legend edition 1991
© 1990 by Orson Scott Card

Printed and bound in Great Britain by
Cox & Wyman Ltd, Reading

ISBN 0 09 9734400

To Robert Stoddard:
For music together,
for journeys apart,
always searching for the narrow road.

The Stories of
The Folk of the Fringe

In America's future, when society has collapsed under
the weight of war, civilization lives on among those folk
whose bonds of faith or tribe or language are still
strong. These interweaving stories tell of people who
are far from the center of these tight-bound com-
munities, finding a life for themselves along the fringe.

the big cities and left whole states nothing but waste land. But Jamie Teague had been a ways northward in his travels, and heard stories from even farther north, and what he learned was this: After the bleeding was over, the survivors had land and tools enough to feed themselves. There was a life, if they could fend off the vagabonds and mobbers, and if the winter didn't kill them, and if they didn't get one of them diseases that was still mutating themselves here and there, and if they wasn't too close to a place where one of the bombs hit. There was enough. They could live.

Here, though, there just wasn't enough. The trees that once made this country beautiful were going fast, cut up for firewood, and bit by bit the folks here were either going to freeze or starve or kill each other off till the population was down. Things would get pretty ugly.

From some stories he heard, Jamie figured things were getting pretty ugly already.

Which is why he skirted his way around Greensboro to the north, keeping his eyes peeled so he saw most folks before they saw him. No, he saw *everybody* before they saw him, and made sure they never saw him at all. That's how a body stayed alive these days. Especially a traveling man, a walking man like him. In some places, being a stranger nowadays was the same as having a death sentence from which you might get an appeal but probably not. Being invisible except when he wanted to be seen had kept Jamie alive right through the worst times of the last five years, the whole world going to hell. He'd learned to walk through the woods so quiet he could pretty near pet the squirrels; and he was so good with throwing rocks that he never fired his rifle at all, not for food, anyway. A rock was all he needed for possum, coon, rabbit, squirrel, or porcupine, and anything bigger would be more meat than he could carry. A walking man can't take a deer along, and he can't stay in one place long enough to smoke it or jerk it or salt it or nothing. So Jamie just didn't look for bigger game. A

3

squirrel was meat enough for him. Wild berries and untended orchards and canned goods in abandoned houses did for the rest of his diet on the road.

Most of all a walking man can't afford to get lonely. You start to feeling like you just got to talk to some human face or you're going to bust, and then what happens? You greet some stranger and he blows your head off. You put in with some woodsy family and they slit your throat in the night and make spoons out of your bones and leather bags out of your skin and your muscle ends up in the smokehouse getting its final cure. It led to no good, wishing for company, so Jamie never did.

That's why he was setting by himself in a tree over the chainlink fence that marked the border of I-40 when he heard some folks singing, so loud he could hear them before he saw them. Singing, if you can believe it, right on the road, right on the *freeway*, which is the same as to say they were out of their minds. The idea of making noise while traveling on I-40 was so brazen that Jamie first thought they must be mobbers. But no, Winston and Greensboro had a right smart highway patrol on horseback, and these folks was coming *from* Winston heading west – no way could they be mobbers. They was just too dumb to live, that's all, normal citizens, refugees or something, people who still thought the world was safe for singing in.

When they came into sight, they were as weird a group as Jamie'd seen since the plague started. Right up front walked a big fat white woman looking like silage in a tent, and she was leading the others in some song. Two men, one white and one black, were each pulling wagons made of bicycles framed together with two-by-fours, loaded with stuff and covered with tarps. There was two black girls about eighteen maybe, and a blond white woman about thirty-five, and a half-dozen little white kids. Looked like a poster pleading for racial unity from back before the plague.

These days you just didn't see blacks and whites

together much. People looked out for their own. There wasn't a lot of race *hatred*, they just didn't have much to do with each other. Like Marine City, where Jamie was just coming back from. There was black Marine City and white Marine City. They all pretended to be part of the same town, but they had separate police and separate courts and you just didn't go into the other folks' part of town. You just didn't. It was pretty much that way anywhere Jamie went.

Yet here they were, black and white, walking along together like they were kin. Jamie knew right off that they couldn't have been traveling together for long – they acted like they still trusted each other, and didn't mind being together. That's how it was for the first few days of traveling in the same company, and how it was again after a few years. And seeing how careless they was, Jamie knew for a fact that they'd never live a week, let alone the years it'd take to get that long-time trust. Besides, thought Jamie, with a bitter taste in his mouth, some folks you can't trust no matter how long you're together, even if it's all your whole life.

The fat lady was singing loud, in between panting – no way was she getting enough breath – and the kids sang along, but the grown-ups didn't sing.

'Pioneer children sang as they walked and walked and walked and walked.'

The song went on like that, the same thing over and over. And when the fat lady stopped singing 'walked and walked,' some of the kids would smartmouth and keep going, 'walked and walked and walked and walked and walked and walked,' until Jamie was sure somebody'd give them a smack and tell them to shut up. But nobody did. The adults just kept going, paying no mind. Pulling their bicycle carts, or carrying packs.

Not one gun. Not one rifle or pistol, nothing at all.

This was a group of walking dead people, Jamie knew that as sure as he knew that the kids were all off pitch in their singing. They were coming to the last border of civilization between here and the Cherokee Reservation. They were going to sing their way right off the edge of the world.

Jamie didn't have any quarrel with himself about what to do. He didn't give no second thought to it. He just knew that their dying might be in his reach to stop, and so he reached out to stop it.

Or rather *stepped* out. He slung his rifle over his shoulder and slid out along the limb that hung over the chain-link fence, then dropped. He scooped up his pack and shrugged it on, then walked on down the embankment. Five years ago it was mowed nice and smooth all year. Now it was half grown with saplings, and it wasn't easy getting through it. By the time he reached the freeway they were a hundred yards on, still singing. A different song this time – 'Give said the little stream, give oh give, give oh give' – but it amounted to the same thing. He could hear them, but they hadn't even heard him rustling through the underbrush, noisy as can be.

'Good evening,' he said.

Now they stopped singing. Those carts stopped moving and the kids were scooped up and most of them were scrambling for the edge of the road before the sound of Jamie's voice had quit ringing in the air. At least they knew enough to be frightened, though by the time a mobber was talking to you, there was no way you could escape just by running. And not one of them had pulled out any kind of gun, even now.

'Hold on,' said Jamie. 'If I meant to kill you, you'd be dead already. I've been watching you for five minutes. And *hearing* you for ten.'

They stopped moving toward the shoulder.

'Besides, folks, you were running toward the median strip. That's like a chicken running from the farmer and jumping in the cookpot to hide.'

They all stayed where they were, except for the black man, who came back out to the middle of the westbound lane. The fat lady was still there, her hand resting on one of the bicycle carts. She didn't look frightened like the others, neither. She didn't look like she knew how to be scared.

Jamie went on talking, knowing how his easy relaxed voice would calm them down. 'See, the mobbers, when they set up to bushwhack folks, they never attack you from just one side. You run to the median strip, and you can count on finding even more of them down there waiting to catch you.'

'Seems you know a lot about mobbers,' said the black man.

'I'm alive and I'm on the road and I'm alone,' said Jamie. 'Of course I know about mobbers. The ones who didn't learn about them real fast are all dead. Like you folks.'

'We aren't dead,' said the fat woman.

'Well, now, I guess that's a matter of opinion,' said Jamie. 'You look dead to me. Oh, still walking, maybe. Still singing at the top of your voices. But forgive me if I'm wrong, I kept thinking you were singing, "Come and kill us, anybody, come and take away our stuff!" '

'We were singing "Give said the little stream," ' said one of the kids, a blond girl about ten years old maybe.

'What he means is we should've kept our mouths shut,' said one of the teenage black girls. The skinny one.

'Which is what *I* said back at the Kernersville exit,' said the one who looked like her bra was about to bust from pressure.

The black man shot them a glare. They looked disgusted, but they shut up.

'My name's Jamie Teague, and I thought I'd give you some advice that would keep you alive maybe five miles farther.'

'We're still safe enough here. We're in Winston.'

'You just passed the Silas Creek Parkway. The Winston Highway Patrol doesn't come out this far too often. And once you pass the 421 exit, they don't come out here at all.'

7

'But bushwhackers wouldn't be this close in to Winston, would they?' said the fat woman.

People were so dumb sometimes. 'What do you think, they wait out in the middle of the wilderness, hoping for some group of travelers who managed to fight off every other band of bushwhackers between here and there? The easy pickings all get picked close in to town. Didn't the highway patrol tell you that?'

The black man looked at the fat woman.

'No, they didn't,' he said.

'Well then,' said Jamie, 'I think you must've offended them somehow, cause they know the interchange at 421 is just about the most dangerous spot to walk through, and they let you head right for it.'

The fat woman's face went even uglier. 'No doubt they were *Christians*,' she said. She didn't spit, but she might as well have.

A sudden thought came to Jamie. 'Aren't you folks Christians?'

'We always thought we were,' said the white guy. He was still at the side of the road, his arm around the blond woman. He talked quiet, but he looked strong. It was almost a relief to have the white guy talk. It was weird to have a black man do most of the talking when a white man was in the group. Not that Jamie thought it *ought* to be the other way. He'd just never seen a group of both colors where a black man was the spokesman.

Now the black man interrupted. 'Thank you for your advice, Mr. – Teague, was it?'

'It wasn't advice. It was the facts. The only safe way out of town for a group your size, since you need a road for them bikes, is to go back to Silas Creek Parkway, go north to Country Club Road, and head west on that. You can hook onto 421 farther west, and it won't be so dangerous.'

'But we're going on I-40 all the way,' said the fat woman.

'All the way to hell, maybe. Where do you plan to

8

go?' asked Jamie.

'None of your business,' said the blond woman. Her voice snapped out like a whip. She was a suspicious one.

'Every overpass on the interstate is taken by one group of mobbers or another,' said Jamie. 'It's shelter for them, and easy to find their way back after raping and killing their way through the countryside. Even if every one of you had a machine gun and those carts were full of ammo, you'd be out of bullets before Hickory and dead before Morganton.'

'How do we know that's true?' asked the blond woman.

'Because I told you,' said Jamie. 'And I told you because it was plain you didn't know. Anybody who knows that stuff and still uses the freeway must *want* to die.'

There was a pause, just a bit of a second where nobody answered, and it came into Jamie's head that maybe they did. Maybe they actually kind of halfway hoped to die. These were definitely crazy people. But then, who wasn't, these days? Anybody still alive had seen terrible things, enough to push sanity right out of their heads. Jamie figured sanity was barely hanging on to most folks by their ears or hair, ready to drop off at the first sign of danger, leaving them all loony as –

'We don't want to die,' said the white man.

'Though the Lord may have his own private plans for us,' said the fat woman.

'Maybe so,' said Jamie. 'But I haven't seen the Lord doing many miracles lately.'

'Me neither,' said the blond woman. Oh, she was bitter.

'I've seen a lot of them,' said the white man, who must be her husband.

'Let me tell you about miracles,' said Jamie. He was enjoying this – he hadn't talked so much in ten days, not since he left Marine City, or Camp Lejeune, as they used to call it. And Jamie *was* a talker. 'If you folks keep

9

going the way you're going, the next ten miles will use up your whole lifetime quota of miracles, and you'll be killed by mile eleven.'

The black man was believing him now. 'So we go back to Silas Creek Parkway, head north to Country Club, and go on out of town that way?'

'I figure.'

'It's a trap,' said the blond woman. 'He's got a gang of mobbers on Country Club, and he wants to steer us that way to get bushwhacked!'

'Ma'am,' said Jamie, 'I suppose that's possible. But what's also possible is this.' Jamie unshouldered his gun and had it pointing right at the black man in a movement so fast nobody even twitched before he had the gun set to shoot. 'Bang,' said Jamie. Then he pointed the gun at each of the grown-ups in turn. 'Bang, bang, bang, bang,' he said. 'I don't need no gang.'

Jamie didn't expect their reaction. One of the children burst into tears. One of them was shaking. A couple of kids ran over and hid behind the fat woman. All of them had such a look of horror in their faces, staring at Jamie like they expected him to mow them all down, kids and all. The grown-ups were worse, if anything. They looked like they almost welcomed the gun, as if they expected it, like it was a relief that death was finally here. The black man closed his eyes, like he was expecting the bullet to be a lover's kiss.

Only the fat woman didn't get weird on him. 'Don't point a gun at us again, boy,' she said coldly. 'Not unless you mean to use it.'

'Sorry,' said Jamie. He shouldered the rifle again. 'I was just trying to show you how easy it is to –'

'We know how easy,' said the fat woman. 'And we're taking your advice. It was decent of you to warn us.'

'The Lord has seen your kindness,' said the black man, 'and he'll reward you for it.'

'Maybe so,' said Jamie, to be polite.

'Even if you do it unto the least of these my brethren,'

said the black man.

'Which is definitely us,' said the fat woman.

'Yeah, well, good luck, then.' Jamie turned his back on them and headed for the shoulder of the road.

'Wait a minute,' said the white man. 'Where you going?'

'That's none of our business,' said the black man. 'He doesn't have to tell us that.'

'I just thought if he was going west, like us, that maybe we could go along together.'

Jamie turned back to face him. 'No way,' he said.

'Why not?' asked the blond woman, as if she was offended.

Jamie didn't answer.

''Cause he thinks we're so dumb we'll get killed anyway,' said the white man, 'and he doesn't want to get killed along with us. Right?'

Jamie still didn't say anything, but that was an answer too.

'You know your way around here,' said the white guy. 'I thought maybe we could hire you to guide us. Partway, anyhow.'

Hire him! What money would they use? What coin was worth anything now? 'I don't think so,' said Jamie.

'Me neither,' said the fat woman.

'We don't trust in the arm of flesh,' said the black man, sounding pious. Was he their minister, then?

'Yeah, the Lord is our Shepherd,' said the fat woman. She *didn't* say it piously. The black man glared at her.

The white man gave it one more try. 'Well it occurs to me that maybe the Lord has shepherded us to meet this guy. He's got a gun and he's traveled a lot and he knows what he's doing, which is more than we can claim. We'd be stupid not to have him with us, if we can.'

'You can't,' said Jamie. Warning them was one thing. Dying with them was something else. He turned his back again and walked back into the scrub forest alongside the road.

He heard them behind him. 'Where'd he go? Like he just disappeared.'

Yeah, and that was with Jamie not even half trying to hide himself. These folks would never even see the bushwhackers that got them. City people.

Once he was up in the tall trees, though, he didn't just head out west on his own path. Without really deciding to, he climbed back into the same tree as before, to see what these people decided to do. Sure enough, they were turning their carts east.

Fine. Jamie was shut of them. He'd done what he could.

So why was he walking eastward, too, parallel to their path? The Lord is their shepherd, not me, thought Jamie. But he had some misgiving, some fear that he couldn't rightly name; and having taken *some* responsibility for them, he felt more.

They didn't even make it back to Silas Creek Parkway. There were twenty highway patrolmen, dismounted and guns at the ready. Jamie had never seen so many all in one place. Were they expecting an invasion of mobbers?

No. They were expecting this little group of travelers. This was what they had come for. Jamie couldn't hear what was said, but he got the message right enough, from the gestures, the attitudes, the gathering despair in the little group of refugees. The highway patrol wasn't letting them back into Winston, not even long enough to take the parkway north to Country Club and out. It made Jamie feel sick inside. He had no doubt that the patrol knew what I-40 was like, knew what would surely happen at the 421 interchange. The highway patrol was planning on having the mobbers do murder for them. For some reason, the highway patrol wanted these people dead. They had probably assembled there to go out and collect the bodies and make a report.

Some favor Jamie had done them. There had been some feeling of hope before as they sang; now the hope

12

was gone, there was no spring in the children's step. They knew now that they were heading for death, and they had seen the faces of the people who wanted them dead.

They had seen such faces before, though, Jamie was sure of it. The adults among them had not been shocked when Jamie pointed a gun at them, and they showed no anger now at the highway patrol. They were convinced already that they had no help, no friends, not from the civilized towns and certainly not from bushwhackers. No wonder the blond woman had been so suspicious of him.

But the white guy had shown some hope in the help of a stranger on the road. He had thought he could strike a deal with Jamie Teague. It made Jamie feel kind of good and kind of bad all at once, that the guy had found some hope in him. And so, as they headed west again, Jamie found himself paralleling them again, and this time going faster, getting ahead of them, crossing the freeway back and forth, as if he were scouting their path on either side.

I *am* scouting their path, he realized.

So it was that Jamie came to the 421 interchange, silently and carefully, moving through the thick woods. He spotted two bushwhacker lookouts, one of them asleep and the other one not very alert. And now he had to decide. Should he kill them? He could, easily enough – these two, anyway. And heaven knows bushwhackers probably did enough murder in a year to give them all the death penalty twice over. The real question in his mind was, do I want to get into a pitched battle with these bushwhackers, or is there another way? It wasn't like he was going to get any help from these people – not a weapon in the bunch, and not a fighter, probably, even if they had a gun. If there was any fighting, he'd have to do it all.

He didn't kill them. He didn't decide not to, he just decided he had time to go get a look at the bushwhacker town under the overpass and then come back and kill these two if need be.

The bushwhacker town was built on the westbound side of I-40, sheltered under the 421 crossover. It was like most he'd seen, made of old cars pushed together to make narrow streets, enough of them to stretch four car lengths beyond the overpass. Outdoor shade from cloths stretched between cars here and there, a few naked children running around shouting, some slovenly women cussing at them or cooking at a fire, and men lolling around sleeping or whittling or whatever, all with guns close to hand. A quick count put the fighting force here above twenty. There was no hope of Jamie taking them on by himself. By surprise he might kill even a half dozen – he was that good a shot, and that quick – but that'd still leave plenty to chase him down in the woods while others stayed and had their way with the refugees coming up the road. Jamie wasn't against killing scum like this, not in principle, but he did figure on its only being worth doing when you had a chance of winning.

Right then he should have just gone on, figuring there was nothing else he could do for them. They were just some more statistics, some more people killed by the destruction of society. The fall of civilization was bound to mash some people, and it wasn't his fault or his job to stop it.

Trouble was that these folks he had seen up close. These folks weren't just numbers. Weren't just the corpses he was always running across in abandoned farmhouses or old dead cars or out in the woods somewhere. They had faces. He had heard their children singing. He had bent them out of their path once, and it was his duty to find some way to do it again.

How did he know that? Nobody had ever told him any such duty. He just knew that this is what a decent person does – he helps if he can. And since he wanted so bad to be a decent person, even though he knew as sharp as ever that he was surely the most inhuman soul as ever walked the face of the earth, he turned around, snuck past the sleeping lookout again, and returned to the refugees before they even got back to the place where he first met them.

Not that he figured on joining up with them, not really. He might lead them west to the Blue Ridge, since he was going there anyway, but after that they'd be on their own. Go their separate ways. He'd have done his part and more by then, and it was none of his business what happened to them after that.

Tina held her peace. Didn't say a thing. But she thought things, oh yes, she told herself a sermon like Mother used to before she died – of a stroke, back before the world fell apart, thank heaven. It was Mother's voice in her head. No use getting mad about it. No use letting it eat your stomach out from the inside, give you colitis, make you do crazy things. No use yelling at those sanctimonious snot-faced highway patrolmen with their snappy uniforms and manure-spouting horses and shiny pistols at their belts. No use saying, You aren't any different than the filth who massacred babies on Pinetop Road. You think you're better cause you don't pull the trigger yourselves? That just means that besides being killers, you're cowards too.

No use saying any of that.

But Tina knew that everybody knew what she thought, even if she did hold her tongue. Long ago she discovered that all her bad feelings got written out in big bold letters on her face. Tender feelings not so much. Soft feelings, they were invisible. But let her feel the tiniest scrap of anger, and people would start shying away from her. 'Tina's on the warpath,' they'd say. 'Tina's mad, I hope not at me.' Sometimes she didn't like being so transparent, but this time she was glad. Because she saw how each one of those patrolmen

15

looked at her while their commander was telling his lies, how each one met her eyes and then looked away, looked at the ground, or even tried to look meaner and tougher, it all came to the same thing. They knew what they were doing.

And Tina capped it by turning her back on the commander while he was still explaining about how he doesn't make the ordinances, the city council does – she turned her back and walked away. Walked slow, because folks her size don't exactly scamper, but *walked* nonetheless. The little orphaned kids from her Primary, Scotty and Mick and Valerie and Cheri Ann, they turned and followed her at once, and when they went, so did the Cinn kids, Nat and Donna. And then their parents, Pete and Annalee; and then those two black girls from the Bennett Ward, Marie and Rona; and only then, when everybody else was walking west, only then did Brother Deaver give up trying to persuade that apprentice hitler to let them pass.

Tina felt guilty about that. To walk off and embarrass Brother Deaver like that. His authority was scanty enough as it was, being second counselor in a bishopric that didn't exist anymore, what with the bishop and the first counselor dead. No need for her to undermine it. But then she'd always had trouble supporting the priesthood. Not in her heart – she was always obedient and supportive. She just kept accidentally doing things that made the men look somewhat indecisive in comparison. Like this time. She hadn't really figured that anybody would follow her. She just couldn't stand it anymore herself, and the only way to show her contempt for the highway patrolmen was to turn away while they were talking. To leave while it was still her choice to leave, instead of when they got fed up and leveled their guns at them and frightened the children. It was the right time to leave, and if Brother Deaver didn't notice that, well, was it Tina's fault?

Her legs hurt. No, that was too vague. With every

16

step, her hip joints crackled, her ankles stabbed, her knees weakened, her soles stung, her arches sagged, her back twisted, her shoulders knotted tighter. Why, this is an honest-to-goodness exercise program, she realized, walking the twenty-five miles from the Guilford College Exit to the place we're going to die. I thought my muscles were in good shape from all that custodial work at the meetinghouse, all the waxing and washing and polishing and chair-moving and table-folding. I had no idea that walking twenty-five miles would make me feel like a mouse that got played with by a half-blind cat.

Tina stopped dead in the middle of the road.

Everybody else stopped, too.

'What's wrong?' asked Peter.

'You see something?' asked Rona.

'I'm tired,' said Tina. 'I ache all over, and I'm tired, and I want to rest.'

'But it's only three in the afternoon,' said Brother Deaver. 'We got three good hours of walking left.'

'You in some hurry to get to the 421 turnoff?' asked Tina.

'It might not be what that man said, you know,' said Annalee Cinn. She always had to take the contrary view; Tina didn't mind, she was used to it.

Besides, Peter had a way of contradicting her without making her mad – which was, Tina figured, why they got married. The world couldn't have handled Annalee Davenport unless somebody stood near her all the time to contradict her without making her mad.

'I thought so, too, honey,' said Peter, till that cop sent us back. *He* knows 421 is death to us.'

'The *real* number of the Beast,' said Rona. Tina winced. Whoever persuaded Rona to read Revelation ought to be . . .

'Now you know you didn't think he might be lying,' said Annalee. 'You wanted to have him join us.'

'Well I can see why he didn't,' said Tina. 'Everybody talks real sorry about what happened, but they all wish

17

the mobbers had finished the job so they didn't have all these leftover Mormons to worry about.'

'Don't call them mobbers,' said Brother Deaver. 'That makes them sound like outsiders. That's just what they want you to think – that nobody from Greensboro – '

'Don't talk about them at all,' said Donna Cinn. For an eleven-year-old, she was pretty plainspoken. No sirs and ma'ams from her. But she spoke plain sense.

'Donna's right,' said Tina. 'And so am I. We might as well rest here by the side of the road. I could use some setting time.'

'Me too,' said Scotty.

It was the voice of the youngest child that decided them. So it was they were sitting in the grass of the median strip, under the shade of a tulip tree, when Jamie came back.

'This isn't such a big tree,' said Annalee. 'Remember when they divided the First Ward into Guilford and Summit?'

It was a question that didn't need answering. There used to be so many Saints in Greensboro that the parking lot was completely full every Sunday. Now they could fit in the shade of a single tulip tree.

'There's still three hundred families in Bennett Ward,' said Rona.

Which was true. But it was a sore point to Tina all the same. The black part of town was just fine. Nobody was going to make *them* leave. Who would've thought, back when they formed a whole ward in the black part of town, that six years later it'd be the only congregation left in Greensboro, with most whites dead and all the white survivors gone off on a hopeless journey to Utah, taking along only a handful of blacks like Deaver himself. It was hard to know whether the blacks who stayed behind were the smartest or the most fearful and faithless; not for me to judge, anyway, Tina decided.

'They're in Bennett Ward,' said Brother Deaver. 'And we're here.'

'I know that,' said Rona.

Everybody knew that. They also knew what it meant. That the black Saints from Bennett Ward were going to stick it out in Greensboro; that out of all of them, only these two girls, for heaven only knew what reason, only Rona Harrison and Marie Speaks had volunteered to journey west. Tina hadn't decided whether this meant they were faithful or crazy. Or both. Tina well knew it was possible to be both.

Anyway, it was in the silence after Rona last spoke that they noticed Jamie Teague was standing there again. He'd come up from the south side of the road, and was standing there in plain sight, watching.

Pete jumped to his feet, and Brother Deaver was mad as hops. 'Don't go sneaking up on folks like that!'

'Hold your voice down,' said Teague softly.

Tina didn't like the way he always spoke so soft. Like a gangster. Like he didn't have to try to talk loud enough – it was *your* business to hear him.

'What did you come back for?' asked Annalee. Sounding hard and suspicious. I hope Teague doesn't think she really means that.

'I saw the patrol turn you away,' said Teague.

'That was an hour ago,' said Brother Deaver. 'More.'

'I also went ahead to see if maybe the mobbers at 421 weren't too much to fight through.'

'And?' asked Pete.

'More than twenty men, and who knows whether their women shoot, too.'

Tina could hear the others sigh, even though they didn't voice it; she could hear the breath go out of them like the air hissing out of a pop-top can. Twenty men. That was how many guns they'd have pointing at them. All these days, and we'll face the guns after all.

'So what I'm thinking is, do you plan to stay here till one of them wanders up here and finds you? Or what?'

Nobody had an answer, so nobody said anything.

'What I'm trying to figure,' said Teague, 'is whether

19

you folks want to die, or whether it's worth the trouble trying to help you get out of this alive?'

'And what I'm trying to figure is what difference it makes to you,' said Annalee.

'Shut your mouth, Annalee,' said Tina, gently. 'I want to know what you have in mind, Mr. Teague.'

'Well it isn't like you're in a car or anything, right? You don't have to wait for an exit to get off the freeway.'

'We do with these carts,' said Pete.

'Are those carts worth dying for?'

'All our food's on there,' said Brother Deaver.

'They come apart,' said Tina.

The others looked at her.

'My husband designed them so you could just take them apart,' she said. 'For fording rivers. He figured at least one bridge was bound to be out.'

'Your husband's a smart man,' said Teague. But there was a question in his eyes.

'My husband's dead,' said Tina. 'But we both knew from the first plagues that we'd end up making this trip, and without gasoline, either. I suppose most Mormons have thought some time or other that there'd come a time when they had to make their way to Utah.'

'Or Jackson County,' said Annalee.

'Somewhere,' said Tina. 'He figured the carts wouldn't be much good if we couldn't ford a river with them. Only in this case, I guess we're fording a freeway.'

'More like a portage around a rapids,' said Teague.

'I like that,' said Pete. 'These carts are boats, the freeway's a river, and the overpasses are waterfalls.'

'A metaphor,' said Brother Deaver. He was smiling. He always got some kind of thrill out of knowing a fancy name for things.

Just like that, and Teague had got them out of despair and into hoping again. Made them all wonder why nobody had thought of taking apart the carts and just walking into the woods. Maybe it was because they were city people who thought of freeways as things you

20

couldn't get off of except at places with an arrow and the word EXIT. But Tina thought it was probably because they all expected to die; some of them were maybe even disappointed they weren't already dead. Or not disappointed, exactly. Ashamed. Living just didn't have all that much attraction to them. Even the children. They weren't ready to walk on and greet death with hymns and rejoicing, but they might well have sat there waiting for death to stumble over them. Till Teague came back.

They moved the carts as far into the underbrush on the north side of the road as they could, then unloaded them and carried all the bundles up to the chain-link fence. Teague carried heavy wire-clippers with him – this wasn't his first time going through a fence, obviously – and he made them notice how he cut low. 'You got to crawl through,' he said, 'but then they can't see the cut from the road, and they're less likely to follow you.'

'You think they aim to follow us?' asked Marie, scared.

'Not the highway patrol,' said Teague. 'I don't think they care. But if the mobbers see a new break in the fence – '

'We'll crawl,' said Tina. And if she was willing to crawl through, nobody else could complain about it. But she had merely spoken what the others needed to hear, to get them moving, to keep them safe. The question of whether she herself was actually going to crawl through anything was still very much undecided.

Once the cart was unloaded, they carefully dismantled the two-by-four frames that bound each pair of bikes together. Teague wouldn't let them do it, though, till he had looked carefully at every lashpoint. Tina liked him better and better. He wasn't in such a hurry that he got himself into a mess. He took the time to make sure he could make things work right later on.

She also noticed that he did none of the unloading and carrying. Instead he watched constantly, looking up

21

and down the freeway and into the woods. One time he ran up the hill, skinnied under the chain-link fence, and climbed a tree fast as a squirrel. He was back down a minute later. 'False alarm,' he said.

'Story of my life,' said Pete.

'Pete's a fireman,' said Annalee.

'Was,' said Brother Deaver.

'I *am* a fireman,' said Pete. ''Till I die I'm a fireman.' He spoke fiercely.

Brother Deaver backed off. 'I meant no harm.'

Teague lost his temper for a second. 'I don't give a flying – '

He didn't finish, cause right then he caught Tina's eye and she looked at him just like a misbehaving child in Primary. She had a look that could tame the wildest brat. She used it on bishops and stake presidents too sometimes, and they calmed down even quicker than the kids.

Brother Deaver felt the need to say the obvious. 'I hope you'll continue to watch your language around the children.'

Teague never took his gaze from Tina's eyes. 'I know I'll sure as heck watch my language around *her*.'

'Tina Monk,' she said.

'*Sister* Monk,' said Brother Deaver.

'Tell those kids not to make a path up there,' said Teague. 'Walk in different places through that open grassy place.'

The bikes and two-by-fours got through fine. So did everybody except Teague and Tina. And there she stood, looking at that little bitty hole and feeling exactly how thick she was from front to back. How tired she was. How she wasn't in the mood to shinny through there with everybody watching. How she wasn't altogether sure she could do it without help. She imagined Brother Deaver or Pete Cinn grabbing two hands onto her wrists and pulling and pulling and finally collapsing in exhaustion. She shuddered.

'Well, go on,' she said to Teague. 'I'll come on later.'

Brother Deaver and Pete Cinn started to argue with her, but Annalee shut them up and made them pull stuff over the crest of the hill.

'Sister Monk,' said Annalee, 'we aren't going nowhere without you, so you might as well make up your mind and get through there.'

'The only way I'll get through is if you cut that fence from top to bottom and I walk through,' she said.

'Can't do that,' said Teague. 'Might as well put up a flashing neon sign.'

'Good-bye and God bless you all,' said Tina. She started walking down the hill.

Teague fell in step right beside her. 'Maybe you're a dumb lady, after all, ma'am, and that's fine with me. But when I scared those little ones, it was you they went to.'

'I can't shimmy under that fence, not uphill,' she said.

'You're about wore out, I guess,' said Teague.

'I'm about a hundred and fifty pounds too heavy, is what.'

'I'll push you.'

'If you lay a hand on me I'll break it off.'

He laid his hand on her shoulder. 'OK, I've touched it. Skin with a lot of fat under it. So what. Get up there and I'll push you under the fence.'

She shuddered at the touch of his hand, but she also knew he was right. There were lots of reasons to die, but dying because you couldn't stand the humiliation of some man pushing his hands into your fat and pushing you up a hill – that wasn't a good enough reason.

'If you get a hernia, don't expect me to knit you a truss,' she said.

Back at the fence, she made Annalee go up the hill. 'You keep everybody on that side. I don't want anybody watching this.'

Tina noted with satisfaction that Annalee may be contrary sometimes, but not when it counts. As soon as she was on her way up the slope, Tina sat down with her back toward the fence, then lay down.

'On your stomach,' said Teague.

'I plan to dig in with my heels.'

'And then how do I push you without giving offense, ma'am? Crawl through and grab saplings on the other side.'

She rolled over. He immediately shoved his hands into her thighs and started pushing. It was a hard shove he had – the boy was strong. And it didn't feel humiliating. It felt plain irresistible. He was moving her at a good clip without her even helping. And uphill, too.

'Maybe I've been losing weight,' she panted. With all her weight on her lungs, she didn't have much breath.

'Shut up, ma'am, and grab onto something.'

She shut up and grabbed a sapling and pulled. With all her strength, sliding herself forward, feeling him pressing upward on her thighs, feeling the grass tear loose under her breasts and belly, the dirt slide into her clothes, the chain-link pushing down on her back. Her arms had never pulled so hard in her life. She could hardly breathe.

'You're through.'

So she was. Covered with dirt and sweat from neck to knees, but through the fence. She got up onto all fours, then rolled over to a sitting position, feeling, as always, like a rotating planet. She sat there to rest for a moment. While she did, Teague rolled the cut flap of chain-link back down and tied one corner of the bottom in place with a short piece of twine he took out of his pocket.

'Let's go,' he said. He held out a hand. She took it, and he pulled her to her feet. Then he stood there, holding her wrist, looking at her face. 'I don't want you carrying anything. I don't want you so much as holding hands with a little kid who gets tired.'

'I'll pull my weight,' she said.

'And nothing else,' he said. 'From the look of you, I'd say you're ten miles from a heart attack.'

'Stroke,' she said. 'In my family, it's strokes.'

'I mean it,' Teague insisted. 'And if you get tired, you make everybody stop and rest.'

'I'm not going to slow them down just because I'm –'

'Fat,' he said.

'Right,' she said.

'I'll tell you, ma'am. They need you, and they need you alive. You pull nothing, you carry nothing, you drink whenever you're thirsty, and you rest whenever you're tired.'

'And I tell you that I'm in better shape than you think. I was custodian at the church, I worked my body all day every day, and furthermore I never smoked a single cigarette or drank a drop of liquor from the day I was born.'

'You're telling me why you ain't dead already,' said Teague. 'I'm telling you how not to be dead tomorrow. You watch. You stay alive on this trip of yours, you'll thin out.'

'Don't tell me what to do.'

'Walk up this hill.'

She turned around and started walking up. Briskly, to show him she could do it. Ten paces later, her right leg just gave out. Gave right out, and she stumbled and fell on her face. Not a bad fall, since she was going uphill anyway. He helped her up, and she let him half-pull her the rest of the way. It was plain that she had used herself up, at least for one day. They made their camp right there on the far side of the hill, just a hundred yards farther on than the gap where they came through. Teague wouldn't let them light a fire, and he spent most of the time till dusk scouting around or climbing trees and looking.

It was a warm night, so they slept right there in the woods on the far side of the hill, out of sight of the road, out of sight of everything. Yet they could hear, not all that far off, the crackling of a fire and folks laughing and talking. Couldn't make out the words, but they were having fun.

'Mobbers?' whispered Pete.

'Barbecue,' said Teague.

Citizens of Winston. Protected by the law. A couple of miles away, mobbers hoping to kill and strip passersby. And in between them, quiet, listening, Tina Monk, breathing heavily, the pain in her unaccustomed muscles making it impossible to sleep, her weariness making it unbearable to be awake. Laughter. Pleasant company. Someone had all those things tonight, all those things that come with peace. How dare they have peace, when their highway patrolmen sent a dozen souls to what they thought was certain death? You are responsible, you laughers, you friends and lovers, you are the ones in whose name those stolid killers acted. You.

Then she slept and dreamed of crawling through tight places. Cramming her bulk into a narrow shaft, her clothing climbing up her body as she thrust herself farther in, farther, until she could put the cover on. Then lying there in the heat, the close air, hearing shooting, the sound of it echoing, amplified through the air-conditioning system; and screams. Every bullet meant for kin of hers. Brothers and sisters, all of them, screaming in pain and terror while Tina Monk, building custodian, Primary president, choir leader, cowered in the air-conditioning system trying to keep her breathing soft enough that no one would find her. They shot her husband at the top of the stairs down into the furnace room. When she finally opened the door, it was Tom's body she had to shove out of the way in order to open it, Tom's blood that made prints of her shoes as she walked up the stairs. His sweet and patient face, she saw it now in her mind as she slept her dark unquiet sleep.

Herman Deaver knew that he had no authority. Bishop Coward could say he was in charge, as the only high

26

priest in the group, but it wasn't spiritual leadership they needed. This wasn't a prophetic journey; there was no Lehi to wake up with dreams that told them where to go; there was no divine gift of a liahona with pointers on it to show the way. There wasn't even a trace of manna on the ground in the morning, just dew soaking them, making the morning stiff and clinging and miserable.

I can explain, very clearly, how Shakespeare's Hamlet is in fact not contemplating suicide in the 'To Be or Not to Be' soliloquy, but rather deciding whether to endure suffering as a Christian or take vengeful action. What Herman Deaver could not explain, to himself or anyone else, was why he, a high priest, a temple-going Saint, a professor of literature, why he was so terribly sorry to be alive. I apologize. My mistake. An oversight. An error of scheduling. If only you had sent a reminder. To be or not to be was not the question at all. Hamlet did not care about vengeance or justice. What he wanted was his father back. Good intentions – but he took away his friend Laertes' father instead. Now we're alike, eh what? Even steven. Get up, Deaver. Set an example, even if you aren't the leader. You're the chaplain now, that's what you are, so at least keep morale up by being perky and chipper and energetic. Ignore that pain from your burning prostate. It isn't agony yet. Not till you take the first leak of the day.

'The boys' lavatory is that stand of bushes over there,' said Sister Monk.

Since his eyes were closed, Deaver didn't know if she meant him or not. But he took it as if she did, and struggled to his feet, squinting to see as the first sunlight slanted through the branches. It burned, it burned, it burned; the sunlight, his prostate, the urine tearing at him as it passed out of his body and sizzled on last year's leaves. When I was young I never thought it would be such agony to do this. I never thought at all. I can feel all my bones.

This much courtesy they still had: they didn't start the meeting till he was back. Or perhaps they hadn't noticed yet that he wasn't in charge. That Peter, so young and strong, that he was more listened to; that Tina Monk, always forceful and now more so than ever, that she now made decisions in her simple forthright way. Perhaps they thought of this as 'giving counsel.' But the decision was made before he spoke. He didn't mind this. He welcomed it. Decisions were not his strong suit. Teaching was his strong suit. They could make decisions; then he would explain to them why it was a good idea. That's the skill of the scholarly critic. Explaining after the fact why somebody was great, who everybody already agrees was great. The metaphor of the freeway as river, with portages around the rapids, that was far easier for him to comprehend than the way this gentile, Teague, made sense of what he saw when he stared at the uninterrupted wall of forest green.

'We need you,' Pete was saying. 'We got no right to ask it, but we need you to guide us or we'll never get there.'

'Get where?' Ah, a sensible question. Of course Teague goes straight to the point. Get where? To heaven, to the celestial glory, Jamie Teague. To life eternal, where we will know the only true God, and Jesus Christ, whom he has sent.

'To Utah,' said Tina. Oh yes. The *immediate* destination. The *short-term* destination. How far-sighted of me. Over-sighted.

'You're crazy,' said Teague.

'Probably,' said Tina.

'Not really,' said Pete. 'Where else can people like us go?'

'That's two thousand miles away. For all you know, all kinds of bombs landed there. It might be hot as D.C.'

'There was still radio for a while. Utah wasn't hit bad.'

'Or wiped out by plague.'

'There'll be something,' said Pete.

28

'You, hope.'

'We *know*.' Pete grinned. 'We may not look like much to you, but out there Mormons are in charge. I promise you that wherever there's four Mormons, there'll be a government. A president, two counselors, and somebody to bring refreshments.'

Deaver laughed. He remembered that jokes like that were funny. Some others joined in. Mostly children who didn't get the joke, but that was good. It was good for the children to laugh.

Deaver couldn't help but be hurt, though, when Teague looked for confirmation, not to him, but to Sister Monk.

'It's true,' she said. 'We've been preparing for this for years. We knew it was coming. We tried to warn everybody. Put no trust in the arm of flesh. Your weapons will mean nothing. Only trust in the Lord, and he will save you.'

'How's he been doing so far for you folks?' asked Teague.

It was a bitter and terrible question, so Deaver knew that he was the only one who could answer it. 'You understand that the promise refers to large groups. America as a whole. The Church as a whole. Many individuals will suffer and die.'

Teague only now seemed to realize that he had maybe given offense. 'I'm sorry,' he said.

'It's a natural question,' said Deaver. 'In the Book of Mormon, the prophets Alma and Amulek were forced to watch as their enemies threw whole families of the faithful into a fire and burned them alive. Why doesn't God reach out and save these people, Amulek asked. And Alma said, Death tastes sweet to them; why should the Lord prevent it? But the wicked must be allowed to do their wickedness, so that everyone will know that their terrible punishment is just. Then Amulek said, Maybe they'll kill us, too. And Alma said, If they do, then we'll die. But I think the Lord won't allow it. Our work is not yet done.'

Deaver could feel their eyes on him, could hear how their breathing had become quiet. The children especially, they listened to him, they watched his lips as he spoke. He knew that they understood what the story meant to them. Our work is not yet done, that's why we're alive.

But don't ask me what our work *is*. Don't ask me what we're supposed to accomplish, if by some miracle we survive a two-thousand-mile journey through hell until we reach the kingdom of God in the mountains.

Teague did not break the silence; Deaver knew from that that he was a sensitive man, despite his youth, despite the fact that he was a gentile. For the first time it occurred to him that Teague might even be a potential convert. Wouldn't that be a miracle, to baptize a new member here in the wilderness!

'The Church will be strong in Utah,' said Tina Monk. 'And you can bet we won't be much safer anywhere else than we were in Greensboro and Winston.'

'You're Mormons, right?' said Teague.

'You mean you only just now guessed that?' said Annalee. She was always disrespectful and sharp-tongued. Deaver heard that marriage had mellowed her. He was grateful he never knew her before.

'You never said right out,' said Teague.

'Does it make a difference?' asked Deaver. Will you not help us, now that you know we are – what is the term? – the cult of the anti-Christ? The secret worshipers of Satan? Secular Humanists masquerading as Christians in order to seduce impressionable young people and lead them into unspeakable abominations?

'It does if you're going to Utah,' said Teague.

'I-40 to Memphis,' said Pete. 'Then up to St. Louis and I-70 to Denver. After that, who knows? They might even have trains running, or buses.'

'Or a weekly space shuttle flight,' said Teague.

'Don't underestimate the resourcefulness of the Mormon people,' said Deaver.

'Don't underestimate how much trouble a few nukes, some biological warfare, and the collapse of civilization can cause,' said Teague. 'Not to mention how the climate's changed. How do you know Utah isn't buried under glaciers?'

'They don't form that fast,' said Pete.

'Two thousand miles,' said Teague. 'With winters colder and longer now than they used to be – how far you think you'll get before September?'

'We didn't expect to do it in one year,' said Deaver.

'We need you,' said Pete. 'We'll hire you.'

Teague laughed. 'And pay me what?'

'A house and a job in Utah,' said Pete.

'You can guarantee that?' said Teague. 'You guarantee that I'll have a little plot of ground? A house with hot and cold running water? A nice little job to go to? Eight to five? What about location – I don't want to have to commute more than fifteen minutes to – '

'Shut up,' said Tina.

Teague shut up.

'We can promise you that there's peace in the mountains of Utah. We can promise you that if you lead us there, you'll be rewarded as best they can. We can promise you that in Utah, you can reap what you plant, you can keep what you make, you can count on being as safe tomorrow as you are today. Where else in all this world are those things true?'

'I'm not about to become a Mormon,' said Teague.

'No one expects it,' said Sister Monk.

'They'll just expect you to be a good man,' said Deaver.

'Then forget it,' said Teague.

'A *good* man,' said Deaver. 'Not a perfect one.'

'How bad can a man be and still be good?'

'You have to be good enough to take a helpless group like us two thousand miles, with no promise of payment beyond our word.'

Deaver saw, with satisfaction, that Teague was being

won over. He halfway suspected that Teague *wanted* to be won over. After all, he had already invested a lot of time and effort in helping them get off the freeway. He was risking a lot, too – if the highway patrol caught them here, they'd no doubt be in trouble. And the fact that there wasn't any shooting last night – the patrol might well notice that and come looking for them.

Maybe Teague thought of that at the same time, because he stood up suddenly. 'I'll think about it. But for now we've got to get moving. It'll be slow going for a while, till we can put the carts back together on a road. Put the heaviest stuff on bikes. I hope those things have airless tires.'

'Of course,' said Tina. 'My husband never considered anything else. What good would bikes be on a cross-country trip, if they're always going flat?'

'The little kids will carry the two-by-fours.'

Annalee started to protest. 'They're too heavy for – '

'They'll rest a lot,' said Teague. 'We're going to do this all in one trip. Grown-ups will be carrying a lot more.'

It turned out that Scotty, Mick, Cheri Ann, and Valerie could only handle four of the two-by-fours, but Pete thought of using the others to make a kind of sedan chair, which he and Deaver bore on their shoulders, with a much heavier burden on the two-by-fours between them than they could possibly have carried on their backs.

Sister Monk started to pick up a bundle of dried food.

'Put it down,' said Teague.

'It's light,' said Sister Monk.

Teague didn't say another word. Just stared at her, and she stared back. To Deaver's surprise, it was Sister Monk who gave in. He'd never seen such a thing in all his years in the Church. Sister Monk backed down to no man, or woman either. But she backed down to this Jamie Teague.

It was the first time Deaver realized what Teague must have seen right off – that Sister Monk wasn't doing so well, physically speaking. Deaver was so used to her being fat, and having that mean nothing as far as her being a hard worker in the Church, that it didn't occur to him that this journey was different. But now that Teague's insistence on her carrying nothing had brought the matter to Deaver's attention, he could see how flushed and weak she looked, how her walk was none too steady even in the morning after a night of sleep. For the first time it occurred to Deaver that she might not make it through the trip.

It made him angry, to realize how much he had unconsciously been depending on this woman. Wasn't he the one with the authority? Wasn't he supposed to lead? Yet *he* was depending on *her*. Well, he wouldn't, that's all. Nobody's indispensable. If we can get along without –

No, he wouldn't start listing the indispensable people who were dead, bulldozed into the mass grave in the parking lot of the stake center on Pinetop Road. There was no point in a census now. They were gone, and this meager handful of Saints was still alive. That meant that the Church was still alive, and would go on, sustained by faith and the Lord and, with any luck, this stranger who came out of nowhere offering help unasked. An angel would have been more useful, but if this Jamie Teague was all the Lord had to offer in the way of help, he'd have to do. If it was, in fact, the Lord who sent him.

They made it in one trip. One long trip, with frequent stops. Teague wasn't actually with them most of the way. He ranged ahead, leaving south and returning from the north. Sister Monk actually led them spotting the marks Teague had made on tree trunks, showing which way to go. At the end of the day they were back on the road. U.S. 421 this time, a two-lane expressway, with the overpass some miles behind them. Exhausted as they were, Teague made them rebuild the carts before they gnawed on their jerky and went to sleep. 'You'll want to be under way at dawn,' he said. 'Not sitting around in the open building carts. That was just one overpass.'

So they rebuilt the carts, and he finally let them build a very small fire so they could boil up some soup and give the children a decent meal. Hungry as they were, the kids could hardly keep their eyes open long enough to eat. And when they were asleep, Teague laid out his conditions for traveling with them.

'I'm not good enough to take you two thousand miles,' he said, looking Deaver in the eye. 'I only promise to take you as far as the Great Smokies. I haven't traveled west of there anyway, only between the mountains and the sea, so I don't know any more about the country than you do. But I've got a cabin there that's good for the winter. It's where I live. I know my neighbors there, I've got trade goods from my traveling to buy food, and we've kept it free of mobbers. It's as much as I can promise, but I think I can teach you a few things along the way, give you a better chance next spring.'

'If that's as far as you go with us,' said Pete, 'then we can't pay you anything at all. We got nothing you need, until we get to Utah.'

Teague pulled up a tuft of grass, started splitting the blades up the middle, one by one. 'You got something I need.'

'What is it?' demanded Annalee.

Teague looked at her coldly.

Deaver offered an explanation. 'Maybe we're people he thinks are going to die if he doesn't help us. Maybe he needs not to see us dead.'

Deaver saw Teague's expression change again. An unreadable look, hiding some strange unnameable emotion. Am I right? Is Teague's motive altruistic? Or is there something else, so shameful Teague can't hardly admit it? Does he plan to betray us at some terrible

34

time? Never mind. If the Lord means us to thrive, he'll protect us from such treason. And if he doesn't, I'd rather die by trusting a man who may not be as good as he seems than by being so suspicious I refuse a true friend.

Sister Monk changed the subject. 'You by yourself, Jamie Teague, you can generally avoid trouble, I imagine. You can pretty much be invisible out in the woods, and stay off the roads. But with us, trouble's *going* to come. We'll be on the roads most of the time, too many of us and too clumsy to hide. Somebody's going to spot us.'

'Might be', said Teague.

'You got the gun, Jamie Teague. But do you figure you can kill a man with it?'

'Reckon so,' said Teague.

A pause.

'*Have* you ever killed anybody?' asked Pete. There was awe in his voice, as if having killed somebody was a magical act that would endow this stranger with supernatural power.

'Reckon so,' said Teague.

'I don't believe it,' snapped Annalee.

'We want him as a guide anyway,' said Deaver, 'not a soldier.'

'Where we're going I don't think there's a difference,' said Sister Monk. 'You're an English professor. Pete's a fireman, trained to save lives, to risk his own life – but none of us has ever killed anybody, I think.'

'Wish I had,' murmured Pete.

Sister Monk ignored him. 'And what if the only way to save us was to sneak up on somebody and kill them. From behind, without even giving them a fair chance. Could you do that, Jamie Teague?'

Teague nodded.

'How do we know that?' said Annalee.

Teague waved her off with a gesture of impatience. 'I killed my mother and father,' he said. 'I can kill anybody.'

'My God,' said Rona Harrison.

35

Deaver turned to snap at the girl about not taking the name of the Lord in vain. But then it occurred to him that with Teague confessing to patricide, saying 'My God' seemed pretty tame by comparison.

'Well now,' said Pete.

'Isn't that what you wanted to hear?' asked Teague. 'Didn't you want to know whether I was bloodthirsty enough to do the killing you need done to save your lives? Don't you want to know that your hired soldier has references?'

'I wasn't trying to pry into things you don't want to talk about,' said Sister Monk.

'They deserved it,' said Teague. 'The court gave me a suspended sentence because everybody agreed they deserved it.'

'Did they abuse you?' asked Annalee. Finally she was curious instead of suspicious. A mind like a grocery store newspaper, thought Deaver.

'Annalee,' said Sister Monk sharply. 'We've all stepped too far.'

'I've answered the question you need to know,' said Teague. 'I can kill when I need to. But *I* decide when I need to. I give orders, I don't take them. That clear? If I tell you to get off the road, you get – no arguments. Right? Cause I don't aim to stick around and kill all comers just cause you aren't willing to do what it takes to avoid a fight.'

'Brother Teague,' said Deaver. He pretended not to notice how startled Teague was to be addressed as *Brother*. 'We will gladly accept your authority about how and when to travel, and on what path. And I assure you that it is the desire of our hearts to kill no one, to harm no one, to leave things undisturbed wherever we go.'

'I don't want you killing anybody for *me* anyhow,' said Marie Speaks.

Everybody looked at her – she'd been talking like a teenager so long that nobody expected her to have an opinion on something serious like this.

'I die myself first, you got that?'

'You crazy,' said Rona. 'You lost your mind, girl.'

'Killing a bushwhacker isn't murder,' said Pete.

'Neither is killing a Mormon,' said Marie. 'So I hear.' Then she got up and walked over to where the little ones were sleeping.

'She's crazy,' said Rona.

'She's Christian,' said Deaver.

'So am I,' said Pete, 'but I know there's times when the Lord lets good people fight back. Think of Captain Moroni and the title of liberty. Think of Helaman and the two thousand young men.'

'Think about sleeping,' said Teague. 'I'm not taking first watch tonight, I'm too tired.'

'Me,' said Pete.

'No, me,' said Deaver.

'You, Mr. Deaver,' said Teague. 'Your timepiece there still work, or is it on your wrist from nostalgia?'

'It's solar,' said Deaver. 'It works fine.'

'Watch till midnight. Then wake Pete. Pete, you wake me at three.'

Then Teague got up and went to the bushes they had designated as the boys' lavatory that night.

'Murder's the unforgivable sin,' said Annalee. 'I don't want a murderer telling us what to do.'

'Judge not lest ye be judged,' said Deaver. 'Let him or her who is without sin cast the first stone.'

That was the end of the discussion, as Deaver knew it would be. There wasn't a one of them who didn't feel guilty for one reason or another. For just being alive with so many others dead, if nothing else. Maybe Marie had learned the right lesson from it after all. Maybe killing was never worth it.

But Deaver heard the people breathing around him, he looked and watched the children's chests rising and falling with each breath, and then he imagined somebody coming and raising a knife to them, or pointing a

gun at them. That's not the same thing as somebody
raising a weapon against me personally. I might have
the courage to let the blow fall and not defend myself.
But there's not a chance in the world that I'd let them
harm a hair on those children's heads. I'd blast the
bushwhackers to hell and back if I thought they'd harm
the children. Now maybe that's murderousness, maybe
that's a secret lust for blood in my heart. But I don't
think so. I think that's the indignation of God. I think
that's what Christ felt when he said it was better to tie a
millstone around your neck and jump into the sea than
to raise your hand to harm a child.

Teague killed his mama and his daddy. That was a
hard one. Not mine to judge. But I'll be watching that
boy differently now. Watching real close. We didn't
escape one band of murderers just to fall in with a
worse one now. Bad enough to kill strangers because
you don't like their religion. But to kill your own mama
and daddy.

Deaver shuddered, and stared into the darkness
beyond the flickering firelight.

The fifth day after Teague joined them, they were heading
toward Wilkesboro. Travel was getting into a regular
rhythm now, and nobody was half as sore as they were
the third day. And it wasn't so scary anymore. A few
times Teague had come rushing back from scouting
ahead and made them get off the road, but this wasn't
freeway now and most times they could run the bikes
up behind some bushes without dismantling the carts.
The only portage was crossing I-77. Mostly it was just
walking, one foot after the other.

One of those times in hiding, Rona made Marie peek
through the bushes and watch the horsemen going by.
They looked like a rough crew, and to Marie it looked
like one of them had three human heads hanging from
his saddle. Three black human heads, and it made her

shudder.

'Canteens,' Teague said, but Marie knew better. She knew lots of things folks didn't think she knew. So now, on the afternoon of the fifth day out of Winston, when Marie was feeling hot and tired and wanted a little entertainment, she got a meanness on her and started doing a number on Rona.

'You got your eye on him,' said Marie.

'Do not,' said Rona. She sounded outraged. This was working fine.

'You say his name in your sleep.'

'Nightmares is what.'

'You were thinking of him just now when you smiled.'

'Was not. And I didn't smile.'

'Then how do you know who I'm talking about?'

'You're a queen bitch, that's what you are,' said Rona.

'Don't you talk to me with words like that,' said Marie. She was the one supposed to be needling, not the other way around.

'Stop acting like a bitch and people won't call you one,' said Rona.

'At least I don't get the hots for murderers,' said Marie. That got her back.

'He isn't.'

'Said he was himself.'

'He had good reason.'

'Oh yeah?'

'They used to torture him.'

'He say that?'

'I know it.'

'Murder is the unforgivable sin,' said Marie. 'He'll be in hell forever, so you just don't even bother thinking about marrying him!'

'Shut your mouth! I'm not thinking about marrying him!'

'And he's white and he's not a Mormon and he'll never never never take you to the temple.'

'Maybe I don't care.'

'If you don't care about the temple, why are you going to Utah?'

Rona looked at her strangely. 'Well it ain't to go to the *temple*.'

Marie didn't know what to make of that, and didn't want to find out what Rona meant. But the meanness wasn't gone out of her yet. So she turned back to the old topic. 'He's going to hell no matter what.'

'No he's *not*!' And Rona gave Marie a shove that nearly knocked her on her butt.

'Hey!'

'What's going on here!' It was Brother Deaver, of course. None of the white folks ever told them off about anything. 'Haven't we got things bad enough without you two tailing into each other?'

'I didn't tail into *her*,' said Marie.

'Saying he was going to hell!'

Marie felt Brother Deaver's hand on the back of her neck. 'The Lord is the judge of men's souls,' he said softly.

Marie squirmed to get free of his grasp. She was eighteen now, not some kid that grown-ups could grab onto whenever they wanted.

'So if you can't keep your heart free of condemnation, Marie, I think you'd better learn to keep your mouth shut. Do you understand me, girl?'

She finally broke free. 'You got no right to tell a black girl what to do!' she said – loudly now, so that others farther back could hear. 'You just teach your own white kids and leave me alone!'

It was a terrible thing to say, she knew it and she was sorry. But it also got him to shut up and leave her alone, which was what she wanted, wasn't it? Besides, he *did* marry a white woman, which was the same thing as saying black women were trash. Well, see what it got him – all of them shot dead along with all the other white Mormons, while he was at A&T, where the white

40

Christian Soldiers didn't dare to go. That's the only reason he wanted her to forgive Teague for being a murderer – because he felt like a murderer, too, him being alive because he was black, while his wife and kids were shot down and bulldozed into a parking lot grave. He wanted everybody to be nice and forgiving. Well she knew the law of heaven, didn't she? She wasn't just a Sunday School Mormon, she studied the doctrine and read all the time, and she knew that Christ's atonement had no force over them as murdered. Though truth to tell, his face looked stricken like he was about to die, and just from her cruel hard words against him. She might even have apologized on the spot, except that right then they heard horses' hoofs and all hell broke loose.

The mobbers came up a side road, just sauntering like they didn't expect trouble. Must have come up since Teague passed that road in his scouting. There was only two of them, and for a minute Marie hoped they'd think this group was too much for them. But the mobbers sized them up quick and didn't even pause a minute. They had guns out before they got to 421.

'We don't mean you no harm,' Brother Deaver said, or started to say, anyway, when the one mobber got off his horse and whipped him across the face with his pistol, knocking him down.

'That's *our* speech,' said the mobber, 'and we do all the talking, got it? Everybody lie down – on your bellies.'

'Look at what they got in the way of women, Zack, if that ain't pitiful.'

'That blond one – '

'Keep your hands off her,' said Pete. He started to get up. The taller one with the long beard gave him a kick that looked like it might tear his head off.

'She's dessert,' said the tall one. 'We got dark meat for dinner.'

Marie thought she was already as scared as she could

41

be, but now when the cold barrel of a shotgun was pressed against her forehead, pressing down real heavy, she tasted terror for the first time in her life.

'Please,' whispered Rona.

'Now you just hold still while I get this off you, honey, and open wide for papa, or Zack's gonna blow your girlfriend's head clean off.'

'I'm a good girl!' Rona whined.

'I'll make you even better,' said the long-bearded man.

'No!' Rona screamed.

Marie felt the painful motion of the gun as Zack drew a charge into the chamber. 'Don't fight with them, Rona,' said Marie. She knew it was a cowardly thing to say, but Rona didn't have the gun at her head.

'You little kids best close your eyes,' said Zack. 'Wouldn't want you finding out the facts of life too young.'

Marie could hear the other one set down his shotgun and start unzipping himself, mumbling to himself about how if she gave him a disease he'd hang her head from his saddle, which told Marie that she *did* see what she thought she saw. It made her gag all over again.

'Hold still,' said Zack, 'or it won't go so nice for you when I – '

Suddenly the gun barrel jammed sharp into her head as Zack slumped on it; not even a second later she heard the crack of a gun going off not far away. Zack's shirt blossomed open and spattered blood; Marie grabbed the shotgun barrel and tore it away from her face.

The other mobber muttered something and fumbled for his gun, but then another cracking sound and he was down, too.

'Teague!' Marie shouted. She got to her feet, her head bleeding. Everybody was getting up. Pete had Zack's shotgun in a second and pointed it at the two mobbers – but they were stone dead, each killed with one shot.

'Catch the horses!' Teague was shouting that. And he was right, had to catch the horses, they could pull the

42

carts, they could carry stuff, had to catch them, but Marie couldn't find them, not with blood pouring down into her eyes –

'Marie honey, here, are you all right?' Sister Monk was dabbing at her with a cloth. It stung like hell.

'Did he shoot Marie?' It was one of the little boys.

'Just jammed his gun in her head when he was dying is all – Donna Cinn, you get the little ones back to the side of the road.' Sister Monk taking charge as usual. And as usual everybody hopped to do it. Only this time Marie didn't mind at all, didn't mind those big old hands dabbing at the blood on her face.

Then she noticed Rona making a grunting noise, and she turned to look. Brother Deaver was tugging at Rona's sleeve, but Rona wouldn't quit stomping her foot down on the bearded mobber's face. It wasn't even human anymore, but she kept stomping and now the skull broke through and her shoe sank down in a ways.

Now Teague came up, leading one horse. He handed the reins to Deaver, stepped astride the dead man's body, and took Rona in his arms and just held her, saying, 'You're OK, you're OK now, you're safe.'

'Took you damn long enough,' said Pete. He had the other horse, and he sounded more scared than mad.

'Came as soon as I heard the horses. Had to make sure it was only the two before I started shooting. Rona, I'm sorry, I'm sorry you got so scared, I'm sorry he treated you so bad, but I had to wait until he set his gun down, don't you see.'

'It's OK, he didn't do nothing,' said Annalee.

Rona screamed into Teague's shirt.

'I don't call it nothing to have her lying there with her skirt up like that,' said Teague.

'I just meant he didn't – '

'If it didn't happen to you then you just shut up about what's nothing or not,' said Teague.

Brother Deaver held out a little blue swatch of cloth. 'Here's your underwear, Rona – '

Rona turned away. Sister Monk snatched the panties out of Brother Deaver's hand. 'For heaven's sake, Brother Deaver, use some sense. He *touched* these! She isn't going to put them back on.'

'Rona, I'm sorry, but we've got to get moving,' said Teague. 'Right now, right this second. Those gunshots are bound to call more of them – these two might have twenty more a mile behind them.'

Rona turned away from him, staggered to Sister Monk. Marie didn't mind much, having Sister Monk switch from nursing her to comforting Rona. It was plain Rona was in worse shape.

Teague got the other two men to help him hoist the corpses onto the horses.

'Leave them here,' said Annalee.

'Got to bury them,' said Teague.

'They don't deserve it.'

Pete explained, real gentle. 'So nobody finds the bodies and chases after us to get even.'

A minute later they were off the road and cutting along the edge of some farmer's field, half-screened by trees. Teague pushed them to go faster, and quieter, too, his voice just a whisper. Finally they were down a hill in a hollow. Teague had Brother Deaver and Brother Cinn dig a single large grave, while Annalee kept the children away from the horses.

'Bury these, too,' said Teague.

That was the first time Marie noticed that both saddles had heads tied to them. They looked even worse close up than the heads Marie had seen from a distance.

'I'll take them down,' said Rona. She set right to untying the thongs from the saddle.

'Me too,' said Marie. She didn't even let herself wonder whether it had been a girl or a boy, a man or a woman.

Teague took his rifle and went back up the hill to keep a watch on the road.

Marie didn't puke and neither did Rona. Mostly Marie was just thinking about how grateful she was that her head wasn't on the horse. Then Marie helped Sister Monk strip the corpses and empty the pockets of everything. Three dozen shotgun shells. All kinds of matches and supplies. They stuffed it all in the saddlebags, which were already near full of stuff the mobbers no doubt stole from other folks just today. In twenty minutes both corpses were in the hole, dressed in their ragged underwear, the heads tucked around them, their limp, filthy clothes tossed in on top of them. Only Marie had noticed how Sister Monk wrapped Rona's blue panties inside one of the dead men's shirts. Rona insisted on helping then, tossing dirt onto the bodies until they were covered up.

Marie couldn't keep from speaking. 'They were *poor*.'

'Everybody's poor,' said Pete. 'But they kept alive by stealing the little that others had, and likely killing them, too.'

'Feels wrong, having their victims' heads buried with them,' said Sister Monk.

'The victims don't mind,' said Brother Deaver, 'and we didn't have time to dig more holes. Marie, can you get up the hill real quiet and tell Brother Teague that we're done here?'

But Teague had already seen from up the hill, and he slid down the slope. 'Nobody coming. These two might've been alone,' he said. 'It's getting late enough, maybe we ought to camp farther on down the hollow here. If I remember right there's water. The horses'll need that. We can work the rest of the afternoon rigging up some kind of harness for the horses to pull the bikes.' Teague looked at the grave. 'Get some dead leaves on here. Something to make the soil not look so fresh-turned. And if this happens again, save out their clothes. Dead people don't need them.'

'We'd never wear them,' said Brother Deaver.

'You would, if it got cold enough, and you got naked enough.'

'I've never been that naked,' said Brother Deaver.

Teague shrugged.

'Brother Teague,' said Marie.

'Yeah?'

'I was wrong about not wanting you to kill for me.'

'I know,' said Teague. And that was all he said to her. 'Mr. Deaver, Mr. Cinn, you got any objection to hanging on to those shotguns?'

'It *they* do, *I* don't,' said Sister Cinn.

Brother Deaver and Brother Cinn kept to themselves any objections they might have had. They slung the shotguns over their shoulders. Brother Cinn dropped a few shells in his pocket; then he dropped some in Brother Deaver's pocket. Brother Deaver looked at him in surprise, then embarrassment. Marie was a little disgusted. Didn't college professors know *anything*?

Mostly, though, Marie watched Teague. That's why she was the only one who saw how Teague kept clenching and unclenching his jaw. How his hand shook a little. And late that night, she was the only one who woke up when he took a walk in the moonlight.

She got up and followed him. He stood beside the grave, looking nowhere in particular, his hands jammed in his pockets. He showed no sign of noticing she was there, but she knew he had heard her coming from the minute she got up from the ground.

'You're such a liar,' said Marie. 'You didn't kill your parents.'

He didn't say a thing.

'You never killed a living soul before today.'

'Believe what you like,' he said.

'You never.'

He just stood there with his hands in his pockets until she went back to the camp. She lay there wondering why a man might want other folks to think he was a murderer when he wasn't. Then she wondered why she wanted so bad to believe a man wasn't a murderer when he said right out that he was. She lay awake a long time, but he didn't come back until after she was asleep.

As for Rona, Marie was sure that girl really did have a crush on Jamie Teague, before. Seeing how Teague saved her from rape and probably from having her head bounce along on some mobber's saddle, you'd think she'd be totally in love with him now. But no, not Rona. From then on it was like Teague didn't even exist, except as just another grown-up. Like he was nothing special.

There's just no understanding some people, Marie decided. Maybe Rona just couldn't be grateful and in love at the same time. Maybe she couldn't forgive Teague for waiting to kill the mobbers till they had her panties off. Of maybe Rona just couldn't ever be married to a man that watched her stamp a dead man's head to mush. Rona never told her, and Marie never asked.

Marie carried a scar on her forehead to the end of her life. She'd touch it now and then, and from the start she was glad to have it. She always remembered that it could have been much worse for her than a gun barrel leaning on her head. She could've been in Rona's place.

Day after next they came to the mountains, where the road sloped upward so steep that they had to stop and rest every twenty minutes or so. Pete was grateful they had the horses now, to pull the carts, though he didn't say so out loud; it didn't do to start saying it was a good thing to have the horses, not with Rona still so upset about how they got them.

Pete concentrated on the children, his own and the orphans. They were the ones who suffered most, he knew that. The youngest of them, Scotty Porter and Valerie Letterman, they weren't even born when the first plague struck. The famous Six Missiles had already fallen before Scotty and Valerie said their first words. He murmured to Annalee one time, 'Think there's any chance of getting them into a college-prep kindergarten?' But she'd either forgotten all that craziness from the old days, or else she didn't think it was funny. She didn't think much was funny these days. Neither did Pete, for that matter. But at least he tried now and then. Some-

47

times, for hours, maybe even days at a time, he didn't think about his father killed in the missile that got D.C., or his stepfather shot by looters, or his mom and Annalee's folks and all their brothers and sisters and nieces and nephews crammed into the cultural hall at the stake center, not being sure what was going to happen to them, but knowing deep down all the time, knowing and being terrified. I was in plays on the stage where the guys with the guns stood. I played basketball on the floor where the bullets gouged up the wood finish and blood soaked in under the polish. I was baptized in the font behind the stage, where the men from the city hooked up the hoses to wash out the blood. The Baptists were already talking about making it a Christian library when Pete went there to lay flowers in the parking lot where he had first kissed Annalee after a dance, where now his kin and his friends lay in a jumbled heap of broken bodies under the dirt.

That was the whole world to these children. It had always been in turmoil – did they even realize that things weren't supposed to be this way? Would they ever trust anything again, now that their parents had been taken away from them?

Teague asked him once, when they were alone together, leading the horses. 'Whose kids are those?'

'Donna, the big one, she's mine, and so's Nat, he's my boy.'

'Any fool can see that, they're so blond,' said Teague. Mick and Scotty Porter, Valerie Letterman, Cheri Ann Bee, they're orphans.'

'Why'd you bring them along? Wasn't there anybody in Greensboro who could've took care of them?'

'That's what took us so long leaving. Fighting everybody to get the right to take them with us.'

'But why? Don't you know how much faster we'd go, how much safer we'd be without them?'

Pete held himself back, kept himself from being angry, like he always tried to do and almost always succeeded. 'It's like this, Teague. If we left them, they would've been raised up Baptists.'

'That ain't so bad,' said Teague.

Pete held himself back again, a long time, before he could answer quiet and calm. 'You see, Teague, it was mostly Baptist preachers who spent fifteen years telling people how Mormons were the anti-Christ, how we had secret rituals in the temple where we worshiped Satan. How we said Jesus and the devil were brothers, and how we weren't Christians but pretended to be so we could steal away their children, how we Mormons owned everything and made sure we got rich while good Christians stayed poor. And then when bad times came, all those Baptist preachers washed their hands and said, "We never told anybody to *kill* Mormons." Well, that's true. They never taught murder. But they taught hate and fear, they told lies and they knew they were doing it. Now, Teague, do you see why we wouldn't let these Mormon kids get raised by people who'd tell such lies about the religion their parents died for?'

Teague thought about that for a while. 'How come these kids got out alive? I heard the Christian Soldiers went through killing the wounded.'

So Teague *had* heard the story. 'These four went to Guilford Primary. When the Christian Soldiers were going around arresting people, they got to Guilford Primary School, and Dr. Sonja Day, the principal, she met them at the door. Didn't have a gun or anything. She just shows them the ashes of the school records, still smoldering. She says to them, "All the children in this school are Mormon today, and me and all the faculty. If you take anybody, you take us all." Faced them down and they finally went away.'

'Guts.'

'Think about it, Teague. Mormon kids were ripped out of class in fifty schools in the county. If more principals had guts –'

'One out of fifty's above average, Cinn.'

49

'That's why America deserves all that's happened to her. That's why the Lord hasn't saved us. America turned to loving evil.'

'Maybe they were just afraid,' said Teague.

'Afraid or weak or evil, all three roads lead to hell.'

'I know,' whispered Teague.

His whisper was so deep and sore that Pete knew he'd touched some wounded place in Teague. Pete wasn't one to push deeper at a time like that. He backed off, let a man be. You don't go poking into a wound, that just gets it all infected. You keep hands off, you let it heal up, you give it time and air and gentleness.

'Teague, I wish you'd take me with you when you scout around or go hunting or whatever.'

'I need you to stay with the rest. I don't figure Deaver to be much good with a shotgun.'

'Maybe not,' said Pete. 'But if you don't go with us beyond these mountains, somebody's got to be able to do some of what you do.'

'I been walking the woods for ten years now, long before the plagues started.'

'I got to start sometime.'

'When we get to the Blue Ridge Parkway, I'll start to take you hunting with me. But you carry no gun.'

'Why not?'

'Take it or leave it. Can you throw?'

'I pitched hardball.'

'A rock?'

'I suppose.'

'If you can't hunt with a rock, you can't hunt. Bullets are for killing things big enough to kill *you*. Because when the bullets run out, there won't be no more.'

The higher they got into the mountains, the more relaxed Teague got. After a while, he stopped having them look for sheltered, hidden places to camp in; they camped right out in the open. 'Mobbers don't come up this high,' said Teague.

'Why not?'

'Because when they do, they don't come back.'

At the Blue Ridge Parkway, Teague laid out a whole new set of rules. 'Walk spaced apart, not bunched up. Stay on the pavement or close to it. Nobody goes off alone. Don't hold anything in your hand, not even a rock. Keep your hands in plain sight all the time. If somebody comes, don't move your hands above your waist, not even to scratch your nose. Just keep walking. Above all, make plenty of noise.'

'I take it we're not afraid of bushwhackers anymore,' said Brother Deaver.

'These are mountain people around here, and Chero-kees beyond Asheville. They don't rob people, but they also don't ask a lot of questions before they kill strangers. If they think you might, just *might* cause them any trouble, you're dead where you stand. So you make it plain that you aren't trying to sneak up on anybody and you stay visible all the time.'

'We can sing again?' asked Sister Monk.

'Anything but that "walked and walked and walked and walked" song.'

It was a glorious time then. The Blue Ridge Parkway crested the hills, so they had sky all round them, and the mountains were as pretty as Pete had ever seen them. His real Dad took them along the parkway most autumns when he was growing up. One year they drove it clear from Harper's Ferry down to the Cherokee Res-ervation. Pete and his brother griped the whole way till their dad was promising to amputate limbs if they didn't shut up, but now the trip was glorious in memory. Sometimes Pete forgot he was a grown-up, walking along here, especially when he walked on ahead so he couldn't see any of them. It wasn't autumn yet, though autumn wasn't far off; still, it felt good, felt like coming home. He'd heard other folks say that, too, about the Blue Ridge. About the Appalachians in general. Felt like coming home even if they grew up in some desolate place like California or North Dakota.

Teague made good his promise. It near drove Pete crazy the first few times, when his rock always missed and Teague's almost never did. But after a while he got the knack of it. It was like pitching with a smaller strike zone. By the time they skirted around Asheville, he could clean a squirrel in two minutes and a rabbit in three. He also learned how to choose a hunting ground. You always look for a cabin and walk up singing, so they know you're coming. Then you ask the owner where it's OK to hunt, and if he'd like you to split your catch with him. To hear these mountain folks talk, you could hunt wherever you liked; but Teague would never so much as pick up a rock unless the folks had said 'That holler down there' or 'Along that slope there,' and even though they always said 'No need to bring me none,' Teague always took the whole catch to them and offered them half. He wouldn't leave until they'd accepted at least one animal. 'They can't claim you stole it then,' said Teague. 'If they took part of it, it wasn't poaching.'

'What's to stop them from lying and *saying* you stole it?' asked Pete.

Teague looked at him like he was stupid. 'These are mountain people.'

Whenever they returned from hunting, Pete loved to hear the sound of the children singing, and the grown-ups too now, more and more. Most of all he loved hearing his Annalee's voice, singing and laughing. When they climbed up out of the piedmont and into the mountains, it was like rising out of hell. This is what redemption feels like, he thought. This is what it's like when Christ forgives you of your sins. Like putting you on the top of a green mountain, with as many clouds below you as above; and all your bad memories just washed away with the rain, got lost in the morning fogs. All those bad memories were lowland troubles, left behind, gone. Pete had been born again.

'I never want to come down out of here,' he told Annalee.

'I know,' she said. 'I feel like that too.'

'Then let's don't go down.'

She looked at him sharply. 'What's got into you, Peter? You talk like Teague, you walk like Teague. If I'd wanted to marry a hillbilly I'd've gone to Appalachian State or Western Carolina.'

'A man belongs up here.'

'A Latter-day Saint belongs in the kingdom of God.'

'Look around you, Annalee, and tell me God doesn't love this place.'

'There's no safety here. You feel good cause we don't have to hide every night. But we aren't staying in the open cause we're safe and free, we're staying in the open so somebody won't shoot our heads off. We'd never belong here. But we're already citizens of Utah. Every Mormon is.'

After that Pete didn't mention his desire to stay in the mountains, not to Annalee, not to anybody. He knew that after a while they'd all come around to his point of view. When you get to heaven, why go farther? That's what Pete thought.

'Sister Monk, your dress is getting longer,' said Valerie Letterman one day.

'I must be getting shorter,' Tina answered.

'You're getting prettier.'

'Child, you're going to make a lot of friends in this world.'

But Valerie was right. Walking more than two hundred miles was every bit as effective as stomach stapling in the old days. She'd already hemmed up the skirts of all her dresses twice, as her bulk evaporated. She could feel the muscles working under the flesh of her arms and legs. She could spring to her feet all at once, instead of step by step – all fours, kneel up, one foot planted, two feet squatting, and the last terrible unbending of the knees. That was ancient history now. She rolled out of her blanket – it was cold at night up here – and got right to her feet and felt like every step she was jumping several feet into the air. All the pills she'd tried, all the doctors, all the diets, all the exercises – but the only thing that worked was to walk from Greensboro to Topton.

No trouble all through the mountains. No danger that felt like danger, except a few tight minutes at the Cherokee border, till somebody came along who recognized Jamie Teague. And at last they left the paved road and climbed up a dirt track, all overgrown now that no cars ever came through, and came to a two-story house completely dwarfed by giant oak trees.

'I thought you called this a cabin, Jamie Teague,' she said.

'My foster parents called it that,' he said. 'They were summer people. But as soon as I was old enough, I stayed year-round.'

Tina caught up that information and remembered it. Teague had foster parents before he was old enough to decide where he was going to live. So if he was fostered out because he killed his parents, he must have killed them when he was young. Probably *very* young.

The door was not locked. Yet inside, the house was untouched by thieves or vandals. It was deep with dust and dead insects – no one had entered all summer, least of all to clean. Yet every implement was in its place, and Annalee immediately set everyone to work cleaning up. Tina knew she should have joined in – she probably knew more about cleaning than everybody else put together – but for some reason she just felt an aversion to it, just didn't want to. And the more she thought she ought to help, the less she felt like helping, until finally she fled the house.

'Stop,' said Teague.

'Why?'

'You don't just walk outside and go where you want,' said Teague.

'Why not?'

'My neighbors don't know you yet.'

'They'll know me soon enough,' she said. 'I've always

54

been a good neighbor.'

'It ain't like neighbors down in the city, Mrs. Monk.'

'If you can't bring yourself to call me Sister Monk, then at least call me Tina.'

Teague grinned. 'Go in there and get everybody ready for an expedition.'

The expedition was a trip to each of four neighbors' houses, singing and talking the whole way. The houses were set so far apart you couldn't see any of them from the other. But that didn't matter. They were neighbors all the same. They were the reason Teague's house was untouched. And they could be deadly.

'Mr. Bicker,' said Teague. 'I see you pulled a good crop of tobacco.'

'Mountain tobacco's only a speck better than chewing dog turds,' said Bicker, 'but I got a few leaves curing anyway.'

'Mr. Bicker, you see these folks I got with me?'

'Do I look blind?'

'I've been with these folks since Winston, and they treated me like kin. We've been eating out of the same pot and walking the same road, and stood back to back a few times. They're staying the winter with me and then they're moving on. I showed them the property line, and they all know what land is mine and what land is yours.'

Bicker sniffed. 'Never knowed city people could tell one tree from another.'

But we can read, thought Tina, and we don't let snot trail on our upper lips. She had sense enough not to say it.

'City people or not, Mr. Bicker, they're *my* people, all of them.'

'Them is colored there.'

'I call that a deep suntan, Mr. Bicker. Or maybe Chero-kee blood. But they'll be gone in spring, and you'll hardly notice they're around.'

Bicker squinted.

'But they'll *be* around,' said Teague. 'Every one of them. Every last one, alive and moving around in the spring.'

'Hope there's no influenza,' said Bicker. Then he went back into his cabin, laughing and laughing.

Teague led them away. 'Sing,' he told Tina, and she led them in singing.

'This is like Christmas caroling,' said Annalee's girl Donna.

'Except we didn't used to sing carols so people wouldn't shoot at us,' said Tina.

'Oh, Bicker's all right,' said Teague. 'He'll be fine.'

'Fine? He practically loaded his shotgun right in front of us.'

'Oh, he's a good neighbor, Tina. You just got to know how to treat him.'

'I don't call it a good neighbor when he merely agrees not to kill you before spring.'

But Tina was pretty sure Teague didn't entirely know what he was talking about. After all, he'd been a boy up here, not a girl. There was one kind of neighborliness between men, which mostly consisted of not stealing from each other and not sleeping with each other's wife. Then there was the neighborliness of women, which Teague wouldn't know a thing about.

So she made sure to go along with him as he started going around trading the things he'd gotten on his trip to the coast. All kinds of tooled metal, threads and needles, buttons, pins, scissors, spoons and knives and forks. A precious pair of binoculars, for which Teague got a queen-size mattress in exchange. Bullets to fit half a dozen different guns. A bottle of vitamin C and a bottle of Extra-Strength Tylenol Caplets, both for an old lady with arthritis.

And right after he got through bartering, Tina would start in talking about how she was near helpless cooking wild game. 'I make a fair broth, and I expect I can use my sweet dumpling recipe with honey for the sugar, but you must know ten dozen herbs and vegetables that I'll just step on thinking they're weeds. I don't want to be a bother, but I can trade sewing for cooking lessons. I've

56

got a decent eye with a needle.' Teague was dumfounded at first – it was obvious that in all the time he'd been trading with the menfolk, talking in words of one or two syllables and sentences of three or four words, he'd never had an inkling of how a woman goes calling, of how women help each other instead of trying to drive a bargain. 'It's called civilization,' she said to Teague, between visits. 'Women invented it, and every time you men blow it all to bits, we just invent it again.'

By Christmas she had Bicker himself coming over for supper every night, bringing his fiddle and a memory of a thousand old songs, none of which he sang on key, which nobody minded except Tina, who had been cursed with pitch so clear she could sing quarter tones in a chromatic scale. Never mind – the kids didn't have to live in fear of getting their feet shot off if they happened to stray over the line into Bicker's land. And Teague just sat there singing and laughing along with everybody else, now and then getting this look of surprise on his face, like he'd never had a notion that folks in these mountains ever did such things as this.

In only one thing did Tina follow Teague's heartfelt advice. She never told a soul, nor did anybody else, that they were Mormons. They never sang a Mormon hymn, and on Sunday mornings, when Brother Deaver and Pete Cinn broke bread and blessed the sacrament and passed it, and then they preached, why, they kept the shutters closed and never sang. It wasn't the hate from the TV preachers and the Baptist ministers of the city that they feared. It was an older kind of loathing. Put a name like *Mormon* on somebody, and he stopped being folks and started being Other. And around here, Other got ostracized at the least, and usually got burnt out before spring planting.

But it was a good winter all the same. And Tina noticed how Teague listened and finally came downstairs during church meetings, and even asked a question now and then about something from the Book of

Mormon or some point of doctrine he'd never heard of before. Sometimes he shook his head like it was the craziest mess he'd ever heard of. And sometimes he kind of almost nodded. At Christmas he even told the Christmas story, pretty much following Luke.

Tina held school every day, at first just for the kids in their group, but pretty soon for whatever mountain kids could make it through the snow. She got Rona and Marie to teach sometimes, so she could divide the classes. Brother Deaver taught grammar to Donna and the older kids from the nearby cabins. The worst thing was, no paper to write on, and nothing to write *with*. They wrote with burnt sticks on the porch, then scrubbed the porch with snow and started over. Mostly, though, they did their writing and arithmetic in their heads, reciting their answers. Tina realized she was growing old when the kids regularly out-ciphered her – she just couldn't hold as many numbers at once as they could. That was when Rona became the permanent arithmetic teacher.

They didn't teach geography at all. Nobody knew geography anymore. Everything had changed.

All through the winter, Teague took Pete along to teach him more about hunting and tracking, and Pete learned pretty well, Tina gathered; at least Teague seemed to get closer to him all the time, approving of him, trusting him. At the same time, Tina noticed that Pete seemed to get more and more distant from his family. There wasn't much room for privacy, but as the only married couple, Pete and Annalee had a room to themselves. The day after Christmas Annalee told Tina that she might as well sleep on the dining room table for all the lovemaking she got anymore. 'I might as well be a widow, he never even talks to me.' And then: 'Tina, I think he isn't planning to go on west with us.'

Tina let things ride through January, watching. Annaless was right. Pete never took part in their

58

frequent speculations about Utah. Teague would tease them all sometimes, when nobody else was around. 'Nothing grows out west,' he'd say. 'They probably all moved on to Seattle. You'll get to Utah and nobody'll be there.'

'You don't know what you're talking about, Jamie Teague,' said Tina one time. 'You don't know our people. If it floods we all go into the boatmaking business. If there's a hurricane we all learn to fly.'

Others picked up on it. 'If the corn crop fails, we learn to eat grass,' said Donna.

'And when the grass gets used up, we chew up the trees!' said Mick Porter.

'And then we eat bugs!' shouted his little brother Scotty.

'And worms!' shouted Mick, even louder.

Annalee put a hand on Mick's mouth. 'Let's keep it down.' Didn't want the neighbors to hear them talking about Utah.

'You can bet they're making gasoline out of shale oil,' Tina said. 'That's no tall tale. I bet there's still tractors plowing there, and fertilizer.'

'I believe the fertilizer,' said Teague. But his eyes danced a little, Tina could see that.

So she pressed her case. 'And what have you got here, Jamie?'

It wasn't Teague who answered. It was Pete. 'He's got everything,' he said. 'Safety. Good land. Enough to eat. Good neighbors. And no reason to move on, ever.'

There it was, out in the open.

But Tina pretended that it was still Teague she was talking to, instead of Pete. 'That's this year, Jamie. You make your trips down into the Carolinas. You go into abandoned houses, you visit places and tell stories and they give you gifts. And what do you collect to bring back here? Needles and pins, scissors and thread, tools and all the things that make life halfway livable. Think about that! Do you think those things will last forever?

Nobody's making them anymore, and someday the scavenging will run out. Someday there'll be no more thread, no more needles. What'll you wear then? Some rag of homespun? Anybody spinning yet?'

'Lady down in Murphy spins and weaves real good,' said Teague. Pete nodded like that answered everything.

'Enough for everybody in the hills? Jamie, don't you see that folks around here are just holding on by their fingernails? It isn't as plain to see here because you don't go to sleep in fear of mobs every night. But it's all slipping away. It's fading. And whoever stays here is going to fade, too. But out west – '

'Out west they might all be dead!' said Pete.

'Out west the temple is still standing, and the wards are all still functioning, just like they always have. They're growing crops on good land – in peace – and there'll still be hospitals and medicines. What if you marry someday, Jamie? What if your kids get some disease? A simple one like measles. And they end up blind. A kidney infection. Appendicitis, for heaven's sake. You see any more doctors growing up around here? Every year you'll slip back another fifty years.'

'It's safe here,' said Pete. But his voice was fainter.

'It isn't safe compared to *safety*,' said Tina. 'It's only safe compared to the open lands where the mob rules. And someday you know the mobbers are coming up here. They'll have killed off or run off everybody down there who isn't protected by an army. Those mobbers aren't going to settle down and learn to *farm*, you know. They won't attack the Cherokees, either. They'll come to places like this – '

'And we'll kill them all,' said Pete.

'Till you run out of bullets. Then there's no more shooting from behind trees. Then you fight out in the open against ten times your number, by hand, till they sweep you under. I tell you there's only one place safe in all America, only one place that's growing upward against all the dying.'

'Says you,' said Pete.

'Says all the history of the Mormon people. We've been driven out and mobbed and massacred before, and all we ever do is move on and settle somewhere else. And wherever we settle there's peace and progress. We never hold still. I'm betting we don't even have to get to the mountains to find them. I'm betting they send people out to meet folks like us and help us safely in. That's what they used to do, in the covered wagon days.'

All this time Tina only looked at Teague, never once at Pete. But out of the corner of her eye she could see how Pete deflated when Teague nodded. 'I guess you aren't crazy to try to get there after all. I just wish I had more hope of your making it.'

'The Lord will protect us,' said Tina.

'He was doing a slim job of it till Teague came along,' said Pete.

'But Jamie came along, didn't you, Jamie? Why do you think you happened to be there when we needed you so bad?'

Teague grinned. 'I reckon I'm just a regular old angel,' he said.

Still, Easter came and no decision had been made. They had a church service on Easter Sunday, but nobody preached this time. They just bore testimony. It wasn't like the old days, when people used to get up and recite the same old I'm-thankful-fors and I-know-thats. This time they spoke from the heart, spoke of terrible things and wonderful things, spoke of love for each other and anger at the Lord and yet in the end spoke of faith that things would all work out.

And after a while they started talking about the thing they'd only hinted at all these months together. The thing that happened back in May, almost a year before. The terrible death of so many of the people they knew and loved and missed so bad. And the even worse thing – that they themselves had not died.

It was Cheri Ann Bee who started it off. She was seven now, and not even baptized yet, but she still bore her testimony, and at the end she said something real simple, but it about broke Tina's heart. 'I'm sorry I didn't get sick that day and stay home,' she said, 'so I could've gone with Mommy and Daddy to visit Heavenly Father.' Cheri Ann didn't cry or anything; she just plain believed that things were better with her mother and father. And as Tina sat there with tears in her eyes, she wasn't sure if she felt like crying out of pity for this girl or if she felt like crying because she herself didn't have such plain and simple faith, and lacked something of that perfect trust that death was just a matter of going to pay a call on God, who would invite you into his house to live with him.

'I'm sorry, too,' said Brother Deaver, and then he *did* cry, tears running down his cheeks. 'I'm sorry I went to work that day. I'm sorry that the Christian Soldiers were so afraid of provoking the black community of Greensboro that they didn't come take me out of class at A&T and let me hold my babies in my arms while they were dying.'

'His kids wasn't babies,' Scotty Porter whispered to Tina. 'They was bigger than me.'

'All children are always babies to their mama and papa,' Tina answered.

'I called my mama that morning,' said Annalee, and wonder of wonders, she was crying, too, looking as soft and vulnerable as a child. 'I told her how Pete was keeping the kids home from school and we were making a picnic of it at the fire station. And she said, I wisht I could come. And then she said, Can't talk now, Anny Leedy, there's somebody at the door. Somebody at the door! It was *them* at the door, and there I was talking to her on the phone and I didn't even say I love you one last time or nothing.'

There was silence for a while, the way there always was in testimony meetings from time to time, when nobody stood up to talk. It always used to be so tense when nobody talked, everybody feeling guilty cause the time was going to waste and hoping somebody else would get up and talk cause they didn't feel like it. This time, though, the silence was just because everybody was so full and there wasn't a thing to say.

'I knew,' said Pete, finally. 'I had a dream the night before. I saw the men coming to the door. I was *shown*. That's why I kept the kids home. That's why I got us all over to the fire station.'

'You never told me this,' said Annalee.

'I thought it was crazy, that's why. I thought I was plain out of my mind to take a nightmare so serious. But I couldn't leave you all home, feeling like I did.' Pete looked around at the others. 'My station, they stood by me. They turned on the hoses and drove them back. My captain said to them, "If you touch any fireman or any fireman's family, don't be surprised to find your own house on fire someday, and the fire engines a little slow to show up and save you." And so they went away, and we were alive.' Suddenly his face twisted up and he sobbed, great and terrible sobs.

'Petey,' said Annalee. She put her arm around him, but he shrugged her off.

'God showed me a vision, don't you see? And all I could think to save was my own family. Not even my brothers and sisters! Not even my mama! I had a chance to save them all, and they're dead because I didn't give warning.'

Brother Deaver tried to soothe him with words. 'Pete, the Lord didn't command you in that dream to give warning. He didn't tell you to call everybody and tell them. So he probably meant to take the others to himself, and spare only a few to suffer further in this vale of tears.'

Pete lifted his face from his hands, and a mask of grief with reddened eyes staring out, wild and terrible. 'He did tell me,' said Pete. 'Warn them all, he said, only

63

I just thought it was a nightmare, I was too embarrassed to claim to have a vision, I thought they'd all think I was crazy. I'm going to hell, don't you see? I can't go to Utah. I'm rejected and cast off from the Lord.'

'Even Jonah was forgiven,' said Brother Deaver.

But Pete wasn't in the mood to be comforted. It was the end of the meeting, but it was a good meeting, Tina knew that. Everybody said the things they'd been holding back all along, or had those things said for them. They'd done what a testimony meeting was supposed to do. They'd confessed their sins, and now there was hope of forgiveness.

It was afternoon of Easter Sunday. The day had warmed up right smart, and Jamie shed his jacket and felt the wind cool on his back and arms, right through his shirt, and felt the sun hot, too, right at the same time. Best kind of weather, best kind of day.

'I guess you got an earful today.'

Jamie turned around. He couldn't believe he hadn't heard a big woman like Tina come lumbering up behind him. But then she wasn't so big these days. And he had a lot of noisy thoughts going round in his head.

'I figured a lot of this out before, anyway,' said Jamie. 'I heard tales of the Greensboro massacre.'

'Is that how they tell it? That our people were massacred?'

'Sometimes,' said Jamie. 'Other times they call it the Purification of Greensboro. Them as says that usually allow as how other places need purification, too.'

'I hope all our people are heading west. I pray they all have sense to go. We should've gone years ago.'

'May be,' said Jamie. But he knew this wasn't what Tina came to say.

'Jamie,' said Tina.

This was it.

'Jamie, what's holding you here?'

Jamie looked around at the trees, at the bright spring grass, at the distant curls of smoke from two dozen chimneys spread out through the hills.

'You hardly speak to your neighbors, leastwise you didn't till we came here, Jamie. You got no close friends in these hills.'

'They leave me alone,' said Jamie Teague.

'Too bad,' said Tina.

'I like it. I like being left alone.'

'Don't tell me lies, Jamie.'

'I was a loner before the collapse, and I'm a loner now. Whole thing made not a speck of difference to me.'

'Don't tell yourself lies, either.'

Jamie felt anger flash out inside him. 'I don't need anybody talking like a mama to me. I had one once and I killed her dead.'

'I don't believe that lie,' said Tina.

'Why?' demanded Jamie. 'Do you think I'm so *nice* I'd just naturally never kill a soul? Then you don't know me at all.'

'I know there's times you kill,' said Tina. 'I just don't believe you killed your mama and papa. Because if you did, then why are you still so mad at them?'

'Leave me alone.' Jamie meant it with all his heart.

But Tina didn't seem interested in leaving him alone. 'You know you love us and you don't want to lose us when we leave.'

'Is that what you think?'

'That's what I know. I see how good you are with the kids. What a friend you been to Peter. Don't you see that's half why he wanted to stay, to be with you? We all count on you, we all lean on you, but you count on us, too, you *need* us.'

She was pushing too hard. Jamie couldn't stand it. 'Back off,' he said. 'Just back off and leave me be.'

'And when we pray, you fall silent, and your lips say Amen when the prayer is over.'

'I got respect for religion, that's all.'

'And today when we all confessed the blackest things that hurt us to the soul, you wanted to confess, too.'

'I confessed a long time ago.'

'You confessed a terrible lie. That's what I keep wondering about, Jamie Teague. What sin are you hiding that you think is so bad that it's easier to confess to killing your mama and papa?'

'Leave me alone!' shouted Jamie. Then he ran off from her, ran off up the hill, scrambling fast so he knew there was no hope of her keeping up. Didn't matter. She didn't chase him.

Mick Porter took his brother Scotty with him everywhere. Never let that little boy out of his sight. Have to look out for a kid like Scotty, always running off, always getting into things like he shouldn't.

In the old days it wasn't like that, of course. In the old days Mick used to complain to Mom about how Scotty always had to do everything the same as him. Mick used to wallop Scotty sometimes, and Scotty'd break down whatever Mick made out of legos or blocks, and it got to be like a war. But that all ended. Just didn't happen no more, on account of who'd break up their fights and send them to their rooms till they could just treat each other like civilized human beings now? Mick felt like he was almost Scotty's dad. I am his only kin, and he's my only kin, so look out, everybody else, and that's all.

So Mick had Scotty tagging right along with him, gathering fallen sticks for kindling and getting in some rock-throwing practice, too. Mick wasn't up to getting squirrels, yet. He still had kind of a hard time hitting the same tree he was aiming at. Scotty, of course, had no idea about aim at all. He just felt good if the rock went more than five feet in the general direction he threw it.

Hardly a surprise, then, when Scotty threw his latest rock and it went sideways, whizzing right past Mick's nose and then going thunk, right into something soft not more than a few feet off.

'OK, I'm dead, just skin me gentle so you don't wake me up.'

Mick near to swallowed his tongue he was so surprised. There was Mr. Jamie Teague, sitting right there, and until he spoke Mick hadn't even noticed him. He just held so *still* all the time.

'I hit something!' said Scotty.

'You hit my jeans,' said Mr. Teague. 'If I was a squirrel I might not be dead, but I'd sure be crippled.'

'We can't cook *you*,' said Scotty.

'Guess not,' said Mr. Teague. 'I'm sorry about that.'

'We don't eat people anyhow,' Mick told Scotty.

'I know that,' Scotty said, his voice full of scorn.

Mick turned his attention to Mr. Teague. 'What you doing just setting there?'

'Setting here.'

'I just said that.'

'And thinking.'

'Of course you were thinking,' said Mick. 'Everybody's always thinking. You can't turn it off.'

'And ain't that a damn shame, too,' said Mr. Teague.

Scotty gasped and covered his mouth.

'I'm sorry,' said Mr. Teague. 'I grew up in a family where "damn" was the *nice* way of saying stuff.'

'I know a worser word,' said Scotty.

'No you don't,' said Mick.

'He might,' said Mr. Teague. 'You never know.'

'It's another word for poop,' said Scotty.

'Don't that beat all,' said Mr. Teague. 'Better not teach me what it is, now, Scotty. I might slip and use it in polite company.'

Mick sat down near Mr. Teague's leg, and looked him in the eye. 'Sister Monk says you didn't really kill your mama and daddy.'

'Does she now.'

'I heard her,' said Scotty.

'Is she right?' asked Mick.

'I used to dream about killing them. But after they took us kids away from them, nobody ever told us where they were. Jail, I guess. I always meant to look for them and kill them when I got eighteen and could leave my foster parents, so-called, but the collapse came before I could get a fair start. So you see I meant to do it, and it wasn't my fault I didn't do it, so the way I figure it, I did it in my heart so I'm a murderer.'

'No sir,' said Mick. 'You never did it. You got to kill somebody to be a murderer.'

'Maybe so,' said Mr. Teague.

'Then you'll come with us?'

Mr. Teague laughed out loud. He pulled his legs up close to his body and hugged them. They were the longest pair of legs Mick ever saw. Even longer than Daddy's legs used to be.

'You think my daddy's a skeleton now?' asked Mick.

Mr. Teague's smile went away. 'Maybe,' he said. 'Hard to say.'

'The Christian Soldiers killed him,' said Mick.

'And Mommy,' said Scotty.

'Those are what murderers are,' said Mick.

'I know,' said Mr. Teague.

'Brother Deaver says they killed our mama and daddy because we believe in a living prophet and how Jesus isn't the same person as God the Father.'

'That's right, I guess.'

'What did *your* mama and daddy believe?'

Mr. Teague took in a long breath. He crossed his arms on top of his knees, and then rested his chin on top of his arms. He looked right between Mick and Scotty so long that Scotty started breaking twigs and Mick began to think Mr. Teague just wasn't going to answer, or maybe even he was mad.

'Don't break them sticks, Scotty,' said Mick. 'We can't

68

use it for kindling if it's all broke up.'

Scotty stopped breaking twigs. Didn't sass or stick out his tongue or nothing. It was all different now.

'My mama and daddy believed in getting by,' said Mr. Teague.

'Getting by what?' asked Scotty.

'Just – getting by.'

'That's what you wanted to kill them about?' asked Mick.

Mr. Teague shook his head.

'You aren't making sense, you know,' said Mick.

Mr. Teague grinned. 'Guess not.' He reached out a long arm, and with a single long finger he lifted Mick's chin. Mick didn't like it when grown-ups started moving parts of his body around or grabbing his hand or whatever, like they thought he was a puppet. But it wasn't so bad when Mr. Teague did it, especially because he didn't act like he was planning to make Mick do something or yell at him or anything. 'You love your little brother, don't you?'

Mick shrugged.

Scotty looked at him.

'Course,' said Mick.

'Not when you're mad at me,' said Scotty.

'I'm never mad at you anymore,' said Mick.

'No,' said Scotty, as if he was realizing it for the first time.

'I had a little brother,' said Mr. Teague.

'Did you love him?' asked Mick.

'Yes,' said Mr. Teague.

'Where is he?'

'Dead I guess,' said Mr. Teague.

'Don't you know?'

'They put him in a mental hospital same time they locked up my folks. Put my little sister in a mental hospital, too. Then they farmed out me and my older brothers to foster homes. Never saw any of them again, but I reckon my little brother, being crazy like he was, I

69

reckon he didn't last long after the collapse.'

Mr. Teague was breathing kind of fast, and not looking Mick in the eye anymore. It was kind of scary, like Mr. Teague was a little crazy himself. 'How'd he get crazy?' asked Mick. He wondered if the same thing was happening to Mr. Teague.

'Does he scream?' asked Scotty. 'Crazy people scream.'

'Sometimes he screamed. Mostly he just sat there, looking past you. He'd never look folks in the eye. It was like you wasn't even there. Like he was erasing you in his own mind. But he looked at *me*.'

'How come you?'

'Because I brought him food.'

'Not your mama?'

Mr. Teague shook his head. 'It was when I was five. Your age, Scotty. And my little brother, he was three.'

'I'm five and a half,' said Scotty.

'And my little sister, she was only two.'

'Was she crazy?' asked Mick.

'Not then. But she was sick. And so was my little brother. Both of them, all the time. Ever since they was born. My brother got pneumonia and cried all the time. Lots of bills to pay. My little sister was fussy, too. I used to hear Mama and Daddy yelling at each other all the time, about money, about too damn many kids. Fighting and screaming, and Mama screaming about how she just couldn't take any more, she just couldn't stand it if us kids didn't just shut *up* and let her be for just a couple of hours, that's all she wanted, just a couple of hours of silence, and she was going to have it by God or she'd kill herself, see if I don't, she said, I'm going to cut my wrists and die if you don't shut up. And me, I'd shut up all right, I kept my mouth shut. The older kids, they were in school. But my little brother, he was just sick and out of sorts and he just kept crying and whimpering and the more she yelled the more he whimpered and then my sister, she woke up from her nap and she

70

started crying even louder than my brother did, they just screamed and screamed, and my mama screamed even louder, she just got this horrible face, and she picked up my sister and I thought she was going to throw her on the floor, but she didn't do it. She just took her and grabbed my brother by his arm and dragged him along, dragged them over to the cedar closet that had a lock on the door and she opened it up and shoved them inside and closed the door and locked it. Cry and whine all you want to but I'm not going to hear any more, do you understand me? I just can't stand it any more I'm going to have some *peace*.'

'Daddy locked me in the bathroom one time when I was bad,' said Mick.

'Did they have a light in there?' asked Scotty.

'They had a light. There was a switch and my brother could stand on a box in there and turn it on, so he did. But they didn't like being in there. They screamed and yelled and cried like it was the worst thing in the world, and my brother banged on the door and rattled the handle and kicked the door and stamped his feet. But Mama just went downstairs and turned on the dish-washer and went into the living room and turned on the stereo and laid there on the couch listening to the radio until she fell asleep. Every now and then my brother and sister, they let up on their yelling, but then they'd start all over again. When the older kids got home from school they knew right off to stay away from Mom, and they didn't even ask where the little ones were. They knew you don't mess with Mom in a mood like that. Anyway, Mom got up and fixed dinner, and when Dad came home we ate, and Dad asked where the little kids were, and Mom said, Learning to be quiet. And when she said that, Dad knew not to mess with her, either. Except at the end of the meal he said, Aren't they going to eat? And so Mom slopped food onto a couple of plates and put spoons on them and then she handed me the key and said, Take them their dinner, Jamie. But if you let them out I'll kill myself, do you understand?'

'They was really in trouble I guess,' said Scotty.

'When I opened the door my brother tried to get out, but I pushed him back in. He screamed and cried louder than ever, except he was hoarse by then. My sister was just setting in a corner with her face all red and covered with snot, but he kicked me and tried to shove me out of the way, but I knocked him down and then I knocked him down again and then I slid their plates in with my foot and slammed the door and locked it. My brother kicked and yelled and screamed for a while, but then he quieted down and I guess they ate their dinner. Later on they screamed and yelled some more, about going to the bathroom, but Mom just pretended not to hear, she just shook her head. They're not getting out by yelling, they're not getting their way by yelling.'

'They spent the night in there?' asked Mick.

'Next morning she gave me the key and one bowl of oatmeal and two spoons. This time they were both back in the corner. They'd made themselves pillows and beds kind of, out of the rags in there, we kept the old rags in that closet. And my sister looked like she was afraid of getting hit, and it stunk real bad, because she'd done her poop in a shoebox, but what could she do, if Mom wouldn't let her out to use the toilet? I told Mom, and she just said, Empty it and put it back. I didn't want to, but you don't argue with Mom when she's like that.'

'Gross,' said Mick.

Scotty just stared. Mick knew it was because he messed his pants a couple of times lately, after the Christian Soldiers killed Mama and Daddy, and so talking about pooping in a shoebox kind of embarrassed him.

'I kept thinking, Mom's going to let them out pretty soon. I kept thinking that. But every morning I took them breakfast and emptied the shoebox and the mason jar we left in there for them to piss in. And every night I took them dinner on a plate. Sometimes I could hear them talking in there. Sometimes they played. That was all at first though. After a while it was always quiet, except when one of them was sick and coughed a lot. When the bulb burned out I told Mom but she just didn't say anything. I said, The bulb's out in the cedar closet, but she just looked at me like she'd never even heard of a cedar closet. I finally got my big brother to change the bulb while I watched the door so they couldn't get out. That first time – other times from then on he wouldn't do it, so I had to tie my little brother's hands and feet together so I could change the bulb. When I started first grade, I'd feed them and do the box in the morning before school, and take them dinner at night, just the same thing, day after day, week after week. Most of the time my brother and sister just sat there when I opened the door, not looking at me, just staring at each other or at nothing at all. But every now and then my brother would scream and run at me like he wanted to kill me, and I'd knock him down and slam the door and lock it. I was so mean to him and so angry and so scared that somebody would find out what I was doing to my own brother and sister, how I was keeping them locked in a closet. Nobody else in the family ever even saw them after my brother changed the light bulb that time. Mom didn't even make up the plates for them, I had to do it after everybody left the kitchen. When they grew out of their clothes, I tried to sneak some of the clothes I grew out of, but then Mom would say, What happened to those pants of yours, what happened to that blue shirt, and I'd say, They're in the cedar closet, and she'd look at me that way and say, Those are perfectly good clothes and if they don't fit you anymore we'll give them away to the poor. Can you believe that?'

'We used to give old clothes to Goodwill,' said Scotty.

'They were naked in there, and their skin was white and they looked like ghosts, their eyes empty and never looking at me except when my brother screamed at me and ran at me, and every time I slammed the door and locked it, I wanted to kill them, I wanted to die, I hated it. I'd go to school and look around and I knew that I was the most evil person there, because I kept my little brother and sister naked locked up in a closet. Nobody even knew I *had* a little brother and sister. And I never told them. I never even walked up to a teacher and said, Miss Erbison, or Mrs. Ryan, or whoever, any of them, I could have said, I got me a little brother and sister at home that we've kept locked in the cedar closet since they was three and two years old. If I'd've done that, maybe my brother wouldn't have gone so crazy, maybe my sister wouldn't have forgotten how to walk, maybe they could've been saved in *time*, but I was so scared of what my mom would do, and I was too ashamed to tell anybody what a terrible person I was, they all thought I was an OK guy.'

He stopped talking for a while.

'Didn't they *ever* get out?' asked Scotty.

'When I was in seventh grade. I did a report on Nazi Germany and the concentration camps. I read about the tortures they did. And I thought, That's me. I'm a Nazi. And I read about how all them Nazis, they all said, I was just following orders. Well that was me, just following orders. And then I read how after the war they put them on trial, all those Nazis, and they sentenced them to death for what they did, and then I knew I was right all along. I knew I deserved to die, and my mom and dad deserved to die, but my little brother and sister, they deserved to go free, they deserved to have a day of liberation. So one afternoon when my little brother got hate in his eyes and ran at me, I didn't knock him down. I stepped out of his way and let him run by me. He ran out of the closet and looked around, like he'd never seen the hall before, and I guess he never had, really, he never remembered it. And then he sat down on the top step and bumped his way down the stairs, like he always did when he was a little kid, and I realized that he'd forgotten how to go down stairs. And then all of a sudden I thought, he's going to go in the kitchen and Mom's going to see him and get mad. And I got scared, and I thought, I got to catch him and put him back, or Mom will kill me. So I started to chase down the stairs, but he didn't go into the kitchen, he ran right out the front door, stark naked, I never thought he'd do that, but what did he care about naked, he never wore clothes in seven years. He just ran down the street, screaming and screaming like a creature from space, and I ran after him. I would've called out to him, yelled for him to stop, but I couldn't.'

'Why not?' asked Mick.

'I didn't remember his name.' Brother Teague began to cry. 'I couldn't even remember what his name was.'

It was only then, with Brother Teague crying into his hands like a little baby, that Mick even noticed that Sister Monk and Brother Deaver had both come up sometime, they were both there listening, they probably heard the whole story. Sister Monk came over and knelt down by Brother Teague and gathered him into her arms and let him cry all over her dress. Brother Deaver bowed his head like he was praying, only silently. Scotty noticed that, too, and bowed his head, but then when nobody said a prayer he lifted his head and looked over to Mick.

Mick didn't know what to do, except that it was a terrible story, a terrible thing that happened to Brother Teague's crazy sister and brother. Mick never heard of anybody forgetting how to walk or climb down stairs, or forgeting his own brother's name. When he tried to imagine somebody locking Scotty into a closet and never letting him out, it made Mick so mad he wanted to kill them for doing that. But then he tried to imagine if it was his own mama who locked Scotty up, what then? What would he do then? His mama never would've done such a thing, but what if she did?

It was just too hard to figure out by himself. All he knew was that Brother Teague was crying like Mick never heard anybody cry before in his whole life. Finally he just had to reach over and take hold of Brother Teague's ankle, which was the only part of him that Mick could reach. Mick's hand was so small he couldn't even grab, it was like he was just pressing his hand against Brother Teague's leg.

'You shouldn't feel bad, Brother Teague,' said Mick. 'You're the one who let him out.'

Brother Teague shook his head, still crying.

'I wish these kids hadn't heard that story,' said Brother Deaver.

'Some things you can only tell to children,' said Sister Monk. 'It'll do them no harm.'

Brother Teague pulled his face away from Sister Monk's dress. 'I knew when you came. I was telling *you*. Isn't that how it's done in your testimonies?'

'That's right, Jamie,' said Sister Monk. 'That's how you do it.'

'Now you see why I'll never be a worthy man, Mormon or not,' said Brother Teague. 'There's no place for me out west.'

'It was your mama made you do it,' said Mick.

'I was the one who pushed him back inside,' said Brother Teague. His voice was awful. 'I was the one who turned the key.' Then he reached down inside his shirt and pulled up a key on a leather thong. A common ordinary door key. 'This key,' he said. 'I had the key all along.'

'But Brother Teague,' said Mick, 'you weren't eight years old yet when it all started. You weren't baptized yet. Don't you know Jesus doesn't blame children for what they do before they're eight? I turn eight next week, and when I'm baptized I'll be like I was born all over again, pure and clean, isn't that right, Brother Deaver?'

Brother Deaver nodded. 'Mm-hm,' he said. He was crying now, too, though Mick couldn't figure why, seeing how it was Brother Deaver himself who interviewed

76

him for baptism and taught him half this stuff right after testimony meeting today.

Scotty must have been getting bored now that the story was over. He got up and walked over to Brother Teague and poked him on the shoulder to get his attention. 'Brother Teague,' he said. 'Brother Teague.'

Brother Teague looked up just as Sister Monk said, 'Leave him be, now, you hear?'

'What do you want, Scotty?' asked Brother Teague.

'Now that we're calling you Brother Teague, does that mean you're going west with us to Utah?'

Brother Teague didn't say anything. He just rubbed his eyes and then sat there with his face covered up. Sister Monk and Brother Deaver stayed with him, but Mick couldn't figure out what was going on anymore, and besides, he had to think about the story, and anyway he needed to take a leak and he couldn't do it in the woods unless he got a lot farther away from Sister Monk. So he took Scotty by the hand and led him off to a bunch of bushes higher up the hill.

The whole next week everybody ignored Mick and Scotty and the other kids. There was no school, just packing up and getting ready to go. On Saturday they went down to a deep slow place in the river and baptized Mick in his underwear, because he didn't have any white clothes except his shorts and t-shirt, and Brother Teague had to be baptized in his most faded boxers and a t-shirt he borrowed from Brother Cinn, because Brother Teague didn't have any white clothes at all. Brother Teague came out of the water shivering just as bad as Mick did.

'Water's cold, ain't it?' said Mick.

'Isn't it,' said Sister Cinn.

'Damn cold,' said Brother Teague.

Funny thing was, nobody so much as blinked that Brother Teague swore, right after his baptism, too. Mick couldn't say *ain't*, but Brother Teague could cuss. Which just goes to show you that kids just can't get away with anything, Mick figured.

'That's done it,' said Brother Deaver. 'You're one of us now.'

'Guess so,' said Brother Teague. He looked as goofy as a kindergartner, with his hair all wet and sticking out and that smile on his face.

'It's just a sneaky Mormon trick,' said Brother Cinn. 'Once you're baptized, we don't have to pay you for leading us anymore.'

'I been paid,' said Brother Teague.

Next morning they had a prayer meeting and headed off west toward Chattanooga. They only made it to somewhere between St. Louis and Kansas City that summer, what with getting arrested in Memphis and nearly lynched in Cape Girardeau. Winter was hard, so far north, but they made it, trading tales of how the Saints suffered through the deadly winter in Winter Quarters, Iowa, after getting driven out of Nauvoo. We're just following in their footsteps, living out their story.

The next summer, crossing the plains, all of Brother Teague's woodlore came to nothing. Trees got too sparse to hide in, so they had to learn to travel in the low places between the sweeping swells of the rolling prairie land. The mobbers of the plains didn't care much about highways, either; they could come on you any time. All the grown-ups learned how to shoot – it was worth wasting a few bullets now, said Brother Teague, to be sure they'd not be wasted if it came to a fight.

Never did see any mobbers. But there were signs of their passing. And one day they spotted a column of smoke a long ways off to the south, too thick and black to be a cookfire. 'Somebody's getting burned out,' said Brother Teague.

'Think we'd better hunker down and hide?' asked Brother Cinn.

'I think you best keep lookout while everybody waits

78

here in this gully,' said Brother Teague. 'But I need to go see what's going on.'

'Dangerous,' said Sister Monk.

'No lie,' said Brother Teague. 'But we need to know which way the mobbers rode after they got done there.'

'I'll go with you,' said Brother Deaver. 'There might be survivors. You might need help.'

They came back in the evening. Brother Teague had a little boy perched on the horse behind him. 'You can light up a cookfire,' said Brother Teague. 'They rode south.'

Brother Deaver lifted the boy down off Brother Teague's horse. 'Come on, son,' he said. 'You need to eat.'

'What happened?' asked Sister Monk.

'No need talking about it now,' said Brother Deaver. Plainly he meant no use talking about it in front of the boy.

At dinner Mick and Scotty sat on either side of the new boy. It was like he was a foreigner. He looked at the food like he'd never seen mush before. When they spoke to him he didn't even act like he heard them.

'You deaf?' asked Scotty. 'Can't you hear me? You deaf?'

This time the boy shook his head just a little.

'He can hear!' shouted Scotty.

'Course he can hear,' said Sister Monk, from off by the cookfire. 'Don't go pestering him.'

'Your folks get killed?' asked Mick.

The boy shrugged.

'Our folks did. Got shot down back in North Carolina couple years ago.'

The boy shrugged again.

'What's your name?' asked Mick.

The boy went still, like a statue.

'You got a name, don't you?'

If he did, he never let on. After dinner Brother Teague gave the boy his own bedroll to sleep in. Boy didn't even say thanks. He was a strange one.

But strange or not, Brother Teague never let the new boy out of his sight the whole rest of the way. Always watching out for him, talking to him, pointing things out. Mick couldn't help but feel a stab of envy – Brother Teague was doing all the things he used to do with Mick, and here the new boy didn't even bother to answer. It was Scotty who cleared it up for Mick. 'It's like Brother Teague got to talk to his little brother again,' he said. It made sense to Mick, then, and so he didn't try to butt in, and it hardly bothered him at all to see the new boy perched on Brother Teague's horse with him all the time, or Brother Deaver's whenever Brother Teague was off scouting or doing something dangerous.

It wasn't two weeks later that outriders from Utah found them and led them the rest of the way home, with spare horses no less, so they could all ride. They made a wide circle around the ruins of Denver, but once they were up in the mountains it was Mormon country. 'Didn't used to be,' said Sister Monk. But it was Mormon country now, and the locals were glad enough about it, seeing how the Mormons brought law and order, and places without Mormons were dying or dead.

They ended up in a tent city called Zarahemla, which was going to be the new capital; Salt Lake City was mostly evacuated now, since the scientists said the Great Salt Lake was just getting started on flooding the valleys. Tina Monk took the children up to Temple Square for a picnic, so they'd get a look at what used to be the great Mormon city. 'Now it's going to be the Mormon Sea,' she told them. 'But you remember what it was.' There were sailboats on State Street, and the water was lapping at South Temple; Temple Square was still dry because of a levee of sandbags. People were crammed into Temple Square, looking at things, saying good-bye. The temple was a mountain of granite. It wasn't going anywhere, ever. But the basement levels were already flooded, and soon it would no longer be part of the life of the Church.

'Mankind was too wicked,' Sister Monk told the children. 'But maybe the Lord is just going to hide the temple from us for a while, until we're worthy to get it back.'

The story of the Greensboro Massacre and their trek from North Carolina spread pretty quick. They met the new governor, Sam Monson, who just got elected under the new constitution of the State of Deseret. He was a young man, not all that much older than Brother Teague and a good sight younger than Brother Deaver. But he greeted them all with respect, promised jobs for the grown-ups, and kept his word.

What he couldn't do was keep them together. The orphan laws required kids with both parents dead and no kin to be fostered with families that had both a mother and a father. There was an awful lot of orphans these days. Best they could do for Mick and Scotty was to foster them to the same home together.

Mick was sure that if Brother Teague had been a married man then, he would have adopted that new boy they found; as it was, it near broke Brother Teague's heart to turn him over to the authorities. But he couldn't argue. More than any of them, the new boy needed a family to take care of the boy day and night, something Brother Teague just couldn't do, especially since his new job was being an outrider, which meant finding folks heading toward Deseret and guiding them back safely. A good job for him, and he knew it, but it meant he was gone six weeks at a time.

It might have been they could've lost touch with each other; that's what happened with most companies. But being the sole company ever to come in from the Greensboro massacre, that gave them a story that bound them together. Tina Monk visited and wrote letters; Brother Deaver came every now and then and brought Mick and Scotty along with him when he was

81

in town giving a faith-promoting talk in a nearby ward. The only one they lost track of was the new boy, him being with them only a couple of weeks, and never saying a word or even telling them his name. Mick felt bad about that sometimes, but it couldn't be helped. They'd helped him somewhat, as best they could, but he just wasn't one of them, just hadn't been through it all with them. There was no blame attached to losing touch with him. That's just the way of it – everybody doing his best, fitting in and helping others all he can.

Mick remembered that journey all the days of his life, as clear as if it happened yesterday, and whenever he saw Jamie Teague after that, like at Jamie's wedding with Marie Speaks, and once when they ran into each other at Conference, times like that they'd greet each other and laugh and tell folks that they were the very same age, they had the very same birthday. And it was true, too, because they were born again in ice cold water on that spring morning in the Appalachians.

Salvage

The road began to climb steeply right from the ferry, so the truck couldn't build up any speed. Deaver just kept shifting down, wincing as he listened to the grinding of the gears. Sounded like the transmission was chewing itself to gravel. He'd been nursing it all the way across Nevada, and if the Wendover ferry hadn't carried him these last miles over the Mormon Sea, he would have had a nice long hike. Lucky. It was a good sign. Things were going to go Deaver's way for a while.

The mechanic frowned at him when he rattled in to the loading dock. 'You been ridin the clutch, boy?'

Deaver got down from the cab. 'Clutch? What's a clutch?'

The mechanic didn't smile. 'Couldn't you hear the transmission was shot?'

'I had mechanics all the way across Nevada askin to fix it for me, but I told em I was savin it for you.'

The mechanic looked at him like he was crazy. 'There ain't no mechanics in Nevada.'

If you wasn't dumb as your thumb, thought Deaver, you'd know I was joking. These old Mormons were so straight they couldn't sit down, some of them. But Deaver didn't say anything. Just smiled.

'This truck's gonna stay here a few days,' said the mechanic.

Fine with me, thought Deaver. I got plans. 'How many days you figure?'

'Take three for now, I'll sign you off.'

'My name's Deaver Teague.'

'Tell the foreman, he'll write it up.' The mechanic

lifted the hood to begin the routine checks while the dockboys loaded off the old washing machines and refrigerators and other stuff Deaver had picked up on this trip. Deaver took his mileage reading to the window and the foreman paid him off.

Seven dollars for five days of driving and loading, sleeping in the cab and eating whatever the farmers could spare. It was better than a lot of people lived on, but there wasn't any future in it. Salvage wouldn't go on forever. Someday he'd pick up the last broken-down dishwasher left from the old days, and then he'd be out of a job.

Well, Deaver Teague wasn't going to wait around for that. He knew where the gold was, he'd been planning how to get it for weeks, and if Lehi had got the diving equipment like he promised then tomorrow morning they'd do a little freelance salvage work. If they were lucky they'd come home rich.

Deaver's legs were stiff but he loosened them up pretty quick and broke into an easy, loping run down the corridors of the Salvage Center. He took a flight of stairs two or three steps at a time, bounded down a hall, and when he reached a sign that said SMALL COMPUTER SALVAGE, he pushed off the doorframe and rebounded into the room. 'Hey Lehi!' he said. 'Hey it's quittin time!'

Lehi McKay paid no attention. He was sitting in front of a TV screen, jerking at a black box he held on his lap.

'You do that and you'll go blind,' said Deaver.

'Shut up, carpface.' Lehi never took his eyes off the screen. He jabbed at a button on the black box and twisted on the stick that jutted up from it. A colored blob on the screen blew up and split into four smaller blobs.

'I got three days off while they do the transmission on the truck,' said Deaver. 'So tomorrow's the temple expedition.'

Lehi got the last blob off the screen. More blobs appeared.

'That's real fun,' said Deaver, 'like sweepin the street and then they bring along another troop of horses.'

'It's an Atari. From the sixties or seventies or something. Eighties. Old. Can't do much with the pieces, it's only eight-bit stuff. All these years in somebody's attic in Logan, and the sucker still runs.'

'Old guys probably didn't even know they had it.'

'Probably.'

Deaver watched the game. Same thing over and over again. 'How much a thing like this use to cost?'

'A lot. Maybe fifteen, twenty bucks.'

'Makes you want to barf. And here sits Lehi McKay, toodling his noodle like the old guys use to. All it ever got *them* was a sore noodle, Lehi. And slag for brains.'

'Drown it. I'm trying to concentrate.'

The game finally ended. Lehi set the black box up on the workbench, turned off the machine, and stood up.

'You got everything ready to go underwater tomorrow?' asked Deaver.

'That was a good game. Having fun must've took up a lot of their time in the old days. Mom says the kids used to not even be able to get jobs till they was sixteen. It was the law.'

'Don't you wish,' said Deaver.

'It's true.'

'You don't know your tongue from dung, Lehi. You don't know your heart from a fart.'

'You want to get us both kicked out of here, talkin like that?'

'I don't have to follow school rules now, I graduated sixth grade, I'm nineteen years old, I been on my own for five years.' He pulled his seven dollars out of his pocket, waved them once, stuffed them back in carelessly. 'I do OK, and I talk like I want to talk. Think I'm afraid of the Bishop?'

'Bishop don't scare me. I don't even go to church

except to make Mom happy. It's a bunch of bunny turds.'

Lehi laughed, but Deaver could see that he was a little scared to talk like that. Sixteen years old, thought Deaver, he's big and he's smart but he's such a little kid. He don't understand how it's like to be a man. 'Rain's comin.'

'Rain's always comin. What the hell do you think filled up the lake?' Lehi smirked as he unplugged everything on the workbench.

'I meant *Lor*raine Wilson.'

'I know what you meant. She's got her boat?'

'And she's got a mean set of fenders.' Deaver cupped his hands. 'Just need a little polishing.'

'Why do you always talk dirty? Ever since you started driving salvage, Deaver, you got a gutter mouth. Besides, she's built like a sack.'

'She's near fifty, what do you expect?' It occurred to Deaver that Lehi seemed to be stalling. Which probably meant he botched up again as usual. 'Can you get the diving stuff?'

'I already got it. You thought I'd screw up.' Lehi smirked again.

'You? Screw up? You can be trusted with *anything*.' Deaver started for the door. He could hear Lehi behind him, still shutting a few things off. They got to use a lot of electricity in here. Of course they had to, because they needed computers all the time, and salvage was the only way to get them. But when Deaver saw all that electricity getting used up at once, to him it looked like his own future. All the machines he could ever want, new ones, and all the power they needed. Clothes that nobody else ever wore, his own horse and wagon or even a car. Maybe he'd be the guy who started *making* cars again. He didn't need stupid blob-smashing games from the past. 'That stuff's dead and gone, duck lips, dead and gone.'

'What're you talkin about?' asked Lehi.

'Dead and gone. All your computer things.'

It was enough to set Lehi off, as it always did. Deaver grinned and felt wicked and strong as Lehi babbled along behind him. About how we use the computers more than they ever did in the old days, the computers kept everything going, on and on and on, it was cute, Deaver liked him, the boy was so *intense*. Like everything was the end of the world. Deaver knew better. The world was dead, it had already ended, so none of it mattered, you could sink all this stuff in the lake.

They came out of the Center and walked along the retaining wall. Far below them was the harbor, a little circle of water in the bottom of a bowl, with Bingham City perched on the lip. They used to have an open-pit copper mine here, but when the water rose they cut a channel to it and now they had a nice harbor on Oquirrh Island in the middle of the Mormon Sea, where the factories could stink up the whole sky and no neighbors ever complained about it.

A lot of other people joined them on the steep dirt road that led down to the harbor. Nobody lived right in Bingham City itself, because it was just a working place, day and night. Shifts in, shifts out. Lehi was a shift boy, lived with his family across the Jordan Strait on Point-of-the-Mountain, which was as rotten a place to live as anybody ever devised, rode the ferry in every day at five in the morning and rode it back every afternoon at four. He was supposed to go to school after that for a couple of hours but Deaver thought that was stupid, he told Lehi that all the time, told him again now. School is too much time and too little of everything, a waste of time.

'I gotta go to school,' said Lehi.

'Tell me two plus two, you haven't got two plus two yet?'

'*You* finished, didn't you?'

'Nobody needs anything after fourth grade.' He

shoved Lehi a little. Usually Lehi shoved back, but this time no.

'Just try getting a real job without a sixth-grade diploma, OK? And I'm pretty close now.' They were at the ferry slip. Lehi got out his pass.

'You with me tomorrow or not?'

Lehi made a face. 'I don't know, Deaver. You can get arrested for going around there. It's a dumb thing to do. They say there's real weird things in the old skyscrapers.'

'We aren't going *in* the skyscrapers.'

'Even worse in *there*, Deaver. I don't want to go there.'

'Yeah, the Angel Moroni's probably waiting to jump out and say booga-booga-booga.'

'Don't talk about it, Deaver.' Deaver was tickling him; Lehi laughed and tried to shy away. 'Cut it out, chiggerhead. Come on. Besides, the Moroni statue was moved to the Salt Lake Monument up on the mountain. And that has a guard all the time.'

'The statue's just gold plate anyway. I'm tellin you those old Mormons hid tons of the stuff down in the Temple, just waitin for somebody who isn't scared of the ghost of Bigamy Young to –'

'Shut *up*, snotsucker, OK? People can hear! Look around, we're not alone!'

It was true, of course. Some of the older people were glaring at them. But then, Deaver noticed that older people liked to glare at younger ones. It made the old farts feel better about kicking off. It was like they were saying, OK, I'm dying, but at least you're stupid. So Deaver looked right at a woman who was glaring at him and murmured, 'OK, I'm stupid, but at least I won't die.'

'Deaver, do you always have to say that where they can hear you?'

'It's true.'

'In the first place, Deaver, they aren't dying. And in the second place, you're definitely stupid. And in the third place, the ferry's here.' Lehi punched Deaver lightly in the stomach.

Deaver bent over in mock agony. 'Ay, the laddie's ungrateful, he is, I give him me last croost of bread and this be the thanks I gets.'

'*Nobody* has an accent like that, Deaver!' shouted Lehi. The boat began to pull away.

'Tomorrow at five-thirty!' shouted Deaver.

'You'll never get up at four-thirty, don't give me that, you never get up . . .' But the ferry and the noise of the factories and machines and trucks swallowed up the rest of his insults. Deaver knew them all, anyway. Lehi might be only sixteen, but he was OK. Someday Deaver'd get married but his wife would like Lehi, too. And Lehi'd even get married, and his wife would like Deaver. She'd better, or she'd have to swim home.

He took the trolley home to Fort Douglas and walked to the ancient barracks building where Rain let him stay. It was supposed to be a storage room, but she kept the mops and soap stuff in her place so that there'd be room for a cot. Not much else, but it was on Oquirrh Island without being right there in the stink and the smoke and the noise. He could sleep and that was enough, since most of the time he was out on the truck.

Truth was, his room wasn't home anyway. Home was pretty much Rain's place, a drafty room at the end of the barracks with a dumpy frowzy lady who served him good food and plenty of it. That's where he went now, walked right in and surprised her in the kitchen. She yelled at him for surprising her, yelled at him for being filthy and tracking all over her floor, and let him get a slice of apple before she yelled at him for snitching before supper.

He went around and changed light bulbs in five rooms before supper. The families there were all crammed into two rooms each at the most, and most of them had to share kitchens and eat in shifts. Some of the rooms were nasty places, family warfare held off only as long as it took him to change the light, and sometimes even that truce wasn't observed. Others were doing fine, the place was small but they liked each other. Deaver was pretty sure his family must have been one of the nice ones, because if there'd been any yelling he would have remembered.

Rain and Deaver ate and then turned off all the lights while she played the old record player Deaver had wangled away from Lehi. They really weren't supposed to have it, but they figured as long as they didn't burn any lights it wasn't wasting electricity, and they'd turn it in as soon as anybody asked for it.

In the meantime, Rain had some of the old records from when she was a girl. The songs had strong rhythms, and tonight, like she sometimes did, Rain got up and moved to the music, strange little dances that Deaver didn't understand unless he imagined her as a lithe young girl, pictured her body as it must have been then. It wasn't hard to imagine, it was there in her eyes and her smile all the time, and her movements gave away secrets that years of starchy eating and lack of exercise had disguised.

Then, as always, his thoughts went off to some of the girls he saw from his truck window, driving by the fields where they bent over, hard at work, until they heard the truck and then they stood and waved. Everybody waved at the salvage truck, sometimes it was the only thing with a motor that ever came by, their only contact with the old machines. All the tractors, all the electricity were reserved for the New Soil Lands; the old places were dying. And they turned and waved at the last memories. It made Deaver sad and he hated to be sad, all these people clinging to a past that never existed.

'It never existed,' he said aloud.

'Yes it did,' Rain whispered. 'Girls just wanna have fu-un,' she murmured along with the record. 'I hated this song when I was a girl. Or maybe it was my mama who hated it.'

'You live here then?'

'Indiana,' she said. 'One of the states, way east.'

'Were you a refugee, too?'

'No. We moved here when I was sixteen, seventeen, can't remember. Whenever things got scary in the world, a lot of Mormons moved home. This was always home, no matter what.'

The record ended. She turned it off, turned on the lights.

'Got the boat all gassed up?' asked Deaver.

'You don't want to go there,' she said.

'If there's gold down there, I want it.'

'If there was gold there, Deaver, they would've taken it out before the water covered it. It's not as if nobody got a warning, you know. The Mormon Sea wasn't a flash flood.'

'If it isn't down there, what's all the hush-hush about? How come the Lake Patrol keeps people from going there?'

'I don't know, Deaver. Maybe because a lot of people feel like it's a holy place.'

Deaver was used to this. Rain never went to church, but she still talked like a Mormon. Most people did, though, when you scratched them the wrong place. Deaver didn't like it when they got religious. 'Angels need police protection, is that it?'

'It used to be real important to the Mormons in the old days, Deaver.' She sat down on the floor, leaning against the wall under the window.

'Well it's nothin now. They got their other temples, don't they? And they're building the new one in Zarahemla, right?'

'I don't know, Deaver. The one here, it was always the real one. The center.' She bent sideways, leaned on her hand, looked down at the floor. 'It still is.'

Deaver saw she was getting really somber now, really sad. It happened to a lot of people who remembered the old days. Like a disease that never got cured. But

91

Deaver knew the cure. For Rain, anyway. 'Is it true they used to kill people in there?'

It worked. She glared at him and the languor left her body. 'Is that what you truckers talk about all day?'

Deaver grinned. 'There's stories. Cuttin people up if they told where the gold was hid.'

'You know Mormons all over the place, now, Deaver, do you really think we'd go cuttin people up for tellin secrets?'

'I don't know. Depends on the secrets, don't it?' He was sitting on his hands, kind of bouncing a little on the couch.

He could see that she was a little mad for real, but didn't want to be. So she'd pretend to be mad for play. She sat up, reached for a pillow to throw at him.

'No! No!' he cried. 'Don't cut me up! Don't feed me to the carp!'

The pillow hit him and he pretended elaborately to die.

'Just don't joke about things like that,' she said.

'Things like what? You don't believe in the old stuff anymore. Nobody does.'

'Maybe not.'

'Jesus was supposed to come again, right? There was atom bombs dropped here and there, and he was supposed to come.'

'Prophet said we was too wicked. He wouldn't come cause we loved the things of the world too much.'

'Come on, if he was comin he would've come, right?'

'Might still,' she said.

'Nobody believes that,' said Deaver. 'Mormons are just the government, that's all. The Bishop gets elected judge in every town, right? The president of the elders is always mayor, it's just the government, just politics, nobody believes it now. Zarahemla's the capital, not the holy city.'

He couldn't see her because he was lying flat on his back on the couch. When she didn't answer, he got up and looked for her. She was over by the sink, leaning on the counter. He snuck up behind her to tickle her, but something in her posture changed his mind. When he got close, he saw tears down her cheeks. It was crazy. All these people from the old days got crazy a lot.

'I was just teasin,' he said.

She nodded.

'It's just part of the old days. You know how I am about that. Maybe if I remembered, it'd be different. Sometimes I wish I remembered.' But it was a lie. He never wished he remembered. He didn't like remembering. Most stuff he couldn't remember even if he wanted to. The earliest thing he could bring to mind was riding on the back of a horse, behind some man who sweated a lot, just riding and riding and riding. And then it was all recent stuff, going to school, getting passed around in people's homes, finally getting busy one year and finishing school and getting a job. He didn't get misty-eyed thinking about any of it, any of those places. Just passing through, that's all he was ever doing, never belonged anywhere until maybe now. With Lehi and Rain, the two of them, they were both home. He belonged here. 'I'm sorry,' he said.

'It's fine,' she said.

'You still gonna take me there?'

'I said I would, didn't I?'

She sounded just annoyed enough that he knew it was OK to tease her again. 'You don't think they'll have the Second Coming while we're there, do you? If you think so, I'll wear my tie.'

She smiled, then turned to face him and pushed him away. 'Deaver, go to bed.'

'I'm gettin up at four-thirty, Rain, and then you're one girl who's gonna have fun.'

'I don't think the song was about early morning boat trips.'

She was doing the dishes when he left for his little room.

*

93

Lehi was waiting at five-thirty, right on schedule. 'I can't believe it,' he said. 'I thought you'd be late.'

'Good thing you were ready on time,' said Deaver, 'cause if you didn't come with us you wouldn't get a cut.'

'We aren't going to find any gold, Deaver Teague.'

'Then why're you comin with me? Don't give me that stuff, Lehi, you know the future's with Deaver Teague, and you don't want to be left behind. Where's the diving stuff?'

'I didn't bring it *home*, Deaver. You don't think my mom'd ask questions then?'

'She's always askin questions,' said Deaver.

'It's her job,' said Rain.

'I don't want anybody askin about everything I do,' said Deaver.

'Nobody has to ask,' said Rain. 'You always tell us whether we want to hear or not.'

'If you don't want to hear, you don't have to,' said Deaver.

'Don't get touchy,' said Rain.

'You guys are both gettin wet-headed on me, all of a sudden. Does the temple make you crazy, is that how it works?'

'I don't mind my mom askin me stuff. It's OK.'

The ferries ran from Point to Bingham day and night, so they had to go north a ways before cutting west to Oquirrh Island. The smelter and the foundries put orange-bellied smoke clouds into the night sky, and the coal barges were getting offloaded just like in daytime. The coal-dust cloud that was so grimy and black in the day looked like white fog under the floodlights.

'My dad died right there, about this time of day,' said Lehi.

'He loaded coal?'

'Yeah. He used to be a car salesman. His job kind of disappeared on him.'

'You weren't there, were you?'

'I heard the crash. I was asleep, but it woke me up. And then a lot of shouting and running. We lived on the island back then, always heard stuff from the harbor. He got buried under a ton of coal that fell from fifty feet up.'

Deaver didn't know what to say about that.

'You never talk about your folks,' said Lehi. 'I always remember my dad, but you never talk about your folks.'

Deaver shrugged.

'He doesn't remember em,' Rain said quietly. 'They found him out on the plains somewhere. The mobbers got his family, however many there was, he must've hid or something, that's all they can figure.'

'Well what was it?' asked Lehi. 'Did you hide?'

Deaver didn't feel comfortable talking about it, since he didn't remember anything except what people told him. He knew that other people remembered their childhood, and he didn't like how they always acted so surprised that he didn't. But Lehi was asking, and Deaver knew that you don't keep stuff back from friends. 'I guess I did. Or maybe I looked too dumb to kill or somethin.' He laughed. 'I must've been a real dumb little kid, I didn't even remember my own name. They figure I was five or six years old, most kids know their names, but not me. So the two guys that found me, their names were Teague and Deaver.'

'You gotta remember somethin.'

'Lehi, I didn't even know how to talk. They tell me I didn't even say a word till I was nine years old. We're talkin about a slow learner here.'

'Wow.' Lehi was silent for a while. 'How come you didn't say anything?'

'Doesn't matter,' said Rain. 'He makes up for it now, Deaver the talker. Champion talker.'

They coasted the island till they got past Magna. Lehi led them to a storage shed that Underwater Salvage had put up at the north end of Oquirrh Island. It was unlocked and full of diving equipment. Lehi's friend

95

had filled some tanks with air. They got two diving out-fits and underwater flashlights. Rain wasn't going underwater, so she didn't need anything.

They pulled away from the island, out into the regular shipping lane from Wendover. In that direction, at least, people had sense enough not to travel at night, so there wasn't much traffic. After a little while they were out into open water. That was when Rain stopped the little outboard motor Deaver had scrounged for her and Lehi had fixed. 'Time to sweat and slave,' said Rain.

Deaver sat on the middle bench, settled the oars into the locks, and began to row.

'Not too fast,' Rain said. 'You'll give yourself blisters.'

A boat that might have been Lake Patrol went by once, but otherwise nobody came near them as they crossed the open stretch. Then the skyscrapers rose up and blocked off large sections of the starry night.

'They say there's people who was never rescued still livin in there,' Lehi whispered.

Rain was disdainful. 'You think there's anything left in there to keep anybody alive? And the water's still too salty to drink for long.'

'Who says they're alive?' whispered Deaver in his most mysterious voice. A couple of years ago, he could have spooked Lehi and made his eyes go wide. Now Lehi just looked disgusted.

'Come on, Deaver, I'm not a kid.'

It was Deaver who got spooked a little. The big holes where pieces of glass and plastic had fallen off looked like mouths, waiting to suck him in and carry him down under the water, into the city of the drowned. He some-times dreamed about thousands and thousands of people living under water. Still driving their cars around, going about their business, shopping in stores, going to movies. In his dreams they never did anything bad, just went about their business. But he always woke up sweating and frightened. No reason. Just spooked him. 'I think they should blow up these things before they fall down

96

and hurt somebody,' said Deaver.

'Maybe it's better to leave em standing,' said Rain. 'Maybe there's a lot of folks like to remember how tall we once stood.'

'What's to remember? They built tall buildings and then they let em take a bath, what's to brag for?'

Deaver was trying to get her not to talk about the old days, but Lehi seemed to like wallowing in it. 'You ever here before the water came?'

Rain nodded. 'Saw a parade go right down this street. I can't remember if it was Third South or Fourth South. Third I guess. I saw twenty-five horses all riding together. I remember that I thought that was really something. You didn't see many horses in those days.'

'I seen too many myself,' said Lehi.

'It's the ones I don't see that I hate,' said Deaver. 'They ought to make em wear diapers.'

They rounded a building and looked up a north-south passage between towers. Rain was sitting in the stern and saw it first. 'There it is. You can see it. Just the tall spires now.'

Deaver rowed them up the passage. There were six spires sticking up out of the water, but the four short ones were under so far that only the pointed roofs were dry. The two tall ones had windows in them, not covered at all. Deaver was disappointed. Wide open like that meant that anybody might have come here. It was all so much less dangerous than he had expected. Maybe Rain was right, and there was nothing there.

They tied the boat to the north side and waited for daylight. 'If I knew it'd be so easy,' said Deaver, 'I could've slept another hour.'

'Sleep now,' said Rain.

'Maybe I will,' said Deaver.

He slid off his bench and sprawled in the bottom of the boat.

He didn't sleep, though. The open window of the steeple was only a few yards away, a deep black surrounded by the starlit grey of the temple granite. It was down there, waiting for him; the future, a chance to get something better for himself and his two friends. Maybe a plot of ground in the south where it was warmer and the snow didn't pile up five feet deep every winter, where it wasn't rain in the sky and lake everywhere else you looked. A place where he could live for a very long time and look back and remember good times with his friends, that was all waiting down under the water.

Of course they hadn't *told* him about the gold. It was on the road, a little place in Parowan where truckers knew they could stop in because the iron mine kept such crazy shifts that the diners never closed. They even had some coffee there, hot and bitter, because there weren't so many Mormons there and the miners didn't let the Bishop push them around. In fact they even called him Judge there instead of Bishop. The other drivers didn't talk to Deaver, of course, they were talking to each other when the one fellow told the story about how the Mormons back in the gold rush days hoarded up all the gold they could get and hid it in the upper rooms of the temple where nobody but the prophet and the twelve apostles could ever go. At first Deaver didn't believe him, except that Bill Horne nodded like he knew it was true, and Cal Silber said you'd never catch him messin with the Mormon temple, that's a good way to get yourself dead. The way they were talking, scared and quiet, told Deaver that they believed it, that it was true, and he knew something else, too: if anyone was going to get that gold, it was him.

Even if it *was* easy to get here, that didn't mean anything. He knew how Mormons were about the temple. He'd asked around a little, but nobody'd talk about it. And nobody ever went there, either, he asked a lot of people if they ever sailed on out and looked at it, and they all got quiet and shook their heads no or changed the subject. Why should the Lake Patrol guard it, then, if everybody was too scared to go? Everybody but Deaver Teague and his two friends.

'Real pretty,' said Rain.

Deaver woke up. The sun was just topping the mountains; it must've been light for some time. He looked where Rain was looking. It was the Moroni tower on the top of the mountain above the old capitol, where they'd put the temple statue a few years back. It was bright and shiny, the old guy and his trumpet. But when the Mormons wanted that trumpet to blow, it had just stayed silent and their faith got drowned. Now Deaver knew they only hung on to it for old times' sake. Well, Deaver lived for new times.

Lehi showed him how to use the underwater gear, and they practiced going over the side into the water a couple of times, once without the weight belts and once with. Deaver and Lehi swam like fish, of course – swimming was the main recreation that everybody could do for free. It was different with the mask and the air hose, though.

'Hose tastes like a horse's hoof,' Deaver said between dives.

Lehi made sure Deaver's weight belt was on tight. 'You're the only guy on Oquirrh Island who knows.' Then he tumbled forward off the boat. Deaver went down too straight and the air tank bumped the back of his head a little, but it didn't hurt too much and he didn't drop his light, either.

He swam along the outside of the temple, shining his light on the stones. Lots of underwater plants were rising up the sides of the temple, but it wasn't covered much yet. There was a big metal plaque right in the front of the building, about a third of the way down. THE HOUSE OF THE LORD it said. Deaver pointed it out to Lehi.

When they got up to the boat again, Deaver asked about it. 'It looked kind of goldish,' he said.

'Used to be another sign there,' said Rain. 'It was a little

different. That one might have been gold. This one's
plastic. They made it so the temple would still have a
sign, I guess.'

'You sure about that?'

'I remember when they did it.'

Finally Deaver felt confident enough to go down into
the temple. They had to take off their flippers to climb
into the steeple window; Rain tossed them up after. In
the sunlight there was nothing spooking about the window. They sat there on the sill, water lapping at their
feet, and put their fins and tanks on.

Halfway through getting dressed, Lehi stopped. Just
sat there.

'I can't do it,' he said.

'Nothin to be scared of,' said Deaver. 'Come on,
there's no ghosts or nothin down there.'

'I can't,' said Lehi.

'Good for you,' called Rain from the boat.

Deaver turned to look at her. 'What're you talkin
about?'

'I don't think you should.'

'Then why'd you bring me here?'

'Because you wanted to.'

Made no sense.

'It's holy ground, Deaver,' said Rain. 'Lehi feels it, too.
That-why he isn't going down.'

Deaver looked at Lehi.

'It just don't feel right,' said Lehi.

'It's just stones,' said Deaver.

Lehi said nothing. Deaver put on his goggles, took a
light, put the breather in his mouth, and jumped.

Turned out the floor was only a foot and a half down.
It took him completely by surprise, so he fell over and
sat on his butt in eighteen inches of water. Lehi was just
as surprised as he was, but then he started laughing, and
Deaver laughed, too. Deaver got to his feet and started
flapping around, looking for the stairway. He could
hardly take a step, his flippers slowed him down so much.

100

'Walk backward,' said Lehi.

'Then how am I supposed to see where I'm going?'

'Stick your face under the water and look, chiggerhead.'

Deaver stuck his face in the water. Without the reflection of why he isn't going down.'

Deaver looked at Lehi.

'It just don't feel right,' said Lehi.

'It's just stones,' said Deaver.

Lehi said nothing. Deaver put daylight on the surface, he could see fine. There was the stairway.

He got up, looked toward Lehi. Lehi shook his head. He still wasn't going.

'Suit yourself,' said Deaver. He backed through the water to the top step. Then he put in his breathing tube and went down.

It wasn't easy to get down the stairs. They're fine when you aren't floating, thought Deaver, but they're a pain when you keep scraping your tanks on the ceiling. Finally he figured out he could grab the railing and pull himself down. The stairs wound around and around. When they ended, a whole bunch of garbage had filled up the bottom of the stairwell, partly blocking the doorway. He swam above the garbage, which looked like scrap metal and chips of wood, and came out into a large room.

His light didn't shine very far through the murky water, so he swam the walls, around and around, high and low. Down here the water was cold, and he swam faster to keep warm. There were rows of arched windows on both sides, with rows of circular windows above them, but they had been covered over with wood on the outside; the only light was from Deaver's flashlight. Finally, though, after a couple of times around the room and across the ceiling, he figured it was just one big room. And except for the garbage all over the floor, it was empty.

Already he felt the deep pain of disappointment. He forced himself to ignore it. After all, it wouldn't be right

101

out here in a big room like this, would it? There had to be a secret treasury.

There were a couple of doors. The small one in the middle of the wall at one end was wide open. Once there must have been stairs leading up to it. Deaver swam over there and shone his light in. Just another room, smaller this time. He found a couple more rooms, but they had all been stripped, right down to the stone. Nothing at all.

He tried examining some of the stones to look for secret doors, but he gave up pretty soon – he couldn't see well enough from the flashlight to find a thin crack even if it was there. Now the disappointment was real. As he swam along, he began to wonder if maybe the truckers hadn't known he was listening. Maybe they made room it all up just so someday he'd do this. Some joke, where they wouldn't even see him make a fool of himself.

But no, no, that couldn't be it. They believed it, all right. But he knew now what they didn't know. Whatever the Mormons did here in the old days, there wasn't any gold in the upper rooms now. So much for the future. But what the hell, he told himself, I got here, I saw it, and I'll find something else. No reason not to be cheerful about it.

He didn't fool himself, and there was nobody else down here to fool. It was bitter. He'd spent a lot of years thinking about bars of gold or bags of it. He'd always pictured it hidden behind a curtain. He'd pull on the curtain and it would billow out in the water, and here would be the bags of gold, and he'd just take them out and that would be it. But there weren't any curtains, weren't any hidey-holes, there was nothing at all, and if he had a future, he'd have to find it somewhere else.

He swam back to the door leading to the stairway. Now he could see the pile of garbage better, and it occurred to him to wonder how it got there. Every other room was completely empty. The garbage couldn't

102

have been carried in by the water, because the only windows that were open were in the steeple, and they were above the water line. He swam close and picked up a piece. It was metal. They were all metal, except a few stones, and it occurred to him that this might be it after all. If you're hiding a treasure, you don't put it in bags or ingots, you leave it around looking like garbage and people leave it alone.

He gathered up as many of the thin metal pieces as he could carry in one hand and swam carefully up the stairwell. Lehi would have to come down now and help him carry it up; they could make bags out of their shirts to carry lots of it at a time.

He splashed out into the air and then walked backward up the last few steps and across the submerged floor. Lehi was still sitting on the sill, and now Rain was there beside him, her bare feet dangling in the water. When he got to them he turned around and held out the metal in his hands. He couldn't see their faces well, because the outside of the facemask was blurry with water and kept catching sunlight.

'You scraped your knee,' said Rain.

Deaver handed her his flashlight and now that his hand was free, he could pull his mask off and look at them. They were very serious. He held out the metal pieces toward them. 'Look what I found down there.'

Lehi took a couple of the metal pieces from him. Rain never took her eyes from Deaver's face.

'It's old cans, Deaver,' Lehi said quietly.

'No it isn't,' said Deaver. But he looked at his fistful of metal sheets and realized it was true. They had been cut down the side and pressed flat, but they were sure enough cans.

'There's writing on it,' said Lehi. 'It says, Dear Lord heal my girl Jenny please I pray.'

Deaver set down his handful on the sill. Then he took one, turned it over, found the writing. 'Forgive my adultery I will sin no more.'

103

Lehi read another. 'Bring my boy safe from the plains O Lord God.'

Each message was scratched with a nail or a piece of glass, the letters crudely formed.

'They used to say prayers all day in the temple, and people would bring in names and they'd say the temple prayers for them,' said Rain. 'Nobody prays here now, but they still bring the names. On metal so they'll last.'

'We shouldn't read these,' said Lehi. 'We should put them back.'

There were hundreds, maybe thousands of those metal prayers down there. People must come here all the time, Deaver realized. The Mormons must have a regular traffic coming here and leaving these things behind. But nobody told me.

'Did you know about this?'

Rain nodded.

'You brought them here, didn't you.'

'Some of them. Over the years.'

'You knew what was down there.'

She didn't answer.

'She told you not to come,' said Lehi.

'You knew about this too?'

'I knew people came, I didn't know what they did.'

And suddenly the magnitude of it struck him. Lehi and Rain had both known. All the Mormons knew, then. They all knew, and he had asked again and again, and no one had told him. Not even his friends.

'Why'd you let me come out here?'

'Tried to stop you,' said Rain.

'Why didn't you tell me this?'

She looked him in the eye. 'Deaver, you would've thought I was givin you the runaround. And you would have laughed at this, if I told you. I thought it was better if you saw it. Then maybe you wouldn't go tellin people how dumb the Mormons are.'

'You think I would?' He held up another metal prayer and read it aloud. 'Come quickly, Lord Jesus, before I die.' He shook it at her. 'You think I'd laugh at these people?'

'You laugh at everything, Deaver.'

Deaver looked at Lehi. This was something Lehi had never said before. Deaver would never laugh at something that was really important. And this was really important to them, to them both.

'This is yours,' Deaver said. 'All this stuff is yours.'

'I never left a prayer here,' said Lehi.

But when he said *yours* he didn't mean just them, just Lehi and Rain. He meant all of them, all the people of the Mormon Sea, all the ones who had known about it but never told him even though he asked again and again. All the people who belonged here. 'I came to find something here for *me*, and you knew all the time it was only *your* stuff down there.'

Lehi and Rain looked at each other, then back at Deaver.

'It isn't ours,' said Rain.

'I never been here before,' said Lehi.

'It's your stuff.' He sat down in the water and began taking off the underwater gear.

'Don't be mad,' said Lehi. 'I didn't know.'

You knew more than you told me. All the time I thought we were friends, but it wasn't true. You two had this place in common with all the other people, but not with me. Everybody but me.

Lehi carefully took the metal sheets to the stairway and dropped them. They sank at once, to drift down and take their place on the pile of supplications.

Lehi rowed them through the skyscrapers to the east of the old city, and then Rain started the motor and they skimmed along the surface of the lake. The Lake Patrol didn't see them, but Deaver knew now that it didn't matter much if they did. The Lake Patrol was mostly Mormons. They undoubtedly knew about the traffic here, and let it happen as long as it was discreet. Probably the only people they stopped were the people who weren't in on it.

All the way back to Magna to return the underwater gear, Deaver sat in the front of the boat, not talking to the others. Where Deaver sat, the bow of the boat seemed to curve under him. The faster they went, the less the boat seemed to touch the water. Just skimming over the surface, never really touching deep; making a few waves, but the water always smoothed out again.

Those two people in the back of the boat, he felt kind of sorry for them. They still lived in the drowned city, they belonged down there, and the fact they couldn't go there broke their hearts. But not Deaver. His city wasn't even built yet. His city was tomorrow.

He'd driven a salvage truck and lived in a closet long enough. Maybe he'd go south into the New Soil Lands. Maybe qualify on a piece of land. Own something, plant in the soil, maybe he'd come to belong there. As for this place, well, he never had belonged here, just like all the foster homes and schools along the way, just one more stop for a year or two or three, he knew that all along. Never did made any friends here, but that's how he wanted it. Wouldn't be right to make friends, cause he'd just move on and disappoint them. Didn't see no good in doing that to people.

The Fringe

LaVon's book report was drivel, of course. Carpenter knew it would be from the moment he called on the boy. After Carpenter's warning last week, he knew LaVon would have a book report – LaVon's father would never let the boy be suspended. But LaVon was too stubborn, too cocky, too much the leader of the other sixth-graders' constant rebellion against authority to let Carpenter have a complete victory.

'I really, truly loved *Little Men*,' said LaVon. 'It just gave me goose bumps.'

The class laughed. Excellent comic timing, Carpenter said silently. But the only place that comedy is useful here in the New Soil country is with the gypsy pageant wagons. That's what you're preparing yourself for, LaVon, a career as a wandering parasite who lives by sucking laughter out of weary farmers.

'Everybody nice in this book has a name that starts with *d*. Demi is a sweet little boy who never does anything wrong. Daisy is so good that she could have seven children and still be a virgin.'

He was pushing the limits now. A lot of people didn't like mention of sexual matters in the school, and if some pin-headed child decided to report this, the story could be twisted into something that could be used against Carpenter. Out here near the fringe, people were desperate for entertainment. A crusade to drive out a teacher for corrupting the morals of youth would be more fun than a traveling show, because everybody could feel righteous and safe when he was gone. Carpenter had seen it before. Not that he was afraid of it, the way most teachers were. *He* had a career no matter what. The university would take him back, eagerly; they thought he was crazy to go out and teach in the low schools. I'm safe, absolutely safe, he thought. They can't wreck my career. And I'm not going to get prissy about a perfectly good word like *virgin*.

'Dan looks like a big bad boy, but he has a heart of gold, even though he does say real bad words like *devil* sometimes.' LaVon paused, waiting for Carpenter to react. So Carpenter did not react.

'The saddest thing is poor Nat, the street fiddler's boy. He tries hard to fit in, but he can never amount to anything in the book, because his name doesn't start with *d*.'

The end. LaVon put the single paper on Carpenter's desk, then went back to his seat. He walked with the careful elegance of a spider, each long leg moving as if it were unconnected to the rest of his body, so that even walking did not disturb the perfect calm. The boy rides on his body the way I ride in my wheelchair, thought Carpenter. Smooth, unmoved by his own motion. But *he* is graceful and beautiful, fifteen years old and already a master at winning the devotion of the weak-hearted children around him. *He* is the enemy, the torturer, the strong and beautiful man who must confirm his beauty by preying on the weak. I am not as weak as you think.

LaVon's book report was arrogant, far too short, and flagrantly rebellious. That much was deliberate, calculated to annoy Carpenter. Therefore Carpenter would not show the slightest trace of annoyance. The book report had also been clever, ironic, and funny. The boy, for all his mask of languor and stupidity, had brains. He was better than this farming town; he could do something that mattered in the world besides driving a tractor in endless contour patterns around the fields. But the way he always had the Fisher girl hanging on him, he'd no doubt have a baby and a wife and stay here forever. Become a big shot like his father, maybe, but never leave a mark in the world to show he'd been there. Tragic, stupid waste.

But don't show the anger. The children will misunderstand, they'll think I'm angry because of LaVon's rebelliousness, and it will only make this boy more of a hero in their eyes. Children choose their heroes with unerring stupidity. Fourteen, fifteen, sixteen years old, all they know of life is cold and bookless classrooms interrupted now and then by a year or two of wrestling with this stony earth, always hating whatever adult it is who keeps them at their work, always adoring whatever fool gives them the illusion of being free. You children have no practice in surviving among the ruins of your own mistakes. We adults who knew the world before it fell, we feel the weight of the rubble on our backs.

They were waiting for Carpenter's answer. He reached out to the computer keyboard attached to his wheelchair. His hands struck like paws at the oversized keys. His fingers were too stupid for him to use them individually. They clenched when he tried to work them, tightened into a fist, a little hammer with which to strike, to break, to attack; he could not use them to grasp or even hold. Half the verbs of the world are impossible to me, he thought as he often thought. I learn them the way the blind learn words of seeing – by rote, with no hope of ever knowing truly what they mean.

The speech synthesizer droned out the words he keyed. 'Brilliant essay, Mr. Jensen. The irony was powerful, the savagery was refreshing. Unfortunately, it also revealed the poverty of your soul. Alcott's title was ironic, for she wanted to show that despite their small size, the boys in her book were great-hearted. You, however, despite your large size, are very small of heart indeed.'

LaVon looked at him through heavy-lidded eyes. Hatred? Yes, it was there. Do hate me, child. Loathe me enough to show me that you can do anything I ask you to do. Then I'll own you, then I can get something decent out of you, and finally give you back to yourself as a human being who is worthy to be alive.

Carpenter pushed outward on both levers, and his wheelchair backed up. The day was nearly over, and tonight he knew some things would change, painfully, in the life of the town of Reefrock. And because in a way the arrests would be his fault, and because the imprisonment of a father would cause upheaval in some of these children's families, he felt it his duty to prepare them as best he could to understand why it had to happen, why, in the larger view, it was good. It was too much to expect that they would actually understand, today; but they might remember, might forgive him someday for what they would soon find out that he had done to them.

So he pawed at the keys again. 'Economics,' said the computer. 'Since Mr. Jensen has made an end of literature for the day.' A few more keys, and the lecture began. Carpenter entered all his lectures and stored them in memory, so that he could sit still as ice in his chair, making eye contact with each student in turn, daring them to be inattentive. There were advantages in letting a machine speak for him; he learned many years ago that it frightened people to have a mechanical voice speak his words, while his lips were motionless. It was monstrous, it made him seem dangerous and strange. Which he far preferred to the way he looked, weak as a worm, his skinny, twisted, palsied body rigid in his chair; his body looked strange, but pathetic. Only when the synthesizer spoke his acid words did he earn respect from the people who always, always looked downward at him.

'Here in the settlements just behind the fringe,' his voice went on, 'we do not have the luxury of a free economy. The rains sweep onto this ancient desert and find nothing here but a few plants growing in the sand. Thirty years ago, nothing lived here; even the lizards had to stay where there was something for insects to eat, where there was water to drink. Then the fires we lit put a curtain in the sky, and the ice moved south, and the rains that had always passed north of us now raked and scoured the desert. It was opportunity.'

LaVon smirked as Kippie made a great show of dozing off. Carpenter keyed an interruption in the lecture. 'Kippie, how well will you sleep if I send you home now for an afternoon nap?'

Kippie sat bolt upright, pretending terrible fear. But the pretense was also a pretense; he *was* afraid, and so to conceal it he pretended to be pretending to be afraid. Very complex, the inner life of children, thought Carpenter.

'Even as the old settlements were slowly drowned under the rising Great Salt Lake, your fathers and mothers began to move out into the desert, to reclaim it. But not alone. We can do nothing alone here. The fringers plant their grass. The grass feeds the herds and puts roots into the sand. The roots become humus, rich in nitrogen. In three years the fringe has a thin lace of soil across it. If at any point a fringer fails to plant, if at any point the soil is broken, then the rains eat channels under it, and tear away the fringe on either side, and eat back into farmland behind it. So every fringer is responsible to every other fringer, and to us. How would you feel about a fringer who failed?'

'The way I feel about a fringer who succeeds,' said Pope. He was the youngest of the sixth-graders, only thirteen years old, and he sucked up to LaVon disgracefully.

Carpenter punched four codes. 'And how is that?' asked Carpenter's metal voice.

Pope's courage fled. 'Sorry.'

Carpenter did not let go. 'What is it you call fringers?' he asked. He looked from one child to the next, and they would not meet his gaze. Except LaVon.

'What do you call them?' he asked again.

'If I say it, I'll get kicked out of school,' said LaVon. 'You want me kicked out of school?'

'You accuse them of fornicating with cattle, yes?'

A few giggles.

'Yes sir,' said LaVon. 'We call them cow-fornicators, sir.'

Carpenter keyed in his response while they laughed. When the room was silent, he played it back. 'The bread you eat grows in the soil they created, and the manure of their cattle is the strength of your bodies. Without fringers you would be eking out a miserable life on the shores of the Mormon Sea, eating fish and drinking sage tea, and don't forget it.' He set the volume of the synthesizer steadily lower during the speech, so that at the end they were straining to hear.

Then he resumed his lecture. 'After the fringers came your mothers and fathers, planting crops in a scientifically planned order: two rows of apple trees, then six meters of wheat, then six meters of corn, then six meters of cucumbers, and so on, year after year, moving six more meters out, following the fringers, making more land, more food. If you didn't plant what you were told, and harvest it on the right day, and work shoulder to shoulder in the fields whenever the need came, then the plants would die, the rain would wash them away. What do you think of the farmer who does not do his labor or take his work turn?'

'Scum,' one child said. And another: 'He's a wallow, that what he is.'

'If this land is to be truly alive, it must be planted in a careful plan for eighteen years. Only then will your family have the luxury of deciding what crop to plant. Only then will you be able to be lazy if you want to, or work extra hard and profit from it. Then some of you can get rich, and others can become poor. But now, today, we do everything together, equally, and so we share equally in the rewards of our work.'

LaVon murmured something.

112

'Yes, LaVon?' asked Carpenter. He made the computer speak very loudly. It startled the children.

'Nothing,' said LaVon.

'You said: Except teachers.'

'What if I did?'

'You are correct,' said Carpenter. 'Teachers do not plow and plant in the fields with your parents. Teachers are given much more barren soil to work in, and most of the time the few seeds we plant are washed away with the first spring shower. You are living proof of the futility of our labour. But we try, Mr. Jensen, foolish as the effort is. May we continue?'

LaVon nodded. His face was flushed. Carpenter was satisfied. The boy was not hopeless – he could still feel shame at having attacked a man's livelihood.

'There are some among us,' said the lecture, 'who believe they should benefit more than others from the work of all. These are the ones who steal from the common storehouse and sell the crops that were raised by everyone's labor. The black market pays high prices for the stolen grain, and the thieves get rich. When they get rich enough, they move away from the fringe, back to the cities of the high valleys. They wives will wear fine clothing, their sons will have watches, their daughters will own land and marry well. And in the meantime, their friends and neighbors, who trusted them, will have nothing, will stay on the fringe, growing the food that feeds the thieves. Tell me, what do you think of a black marketeer?'

He watched their faces. Yes, they knew. He could see how they glanced surreptitiously at Dick's new shoes, at Kippie's wristwatch. At Yutonna's new city-bought blouse. At LaVon's jeans. They knew, but out of fear they had said nothing. Or perhaps it wasn't fear. Perhaps it was the hope that their own father would be clever enough to steal from the harvest, so they could move away instead of earning out their eighteen years.

'Some people think these thieves are clever. But I tell

you they are exactly like the mobbers of the plains. They are the enemies of civilization.'

'*This* is civilization?' asked LaVon.

'Yes.' Carpenter keyed an answer. 'We live in peace here, and you know that today's work brings tomorrow's bread. Out on the prairie, they don't know that. Tomorrow a mobber will be eating their bread, if they haven't been killed. There's no trust in the world, except here. And the black marketeers feed on trust. Their neighbor's trust. When they've eaten it all, children, what will you live on then?'

They didn't understand, of course. When it was story problems about one truck approaching another truck at sixty kleeters and it takes an hour to meet, how far away were they? – the children could handle that, could figure it out laboriously with pencil and paper and prayers and curses. But the questions that mattered sailed past them like little dust devils, noticed but untouched by their feeble, self-centered little minds.

He tormented them with a pop quiz on history and thirty spelling words for their homework, then sent them out the door.

LaVon did not leave. He stood by the door, closed it, spoke. 'It was a stupid book,' he said.

Carpenter clicked the keyboard. 'That explains why you wrote a stupid book report.'

'It wasn't stupid. It was funny. I read the damn book, didn't I?'

'And I gave you a B.'

LaVon was silent a moment, then said, 'Do me no favors.'

'I never will.'

'And shut up with that goddam machine voice. You can make a voice yourself. My cousin's got palsy and she howls to the moon.'

'You may leave now, Mr. Jensen.'

'I'm gonna hear you talk in your natural voice someday, Mr. Machine.'

114

'You had better go home now, Mr. Jensen.'

LaVon opened the door to leave, then turned abruptly and strode the dozen steps to the head of the class. His legs now were tight and powerful as horses' legs, and his arms were light and strong. Carpenter watched him and felt the same old fear rise within him. If God was going to let him be born like this, he could at least keep him safe from the torturers.

'What do you want, Mr. Jensen?' But before the computer had finished speaking Carpenter's words, LaVon reached out and took Carpenter's wrists, held them tightly. Carpenter did not try to resist; if he did, he might go tight and twist around on the chair like a slug on a hot shovel. That would be more humiliation than he could bear, to have this boy see him writhe. His hands hung limp from LaVon's powerful fists.

'You just mind your business,' LaVon said. 'You only been here two years, you don't know nothin, you understand? You don't see nothin, you don't say nothin, you understand?'

So it wasn't the book report at all. LaVon had actually understood the lecture about civilization and the black market. And knew that it was LaVon's own father, more than anyone else in town, who was guilty. Nephi Delos Jensen, bigshot foreman of Reefrock Farms. Have the marshals already taken your father ? Best get home and see.

'Do you understand me?'

But Carpenter would not speak. Not without his computer. This boy would never hear how Carpenter's own voice sounded, the whining, baying sound, like a dog trying to curl its tongue into human speech. You'll never hear my voice, boy.

'Just try to expel me for this, Mr. Carpenter. I'll say it never happened. I'll say you had it in for me.'

Then he let go of Carpenter's hands and stalked from the room. Only then did Carpenter's legs go rigid, lifting him on the chair so that only the computer over his lap kept him from sliding off. His arms pressed outward, his neck twisted, his jaw opened wide. It was what his body did with fear and rage; it was why he did his best never to feel those emotions. Or any others, for that matter. Dispassionate, that's what he was. He lived the life of the mind, since the life of the body was beyond him. He stretched across his wheelchair like a mocking crucifix, hating his body and pretending that he was merely waiting for it to calm, to relax.

And it did, of course. As soon as he had control of his hands again, he took the computer out of speech mode and called up the data he had sent on to Zarahemla yesterday morning. The crop estimates for three years, and the final weight of the harvested wheat and corn, cukes and berries, apples and beans. For the first two years, the estimates were within two percent of the final total. The third year, the estimates were higher, but the harvest stayed the same. It was suspicious. Then the Bishop's accounting records. It was a sick community. When the Bishop was also seduced into this sort of thing, it meant the rottenness touched every corner of village life. Reefrock Farms looked no different from the hundred other villages just this side of the fringe, but it was diseased. Did Kippie know that even his father was in on the black marketeering? If you couldn't trust the Bishop, who was left?

The words of his own thoughts tasted sour in his mouth. Diseased. They aren't so sick, Carpenter, he told himself. Civilization has always had its parasites, and survived. But it survived because it rooted them out from time to time, cast them away and cleansed the body. Yet they made heroes out of the thieves and despised those who reported them. There's no thanks in what I've done. It isn't love I'm earning. It isn't love I feel. Can I pretend that I'm not just a sick and twisted body taking vengeance on those healthy enough to have families, healthy enough to want to get every possible advantage for them?

He pushed the levers inward and the chair rolled forward. He skillfully maneuvered between the chairs, but it still took nearly a full minute to get to the door. I'm a snail. A worm living in a metal carapace, a water snail creeping along the edge of the aquarium glass, trying to keep it clean from the filth of the fish. I'm the loathsome one; they're the golden ones that shine in the sparkling water. They're the ones whose death is mourned. But without me they'd die. I'm as responsible for their beauty as they are. More, because I work to sustain it, and they simply – are.

It came out this way whenever he tried to reason out an excuse for his own life. He rolled down the corridor to the front door of the school. He knew, intellectually, that his work in crop rotation and timing had been the key to opening up the vast New Soil Lands here in the eastern Utah desert. Hadn't they invented a civilian medal for him, and then, for good measure, given him the same medal they gave to the freedom riders who went out and brought immigrant trains safely into the mountains? I was a hero, they said, this worm in his wheelchair house. But Governor Monson had looked at him with those distant, pitying eyes. He, too, saw the worm; Carpenter might be a hero, but he was still Carpenter.

They had built a concrete ramp for his chair after the second time the students knocked over the wooden ramp and forced him to summon help through the computer airlink network. He remembered sitting on the lip of the porch, looking out toward the cabins of the village. If anyone saw him, then they consented to his imprisonment, because they didn't come to help him. But Carpenter understood. Fear of the strange, the unknown. It wasn't *comfortable* for them, to be near Mr. Carpenter with the mechanical voice and the electric rolling chair. He understood, he really did, he was human too, wasn't he? He even agreed with them. Pretend Carpenter isn't there, and maybe he'll go away.

117

The helicopter came as he rolled out onto the asphalt of the street. It landed in the Circle, between the storehouse and the chapel. Four marshals came out of the gash in its side and spread out through the town.

It happened that Carpenter was rolling in front of Bishop Anderson's house when the marshal knocked on the door. He hadn't expected them to make the arrests while he was still going down the street. His first impulse was to speed up, to get away from the arrest. He didn't want to see. He liked Bishop Anderson. Used to, anyway. He didn't wish him ill. If the Bishop had kept his hands out of the harvest, if he hadn't betrayed his trust, he wouldn't have been afraid to hear the knock on the door and see the badge in the marshal's hand.

Carpenter could hear Sister Anderson crying as they led her husband away. Was Kippie there, watching? Did he notice Mr. Carpenter passing by on the road? Carpenter knew what it would cost these families. Not just the shame, though it would be intense. Far worse would be the loss of their father for years, the extra labor for the children. To break up a family was a terrible thing to do, for the innocent would pay as great a cost as their guilty father, and it wasn't fair, for they had done no wrong. But it was the stern necessity, if civilization was to survive.

Carpenter slowed down his wheelchair, forcing himself to hear the weeping from the Bishop's house, to let them look at him with hatred if they knew what he had done. And they would know: he had specifically refused to be anonymous. If I can inflict stern necessity on them, then I must not run from the consequences of my own actions. I will bear what I must bear, as well – the grief, the resentment, and the rage of the few families I have harmed for the sake of all the rest.

The helicopter had taken off again before Carpenter's chair took him home. It sputtered overhead and disappeared into the low clouds. Rain again tomorrow, of course. Three days dry, three days wet, it had been the weather pattern all spring. The rain would come pounding tonight. Four hours till dark. Maybe the rain wouldn't come until dark.

He looked up from his book. He *had* heard footsteps outside his house. And whispers. He rolled to the window and looked out. The sky was a little darker. The computer said it was four-thirty. The wind was coming up. But the sounds he heard hadn't been the wind. It was three-thirty when the marshals came. Four-thirty now, and footsteps and whispers outside his house. He felt the stiffening in his arms and legs. Wait, he told himself. There's nothing to fear. Relax. Quiet. Yes. His body eased. His heart pounded, but it was slowing down.

The door crashed open. He was rigid at once. He couldn't even bring his hands down to touch the levers so he could turn to see who it was. He just spread there helplessly in his chair as the heavy footfalls came closer.

'There he is.' The voice was Kippie's.

Hands seized his arms, pulled on him; the chair rocked as they tugged him to one side. He could not relax. 'Son of a bitch is stiff as a statue.' Pope's voice. Get out of here, little boy, said Carpenter, you're in something too deep for you, too deep for any of you. But of course they did not hear him, since his fingers couldn't reach the keyboard where he kept his voice.

'Maybe this is what he does when he isn't at school. Just sits here and makes statues at the window.' Kippie laughed.

'He's scared stiff, that's what he is.'

'Just bring him out, and fast.' LaVon's voice carried authority.

They tried to lift him out of the chair, but his body was too rigid; they hurt him, though, trying, for his thighs pressed up against the computer with cruel force, and they wrung at his arms.

'Just carry the whole chair,' said LaVon.

They picked up the chair and pulled him toward the door. His arms smacked against the corners and the doorframe. 'It's like he's dead or something,' said Kippie. 'He don't say nothin.'

He was shouting at them in his mind, however. What are you doing here? Getting some sort of vengeance? Do you think punishing me will bring your fathers back, you fools?

They pulled and pushed the chair into the van they had parked in front. The Bishop's van – Kippie wouldn't have the use of *that* much longer. How much of the stolen grain was carried in here?

'He's going to roll around back here,' said Kippie.

'Tip him over,' said LaVon.

Carpenter felt the chair fly under him; by chance he landed in such a way that his left arm was not caught behind the chair. It would have broken then. As it was, the impact with the floor bent his arm forcibly against the strength of his spasmed muscles; he felt something tear, and his throat made a sound in spite of his effort to bear it silently.

'Did you hear that?' said Pope. 'He's got a voice.'

'Not for much longer,' said LaVon.

For the first time, Carpenter realized that it wasn't just pain that he had to fear. Now, only an hour after their fathers had been taken, long before time could cool their rage, these boys had murder in their hearts.

The road was smooth enough in town, but soon it became rough and painful. From that, Carpenter knew they were headed toward the fringe. He could feel the cold metal of the van's corrugated floor against his face; the pain in his arm was settling down to a steady throb. Relax, quiet, calm, he told himself. How many times in your life have you wished to die? Death means nothing to you, fool, you decided that years ago, death is nothing but a release from this corpse. So what are you afraid of? Calm, quiet. His arms bent, his legs relaxed.

'He's getting soft again,' reported Pope. From the front of the van Kippie guffawed. 'Little and squirmy. Mr. Bug. We always call you that, you hear me, Mr. Bug? There was always two of you. Mr. Machine and Mr. Bug. Mr. Machine was mean and tough and smart, but Mr. Bug was weak and squishy and gross, with wiggly legs. Made us want to puke, looking at Mr. Bug.'

I've been tormented by master torturers in my childhood, Pope Griffith. You are only a pathetic echo of their talent. Carpenter's words were silent, until his hands found the keys. His left hand was almost too weak to use, after the fall, so he coded the words clumsily with his right hand alone. 'If I disappear the day of your father's arrest, Mr. Griffith, don't you think they'll guess who took me?'

'Keep his hands away from the keys!' shouted LaVon. 'Don't let him touch the computer.'

Almost immediately, the van lurched and took a savage bounce as it left the roadway. Now it was clattering over rough, unfinished ground. Carpenter's head banged against the metal floor, again and again. The pain of it made him go rigid; fortunately, spasms always carried his head upward to the right, so that his rigidity kept him from having his head beaten to unconsciousness.

Soon the bouncing stopped. The engine died. Carpenter could hear the wind whispering over the open desert land. They were beyond the fields and orchards, out past the grassland of the fringe. The van doors opened. LaVon and Kippie reached in and pulled him out, chair and all. They dragged the chair to the top of a wash. There was no water in it yet.

'Let's just throw him down,' said Kippie. 'Break his spastic little neck.' Carpenter had not guessed that anger could burn so hot in these languid, mocking boys.

But LaVon showed no fire. He was cold and smooth as snow. 'I don't want to kill him yet. I want to hear him talk first.'

Carpenter reached out to code an answer. LaVon

121

slapped his hands away, gripped the computer, braced a foot on the wheelchair, and tore the computer off its mounting. He threw it across the arroyo; it smacked against the far side and tumbled down into the dry wash. Probably it wasn't damaged, but it wasn't the computer Carpenter was frightened for. Until now Carpenter could cling to a hope that they just meant to frighten him. But it was unthinkable to treat precious electronic equipment that way, not if civilization still had any hold on LaVon.

'With your *voice*, Mr. Carpenter. Not the machine, your own voice.'

Not for you, Mr. Jensen. I don't humiliate myself for you.

'Come on,' said Pope. 'You know what we said. We just take him down into the wash and leave him there.'

'We'll send him down the quick way,' said Kippie. He shoved at the wheelchair, teetering it toward the brink.

'We'll *take* him down!' shouted Pope. 'We aren't going to kill him! You promised!'

'Lot of difference it makes,' said Kippie. 'As soon as it rains in the mountains, this sucker's gonna fill up with water and give him the swim of his life.'

'We won't kill him,' insisted Pope.

'Come on,' said LaVon. 'Let's get him down into the wash.'

Carpenter concentrated on not going rigid as they wrestled the chair down the slope. The walls of the wash weren't sheer, but they were steep enough that the climb down wasn't easy. Carpenter tried to concentrate on mathematics problems so he wouldn't panic and writhe for them again. Finally the chair came to rest at the bottom of the wash.

'You think you can come here and decide who's good and who's bad, right?' said LaVon. 'You think you can sit on your little throne and decide whose father's going to jail, is that it?'

Carpenter's hands rested on the twisted mountings

that used to hold his computer. He felt naked, defenseless without his stinging, frightening voice to whip them into line. LaVon was smart to take away his voice. LaVon knew what Carpenter could do with words.

'Everybody does it,' said Kippie. 'You're the only one who doesn't black the harvest, and that's only because you can't.'

'It's easy to be straight when you can't get anything on the side anyway,' said Pope.

Nothing's easy, Mr. Griffith. Not even virtue.

'My father's a good man!' shouted Kippie. 'He's the Bishop, for Christ's sake! And you sent him to jail!'

'If he ain't shot,' said Pope.

'They don't shoot you for blacking anymore,' said LaVon. 'That was in the old days.'

The old days. Only five years ago. But those were the old days for these children. Children are innocent in the eyes of God, Carpenter reminded himself. He tried to believe that these boys didn't know what they were doing to him.

Kippie and Pope started up the side of the wash. 'Come on,' said Pope. 'Come on, LaVon.'

'Minute,' said LaVon. He leaned close to Carpenter and spoke softly, intensely, his breath hot and foul, his spittle like sparks from a cookfire on Carpenter's face. 'Just ask me,' he said. 'Just open your mouth and beg me, little man, and I'll carry you back up to the van. They'll let you live if I tell them to, you know that.'

He knew it. But he also knew that LaVon would never tell them to spare his life.

'Beg me, Mr. Carpenter. Ask me please to let you live, and you'll live. Look. I'll even save your little talkbox for you.' He scooped up the computer from the sandy bottom and heaved it up out of the wash. It sailed over Kippie's head just as he was emerging from the arroyo.

'What the hell was that, you trying to kill me?'

LaVon whispered again. 'You know how many times

you made me crawl? And now I gotta crawl forever, my father's a jailbird thanks to you, I got little brothers and sisters, even if you hate me, what've you got against them, huh?'

A drop of rain struck Carpenter in the face. There were a few more drops.

'Feel that?' said LaVon. 'The rain in the mountains makes this wash flood every time. You crawl for me, Carpenter, and I'll take you up.'

Carpenter didn't feel particularly brave as he kept his mouth shut and made no sound. If he actually believed LaVon might keep his promise, he would swallow his pride and beg. But LaVon was lying. He couldn't afford to save Carpenter's life now, even if he wanted to. It had gone too far, the consequences would be too great. Carpenter had to die, accidently drowned, no witnesses, such a sad thing, such a great man, and no one the wiser about the three boys who carried him to his dying place.

If he begged and whined in his hound voice, his cat voice, his bestial monster voice, then LaVon would smirk at him in triumph and whisper, 'Sucker.' Carpenter knew the boy too well. Tomorrow LaVon would have second thoughts, of course, but right now there'd be no softening. He only wanted his triumph to be complete, that's why he held out a hope. He wanted to watch Carpenter twist like a worm and bay like a hound before he died. It was a victory, then, to keep silence. Let him remember me in his nightmares of guilt, let him remember I had courage enough not to whimper.

LaVon spat at him; the spittle struck him in the chest. 'I can't even get it in your ugly little worm face,' he said. Then he shoved the wheelchair and scrambled up the bank of the wash.

For a moment the chair hung in balance; then it tipped over. This time Carpenter relaxed during the fall and rolled out of the chair without further injury. His back was to the side of the wash they had climbed; he couldn't see if they were watching him or not. So he held still, except for a slight twitching of his hurt left arm. After a while the van drove away.

Only then did he begin to reach out his arms and paw at the sand of the arroyo bottom. His legs were completely useless, dragging behind him. But he was not totally helpless without his chair. He could control his arms, and by reaching them out and then pulling his body onto his elbows he could make good progress across the sand. How did they think he got from his wheelchair to bed, or to the toilet? Hadn't they seen him use his hands and arms? Of course they saw, but they assumed that because his arms were weak, they were useless.

Then he got to the arroyo wall and realized that they *were* useless. As soon as there was any slope to climb, his left arm began to hurt badly. And the bank was steep. Without being able to use his fingers to clutch at one of the sagebrushes or tree starts, there was no hope he could climb out.

The lightning was flashing in the distance, and he could hear the thunder. The rain here was a steady plick plick plick on the sand, a tiny slapping sound on the few leaves. It would already be raining heavily in the mountains. Soon the water would be here.

He dragged himself another meter up the slope despite the pain. The sand scraped his elbows as he dug with them to pull himself along. The rain fell steadily now, many large drops, but still not a downpour. It was little comfort to Carpenter. Water was beginning to dribble down the sides of the wash and form puddles in the streambed.

With bitter humor he imagined himself telling Dean Wintz, 'On second thought, I don't want to go out and teach sixth grade. I'll just go right on teaching them here, when they come off the farm. Just the few who want to learn something beyond sixth grade, who want a university education. The ones who love books and numbers and languages, the ones who understand civilization and want to keep it alive. Give me the children who *want* to learn, instead of these poor sandscrapers who only go to school because the law commands that six years out of their first fifteen years have to be spent as captives in the prison of learning.

Why do the fire-eaters go out searching for the old missile sites and risk their lives disarming them? To preserve civilization. Why do the freedom riders leave their safe homes and go out to bring the frightened, lonely refugees in to the safety of the mountains? To preserve civilization.

And why had Timothy Carpenter informed the marshals about the black marketeering he had discovered in Reefrock Farms? Was it, truly, to preserve civilization?

Yes, he insisted to himself.

The water was flowing now along the bottom of the wash. His feet were near the flow. He painfully pulled himself up another meter. He had to keep his body pointed straight toward the side of the wash, or he would not be able to stop himself from rolling to one side or the other. He found that by kicking his legs in his spastic, uncontrolled fashion, he could root the toes of his shoes into the sand just enough that he could take some pressure off his arms, just for a moment.

No, he told himself. It was not just to preserve civilization. It was because of the swaggering way their children walked, in their stolen clothing, with their full bellies and healthy skin and hair, cocky as only security can make a child feel. Enough and to spare, that's what they had, while the poor suckers around them worried whether there'd be food enough for the winter, and if their mother was getting enough so the nursing baby wouldn't lack, and whether their shoes could last another summer. The thieves could take a wagon up the long road to Price or even to Zarahemla, the shining city on the Mormon Sea, while the children of honest men never saw anything but the dust and sand and ruddy mountains of the fringe.

126

Carpenter hated them for that, for all the differences in the world, for the children who had legs and walked nowhere that mattered, for the children who had voices and used them to speak stupidity, who had deft and clever fingers and used them to frighten and compel the weak. For all the inequalities in the world he hated them and wanted them to pay for it. They couldn't go to jail for having obedient arms and legs and tongues, but they could damn well go for stealing the hard-earned harvest of trusting men and women. Whatever his own motives might be, that was reason enough to call it justice.

The water was rising many centimeters every minute. The current was tugging at his feet now. He released his elbows to reach them up for another, higher purchase on the bank, but no sooner had he reached out his arms than he slid downward and the current pulled harder at him. It took great effort just to return to where he started, and his left arm was on fire with the tearing muscles. Still, it was life, wasn't it? His left elbow rooted him in place while he reached with his right arm and climbed higher still, and again higher. He even tried to use his fingers to cling to the soil, to a branch, to a rock, but his fists stayed closed and hammered uselessly against the ground.

Am I vengeful, bitter, spiteful? Maybe I am. But whatever my motive was, they were thieves, and had no business remaining among the people they betrayed. It was hard on the children, of course, cruelly hard on them, to have their father stripped away from them by the authorities. But how much worse would it be for the fathers to stay, and the children to learn that trust was for the stupid and honor for the weak? What kind of people would we be then, if the children could do their numbers and letters but couldn't hold someone else's plate and leave the food on it untouched?

The water was up to his waist. The current was rocking him slightly, pulling him downstream. His legs were

127

floating behind him now, and water was trickling down the bank, making the earth looser under his elbows. So the children wanted him dead now, in their fury. He would die in a good cause, wouldn't he?

With the water rising faster, the current swifter, he decided that martyrdom was not all it was cracked up to be. Nor was life, when he came right down to it, something to be given up lightly because of a few inconveniences. He managed to squirm up a few more centimeters, but now a shelf of earth blocked him. Someone with hands could have reached over it easily and grabbed hold of the sagebrush just above it.

He clenched his mouth tight and lifted his arm up onto the shelf of dirt. He tried to scrape some purchase for his forearm, but the soil was slick. When he tried to place some weight on the arm, he slid down again.

This was it, this was his death, he could feel it, and in the sudden rush of fear his body went rigid. Almost at once his feet caught on the rocky bed of the river and stopped him from sliding farther. Spastic, his legs were of some use to him. He swung his right arm up, scraped his fist on the sagebrush stem, trying to pry his clenched fingers open.

And, with agonizing effort, he did it. All but the smallest finger opened enough to hook the stem. Now the clenching was some help to him. He used his left arm mercilessly, ignoring the pain, to pull him up a little farther, onto the shelf; his feet were still in the water, but his waist wasn't, and the current wasn't strong against him now.

It was a victory, but not much of one. The water wasn't even a meter deep yet, and the current wasn't yet strong enough to have carried away his wheelchair. But it was enough to kill him, if he hadn't come this far. Still, what was he really accomplishing? In storms like this, the water came up near the top; he'd have been dead for an hour before the water began to come down again.

He could hear, in the distance, a vehicle approaching on the road. Had they come back to watch him die? They couldn't be that stupid. How far was this wash from the highway? Not far – they hadn't driven that long on the rough ground to get here. But it meant nothing. No one would see him, or even the computer that lay among the tumbleweeds and sagebrush at the arroyo's edge.

They might hear him. It was possible. If their window was open – in a rainstorm? If their engine was quiet – but loud enough that he could hear them? Impossible, impossible. And it might be the boys again, come to hear him scream and whine for life; I'm not going to cry out now, after so many years of silence –

But the will to live, he discovered, was stronger than shame; his voice came unbidden to his throat. His lips and tongue and teeth that in childhood had so painstakingly practiced words that only his family could ever understand now formed a word again: 'Help!' It was a difficult word; it almost closed his mouth, it made him too quiet to hear. So at last he simply howled, saying nothing except the terrible sound of his voice.

The brake squealed, long and loud, and the vehicle rattled to a stop. The engine died. Carpenter howled again. Car doors slammed.

'I tell you it's just a dog somewhere, somebody's old dog –'

Carpenter howled again.

'Dog or not, it's alive, isn't it?'

They ran along the edge of the arroyo, and someone saw him.

'A little kid!'

'What's he doing down there!'

'Come on, kid, you can climb up from there!'

I nearly killed myself climbing this far, you fool, if I *could* climb, don't you think I *would* have? Help me! He cried out again.

'It's not a little boy. He's got a beard –'

'Come on, hold on, we're coming down!'

'There's a wheelchair in the water –'

'He must be a cripple.'

There were several voices, some of them women, but it was two strong men who reached him, splashing their feet in the water. They hooked him under the arms and carried him to the top.

'Can you stand up? Are you all right? Can you stand?'

Carpenter strained to squeeze out the word: 'No.'

The older woman took command. 'He's got palsy, as any fool can see. Go back down there and get his wheelchair, Tom, no sense in making him wait till they can get him another one, go on down! It's not that bad down there, the flood isn't here yet!' Her voice was crisp and clear, perfect speech, almost foreign it was so precise. She and the young woman carried him to the truck. It was a big old flatbed truck from the old days, and on its back was a canvas-covered heap of odd shapes. On the canvas Carpenter read the words SWEETWATER'S MIRACLE PAGEANT. Traveling show people, then, racing for town to get out of the rain, and through some miracle they had heard his call.

'Your poor arms,' said the young woman, wiping off grit and sand that had sliced his elbows. 'Did you climb that far out of there with just your arms?'

The young men came out of the arroyo muddy and cursing, but they had the wheelchair. They tied it quickly to the back of the truck; one of the men found the computer, too, and took it inside the cab. It was designed to be rugged, and to Carpenter's relief it still worked.

'Thank you,' said his mechanical voice.

'I told them I heard something and they said I was crazy,' said the old woman. 'You live in Reefrock?'

'Yes,' said his voice.

'Amazing what those old machines can still do, even after being dumped there in the rain,' said the old

130

woman. 'Well, you came close to death, there, but you're all right, it's the best we can ask for. We'll take you to the doctor.'

'Just take me home. Please.'

So they did, but insisted on helping him bathe and fixing him dinner. The rain was coming down in sheets when they were done. "All I have is a floor,' he said, 'but you can stay.'

'Better than trying to pitch the tents in this.' So they stayed the night.

Carpenter's arms ached too badly for him to sleep, even though he was exhausted. He lay awake thinking of the current pulling him, imagining what would have happened to him, how far he might have gone downstream before drowning, where his body might have ended up. Caught in a snag somewhere, dangling on some branch or rock as the water went down and left his slack body to dry in the sun. Far out in the desert somewhere, maybe. Or perhaps the floodwater might have carried him all the way to the Colorado and tumbled him head over heels down the rapids, through the canyons, past the ruins of the old dams, and finally into the Gulf of California. He'd pass through Navaho territory then, and the Hopi Protectorate, and into areas that Chihuahua claimed and threatened to go to war to keep. He'd see more of the world than he had seen in his life.

I saw more of the world tonight, he thought, than I ever thought to see. I saw death and how much I feared it.

And he looked into himself, wondering how much he had changed.

Late in the morning, when he finally awoke, the pageant people were gone. They had a show, of course, and had to do some kind of parade to let people know. School would let out early so they could put on the show without having to waste power on lights. There'd be no school this afternoon. But what about his morning classes? There must have been some question when he didn't show up; someone would have called, and if he didn't answer the phone someone would have come by. Maybe the show people had still been here when they came. The word would have spread through school that he was still alive.

He tried to imagine LaVon and Kippie and Pope hearing that Mr. Machine, Mr. Bug, Mr. Carpenter was still alive. They'd be afraid, of course. Maybe defiant. Maybe they had even confessed. No, not that. LaVon would keep them quiet. Try to think of a way out. Maybe even plan an escape, though finding a place to go that wasn't under Utah authority would be a problem.

What am I doing? Trying to plan how my enemies can escape retribution? I should call the marshals again, tell them what happened. If someone hasn't called them already.

His wheelchair waited by his bed. The show people had shined it up for him, got rid of all the muck. Even straightened the computer mounts and tied it on, jury-rigged it but it would do. Would the motor run, after being under water? He saw that they had even changed batteries and had the old one set aside. They were good people. Not at all what the stories said about show gypsies. Though there was no natural law that people who help cripples can't also seduce all the young girls in the village.

His arms hurt and his left arm was weak and trembly, but he managed to get into the chair. The pain brought back yesterday. I'm alive today, and yet today doesn't feel any different from last week, when I was also alive. Being on the brink of death wasn't enough; the only transformation is to die.

He ate lunch because it was nearly noon. Eldon Finch came by to see him, along with the sheriff. 'I'm the new bishop,' said Eldon.

'Didn't waste any time,' said Carpenter.

'I gotta tell you, Brother Carpenter, things are in a

132

tizzy today. Yesterday, too, of course, what with aveng-
ing angels dropping out of the sky and taking away people we all trusted. There's some says you shouldn't've
told, and some says you did right, and some ain't sayin
nothin cause they're afraid somethin'll get told on *them*.
Ugly times, ugly times, when folks steal from their
neighbors.'

Sheriff Budd finally spoke up. 'Almost as ugly as tryin
to drownd em.'

The Bishop nodded. 'Course you know the reason we
come, Sheriff Budd and me, we come to find out who
done it.'

'Done what?'

'Plunked you down that wash. You aren't gonna tell
me you drove that little wheelie chair of yours out there
past the fringe. What, was you speedin so fast you lost
control and spun out? Give me peace of heart, Brother
Carpenter, give me trust.' The Bishop and the sheriff
both laughed at that. Quite a joke.

Now's the time, thought Carpenter. Name the
names. The motive will be clear, justice will be done.
They put you through the worst hell of your life, they
made you cry out for help, they taught you the taste of
death. Now even things up.

But he didn't key their names into the computer. He
thought of Kippie's mother crying at the door. When
the crying stopped, there'd be years ahead. They were a
long way from proving out their land. Kippie was
through with school, he'd never go on, never get out.
The adult burden was on those boys now, years too
young. Should their families suffer even more, with
another generation gone to prison? Carpenter had
nothing to gain, and many who were guiltless stood to
lose too much.

'Brother Carpenter,' said Sheriff Budd. 'Who was it?'

He keyed in his answer. 'I didn't get a look at them.'

'Their voices, didn't you know them?'

'No.'

133

The Bishop looked steadily at him. 'They tried to kill you, Brother Carpenter. That's no joke. You like to died, if those show people hadn't happened by. And I have my own ideas who it was, seein who had reason to hate you unto death yesterday.'

'As you said, a lot of people think an outsider like me should have kept his nose out of Reefrock's business.'

The Bishop frowned at him. 'You scared they'll try again?'

'No.'

'Nothin I can do,' said the sheriff. 'I think you're a damn fool, Brother Carpenter, but nothin I can do if you don't even care.'

'Thanks for coming by.'

He didn't go to church Sunday. But on Monday he went to school, same time as usual. And there were LaVon and Kippie and Pope, right in their places. But not the same as usual. The wisecracks were over. When he called on them, they answered if they could and didn't if they couldn't. When he looked at them, they looked away.

He didn't know if it was shame or fear that he might someday tell; he didn't care. The mark was on them. They would marry someday, go out into even newer lands just behind the ever-advancing fringe, have babies, work until their bodies were exhausted, and then drop into a grave. But they'd remember that one day they left a cripple to die. He had no idea what it would mean to them, but they would remember.

Within a few weeks LaVon and Kippie were out of school; with their fathers gone, there was too much fieldwork and school was a luxury their families couldn't afford for them. Pope had an older brother still at home, so he stayed out the year.

One time Pope almost talked to him. It was a windy day that spattered sand against the classroom window, and the storm coming out of the south looked to be a nasty one. When class was over, most of the kids ducked their heads and rushed outside, hurrying to get home before the downpour began. A few stayed, though, to talk with Carpenter about this and that. When the last one left, Carpenter saw that Pope was still there. His pencil was hovering over a piece of paper. He looked up at Carpenter, then set the pencil down, picked up his books, started for the door. He paused for a moment with his hand on the doorknob. Carpenter waited for him to speak. But the boy only opened the door and went on out.

Carpenter rolled over to the door and watched him as he walked away. The wind caught at his jacket. Like a kite, thought Carpenter, it's lifting him along.

But it wasn't true. The boy didn't rise and fly. And now Carpenter saw the wind like a current down the village street, sweeping Pope away. All the bodies in the world, caught in that same current, that same wind, blown down the same rivers, the same streets, and finally coming to rest on some snag, through some door, in some grave, God knows where or why.

Pageant Wagon

Deaver's horse took sick and died right under him. He was setting on her back, writing down notes about how deep the erosion was eating back into the new grassland, when all of a sudden old Bette shuddered and coughed and broke to her knees. Deaver slid right off her, of course, and unsaddled her, but after that all he could do was pat her and talk to her and hold her head in his lap as she laid there dying.

If I was an outrider it wouldn't be like this, thought Deaver. Royal's Riders go two by two out there on the eastern prairie, never alone like us range riders here in the old southern Utah desert. Outriders got the best horses in Deseret, too, never an old nag like Bette having to work out her last breath riding the grass edge. And the outriders got guns, so they wouldn't have to sit and watch a horse die, they could say farewell with a hot sweet bullet like a last ball of sugar.

Didn't do no good thinking about the outriders, though. Deaver'd been four years on the waiting list, just for the right to apply. Most range riders were on that list, aching for a chance to do something important and dangerous – bringing refugees in from the prairie, fighting mobbers, disarming missiles. Royal's Riders were all heroes, it went with the job, whenever they come back from a mission they got their picture in the papers, a big write-up. Range riders just got lonely and shaggy and smelly. No wonder they all dreamed of riding with Royal Aal. With so many others on the list, Deaver figured he'd probably be too old and they'd take his name off before he ever got to the top. They wouldn't

136

take applications from anybody over thirty, so he only had about a year and a half left. He'd end up doing what he was doing now, riding the edge of the grassland, checking out erosion patterns and bringing in stray cattle till he dropped out of the saddle and then it'd be his horse's turn to stand there and watch *him* die.

Bette twitched a leg and snorted. Her eye was darting every which way, panicky, and then it stopped moving at all. After a while a fly landed on it. Deaver eased himself out from under her. The fly stayed right there. Probably already laying eggs. This country didn't waste much time before it sucked every last hope of life out of anything that held still long enough.

Deaver figured to do everything by the book. Put Bette's anal scrapings in a plastic tube so they could check for disease, pick up his bedroll, his notebooks, and his canteen, and then hike into the first fringe town he could find and call in to Moab.

Deaver was all set to go, but he couldn't just walk off and leave the saddle. The rulebook said a rider's life is worth more than a saddle, but the guy who wrote that didn't have a five-dollar deposit on it. A week's wages. It wasn't like Deaver had to carry it far. He passed a road late yesterday. He'd go back and sit on the saddle and wait a couple of days for some truck to come by.

Anyway he wanted it on his record – Deaver Teague come back saddle and all. Bad enough to lose the horse. So he hefted the saddle onto his back and shoulders. It was still warm and damp from Bette's body.

He didn't follow Bette's hoofprints back along the edge of the grassland – no need to risk his own footsteps causing more erosion. He struck out into the thicker, deeper grass of last year's planting. Pretty soon he lost sight of the grey desert sagebrush, it was too far off in the wet hazy air. Folks talked about how it was in the old days, when the air was so clear and dry you could see mountains you couldn't get to in two days' riding. Now the farthest he could see was to the redrock sentinels sticking up out of the grass, bright orange when he was close, dimmer and greyer a mile or two ahead or behind. Like soldiers keeping watch in the fog.

Deaver's eyes never got used to seeing those pillars of orange sandstone, tortured by the wind into precarious dream shapes, standing right out in the middle of wet-looking deep green grassland. They didn't belong together, those colors, that rigid stone and bending grass. Wasn't natural.

Five years from now, the fringe would move out into this new grassland, and there'd be farmers turning the plow to go around these rocks, never even looking up at these last survivors of the old desert. In his mind's eye, Deaver saw those rocks seething hot with anger as the cool sea of green swept on around them. People might tame the soil of the desert, but never these temperamental, twisted old soldiers. In fifty years or a hundred or two hundred maybe, when the Earth healed itself from the war and the weather changed back and the rains stopped coming, all this grass, all those crops, they'd turn brown and die, and the new orchard trees would stand naked and dry until they snapped off in a sandstorm and blew away into dust, and then the grey sagebrush would cover the ground again, and the stone soldiers would stand there, silent in their victory.

That's going to happen someday, all you fringe people with your rows of grain and vegetables and trees, your towns full of people who all know each other and go to the same church. You think you all belong where you are, you each got a spot you fill up snug as a cork in a bottle. When I come into town you look hard at me with your tight little eyes because you never seen my face before, I got no place with you, so I better do my business and get on out of town. But that's how the desert thinks about you and your plows and houses. You're just passing through, you got no place here, pretty soon you and all your planting will be gone.

Beads of sweat tickled his face and dropped down

onto his eyes, but Deaver didn't let go of the saddle to wipe his forehead. He was afraid if once he set it down he wouldn't pick it up again. Saddles weren't meant to fit the back of a man, and he was sore from chafing and bumping into it. But he'd carried the saddle so far he'd feel like a plain fool to drop it now, so never mind the raw spots on his shoulders and how his fingers and wrists and the backs of his arms hurt from hanging onto it.

At nightfall he hadn't made the road. Even bundled up in his blanket and using the saddle as a windbreak, Deaver shivered half the night against the cold breeze poking here and there over the grass. He woke up stiff and tired with a runny nose. Wasn't till halfway to noon next day that he finally got to the road.

It was a thin ribbon of ancient grey oil and gravel, an old two-lane that was here back when it was all desert and nobody but geologists and tourists and the stubbornest damn cattle ranchers in the world ever drove on it. His arms and back and legs ached so bad he couldn't sit down and he couldn't stand up and he couldn't lay down. So he set down the saddle and bedroll and walked along the road a little to work the pain out. Felt like he was light as cottonwood fluff, now he didn't have the saddle on his back.

First he went south toward the desert till the saddle was almost out of sight in the haze. Then he walked back, past the saddle, toward the fringe. The grass got thicker and taller that direction. Range riders had a saying: 'Grass to the stirrup, pancakes and syrup.' It meant you were close to where the orchards and cropland started, which meant a town, and since most riders were Mormons, they could brother-and-sister their way into some pretty good cooking. Deaver got sandwiches, or dry bread in towns too small to have a diner.

Deaver figured it was like all those Mormons, together they formed a big piece of cloth, all woven together through the whole state of Deseret, each person like a thread wound in among the others to make a fabric, tough and strong and complete right out to the edge – right out to the fringe. Those Mormon range riders, they might stray out into the empty grassland, but they were still part of the weave, still connected. Deaver, he was like a wrong-colored thread that looks like it's hanging from the fabric, but when you get up close, why, you can see it isn't attached anywhere, it just got mixed up in the wash, and if you pull it away it comes off easy, and the cloth won't be one whit weaker or less complete.

But that was fine with Deaver. If the price of a hot breakfast was being a Mormon and doing everything the Bishop told you because he was inspired by God, then bread and water tasted pretty good. To Deaver the fringe towns were as much a desert as the desert itself. No way he could live there long, unless he was willing to turn into something other than himself.

He walked back and forth until it didn't hurt to sit down, and then he sat down until it didn't hurt to walk again. All day and no cars. Well, that was his kind of luck – government probably cut back the gas ration again and nobody was moving. Or they sealed off the road cause they didn't want folks driving through the grassland even on pavement. For all Deaver knew the road got washed through in the last rain. He might be standing here for nothing, and he only had a couple days' water in his canteen. Wouldn't that be dumb, to die of thirst because he rested a whole day on a road that nobody used.

Wasn't till the middle of the night when the rumble of an engine and the vibration of the road woke him up. It was a long way off still, but he could see the headlights. A truck, from the shaking and the noise it made. And not going fast, from how long it took those lights to get close. Still, it was night, wasn't it? And even going thirty, it was a good chance they wouldn't see him.

Deaver's clothes were all dark, except his t-shirt. So, cold as it was at night, he stripped off his jacket and flannel shirt and stood in the middle of the road, letting his undershirt catch the headlights, his arms spread out and waving as the truck got closer.

He figured he looked like a duck trying to take off from a tar patch. And his t-shirt wasn't clean enough for anybody to call it exactly white. But they saw him and laid on the brakes. Deaver stepped out of the way when he saw the truck couldn't stop in time. The brakes squealed and howled and it took them must be a hundred yards past Deaver before they stopped.

They were nice folks – they even backed up to him instead of making him carry the saddle and all up to where they finally got it parked.

'Thank heaven you weren't a baby in the road,' said a man from the back of the truck. 'You wouldn't happen to have brake linings with you, young man?'

The man's voice was strange. Loud and big-sounding, with an accent like Deaver never heard before. Every single letter sounded clear, like the voice of God on Mount Sinai. It didn't occur to Deaver that it was the man might be making a joke, not in *that* voice. Instead he felt like it was a sin that he didn't have brake linings. 'No, sir, I'm sorry.'

The Voice of God chuckled. 'There was an era, before you remember, when no American in his right mind would have stopped to pick up a dangerous-looking stranger like you. Who says America has not improved since the collapse?'

'I'd like a bag of nacho Doritos,' said a woman. 'That would be an improvement.' Her voice was warm and friendly, but she had that same strange way of pronouncing every bit of every word. Jackrabbits could learn English hearing her talk.

'I speak of trust, and she speaks of carnal delights,' said the Voice of God. 'Is that a saddle?'

'Government property, registered in Moab.' He said

141

it right off, so there'd be no thought of maybe making that saddle disappear.

The man chuckled. 'Range rider, then?'

'Yes sir.'

'Well, range rider, it seems trust among strangers isn't perfect yet. No, we wouldn't steal your saddle, even to make brake linings.'

Deaver was plain embarrassed. 'I didn't mean to say –'

'You did right, lad,' said the woman.

The truck was a flatbed with high fencing staked around – ancient, but so were most trucks. Detroit wasn't exactly churning them out anymore. Inside the fence panels, straining against them, was a crazy jumble of tarps, tents, and crates stacked up in a way that made no sense, not in the dark anyway. Somebody flung their arm over the top of one of the softer-looking bundles, and then a sleepy-looking, mussy-haired girl about maybe twelve years old stuck her head up and said, 'What's going on?' It was a welcome sound, her voice – none of that too-crisp talking from *her*.

'Nothing, Janie,' said the woman. She turned back to Deaver. 'And as for you, young man, show some sense and get your shirt back on, it's cold out here.'

So it was. He started to put it on. As soon as she saw he was doing what she wanted, she climbed back into the cab.

He could hear the man tossing his saddlebags onto the truck. Deaver put his foot on the saddle till he had his shirt on, so the man wouldn't come back and try to lift it. Not that he could tell for sure, but by the little light from a sliver of moon, he didn't look like a young man, exactly, and Deaver wouldn't have an old guy lift his saddle for him.

Somebody else came around the front of the truck. A young man, with an easy walk and a smile so full of teeth it caught the moonlight brighter than a car bumper. He stuck out his hand and said, 'I'm his son. My name's Ollie.'

Well, if Deaver thought the Voice of God was weird, his son was even weirder. Deaver'd picked up a lot of riders back in his salvage days, and he'd been picked up himself more times than he could remember. Only a couple of people ever gave or asked for a name, and that was only at the end of the ride, and only if you talked a lot and liked each other. Here was a guy expecting to shake hands, like he thought Deaver was famous – or thought *he* was famous. When Deaver took his hand, Ollie squeezed hard. Like there was real feeling in it. There in the dark, people talking and acting strange, Deaver still half asleep, he felt like he was inside a dream, one that hadn't decided yet whether to be a nightmare.

Ollie let go of Deaver's hand, bent over, and slid the saddle right out from under Deaver's foot. 'Let me get this up onto the truck for you.'

It was plain that Ollie had never hoisted many saddles in his life. He was strong enough, but awkward. Deaver took hold of one end.

'Do horses really wear these things?' asked Ollie.

'Yep,' said Deaver. Deaver knew the question was a joke, but he didn't know why it was funny, or who was supposed to laugh. At least Ollie didn't talk like the older man and woman – he had a natural sound to his voice, an easy way of talking, like you'd already been friends for years. They got the saddle onto the truck. Then Ollie swung up onto the truck and slid the saddle back behind something covered with canvas.

'Heading for Moab, right?' asked Ollie.

'I guess,' said Deaver.

'We're heading to Hatchville,' Ollie said. 'We'll spend no more than two days there, and then it happens we'll be passing through Moab next.' Ollie glanced over at his father, who was just coming back around the truck. Ollie was grinning his face off, and he spoke real loud now, as if to make sure his father heard him. 'Unless you have a faster ride, how about you travel with us the whole way to Moab?'

The Voice of God didn't say a word, and it was too dark to read much expression on his face. Still, as long as Deaver didn't hear him saying, 'Yes, Ollie's right, come ride with us,' the message was plain enough. The son might've shook his hand, but the father didn't hanker for his company past morning.

Truth was Deaver didn't mind a bit. Seemed to him these people didn't have all their axles greased, and he wasn't thinking about their truck, either. He wasn't about to turn down a ride with them tonight – who knew when the next vehicle would come through here? – but he wasn't eager to hang around with them for two days, listening to them talk funny. 'Hatchville's all I need,' said Deaver.

Only after Deaver had turned down the offer did the Voice of God speak again. 'I assure you, it would have been no trouble to take you on to Moab.'

That's right, thought Deaver. It would've been no trouble, but you still didn't want to do it and that's fine with me.

'Come on, get aboard,' said Ollie. 'You'll have to ride in the cab – all the beds are occupied.'

As Deaver walked up to the cab, he saw two more people leaning over the railing of the truck to get a look at him – a really old man and woman, white-haired, almost ghost-like. How many people were there? Ollie and the Voice of God, these two really old ones, the lady who was probably Ollie's mother, and that young girl named Janie. Six at least. At least they were trying to fit in with the government's request for folks to carry the most possible riders per vehicle.

Ollie's father got up into the cab before Deaver, giving him the window. The woman was already in the middle, and when Ollie got into the driver's seat on the other side, it made for a tight fit all across. Deaver didn't mind, though. The cab was cold.

'It'll warm up again when we get going,' said the

woman. 'The heater works, but the fan doesn't.'

'Do you have a name, range rider?' asked the Voice of God.

Deaver couldn't understand this curiosity about names. I'm not renting a room with you people, I'm just taking a ride.

'Maybe he doesn't want to share his name, Father,' said Ollie.

Deaver could feel Ollie's father stiffen beside him. Why was it such a big deal? 'Name's Deaver Teague.'

Now it was Ollie who seemed to tighten up. His smile got kind of set as he started the engine and put the truck in gear. Was this a bet? Whoever got Deaver to say his name won, and Ollie was mad because he had to pay off?

'Do you hail from anywhere in particular?' asked Ollie's father.

'I'm an immigrant,' said Deaver.

'In the long run, so are we all. Immigrant from where?'

Am I applying for a job or something? 'I don't remember.'

The father and mother glanced at each other. Of course they assumed he was lying, and now they were probably thinking he was a criminal or something. So like it or not, Deaver had to explain. 'Outriders picked me up when I was maybe four. All my people was killed by mobbers on the prairie.'

Immediately the tension eased out of the parents. 'Oh, I'm sorry,' said the woman. Her voice was so thick with sympathy that Deaver had to look at her to make sure she wasn't making fun.

'Doesn't matter,' Deaver said. He didn't even remember them, so it wasn't like he missed his folks.

'Listen to us,' said the woman. 'Prying at him, when we haven't so much as told him who we are.'

So at least she noticed they were prying.

'I told him *my* name,' said Ollie. There was a trace of

145

nastiness in the way he said it, and suddenly Deaver knew why he got mad a minute ago. When Ollie introduced himself outside the truck, Deaver didn't give back his own name, but then when Ollie's father asked, Deaver told his name easy enough. It was about the stupidest thing to get mad over that Deaver ever heard of, but he was used to that. Deaver was always doing that, giving offense without meaning to, because people were all so prickly. Or maybe he just wasn't smart about dealing with strangers. You'd think he'd be better at it, since strangers was all he ever had to deal with.

The Voice of God was talking like he didn't even know Ollie was mad. 'We who travel in, on, and around this truck are minstrels of the open road. Madrigals and jesters, thespians and dramaturges, the second-rate sophoclean substitute for NBC, CBS, ABC, and, may the Lord forgive us, PBS.'

The only answer Deaver could think of was a kind of smile, knowing he looked like an idiot, but what could he say that wouldn't let the man know that Deaver didn't understand a word he said?

Ollie grinned over at him. Deaver was glad to see he wasn't mad anymore, and so he smiled back. Ollie grinned even more. This is like a conversation between two people pretending not to be deaf, thought Deaver.

Finally Ollie translated what his father had said. 'We're a pageant wagon.'

'Oh,' said Deaver. He was a fool for not guessing it already. Show gypsies. It explained so many people on one truck and the strange-shaped objects under the canvas and most of all it explained the weird way Ollie's father and mother talked. 'A *pageant* wagon.'

But apparently Deaver said it the wrong way or something, because Ollie's father winced and Ollie snapped off the inside light and the truck sped up, rattling more than ever. Maybe they were mad because they knew all the stories that got told about show gypsies, and they figured Deaver was being snide when he said

146

'*pageant* wagon' like that. Fact was Deaver didn't much care whether pageant wagons left behind them a string of pregnant virgins and empty chicken coops. They weren't his daughters and they weren't his chickens.

Deaver moved around so much that a traveling show never come to any town he was in, at least that he knew about. In Zarahemla he knew they had an actual walk-in theatre, but for that you had to dress nicer than any clothes Deaver owned. And the pageant wagons only traveled out in the hick towns, where Deaver never hung around long enough to know if there was a show going on or not. Only thing he knew about pageant wagons was what he found out tonight – they talked weird and got mad over nothing.

But he didn't want them thinking he had a low opinion of pageant wagons. 'You doing a show in Hatchville?' asked Deaver. He tried to sound favorable to the idea.

'We have an appointment,' said Ollie's father.

'Deaver Teague,' said the woman, obviously changing the subject. 'Do you know why your parents gave you two last names?'

Seemed like whenever these people ran out of stuff to talk about, they always got back to names. But it was better than having them mad. 'The immigrants who found me, there was a guy named Deaver and a guy named Teague.'

'How awful, to take away your given name!' she said.

What was Deaver supposed to say to that?

'Maybe he likes his name,' said Ollie.

Immediately Ollie's mother got flustered. 'Oh, I wasn't criticizing –'

Ollie's father jumped right in to smooth things over. 'I think Deaver Teague is a very distinguished-sounding name. The name of a future governor.'

Deaver smiled a little at that. Him, a governor. The chance of a non-Mormon governor in Deseret was about as likely as the fish electing a duck to be king of the pond. He may be in the water, but he sure ain't one of *us*.

'But our manners,' said the woman. 'We still haven't introduced ourselves. I'm Scarlett Aal.'

'And I'm Marshall Aal,' said the man. 'Our driver is our second son, Laurence Olivier Aal.'

'Ollie,' said the driver. 'For the love of Mike.'

What Deaver mostly heard was the last name. 'Aal like A-A-L?'

'Yes,' said Marshall. He looked off into the distance even though there was nothing to see in the dark.

'Any relation to Royal Aal?'

'Yes,' said Marshall. He was very curt.

Deaver couldn't figure out why Marshall was annoyed. Royal's Riders were the biggest heroes in Deseret.

'My husband's brother,' said Scarlett.

'They're very close,' said Ollie. Then he gave a single sharp hoot of laughter.

Marshall just raised his chin a little, as if to say he was above such tomfoolery. So Marshall didn't like being related to Royal. But definitely they were brothers. Now that Deaver was looking for it, Marshall Aal even looked kind of like Royal's pictures in the paper. Not enough to mistake them for each other. Royal had that ragged, lean, hard-jawed look of a man who doesn't much care where he sleeps; his brother, here in the cab of the pageant wagon, his face was softer.

No, not softer. Deaver couldn't call this sharp-featured man *soft*. Nor delicate. Elegant maybe. Your majesty.

Their names were backward. It was Marshall here who looked like a king, and Royal who looked like a soldier. Like they got switched in the cradle.

'Do you know my Uncle Roy?' asked Ollie. He sounded real interested.

It was plain that Marshall didn't want another word about his brother, but that didn't seem to bother Ollie. Deaver didn't know much about brothers, or about fathers and sons, not having been any such himself, but why would Ollie want to make his father mad on purpose?

148

'Just from the papers,' said Deaver.

Nobody said anything. Just the sound of the engine rumbling on, the feel of the cab vibrating from the road underneath them.

Deaver had that sick feeling he always got when he knew he just didn't belong where he was. He'd already managed to offend everybody, and they'd offended him a few times, too. He just wished somebody else had picked him up. He twisted a little on the seat and leaned his head against the window. If he could go to sleep till they got to Hatchville, then he could get out and never have to face them again.

'Here we've been talking all this time,' said Scarlett, 'and the poor boy is so tired he can hardly stay awake.' Deaver felt her hand pat his knee. Her words, her voice, her touch – they were just what he needed to hear. She was telling him he hadn't offended everybody after all. She was telling him he was still welcome.

He could feel himself unclench inside. He eased down into the seat, breathed a little slower. He didn't open his eyes, but he could still picture the woman's face the way she looked before, smiling at him, her face showing so much sympathy it was like she thought he was her own son.

But of course she could look like that whenever she wanted to – she was an actress. She could make her face and voice seem any old way she chose. Wasn't no particular reason Deaver should believe her. Smarter if he didn't.

What was her name again? Scarlett. He wondered if her hair had once been red.

The sky was just pinking up with dawn, clear and cold outside the heated cab, when they rattled over a rough patch in the road. Deaver wasn't awake and then he was awake. First words he said were from his dream even as it skittered away from him just out of reach. 'It's your stuff,' he said.

'Don't get mad at *me* about it,' said the woman sitting next to him. It took him a moment to realize that it wasn't Scarlett's voice.

In the night sometime the pageant wagon people must have stopped and switched places. Now that he thought about it, Deaver had half-awake memories of Scarlett and other people talking soft and the seat bouncing. Marshall and Scarlett were gone, and so was Ollie. The man at the wheel wasn't one of the people Deaver saw last night. They had called Ollie their second son; this must be his older brother. The young girl he saw on the back of the truck last night – Janie – she was asleep leaning on the driver's shoulder. And next to Deaver was about the prettiest woman he could remember seeing in his life. Of course women got to looking nicer and nicer the more time you spent on the range, but it was sure she was the best-looking woman he ever woke up next to. Not that he'd ever say such a thing. He was plain embarrassed even to think it.

She was smiling at him.

'Sorry. I must have been –'

'Oh, it was some dream,' she said.

I look at you and I think maybe I'm still dreaming. The words were so clear in his mind that he moved his lips without meaning to.

'What?' she asked.

She looked at him like she'd never look at another soul until he answered. Deaver was plain embarrassed. He blurted out something like what he was thinking. 'I said if you're part of the dream I don't want to wake up.'

The man at the wheel laughed. Pleasantly. Deaver liked his laugh. The woman didn't laugh, though. She just smiled and crinkled up her eyes, then looked down at her lap. It was the absolutely perfect thing for her to do. So perfect that Deaver felt like he was starting to float.

'You've done it to this poor ranger man already,

150

Katie,' said the driver. 'Pay no attention to her, my friend. She specializes in enchanting handsome strangers she discovers in the cab of her family's truck. If you kiss her she turns into a frog.'

'You wake up very sweetly,' said Katie. 'And you turn a compliment so a woman can almost believe it's true.'

Only now did Deaver really come awake and realize he was talking to strangers and had no business saying what came to mind, or trying to make his jokes. In the roadside inns where he used to stop while he was driving a scavenger truck, he always talked to the waitresses like that, giving them the most elegant compliments that he thought they might believe. At first he was flirting, teasing them, which was the only way he knew to talk to a woman – he couldn't bring himself to talk crude like the older drivers, so he talked pretty. Soon, though, he stopped making it a joke, because those women would always look at him sharp to see if he was mocking them, and if they saw he wasn't, why, it brightened them, like pulling the chain on a light inside their eyes.

But that was back when he was seventeen, eighteen years old, lots younger than the women he met. They liked him, treated him like a sweet-talking little brother. This woman, though, she was younger than him, and sitting tight up against him in a cab so small it caught all her breath so he could breathe it after, and the sky outside was dim and the light made soft pink shadows on her face. He was wide awake now, and shy.

You don't flirt with a woman in front of her brother.

'I'm Deaver Teague,' he said. 'I didn't see you last night.'

'I didn't exist last night,' she said. 'You dreamed me up and here I am.'

She laughed and it wasn't a giggle or a cackle, it was a low-pitched sound in her throat, warm and inviting.

'Deaver Teague,' said the driver, 'I urge you to remember that my sister Katie Hepburn Aal is the best actress in Deseret, and what you're seeing right now is Juliet.'

151

'Titania,' she said. In that one word she suddenly became elegant and dangerous, her voice even more precise than her mother's had been, like she was queen of the universe.

'Medea,' her brother retorted nastily.

Deaver figured they were calling names, but didn't know what they meant.

'I'm Toolie,' said the driver.

'Peter O'Toole Aal,' said Katie. 'After the great actor.'

Toolie grinned. 'Daddy wasn't subtle about wanting us to go into the family business. Nice to meet you, Deaver.'

All this time Katie didn't take her eyes off Deaver. 'Ollie said you know Uncle Royal.'

'No,' said Deaver. 'I just know about him.'

'I thought you range riders worked under him.'

Was that why she was sitting next to him? Hoping he'd talk about their famous uncle? 'He's over the out-riders.'

'You want to be an outrider?'

It wasn't something he talked about much to anybody. Most young men who signed on as rangers were hoping someday to get into Royal's Riders, but the ones who got in usually made it before they reached twenty-five, which meant they had five or six years on horseback before they applied to the outriders. Deaver was twenty-five when he joined up, and he hadn't had four years as a range rider yet. Except for a couple of older guys, most rangers would have a good laugh if they knew how much Deaver wanted to ride with Royal Aal.

'It's something that might happen,' said Deaver.

'I hope you get your wish,' she said.

This time it was his turn to search her face to see if she was making fun. But she wasn't. He could see that. She really hoped for something good to happen to him. He nodded, not knowing what else to say.

'Riding out there,' she said, 'helping people make it here to safety.'

'Taking apart the missiles,' said Toolie.

'Ain't too many missiles now,' said Deaver.

Which pretty much ended the conversation. Deaver was used to that, having his words be the ones that hung in the air, nobody saying a thing afterward. A long time ago he tried to apologize or explain what he said, something to make that embarrassed silence go away. Last few years, though, he realized he probably hadn't said something wrong. Other people just had a hard time talking to him for long, that's all. Nothing against him. He just wasn't the kind of person you talk to.

Deaver wished he actually knew their uncle, so he could tell them about him. It was plain they were hungry for word about him. If their father'd been feuding with Royal for a long time, they might hardly know him. That'd be strange, for the kinfolk of the best-loved hero of Deseret not to know a bit more about him than any stranger just reading the paper.

They crested a hill. Toolie pointed. 'There's Hatchville.'

Deaver had no idea how long ago they left the grassland and came into the fringe, but from the size of Hatchville he figured this town was probably twelve, fifteen years old. Well back from the edge now, really not fringe at all anymore. Lots of people.

Toolie slowed enough to gear down the truck. Deaver listened with an ear long attuned to motors from his years nursing scavenger trucks from one place to another. 'Engine's pretty good for one this old,' said Deaver.

'You think so?' said Toolie. He perked right up, talking about the engine. These folks made a living only as long as the motor kept going.

'Needs a tune-up.'

Toolie made a wry face. 'No doubt.'

'Probably the mix in the carburetor's none too good.'

Toolie laughed in embarrassment. 'Do carburetors mix something? I always thought they just sat there and carbureted.'

153

'Ollie takes care of the truck,' Katie said.

The little girl between them woke up. 'Are we there yet?'

They were passing the first houses on the outskirts of town. The sky was pretty light now. Almost sunrise.

'You remember where the pageant field is in Hatchville, Katie?' Toolie asked.

'I can't tell Hatchville from Heber,' said Katie.

'Heber's the one with mountains all around like a bowl,' said Janie.

'Then this is Hatchville,' said Katie.

'I knew that,' said Toolie.

They ended up at the town hall, where everybody stood around the truck in the cold morning air while Ollie and Katie went in looking for somebody to give them a permit for a place to set up for the pageant. Deaver figured that this time of morning the only one on duty'd be the night man who did the data linkups with Zarahemla – every town had one – so he didn't bother going in on his own business. As for them going in, well, it was their business, not his.

Sure enough, they came out empty-handed. 'The night guy couldn't give us a permit,' said Ollie, 'but the pageant field's up on Second North and then out east to the first field that's got no fence.'

'And he gave us such a *Christian* welcome,' said Katie. Her smile was full of mischief. Ollie hooted. Deaver was having fun just watching them.

Toolie shook his head. 'Small-town pinheads.'

Katie launched into a thick hicktown accent, full of *r*'s so hard Deaver thought she must have her tongue tickling the back of her throat. 'And you bette*r* stay the*r*e till you come back in at nine and get a pe*r*mit, cause we *r*espect the law a*r*ound he*r*e.'

Deaver couldn't help but laugh with the others, even though the accent she was making fun of, that was pretty much the way he talked.

Marshall, though, he wasn't laughing as he stood

154

there combing his sleep-crazy hair with his fingers. 'Ungrateful, suspicious, small-minded bigots, all of them. I wonder how they'd like to pass this autumn without a single visit from a pageant wagon. There's nothing to stop us from driving on through.' This early in the morning he didn't talk so careful. Deaver heard a little naturalness in his speech, and even though it was only by accident, it kind of made Deaver feel better to know that the real person Marshall used to be wasn't hidden all that deep after all.

'Now Marsh,' said Scarlett. 'You know that our calling comes from the Prophet, not from these small-town people. If their minds are little and ugly and closed, isn't it our job to bring them a broader vision? Isn't that why we're here?'

Katie sighed pointedly. 'Why does it always have to come back to the Church, Mother? We're here to make a living.'

She didn't speak harsh or nasty, but people acted like she'd slapped her mother. Scarlett immediately put her hands to her cheeks and turned away, tears filling her eyes. Marshall looked like he was about to tear into Katie with words so hot they could start a brushfire, and Ollie was grinning like this was the best thing he'd seen all year.

But right then Toolie took a step toward Deaver and said, 'Well, Deaver Teague, you can see how it is with show people. We have to make a grand scene out of everything.'

That reminded folks that there was a stranger among them, and all at once they changed. Scarlett smiled at Deaver. Katie laughed lightly like it was all a joke. Marshall started nodding wisely, and Deaver knew the next words he said would be as elegant as ever.

It was plainly time for Deaver to say thank you and get his saddle off the truck and go take a nap somewhere out of the wind till it got time to report in to Moab. Then the Aals could quarrel with each other all they liked. Parting would be fine with Deaver – he'd been a bit of painless charity to them, and they'd been a ride into town for him. Everybody got what they needed and good-bye.

What messed things up was that when Marshall got pretty much the same idea – that it was time for Deaver to go – he didn't trust Deaver to have sense enough to figure it out himself. So Marshall smiled and nodded and put his arm around Deaver's shoulder. 'I suppose, Son, that you'll want to stay here and wait until the offices open up at eight o'clock.'

Deaver didn't take offense at what he said – he was just hinting for Deaver to do what he already meant to do, so that was fine. Folks had a right to keep their family squabbles away from strangers. But giving him a hug and calling him 'son' while telling him to go away, it made Deaver so mad he wanted to hit somebody.

All the time he was growing up Mormons kept doing that same thing to him. They always fostered him out to live in some Mormon family's house who'd always make him go to church every Sunday even though they knew he wasn't a Mormon and didn't want to be one. The other kids knew right off he wasn't one of them and didn't make any bones about it – they left him alone and didn't pretend they liked him or even cared whether he lived or died. But there was always some Relief Society president who patted his head and called him 'sweetie' or 'you dear thing,' and whenever the bishop passed him, he'd put his arm around him and call him 'son,' just like Marshall, and pretend they were only joking when they said, 'How long till you see the light and get baptized?'

That friendly and nice stuff always lasted until Deaver finally told them 'never' loud enough and nasty enough that they believed him. From then on until he got fostered somewhere else, the bishop would never touch him or speak to him, just fix him with a cold stare as Deaver sat there in the congregation and the bishop sat up on the stand being holy. Sometimes Deaver wondered what would have happened if just once, some bishop had kept on being friendly even after Deaver told him he'd never get baptized. If maybe he might've felt different about Mormons if ever their friendship turned out to be real. But it never happened.

So here was Marshall Aal doing just what those bishops always did, and Deaver plain couldn't help himself, he shrugged Marshall's arm off and stepped back so fast that Marshall's arm was still hanging there in the air for a second. His face and his fists must have shown how mad he was, too, because they all stared at him, looking surprised. All except Ollie, who stood there nodding his head.

Marshall looked around at the others. 'Well, I don't know what I . . .' Then he gave up with a shrug.

Funny thing was, Deaver's anger was gone already, gone in a second. He never let rage hold on to him – that only gets you in trouble. Worst of all, now they all thought he was mad because they were sending him away. But he didn't know how to explain that it was OK, he was glad to go. It always ended up like this whenever he left a foster home, too. The family was sending him away because they were tired of him, which was fine cause he never much liked them either. He didn't mind leaving and they were glad to see him go, and yet nobody could just come out and *say* that.

Well, so what. They'd never see him again. 'Let me get my saddle,' Deaver said. He headed for the side of the truck.

'I'll help you,' said Toolie.

'No such thing,' said Scarlett. She caught ahold of Deaver's elbow and held it tight. 'This young man has been out in the grassland for I don't know how many days, and we're *not* sending him away without breakfast.'

Deaver knew she was just saying that for good manners, so he said no thanks as polite as he could. That might have been the end of it except right then Katie came to

157

him and took his left hand – which was his only free hand, since Scarlett had tight hold on his right elbow. 'Please stay,' she said. 'We're all strangers in this town, and I think we ought to stick together till we have to go our separate ways.'

Her smile was so bright that Deaver had to blink. And her eyes looked at him so steady, it was like she was daring him to doubt that she meant it.

Toolie picked up on it and said, 'We could use another hand setting up, so you'd be earning the meal.'

Even Marshall added his bit. 'I meant to ask you myself. I hope you *will* come with us and share our poor repast.'

Deaver was hungry, all right, and he didn't mind looking at Katie's face though he wished she'd let go of his hand, and he particularly wished Scarlett would unclamp his elbow – but he knew he wasn't really wanted, and so he said no thanks again and got his arms back from the women and headed over to get his saddle off the truck. That was when Ollie laughed and said, 'Come on, Teague, you're hungry and Father feels like a jerk and Mother feels guilty and Katie's hot for you and Toolie wants you to do half his work. How can you just walk off and disappoint everybody?'

'Ollie,' said Scarlett sternly.

But by now Katie and Toolie were laughing, too, and Deaver just couldn't help laughing himself.

'Come on, everybody into the truck,' said Marshall. 'Ollie, you know the way, you drive.'

Marshall and Scarlett and Toolie and Ollie piled into the cab, so Deaver had to ride in back with Katie and Janie and a younger brother, Dusty. The two really old people he saw last night were way in the back of the truck. Katie kept Deaver right up front, behind the cab. Deaver couldn't figure out if she was flirting with him or what. And if she was, he sure didn't know why. He knew his clothes stank of dirt and sweat and the horse he'd been riding till it died, and he also knew he wasn't much to look at even when he shaved. Probably she was just being nice, and didn't know how to do that except by using that smile of hers and looking at him under heavy eyelids and touching his arm and his chest whenever she talked to him. It was annoying, except that it also felt pretty nice. Only that made it even more annoying because he knew that it wasn't going anywhere.

The town was finally coming awake as they drove to the pageant field. Deaver noticed they didn't go straight there. No, they drove that noisy truck up and down every road there was in town, most of them just dirt traces since nothing much got paved these days outside Zarahemla. The sound of the rattletrap truck brought people looking out their windows, and children spurted out the doors to lean on picket fences, jumping up and down.

'Is it Pageant Day?' they'd shout.

'Pageant Day!' answered Katie and Janie and Dusty. Maybe the old folks in back were shouting, too – Deaver couldn't hear. Pretty soon the news was ahead of the truck, and people were already lined up along the edge of the road, straining to see them. That was when the Aals started pulling the tarp off a couple of the big pieces. One of them looked like the top of a missile, and another one was a kind of tower – a tall steep pyramid like a picture Deaver saw in school, the Pyramid of the Sun in Mexico City. When the people saw the rocket, they started yelling, 'Man on the moon!' and when they saw the pyramid, which they couldn't see till the truck passed, they'd scream and laugh and call out, 'Noah! Noah! Noah!'

Deaver figured they must have seen the shows before. 'How many different pageants do you do?' he asked.

'Three,' said Katie. She waved at the crowd. 'Pageant Day!' Then, still talking loud so he could hear her over the truck and the crowds and her little brother and sister yelling, she said, 'We do our *Glory of America* pageant,

159

which Grandfather wrote. And *America's Witness for Christ*, which is the old Book of Mormon pageant from the Hill Cumorah – everybody does that one – and at Christmas we do *The Glorious Night*, which Daddy wrote because he thought the regular Christmas pageants were terrible. That's our whole repertoire in towns like this. Pageant Day!'

'So it's all Mormon stuff,' said Deaver.

She looked at him oddly. '*Glory of America* is American. *The Glorious Night* is from the Bible. Aren't you Mormon?'

Here it is, thought Deaver. Here comes the final freeze-out. Or the sudden interest in converting me, leading up to a freeze-out soon enough. He had forgotten, for just a while this morning, that he hadn't told them yet, that they still figured he was one of them, that he basically belonged. The way that these show gypsies were still part of Hatchville, because they were all Mormons. The way most of the other range riders liked being in town, among fellow Mormons. But now, finding out he wasn't one of them, they'd feel like he fooled them, like he stuck himself in where he didn't belong. Now he really regretted letting them talk him into coming along to breakfast like this. They never would've tried to talk him into it if they knew he wasn't one of them.

'Nope,' said Deaver.

He couldn't believe it when she didn't even pause. Just went on like nothing got said. 'We'd rather do other shows, you know, besides those three. When I was little we spent a year in Zarahemla. I played Tiny Tim in *A Christmas Carol*. Do you know what I've always wanted to play?'

He didn't have any idea.

'You have to guess,' she said.

He wasn't sure he'd even heard the name of a play, let alone a person in one. So he seized on the only thing he could halfway remember. 'Titanic?'

She looked at him like he was crazy.

'In the cab. You said you were –'

'Titania! The queen of the fairies from *A Midsummer Night's Dream*. No, no. I've always wanted to play – you won't tell anybody?'

He sort of shrugged and shook his head at the same time. Who would he tell? And if it was a real secret, why would she tell *him*?

'Eleanor of Aquitaine,' she said.

Deaver had never heard that name in his life.

'It was a part Katherine Hepburn played. The actress I was named after. A movie called *A Lion in Winter*.' She almost whispered the title. 'I saw a tape of it once, years ago. Actually I saw it about five times, in one single day, over and over again. We were staying with an old friend of Grandpa's in Cedar City. He had a VCR that still ran on his windmill generator. The movie's banned now, you know.'

Movies didn't mean much to Deaver. Hardly anybody ever got to see them. Out here on the fringe nobody did. Electricity was too expensive to waste on televisions. Besides, a former salvage man like Deaver knew there just weren't enough working televisions in Deseret for more than a couple in each town. It wasn't like the old days, when everybody went home every night and watched TV till they fell asleep. Nowadays folks only had time for a show when a pageant wagon came to town.

They were past the houses now, pulling onto a bumpy field that had been planted in wheat, long since harvested.

Katie's voice suddenly went husky and trembled a little. 'I'd hang you from the nipples, but you'd shock the children.'

'What?'

'She was such a magnificent woman. She was the first to wear pants. The first *woman* to wear them. And she loved Spencer Tracy till he died, even though he was a Catholic and wouldn't divorce his wife to marry her.'

161

The truck pulled to a stop at the eastern edge of the field. Janie and Dusty jumped right off the truck, leaving them alone between the set pieces and the back of the cab.

'I rode bare-breasted halfway to Damascus,' said Katie, in that husky, quavery voice again. 'I damn near died of wind burn, but the troops were dazzled.'

Deaver finally guessed that she was quoting from the movie. 'They did a movie where a woman said *damn*?'

'Did I offend you? I thought since you weren't a Mormon, you wouldn't mind.'

That sort of attitude made Deaver crazy. Just because he wasn't a Latter-day Saint, Mormons thought he'd want to hear their favorite dirty joke, or else they started swearing cause they thought it would make him more comfortable, or they just assumed that he slept with whores all the time and got drunk whenever he could. But he swallowed his anger without showing it. After all, she meant no harm. And he liked having her so close to him, especially since she hadn't moved any farther away when she found out he was a gentile.

'I just wish you could see the movie,' said Katie. 'Katherine Hepburn is – magnificent.'

'Isn't she dead?'

Katie turned to him, her face a mask of sadness. 'The world is poorer because of it.'

He spoke the way he always did to a sad-looking woman who was too close to ignore. 'I guess the world ain't too poor if you're in it.'

Her face brightened at once. 'Oh, if you keep saying things like that I'll *never* let you go.' She took hold of his arm. His hand had just been hanging at his side, but now that she was pressed up against him, he realized his hand was being pressed into the soft curve of her belly just inside her hip bone. If he even twitched his hand he'd be touching her where a man had no right without being asked. Was she asking?

Toolie, standing on the ground beside the truck,

pounded one fist on Deaver's boot and the other on Katie's shoe. 'Come on, Katie, let go of Deaver so we can use him to help with the loading.'

She squeezed his arm again. 'I don't have to,' she said.

'If she gets annoying, Deaver, break her arm. That's what *I* do.'

'You did it once,' said Katie. 'I never let you do it again.' She let go of Deaver and jumped off the truck.

For a moment he stood there, not moving his hand or anything. She just talked to him, that's all. That's all it meant. And even if she meant more, he wasn't going to do anything about it. You don't answer folks' hospitality by diddling with their daughter. After a minute – no just a few seconds – he swung himself off the truck and joined the others.

Except for picking the exact spot to park and leveling the truck, the family didn't set to work right away. They gathered in the field and Parley Aal, the old man from the back of the truck, he said a prayer. He had a grand, rolling voice, but it wasn't so clear-sounding as Marshall's, and Parley said his *r*'s real hard like the Mormons Katie made fun of back in town. The prayer wasn't long. Mostly all he did was dedicate the ground to the service of God, and ask the Lord's Spirit to touch the hearts of the people who came to watch. He also asked God to help them all remember their lines and be safe. So far only Katie knew Deaver wasn't Mormon, and he said amen at the end just like the others. Then he looked up and in the gap between Toolie and Katie, he could see part of the sign on the truck. Miracle, it said. Then they moved, and Deaver read the whole thing. Sweetwater's Miracle Pageant. Why Sweetwater, when everybody in the family was named Aal?

Unloading the truck and setting up for the show was as hard as the hardest work Deaver'd ever done in his life. There was more stuff on that truck than he would ever have thought possible. The tower and the missile had doors in back, and they were packed tight with props and machinery and supplies. It took only an hour to pitch the tents they lived in – four of them, plus the kitchen awning – but that was the easy part. There was a generator to load off the truck on a ramp, then hook up to the truck's gas tank. It was so awkward to handle, so heavy and temperamental, that Deaver wondered how they did it when he wasn't there. It took all the strength he and Toolie and Ollie and Marshall had.

'Oh, Katie and Scarlett usually help,' said Toolie.

So he was saving Katie work. Was that why she was treating him so nice? Well, that was all right with him. He was glad to help, and he didn't expect payment of any coin. What else was he going to do this morning? Call in to Moab and then sit around and wait for instructions, most likely. Might as well be doing this. Best not to remember the way her body pressed against his hand, the way she squeezed his arm.

They carried metal piping and thick heavy blocks of steel out about fifteen yards from the truck, one on each side of where the audience would be, and then assembled them into trees that held the lights. They kept tossing around words that Deaver never heard of – *fresnel, ellipsoidal* – but before long he was getting the hang of what each light was for. Ollie was the one in charge of all the electrical work. Deaver had a little bit of practice with that sort of thing, but he made it a point not to show off. He just did whatever Ollie ordered, fast and correct and without a word unless he had to ask a question. By the time the lights were wired, aimed, and focused, Ollie was talking to Deaver like they were friends since first grade. Making jokes, even teasing a little – 'Do they make some special horse perfume for you range riders to spray on?' – but mostly teaching Deaver everything there was to know about stage lighting. Why the different-colored filters were used, what the specials did, how the light plot was set up, how to wire up the dimmer board. Deaver couldn't figure what good it was ever going to do him, knowing how to light a stage show, but Ollie knew what he was talking about, and Deaver didn't mind learning something new.

Even with the lights set up the work was hardly started. They had breakfast standing around the gas stove. 'We're working you too hard,' said Scarlett, but Deaver just grinned and stuffed another pancake in his mouth. Tasted like they actually had sugar in them. A gas stove, their own generator, pancakes that tasted like more than flour and water – they might live on a truck and sleep in tents, but these pageant wagon people had a few things that people in the fringe towns usually had to do without.

By noon, dripping with sweat and aching all over, Deaver stood away from the truck with Ollie and Toolie and Marshall as they surveyed the stage. The missile had been taken down and replaced with the mast of a ship; the side of the truck had been covered with panels that made it look like the hull of a boat; and the machinery was all set up to make a wave effect with blue cloth out in front of it. A black curtain hid the pyramid from sight. Dusty raised and dropped the curtain while the men watched. Deaver thought it looked pretty exciting to have the pyramid suddenly revealed when the curtain dropped, but Marshall clucked his tongue.

'Getting a little shabby,' said Marshall.

The curtain *was* patched a lot, and there were some tears and holes that hadn't been patched yet.

'It's shabby at noon, Daddy,' said Toolie. 'At night it's good enough.' Toolie sounded a little impatient.

'We need a new one.'

'While we're wishing, we need a new truck a lot more,' said Ollie.

Toolie turned to him – looking a little angry, it seemed to Deaver, though he couldn't think why Toolie should be mad. 'We don't need a new truck, we just need to take better care of this one. Deaver here says it isn't carbureting right.'

All of a sudden the cheerfulness went right out of Ollie's face. He turned to Deaver with eyes like ice. 'Oh, really?' said Ollie. 'Are you a mechanic?'

'I used to drive a truck,' said Deaver. He couldn't believe that all of a sudden he was in the middle of a family argument. 'I'm probably wrong.'

'Oh, you're right enough,' said Ollie. 'But see, I take all the huge amounts of money they give me to buy spare parts and use it all up in every saloon and whorehouse in the fringe, so the engine just never gets repaired.'

Ollie looked too mad to be joking, but what he was saying couldn't possibly be true. There weren't any saloons or whorehouses in the fringe.

'I'm just saying we can't afford a new truck, or a new curtain either,' said Toolie. He looked embarrassed, but then he deserved to – he *had* as much as accused Ollie of doing a lousy job with the truck.

'If that's what you were doing,' said Ollie, 'why'd you have to get Teague here on your side?'

Deaver wanted to grab him and shout straight into his face: I'm not on anybody's side. I'm not part of your family and I'm not part of this argument. I'm just a range rider who needed a lift into town and helped you unload eight tons of junk in exchange for breakfast.

Toolie was trying to calm things down, it looked like, only he wasn't very good at it. 'I'm just trying to tell you and Father that we're broke, and talking about new curtains and new trucks is like talking about falling into a hole in the ground and it turns out to be a gold mine. It just isn't going to happen.'

'I was just *talking*,' said Ollie.

'You were getting sarcastic and nasty, that's what you were doing,' said Toolie.

Ollie just stood there for a second, like some really terrible words were hanging there in his mind, waiting to get flung out where they could really hurt somebody. But he didn't say a thing. Just turned around and

166

walked away, around the back end of the truck.

'There he is, off in a huff again,' said Toolie. He looked at his father with a bitter half-smile. 'I don't know what I did, but I'm sure it's all my fault he's mad.'

'What you did,' said Marshall, 'was humiliate him in front of his friend.'

It took Deaver a moment to realize Marshall was referring to him. The idea of being Ollie's friend took Deaver by surprise. Was that why Ollie worked so close to him so much of the morning, teaching him how the electrical stuff was done – because they were friends? Somehow Deaver'd got himself turned from a total stranger into a friend without anybody so much as asking him if he minded or if he thought it was a good idea.

'You need to learn to be sensitive to other people, Toolie,' said Marshall. 'Thank heaven you don't lead this company, the way you do what you like without a thought for your brother's feelings. You just run rough-shod over people, Toolie.'

Marshall never exactly raised his voice. But he was precise and cruel as he went on and on. Deaver was plain embarrassed to watch Toolie get chewed on. Toolie did kind of pick a fight with Ollie, but he didn't deserve this kind of tongue-lashing, and it sure didn't help matters much to have Deaver standing there watching. But Deaver couldn't figure how to get away without it looking like he disapproved. So he just stood there, kind of looking between Marshall and Toolie so he didn't meet anybody's eyes.

Over at the truck, Katie was sitting on the top of the pyramid, sewing. Dusty and Janie were setting up the fireworks for the end of the show. Ollie had the hood open, fiddling with something inside. Deaver figured he could probably hear every word Marshall said, chewing out Toolie. He could imagine Ollie smiling that mean little smile of his. He didn't like thinking about it, particularly knowing that Ollie thought of him as a friend. So

167

he let his gaze wander to the pyramid, and he watched as Katie worked.

It seemed an odd thing, to sit so high, right in the sun, when there was plenty of shade to sit in. It occurred to Deaver that Katie might be on top of the pyramid just so he'd be sure to see her. But that was pure foolishness. What happened this morning didn't mean a thing – not her talking to him, not her pressing close to him, meant nothing. He must be a plain fool to imagine a smart good-looking woman like her was paying heed to him in the first place. She was on top of the pyramid cause she liked to look out over the town.

She raised her hand and waved to him.

Deaver didn't dare wave back – Marshall was still going strong, ragging on Toolie about things that went back years ago. Deaver looked away from Katie and saw how Toolie just took it, didn't even show anger in his face. Like he switched off all his emotions while his father talked to him.

Finally it ended. Marshall had finally wound down and now he stood there, waiting for Toolie to answer. And all Toolie said was, 'Sorry, sir.' Not angry, not sarcastic, just simple and clean as can be. Sorry, sir. Marshall stalked off toward the truck.

As soon as his father was out of earshot, Toolie turned to Deaver. 'I'm sorry you had to hear that.'

Deaver shrugged. Had no idea what to say.

Toolie gave a bitter little laugh. 'I get that all the time. Except that Father likes it better when there's somebody there to watch.'

'I don't know about fathers,' said Deaver.

Toolie grinned. 'Daddy doesn't live by the standards of other men. Mere logic, simple fairness – those are the crutches of men with inferior understanding.' Then Toolie's face grew sad. 'No, Deaver, I love my father. This isn't about Ollie or how I treat him, just like what I said to Ollie wasn't about the truck. I'm too much like my dad and he knows it and that's what he hates about me.' Toolie looked around him, as if to see what needed doing. 'I guess I better head to town for the official permit, and you need to get in there and report to Moab, don't you?'

'Guess so.'

Toolie stopped with his mother to see if she needed anything from town. Scarlett recited a list, mostly staples – flour, salt, honey. Things they could get without paying, cause it was their right to have it from the community storehouse. As they talked, Ollie came by and tossed a dirty air filter at Toolie's chest. 'I need a new air filter just like that one only clean.'

'Where are you going, Laurence?' asked Scarlett.

'To sleep,' he said. 'I was up all night driving, in case you forgot.' Ollie started to walk away.

'What about brake linings?' asked Toolie.

'Yeah, see if they've got a mechanic who can do that.' Ollie ducked into a tent. Anger was still thick in the air. Deaver noticed that Scarlett didn't even ask why.

She finished telling her list to Toolie, sometimes talking over what they would probably get donated by the audience in a place like Hatchville. Then Toolie set out, Deaver in tow. Deaver wanted to take his saddle with him, but Toolie talked him out of it. 'If they tell you to get a ride today, your driver can come out and pick it up. And if you end up riding to Moab with us day after tomorrow, you might as well leave the saddle here.' As if he was holding the saddle hostage to make sure Deaver came back.

Deaver wasn't sure why he didn't just say no thanks and then pick up the saddle and carry it with him anyway. He knew they hadn't wanted him in the first place, and it was just good manners or maybe guilt or embarrassment or something that made Toolie want to keep the saddle so Deaver had to come back at least one more time. Funny thing, though: Deaver didn't mind. It had been a long time since anybody went to any trouble to try to get him to stay with them. Them saying he was

Ollie's friend. The way Katie treated him. That was part of it. A lot more of his feeling came out of just working alongside them, helping unload the truck and set up for the show. Deaver had enough sweat spilled in this field that he really wasn't hoping to leave for Moab today. He wanted to see what all the fuss was about. He wanted to see the show. That's all it was, nothing more.

Yet even as he reached that conclusion, he knew it was a lie. Sure, he wanted to see the show, but there was something more. An old hunger, one so deep and ancient, so long unsatisfied that Deaver mostly forgot he was even hungry. Like some part of his soul had already starved to death. Only something was happening here to wake up that old hunger, and he couldn't go away without seeing if somehow maybe it could be satisfied. Not Katie. Or not just Katie, anyway. Something more. Maybe by the time he left for Moab, he'd find out what it was he wanted so bad that it made his dream of joining Royal's Riders seem kind of faint and far away.

He and Toolie walked a direct route to the town hall, not winding through the whole village the way they had that morning. There were still children excited to see them, though. 'Who are you!' they called. 'Are you Noah? Are you Jesus? Are you Armstrong?'

Toolie waved at them, smiled, and usually told them, 'No, my daddy plays that part.'

'Are you Alma?'

'Yes, that's one of the parts I play.'

'What's the show tonight?'

'*Glory of America.*'

All the way through town Deaver noticed how bright-eyed the children were, how daring they thought it was to talk right to somebody from the pageant wagon.

'Sounds like your show's the biggest thing they ever see,' Deaver said.

'Kind of sad, isn't it?' said Toolie. 'In the old days, a show like this – it would've been nothing.'

Deaver went with Toolie into the mayor's office. The secretary had neat, close-cropped hair. Plainly he was the kind of man who never spent a week without a barber – or a day without a bath, probably. Deaver wasn't sure whether he despised or envied the man.

'I'm with the pageant wagon,' said Toolie, 'and I need to change our temporary permit to a regular one.' Deaver saw how he put on an especially humble-but-cheerful tone, and he couldn't help but think that his own life would have been a lot easier if he'd only learned how to act like that toward his foster parents or the bishops of the wards he lived in. Of course, Toolie only had to act like that for a few minutes today, while Deaver would've had to keep it up for days and weeks and years on end. Like crossing your eyes – sure, you can do it, but keep it up too long and you get a head-ache.

And then he thought how when he was little, some-body told him that if you cross your eyes too often they'll stick that way. What if acting all humble and sweet worked that way? What if it got to be such a habit you forgot you were acting, the way Marshall's and Scarlett's fancy acting voices came out of their mouths even when they were picking up a range rider in the middle of the night. Do you become whatever you act like?

Deaver had plenty of time to think about all this, because the secretary didn't say a word for the longest time. He just sat there and eyed Toolie up and down, not showing any expression at all on his very clean and untanned face. Then he looked at Deaver. He didn't exactly ask a question, but Deaver knew what he was asking anyway.

'I'm a range rider,' Deaver said. 'They picked me up out on the road. I need to call Moab.'

A range rider – town people pretty much despised them, but at least they knew what to do with them. 'You can go right in there and call.' The secretary indicated an empty office. 'The sheriff's out on a call.'

Deaver went on into the office and sat at the desk. An old salvage desk – might be one of the ones he found and brought in himself in the old days when he was a kid. Not ten years ago.

He couldn't get an operator – the line was tied up – and as he waited, he could hear what went on in the other room.

'Here's our family business license from Zarahemla,' Toolie was saying. 'If you just look us up in the business database –'

'Fill out the forms,' said the secretary.

'We are licensed by the state of Deseret, sir,' said Toolie. Still polite, still humble.

There was no answer. Deaver leaned over the desk and saw Toolie sitting down, filling out the forms. Deaver understood why Toolie was doing it, all right – giving in to get along. This was how the secretary proved he was in charge. This was how he made sure the show gypsies knew they didn't belong here, that they had no *rights* here. So Toolie would fill out the forms, and as soon as he was gone the secretary would call up the business database, verify their license, and throw out the forms. Or maybe he'd go through the forms line by line, looking for some contradiction, some mistake, so he could have grounds to throw the pageant wagon out of Hatchville. And it wasn't right. The Aal family had natural troubles all their own, they didn't need some short-haired overwashed flunky in the mayor's office adding to their trouble supply.

For a moment, pure rage flowed through Deaver, just like this morning when Marshall put his arm around him and called him *son*. His arms trembled, his toes pumped up and down, like he was getting ready to dance or wrestle – or punch some power-hungry bastard right in the face and break his nose and cover him with his own blood, mat it in his hair, all over his clothes, so even when he didn't hurt so bad, there'd be stains in his shirt to remind him that people can only be pushed *so far* and then one day they bust out and do something about it, show you what all your power's good for –

And then Deaver got it under control, calmed himself down. There was no shortage of volunteer self-trained sons-of-bitches in the world, and this secretary wasn't the worst of them, not close. Toolie was doing the right thing, bowing down and letting the man feel important. Letting him have the victory now, so that the family would have the greater victory later. Cause when they left this town, the Aals would still be themselves, still be a family, while this secretary, he wouldn't have a speck of power over them. That was freedom, the power to leave whenever you wanted to. Deaver understood that kind of power. It was the only kind he'd ever had or ever wanted.

He finally got an operator and told him who he was and who he needed to talk to and why. It took the operator forever to check the computer and verify that Deaver was indeed a range rider and that he was therefore authorized to make an unlimited number of calls to regional headquarters in Moab. At last he got through. It was Meech, the regular dispatcher.

'Got the scrapings?' asked Meech.

'Yeah.'

'Fine, then. Come on in.'

'Quick?'

'Not quick enough to pay money for. Just catch a ride. No hurry.'

'Two, three days all right?'

'No rush. Except I got approval here for you to apply to Royal's Riders.'

'Why the hell didn't you say so, dickhead!' cried Deaver into the phone. He'd been on that waiting list for three years.

'I didn't want you to wet your pants right off, that's why,' said Meech. 'Please note that this is just permission to apply.'

173

How could Deaver tell him he never expected to get permission even for that? He figured that was the way they'd freeze non-Mormons out, by keeping them from applying for the job in the first place.

'And I got about five guys, Teague, asking if you'll transfer your right to apply. They're pretty eager.'

It was legal to sign over your spot to somebody farther down the list – it just wasn't legal to accept money for it. Still, the outrider waiting list was long, and there were bound to be some men on it who never meant to apply, who signed up just to make a little money selling their spot when it came along. Deaver knew that if he said yes and Meech gave him the names of those eager applicants, he'd start getting promises and favors. What he wouldn't get, though, was another chance to apply. 'No thanks, Meech.'

The secretary appeared in the doorway, glowering. 'Just a second,' Deaver said, and put his hand over the phone. 'What is it?'

'Are you aware of the public decency laws?' asked the secretary.

It took a second for Deaver to figure out what he was talking about. Had the secretary heard Meech hint about selling the right to apply? No – it was the public decency laws the secretary was talking about. Deaver thought back over his phone conversation. He must have said *hell* too loud. And even though *dickhead* wasn't on the statutory list, it fit quite easily under 'other crude or lascivious expressions or gestures.'

'Sorry,' he said.

'I hope you're *very* sorry.'

'I am.' He did his best to imitate the humble way Toolie'd been talking before. It was especially hard because he was suddenly in the mood to start laughing out loud – they were going to let him apply to the out-riders! – and he figured the secretary wouldn't like it if Deaver suddenly laughed. 'Very sorry, sir.' He picked up that *sir* bit from Toolie, too.

'Because in Hatchville we don't wink at sin.'

In Hatchville you probably don't piss, either, you just hold it all inside until you die. But Deaver didn't say it, just looked right at the secretary as calmly as he could until the man finally took his unbearable burden of righteousness back to his desk.

That's all Deaver needed, a misdemeanor arrest right when he was about to apply to be an outrider. 'You still hanging on there, Meech?'

'By my fingernails.'

'I'll be there in two days. I've got my saddle.'

'Ain't you cool.'

'Am too.'

'Are not.'

'See you, Meech.'

'Give your erosion reports to the reporter there, OK?'

'Got it,' said Deaver. He hung up.

The secretary grudgingly told him where the reporter's office was. Of course the reporter wasn't transmitting – that was done at night, over the same precious phone lines used for voice calls during the day. But he'd enter it into the computer today, and he didn't look thrilled at getting even Deaver's relatively slim notebook.

'All these coordinates,' said the reporter.

'It's my job to write them down,' said Deaver.

'You're very good at it,' said the reporter. 'Yesterday's desert, today's grass, tomorrow's farm.' It was the slogan of the new lands. It meant the conversation was over.

When Deaver got back, Toolie wasn't in the secretary's office anymore. He was in the mayor's office, and because the door was partly open, Deaver could hear pretty well, especially since the mayor wasn't trying very hard to talk softly.

'I don't *have* to give you a permit, Mr. Aal, so don't start flashing your license from Zarahemla. And don't think I'm impressed because your name is Aal. There's no law says a hero's kinfolk got to be worth shit, do you understand me?'

Shit was definitely on the statutory list. Deaver looked at the secretary, but the secretary just moved more papers around. 'Just don't wink,' said Deaver quietly.

'What?' asked the secretary.

If he could hear Deaver's comment, he could sure hear the mayor. But Deaver decided not to make a big deal about it. 'Nothing,' he said. No reason for him to provoke the secretary any further. Since he came into town with the pageant wagon, anything he did to annoy people would put the Aal family in a bad light, and it sounded like they had trouble enough already.

'Young girls see you in those lights and costumes, they think you really are the Prophet Joseph or Jesus Christ or Alma or Neil Armstrong, and so they're suckers for any unscrupulous bastard who doesn't care what he does to a girl.'

Finally Toolie raised his voice, dropping the humility act just for a moment. Deaver was relieved to know Toolie had a breaking point. 'If you have an accusation –'

'The Aal Pageant and Theatrical Association is implicated in a lot of these, do I make myself clear? No warrants, but we'll be watching. Just cause you call yourselves Sweetwater's Miracle Pageant these days doesn't mean we don't know the kind of people you are. You tell everybody in your company, we're watching you.'

Toolie's answer was too mild to hear.

'It will not happen in Hatchville. You will not ruin some girl and then disappear with your commission from the Prophet.'

So somebody *did* believe all those stories about show gypsies. Maybe Deaver used to believe them, too. But once you know people like the Aals, those stories sound pretty stupid. Except in Hatchville, of course, where they don't wink at sin.

Toolie was real quiet when he came out of the mayor's office, but he had the permit and the requisition form for the bishop's storehouse – both signed by the same man, of course, since the mayor *was* the bishop.

Deaver didn't talk about what he heard. Instead he told Toolie all about his getting permission to apply for job change, which meant he at least had a shot at getting into the outriders.

'What do you want to do that for?' asked Toolie. 'It's a terrible life. You travel thousands of miles on horse-back, tired all the time, people looking to kill you if they get a chance, out in the bad weather every day, and for what?'

It was a crazy question. Every kid in Deseret knew why you wanted to be one of Royal's Riders. 'Save people's lives. Bring them here.'

'The outriders mostly deliver mail from one settled area to another. And make maps. It isn't that much more exciting than the work you're doing now.'

So Toolie *had* looked into the work his uncle Royal was doing. How would Marshall feel about that?

'You ever think of joining?' asked Deaver.

'Not me,' said Toolie.

'Come on,' said Deaver.

'Never since I grew up enough to make intelligent choices.' No sooner were the words out of his mouth than Toolie must have realized what he'd said. 'I don't say it isn't an intelligent choice for *you*, Deaver. It's just – if one of us leaves, the family show is pretty well dead. Who'd do my parts? Dusty? Grandpa Parley? We'd have to hire somebody from outside the family – but how long would somebody like that work for nothing but food and shelter, like we do? If anybody leaves the show, then it's over for everybody. What would Dad and Mom do for a living? So how could I go off and join the outriders?'

There was something in Toolie's tone of voice, some-thing in his manner that said, This is real. This is some-thing I'm really afraid of – the family breaking up, the pageant wagon going out of business. And also: This is why I'm trapped. Why I can't have any dreams of my own, like you do. And because he was speaking true, like Deaver was somebody he trusted, Deaver answered the same way, saying stuff he never said out loud to anybody, or not lately, anyway.

'Being an outrider, it's got a name to it. A range rider – what do they call us? Rabbit-stompers. Grass-herders.'

'I've heard worse,' said Toolie. 'Something about getting personal with cows. You rangers have almost as low a name as we do.'

'At least you're somebody every town you go into.'

'Oh, yes, they roll out the red carpet for us.'

'I mean you're Noah or Neil Armstrong or whatever.'

'That's what we *play*. That's not who we are.'

'That's who you are to *them*.'

'To the children,' said Toolie. 'To the grown-ups all a person is is what he does here in town. You're the bishop or the mayor –'

'The bishop *and* the mayor.'

'Or the sheriff or the Sunday school teacher or a farmer or whatever. You're somebody regular. We come in and we don't fit.'

'At least some of them are glad to see you.'

'Sure,' said Toolie. 'I'm not saying we don't have it better than you, some ways. A gentile in a place like this.'

'Oh, Katie told you.' So it *had* mattered to her he wasn't Mormon, enough to tell her brother. Mormons *always* cared when somebody wasn't one of them. In a way, though, it made it so the way Toolie talked to him, like a friend – it meant even more, because he knew Deaver was a gentile all along.

And Toolie had the grace to act a little embarrassed about knowing something Deaver only told to Katie. 'I wondered, so I asked her to find out.'

Deaver tried to put him at ease about it. 'I'm circumcised, though.'

Toolie laughed. 'Well, too bad it isn't Israel where you live. You'd fit right in.'

Some trucker'd told him when he was about sixteen that Mormons were so damned righteous because they couldn't help it – after you get your dick cut all the way around, the sap can't flow anymore. Deaver knew the part about sap flowing wasn't true, but not till this moment did he realize that the trucker was also putting him on about circumcision being part of the Mormon religion. Once again Deaver had said something stupid and offensive without meaning to. 'Sorry. I thought you Mormons –'

But Toolie was just laughing. 'See? The ignorance is thick on every side.' He clapped his hand onto Deaver's shoulder and left it there for a minute as they walked along the street of Hatchville. And this time it didn't make Deaver mad. This time it felt right to have Toolie's hand on him. They got to the storehouse and arranged for a cart to deliver their supplies that afternoon.

'Soldiers of the United States! We could march on Philadelphia and – we could march –'

'March under arms and grind Philadelphia beneath our boots.'

'Soldiers of the United States! We could march under arms and boot Phila –'

'Grind Philadel –'

'Grind Philadelphia beneath our boots, and what then could –'

'What Congress then could –'

'What Congress then could deny our rightful claim upon the treasury of this blood which we created by –'

'Nation which we created –'

'I'll start over, I'm just confused a little, Janie, let me start over.'

Old Parley had gone over George Washington's speech to his troops so many times that Deaver could have recited it word perfect, just from hearing it while he worked on bypassing a relay to the heater fan. With his head buried deep in the truck's engine, one leg holding him in place by hooking across the fender, the sound of Parley memorizing echoed loud. Sweat dripped off Deaver's forehead into his eyes and stung him a little. Nasty work, but as long as the fan kept blowing they'd remember him.

Got it. Now all he had to do was climb out, start up the truck, and try it to see if the fan motor actually worked.

'I've got it now, Janie,' said Parley. 'But are we now, for the sake of money, to deny the very principles of freedom for which we fought, and for which so many of our comrades fell? Help me here Janie, just a word.'

'I.'

'I what?'

'I say.'

'Got it! I say thee, Nay!'

'I say that in America, soldiers are subject to the lawful government, even when that lawful government acts unjustly against them.'

'Don't read me the whole speech!'

'I thought if you heard it once, Grandpa, you could –'

'You are my prompter, not my understudy!'

'I'm sorry, but we've been over it and –'

Deaver started the truck engine. It drowned out the sound of Parley Aal unfairly blaming Janie for his collapsing memory. The fan worked. Deaver turned off the motor.

'– suddenly starting up! I can't work on these lines under these circumstances, I'm not a miracle worker, nobody could hold these long speeches in their heads with –'

It wasn't Janie's voice that answered him now – it was Marshall's. 'The motor's off now, so go ahead now.'

Parley sounded more petulant. Weaker. 'I say the words so often they don't mean anything to me anymore.'

'They don't have to mean anything, you just have to say them.'

'It's too long!'

'We've cut it down to the bare bones. Washington tells them they could seize Philadelphia and break Congress, but then all their fighting would be in vain, so be patient and let democracy work its sluggish will.'

'Why can't I say *that*? It's shorter.'

'It's also not at all what Washington would say. Dad, we can't have a *Glory of America* pageant without George Washington.'

'Then you do it! I just can't do these things anymore! Nobody could remember all these long speeches!'

'You've done them a thousand times before!'

'I'm too old! Do I have to say it that plain, Marshall?' Then, more softly, almost pleading. 'I want to go home.'

'To Royal.' The name was like acid sizzling on wood.

'To *home*.'

'Home is under water.'

'*You* should be doing Washington's speech, and you know it. You've got the voice, and Toolie's ready to play Jefferson.'

'Is he ready to play Noah?' Marshall spoke scornfully, as if the idea was crazy.

'*You* were his age when you started playing Noah, Marshall.'

'Toolie isn't mature enough!'

'Yes he is, and you should be doing my parts, and Donna and I should be home. For the love of heaven, Marsh, I'm seventy-two and my world is gone and I want to have some peace before I die.' Parley's speech ended with a ragged whisper. It was the perfect dramatic touch. Deaver sat in the cab, imagining the scene he couldn't see: Old Parley staring at his son for a long moment, then turning slowly and walking with weary dignity back to the tent. Every argument in this family is played out in set speeches.

The silence lasted long enough that Deaver felt free to open the door and leave the cab. He immediately looked back to where Janie and Parley had been practicing. Both gone. Marshall too.

Under the kitchen awning sat Donna, Parley's wife. She was old and frail, much older-seeming than Parley himself. Once they brought down her rocking chair early in the morning, she just sat there in the shade, sometimes sleeping, sometimes not. She wasn't senile, really; she fed herself, she talked. It was like she wanted to sit in her chair, close her eyes, and pretend she was somewhere else.

Now, though, she was here. As soon as she saw that Deaver was looking at her, she beckoned to him. He came over.

He figured she had in mind to tell him he ought to be more careful. 'I'm sorry for starting the truck right then.'

'Oh, no, the truck was nothing.' She patted a stool sitting in the grass next to her. 'Parley's just an old man who wants to quit his job.'

'I know the feeling,' said Deaver.

She smiled sadly, as if to say that there wasn't a chance in the world he knew that feeling. She looked at him, studying his face. He waited. After all, she had called him over. Finally she said what was on her mind. 'Why are you here, Deaver Teague?'

He took it as a challenge. 'Returning a favor.'

'No, no. I mean why are *you* here?'

'I needed a ride.'

She waited.

'I thought I ought to fix the heater fan.'

Still she waited.

'I want to see the show.'

She raised an eyebrow. 'Katie had nothing to do with it?'

'Katie's a pretty girl.'

She sighed. 'And funny. And lonely. She thinks she wants to get away, but she doesn't. There is no Broadway anymore. The rats have taken over the theatre buildings. They chewed up the NBC peacock and didn't leave a feather.' She giggled at her own joke.

Then, as if she knew she'd lost the thread of her own

182

conversation, she fell silent and stared off into space. Deaver wondered if maybe he ought to just go back to the truck or take a walk or something.

She startled him by turning her head and gazing at him again, her gaze sharper than ever before. 'Are you one of the three Nephites?'

'What?'

'Appearing on the road like that. Just when we needed an angel most.'

'Three Nephites?'

'The ones who chose to stay behind on Earth till Christ comes again. They go about doing good, and then they disappear. I don't know why I thought that, I know you're just an ordinary boy.'

'I'm no angel.'

'But the way the young ones turned to you. Ollie, Katie, Toolie. I thought you came to –'

'To what?'

'Give them what they want most. Well, why don't you anyway? You don't have to be an angel to work miracles, sometimes.'

'I'm not even a Mormon.'

'I'll tell you the truth,' said the old lady. 'Neither was Moses.'

He laughed. So did she. Then she got that faraway look again. After he waited awhile, her eyelids got heavy, flickered, closed. He stood up, stretched, turned around.

Scarlett was standing not five feet away, looking at him.

He waited for her to say something. She didn't.

Voices off in the distance. Scarlett glanced toward them, breaking the silent connection between them. He also turned. Beyond the truck, the first group of townspeople were coming – looked like three families together, with benches and a couple of ancient folding chairs. He heard Katie call out to them, though he couldn't see her behind the truck. The families waved.

The children ran forward. Now he could see Katie emerging, out in the open field. She was wearing the hoop skirts of Betsy Ross – Deaver knew the Betsy Ross scene because he'd had to learn the cue when to raise the flag, so that Janie could help Dusty with the costume change. The children overran her, turned her around; Katie squatted and hugged the two smallest both at once. She stood up then and led them toward the wagon. It was very theatrical; it was a scene played out for the children's parents, and it worked. They laughed, they nodded. They would enjoy the show. They would like the pageant family, because Katie greeted their children with affection. Theatrical – and yet utterly honest. Deaver didn't know how he knew that. He just knew that Katie really did love to meet the audience.

And then, thinking about that, he knew something else. Knew that he'd seen Katie play out some scenes today that she didn't mean, not the same way, not with that fervency that he saw when she greeted the children. This was real. Her flirting with Deaver, that was false. Calculated. Again, Deaver didn't know how he knew it. But he knew. Katie's smile, her touch, her attention, all that she'd given him today, all that she'd halfway promised, it was an act. She was like her father, not like Toolie. And it tasted nasty, just thinking about it. Not so much because she'd been faking it. Mostly because Deaver'd been taken in so completely.

'Who can find a capable wife?' asked Scarlett softly.

Deaver felt himself blush.

But it wasn't a real question. Scarlett was reciting. 'Her worth is far beyond coral. Her husband's whole trust is in her, and children are not lacking.'

He could see how the children clung to Katie. She must be telling them a story. Or just pretending to be Betsy Ross. The children laughed.

'She repays him with good, not evil, all her life long. When she opens her mouth, it is to speak wisely, and loyalty is the theme of her teaching. She keeps her eye on the doings of her household and does not eat the bread of idleness. Her sons with one accord call her happy; her husband, too, and he sings her praises: Many a woman shows how capable she is; but you excel them all.'

It might be a recitation, but it had to have a point to it. Deaver turned to Scarlett, who was smiling merrily. 'Are you proposing to me?' asked Deaver.

'Charm is a delusion and beauty fleeting; it is the God-fearing woman who is honored. Extol her for the fruit of all her toil, and let her own works praise her in the gates.'

As best Deaver could figure it out, Scarlett was trying to get Deaver thinking about a wife when he looked at Katie. 'You hardly know me, Mrs. Aal.'

'I think I do. And call me Scarlett.'

'I'm not a Mormon, either.' He figured she'd probably been told already, but Deaver knew how much store Mormons set by getting married in the temple, and he also knew he never planned to set foot inside another Mormon temple in his life.

But Scarlett seemed to be ready for that objection. 'That's not *Katie's* fault, now is it, so why punish the poor girl?'

He couldn't very well say to her, Woman, if you think your daughter's really in love with me, then you're a plain fool. 'I'm a stranger, Scarlett.'

'You were this morning. But Mother Aal told us who you *really* are.'

Now he understood that she was teasing him. 'If I'm an angel, I got to say the pay isn't too good.'

But she didn't really want to play. She wanted to talk seriously.

'There's something about you, Deaver Teague. You don't say much, and half what you say is wrong, and yet you caught Katie's eye, and Toolie said to me today, 'Too bad Teague has to leave,' and you made a friend of Ollie, who hasn't made a friend in years.' She looked

185

away, looked toward the truck, though nothing was happening there. 'Do you know, Deaver, sometimes I think Ollie is his uncle Roy all over again.'

Deaver almost laughed out loud. Royal? The hero of the outriders shouldn't be compared to Ollie, with his mocking smile, his petulant temper.

'I don't mean Royal the way he is now, and I especially don't mean his carefully constructed public image. You had to know him before, back before the collapse. A wild boy. He had to put his nose in everything. And more than his nose, if you understand me. It seemed as though anything his body craved, he couldn't rest until he got it. Terrible trouble. Stayed out of jail only by luck and praying. Mother Aal's praying, his luck.'

As she spoke, Deaver noticed that her voice was losing that precision, that studied warmth. She sounded more like a normal person. Like as if just remembering the old days made her talk the way she used to, before she got to be an actress.

'He couldn't hold a job,' she said. 'He'd get mad at somebody, he couldn't take getting bossed around or chewed out, couldn't stand doing the same thing day after day. He got married when he was eighteen to a girl who was so pregnant the baby could have tossed the bouquet. He couldn't stay home, he couldn't stay faithful. Right before the Six Missile War, he up and joined the army. Never sent a dime home, and then the government fell apart and all that time, you know who took care of his wife and baby? Babies by then.'

'You?'

'Well, I suppose. But not by *my* choice. *Marsh* took them in, they lived in our basement. I was so angry. There was barely enough for Marsh and me and our children, so every bite they ate, I felt like they were taking it out of the mouths of little Toolie and Katie and Ollie. I said so, too – not to them, but to Marsh. In private. I'm not a complete bitch.'

Deaver blinked at hearing her use that word. 'What

did he say?'

'They're family, that's what he said. Like that was the whole answer. Family looks out for family, he said. He wouldn't even consider turning them out. Even when the university stopped classes and nobody had jobs, when we were eating dandelion greens and planting the whole yard for a garden just so the rain could come down and rip it all out – that terrible first year – rain tearing it out again and again –'

She stopped a moment to remember, to live in those days again. When she finally spoke again, she was brisk, getting on with the story.

'Then he came up with the idea of the pageant wagon. The Aal Family Pageant was the very first, you know. Not a truck, not then – a trailer in those days, so it really was a kind of wagon, and we built the sets and Marsh wrote *Glory of America* and adapted the old Hill Cumorah pageant so we'd have a Book of Mormon show and we went on the road. Oh, we were always a theatrical family. I met Marsh when his mother was directing plays at church.'

She looked down at her mother-in-law, asleep in the chair.

'Whoever would have thought play-acting would keep us alive! It was Marsh took the Aal name and made it stand for something, one end of Deseret to the other. And somehow he made it – *we* made it pay enough to raise our own kids and Royal's too, kept bread on the table for all of us. His wife wasn't easy to live with, never pulled her weight, but we kept her the whole time, too. Until she ran off one day. And we still kept her kids, never put them in foster homes. They knew they could count on a place with us forever.'

She couldn't possibly know how those words stung deep in Deaver's heart, reminding him of foster homes that always began with promises of 'you're here for good' and ended with Deaver putting his ugly little brown cardboard box in the back of somebody else's car and riding off without ever even a letter or postcard from one of the old families. He didn't want to hear any more talk about places you could count on. So he turned the conversation back to Ollie. 'I don't see how Ollie's like Royal. He hasn't left any children behind and run off.'

She got a hard look in her eyes. 'Hasn't he? It isn't for lack of trying.'

Deaver thought of what the mayor said to Toolie this morning. The Aal family was implicated. Getting girls pregnant and running off, that was no joke, that could get a man in jail. And here Scarlett was as much as confessing that the accusation wasn't just smalltown rumors, it was true and she knew it. And after what the mayor said, Deaver knew that if Ollie got caught, it would surely mean the loss of the family's license. They'd be dead broke – what value would their costumes and set pieces have to anybody else? They'd end up on some fringe farm somewhere. Deaver tried to imagine Marshall getting along with other farmers, fitting in. Tried to picture him covered with dirt and sweat, mud high up on his boots. That was what Ollie was flirting with, if Scarlett's accusation was true.

'I bet Ollie wouldn't do that,' said Deaver.

'Ollie is Roy all over again. He can't control himself. He gets a desire, then he'll fulfill it and damn the consequences. We never stay in the same place long enough for him to get caught. He thinks he can go on like this forever.'

'You ever explain it to Ollie like this?'

'You can't explain things to Ollie. Or at least *I* can't, and certainly Marsh and Toolie can't. He just blows up or walks away. But maybe you, Deaver. You're his friend.'

Deaver shook his head. 'That's the kind of thing you don't talk about to somebody you met this morning.'

'I know. But in time –'

'I just got my chance to apply to the outriders.'

Her face went grim. 'So you'll be gone.'

'I was going anyway. To Moab.'

'Range riders come into town. They get mail. We might keep in touch.'

'Same with outriders.'

'Not for us,' she said. Deaver knew it was true. They couldn't stay in touch with one of Royal's Riders. Not with Marshall feeling the way he did.

But still – if Ollie was really like Royal when he was younger, they could find some hope in that. 'Royal came home, didn't he? Maybe Ollie'll grow out of it.'

'Royal never came home.'

'He's got his wife and kids now,' said Ollie. 'I've read about them. In the papers.'

'That's how Royal came home – in the papers. We started reading stories about the outriders, and how the most daring one among them was a man named Royal Aal. In those days we were famous enough that they used to put in a little tag: 'No relation to the theatrical Aal family.' Which meant they were asking him, and he was denying it. His kids were old enough to read, some of them. *We* never denied him. We'd tell the kids, 'Yes, that's your daddy. He's off doing such an important work – saving people's lives, destroying the missiles, fighting the mobbers.' We'd tell them how everybody sacrifices during hard times, and their sacrifice was doing without their daddy for a while. Marshall even wrote to Roy, and so did I, telling him about his children, how they were smart and strong and good. When Joseph, the oldest, fell from a tree and shattered his arm so badly the doctors wanted to take it off, we wrote to him about his son's courage, and how we made them save the arm no matter what – and he never answered.'

It made Deaver sick to think of such a thing. He knew what it was like to grow up without a mother and father. But at least he knew that his parents were dead. He could believe that they *would* have come for him if they could. What would it be like to know your father was alive, that he was famous, and still have him never come, never write, never even send a message. 'Maybe he didn't get the letters.'

She laughed bitterly. 'He got them, all right. One day – Joseph was twelve, he was just ordained a deacon a few weeks before – the sheriff shows up at our campsite in Panguitch, and he's got a court order. A court order, listing Royal and his wife as co-complainants – yes, they were back together now. Telling us to surrender the children of Royal Aal into the sheriff's custody or face kidnapping charges!'

Tears flowed down her face. They weren't beautiful, decorous actress tears; they were hot and bitter, and her face was twisted with emotion.

'He didn't come himself, he didn't write to ask us to send the children, he didn't even thank us for keeping them alive for ten years. Nor did that ungrateful bitch of a wife of his, and she ate at our table for five of those years.'

'What did you do?'

'Marsh and I took his kids into the tent and told them that their father and mother had sent for them, that it was time for them to be together with their family again. You've never seen kids look happier. They'd been reading the papers, you see. That's who they thought Royal Aal was, the great hero. Like finding out that after years of being an orphan, your father the king had finally found you and you were going to be a prince and princesses. They were so happy, they hardly said good-bye to us. We don't blame them for that. They were children, going home. We don't even blame them for never writing to us since then – Royal probably forbade them to. Or maybe he told them lies about us, and now they hate us.' Her left hand was in front of her face; her right hand clenched and unclenched on her lap, gathering folds of her dress in a sodden mass. 'So don't tell me how Royal grew out of it.'

This wasn't exactly the story folks usually told about Royal Aal.

'I read an article about him once,' said Scarlett. 'Several years ago. About him and his oldest son Joseph riding together out on the prairies, a second generation of hero. And they quoted Roy about how he had such a hard family life, that there were so many rules he always felt like he was in prison, but that he had rescued his boy Joseph from that prison.'

Deaver had read that article, the way he read everything about Royal Aal. He thought he understood it when he read it; thought how he was in prison, too, and began to dream that maybe Royal Aal could rescue him, too. But now he'd spent a day with Royal's family. He could see how confining it was. Fights and squabbles. But also working together, everybody with a place that nobody else could fill. The kind of family he always wished for as a kid.

A thousand times over the years Deaver had imagined going to the outrider headquarters in Golden and going up to Royal Aal and shaking his hand, hearing Royal welcome him as one of his outriders. Only now if it really happened he'd be thinking of something else – like Marshall and Scarlett being served that court order. Like kids growing up without a word from their father. Like telling lies to make folks who'd done good to you look bad.

At the same time, Deaver could also see how it might look different to Royal, how as a kid he might have come to hate his brother Marshall – the man really was hard to take sometimes – and Deaver could guess that Parley wasn't the nicest, most understanding father in the world. This wasn't a family full of perfectly nice people. But that didn't mean they deserved dirt from him.

So how could Deaver become an outrider, knowing all this about Royal Aal? How could he follow such a man? Somehow he'd have to put all this out of his mind, forget that he knew it. Maybe someday he'd even get to know Royal well enough that he could sit down by a fire one night and say, What about your family? I met them once – what about them? And then he'd hear Royal's side of the story. That could change everything, knowing the other guy's side of the story.

Only he couldn't imagine any story Roy could tell that would justify what Scarlett went through – what she was still going through, just remembering. 'I can see why you don't like to hear much about Royal now.'

'We don't use our name much anymore,' said Scarlett. 'Do you know what that does to Marsh? Everybody thinks Roy's a hero, while every town we go into, they treat us like we're all thieves and vandals and full-time fornicators. Someone once asked us if we stopped using the Aal name on our pageant wagon in order to protect Roy's reputation.' She laughed – or sobbed. It wasn't too easy to tell. 'It near eats Marsh alive. We still live from the charity of the Church. Every bit of food from the bishop's storehouse. You don't know this, probably, Deaver Teague, but back in the old days, you only ate from the bishop's storehouse if you were down and out. A failure. It still feels that way to Marsh and me. Roy doesn't eat from the storehouse. Nor does his family these days. Roy doesn't move from town to town in the fringe.'

Deaver knew something about how it felt when every bite you ate was somebody's charity, when you being alive at all was a favor other people did for you out of the goodness of their hearts. No wonder there was a touch of anger always under the surface in this family, ready to lash out whenever something went even a little bit wrong.

'And the thing that hurts worst about the way they treat us in these pitiful little towns is that we deserve it.'

'I don't think so,' said Deaver.

'Sometimes I wish Ollie would just run off like Roy – only do it now, *before* he has a wife and children for his brother Toolie to take care of.'

That didn't seem fair to Deaver, and for once he felt

192

bold enough to speak up about it. 'Ollie works hard. I was with him all morning.'

'Yes, yes,' said Scarlett. 'I know that. He isn't Roy. He tries to be good. But he always stands there with that little half-smile, as if he thinks we're all so terribly amusing. I saw that smile on Roy's face the whole time he was with us, before he ran off. That smile's like a sign that says, I may be with you, but I'm no part of you.'

Deaver had noticed the smile, but he never thought that was what it meant. It seemed to Deaver that Ollie mostly smiled when he was embarrassed about the way his family was acting, or when he was trying to be friendly. It wasn't Ollie's fault that when he smiled, his face reminded people of Royal Aal.

'Ollie's old enough to be on his own,' said Deaver. 'When I was his age, I'd been driving a scavenger truck for a couple of years.'

Scarlett looked at Deaver in disbelief. 'Of course Ollie's *old* enough. But if he left, who'd do the lighting? Who'd keep the truck running? Marshall and Toolie and Katie and me – what do we know except the shows?'

Didn't she see the contradiction in what she said? Ollie couldn't go because the family needed him – but all the time he was there, his own mother was wishing he'd run off so he wouldn't cause the harm his uncle caused. There was no sense in it at all. For all Deaver knew, Ollie was nothing at all like his uncle. But if his own mother saw him that way, then it was hard to see how Ollie could ever prove to her it wasn't true.

Deaver had seen a lot of families over the years. Even though he was never really a part of any one of them, he lived right with them, saw how the parents treated their children, saw how the children treated their parents. Better than most people, he understood how it was when something was wrong in a family. Everybody tries to hide it, to pretend everything's OK, but it always squeezes out somewhere. The Aals had all that pain

193

from what Royal did and they couldn't get back at Royal, not a bit. But it so happened that they had a son who was a little bit like Royal. It was bound to squeeze out there, some of that pain. Deaver wondered how long Scarlett had thought of Ollie as being just like Roy. Wondered if Ollie had ever caught a scrap of a sentence about it. Or if one time when she was mad Scarlett had said it right out, 'You're just like your uncle, you're exactly like him!'

That was the kind of thing a kid doesn't forget. One time a foster mother called Deaver a thief, and when it turned out her own kid had stolen the sugar and sold it, even though she made a big deal about apologizing to Deaver, he never forgot it. It was like a wall between them for the months before he was finally fostered somewhere else. You just can't unsay what's been said.

Thinking of that, of people saying cruel things they can't take back, Deaver remembered how Marshall gave a tongue-lashing to Toolie that morning. There was more going on in this family than Ollie reminding his mother of Roy Aal.

'I shouldn't have said any of this to you, Deaver Teague.'

Deaver realized he must have been silent a long time, just standing there. 'No, it's all right,' said Deaver.

'But there's something about you. You're so sure of yourself.'

People had said that to Deaver before. He long since figured out that it was because he didn't talk often, and when he did, he didn't say much. 'I suppose,' he said.

'And when Mother Aal called you an angel –'

Deaver gave a little laugh.

'I thought – maybe the Lord led you to us. Or led us to you. At a time when we are in such great need of healing. Maybe you don't even realize it yourself, but maybe you're here to work a miracle.'

Deaver shook his head.

'Maybe you can work a miracle without even knowing

you're doing it.' She took Deaver's hand – and now the theatricality was back. She was trying to make him feel a certain way, and so she was acting. Deaver was glad to know he could see the difference so clearly. It meant he could believe what she said when she wasn't acting. 'Oh, Deaver,' she said. 'I'm so scared about Ollie.'

'Scared he'll run away? Or scared he won't?'

She whispered. 'I don't know what I want. I just want things to be better.'

'I wish I could help you. But about all I can do is work the flag in the Betsy Ross scene. And rewire the heater fan in the truck.'

'Maybe that's enough, Deaver Teague. Maybe just by being who you are, maybe that'll do it. What if God sent you to us? Is that so impossible?'

Deaver had to laugh. 'God never sent me anywhere.'

'You're a good man.'

'You don't know that.'

'You only have to take one bite of the apple to know if it's ripe.'

'I just happened to come along.'

'Your horse happened to die that day and you happened to walk with your saddle so you arrived just when you did and we had brake trouble so we arrived when *we* did and you just happened to be the first person in years that Ollie's cared for and Katie just happened to take a liking to you. Pure chance.'

'I wouldn't set much store on Katie taking a liking to me,' said Deaver. 'I don't think there's much in it.'

Scarlett looked at him with deep-welling eyes and spoke with well-crafted fervor. 'Save us. We don't have the strength to save ourselves.'

Deaver didn't know what to say. Just shook his head and moved away, out into the grass away from the truck, away from everybody. He could see them all – the crowd out front, the Aals working behind the truck, getting makeup on, setting up the props so they'd be ready to take onstage when they were needed. He walked a little farther away, and everybody got smaller.

If the crowd kept coming like this, there'd be hundreds of people by showtime. Everybody in town, probably. Pageant wagons didn't come through all that often.

The sun was still up, though, and people were still arriving, so Deaver figured he could take a minute to walk off by himself and think. Old Donna was crazy as a loon, calling him an angel. And Scarlett, asking him to somehow stop Ollie from wrecking them. And Katie, wanting whatever it was she wanted.

He only met these people last night. Not twenty-four hours ago. And yet he'd seen them so close and so clear that he felt like he knew them. Could they possibly also know *him*?

No, they were desperate, that's all it was. Wanting to change and using the first person who came along to help them do it. What Deaver couldn't understand was why they wanted to keep up their show-gypsy life in the first place. It wasn't much of a life, as far as Deaver could see. Working too hard, just to put on shows in towns that hated them.

Katie, what do you want?

She was probably part of this conspiracy of women – Scarlett, Donna, and Katie, all trying to get Deaver to stay in hopes he could make things better for them. The worst thing was he halfway wanted to stay. Even knowing Katie was faking it, he still was drawn to her, still couldn't keep his eyes off her without trying. What was it Meech said when a guy left the rangers to marry some woman? 'Testosterone poisoning,' that's what he called it. 'Man gets sick with testosterone poisoning, that's the one disease takes you out of the rangers for good.' Well, I got that disease, and if I wanted to I could plain forget everything else except Katie, at least for a while, long enough to wake up and find myself stuck here with a wife and babies and then I'd never go even if I wanted to, even if I found out Katie was play-acting all the time and never really wanted me at all – I'd never go because

I'm no Royal Aal, I'm no foster father. If I ever got me a family I'd never leave my kids, never. They could count on me till I was dead.

Which is why I can't stay, I can't let myself believe any of this or even care about it. They're actors, and I'm not an actor, and I could no more be a part of them than I could be a part of Hatchville not being a Mormon. And as for Katie, I know better than to think a woman like that could ever love me. I'm a fool for even thinking about staying. They're all so unhappy, I'd just be guaranteeing myself as much misery as they've got. My life's work is out on the prairie with the outriders. Even if Royal Aal is a gold-plated turd, even if I didn't fit in there, either, at least I'd be doing a work that made some difference in the world.

Deaver wound up in the apple orchard about a hundred yards south of the truck. Hatchville was enough years back from the fringe that the trees were big and solid enough to climb. He swung up into a branch. He watched the crowd still coming. It was getting late. The sun was about touching the mountains to the west. He could hear Katie's voice calling. 'Ollie!'

Like hide-and-seek the neighborhood kids played when Deaver was little. Ollie ollie oxen free. Deaver was a champion hider. He'd heard that call more than once.

Then Toolie's voice. And Marshall's. 'Ollie!'

Deaver imagined what would happen if Ollie just didn't come back. If he ran off like Royal did. What would the family do? They couldn't run the show without somebody running lights and firing off the electrical effects. Everybody else was on stage but Ollie.

Then Deaver got a sickening jolt in the pit of his stomach. There *was* one other person who knew something about the lighting and wasn't on stage. Can you help us, Deaver Teague? What would he say then? No, sorry, I got grass to tend, good luck and good-bye.

Hell, he couldn't say no and walk off like that, and Ollie knew it. Ollie sized him up right off, pegged him for to go off and leave people in the lurch. That's why he made such a point of teaching Deaver how the lighting system worked. So Ollie could run off without destroying the family. And here everybody thought Ollie had chosen Deaver as a *friend*. No sir, Deaver Teague wasn't Ollie's friend, he was Ollie's patsy.

But he had to give Ollie some credit here. Scarlett was wrong about him – Ollie wasn't the kind just to run away like Royal did, and to hell with the family and the show. No, Ollie waited till he had a half-likely replacement before he took off. Too bad if Deaver didn't particularly *want* to run lights for the Aal family show – that wasn't Ollie's problem. What did he care about Deaver Teague? Deaver wasn't one of the family, he was an outsider, it was all right to screw around with *his* life because he didn't amount to anything anyway. After all, Deaver didn't have any family or any connections. What did *he* matter, as long as Ollie's family was all right?

Even though Deaver was burning, he couldn't help imagining Katie coming to him, frantic – no actress stuff now, she'd really be upset – saying, 'What'll we do? We can't do the show without somebody running lights.' And Deaver'd say, 'I'll do it.' She'd say, 'But you don't know the changes, Deaver.' And Deaver'd say, 'Give me a script, write them down. I can do it. Whoever isn't on stage can help me.' And then her lips on his, her body pressed up against him after the show, and then her sweet hot breath against his cheek as she murmured, 'Oh, thank you, Deaver. You saved us.'

'Don't *do* that.' It was a girl's voice that snapped Deaver out of his imagination. Not Katie's voice. Behind him and to the north, deeper in the orchard.

'Don't *do* that.' A man's voice, mocking. Deaver turned to look. In the reddish light of sunset, he could see Ollie and a girl from Hatchville. She was giggling. He was kissing her neck and had both hands on her buttocks, gripping so tight she was standing on tiptoes.

Not very far away from Deaver at all. Deaver kept his mouth shut, but he was thinking, Ollie didn't run off after all. What he couldn't decide was whether he was glad of it or ticked off about it.

'You can't,' said the girl. She tore away from him, ran a few steps, then stopped and turned away. Plainly she wanted him to follow her.

'You're right, I can't,' said Ollie. 'Time for the show. But when it's over, you'll be there, won't you?'

'Of course. I'm going to watch it all.'

Suddenly Ollie got all serious-looking. 'Nance,' he said. 'You don't know how much you mean to me.'

'You just only met me a few minutes ago.'

'I feel like I've known you so long. I feel like – I feel like I've been lonely for you my whole life and didn't know it till now.'

She liked that. She smiled and looked down, looked away. Deaver thought: Ollie's as much of an actor as anybody else in the Aal family. I ought to be taking notes on how to seduce a Mormon girl.

'I know it's right between us,' said Ollie. 'I know – you don't have to believe me, I can hardly believe it myself – but I know we were *meant* to find each other. Like this. Tonight.'

Then Ollie reached out his hand. She tentatively put her hand in his. Slowly he raised her hand to his lips, kissed her fingers gently one by one. She put a finger of the other hand in her mouth, watching him intently.

Still holding her hand, he reached out and caressed her cheek with his other hand, just the backs of his fingers brushing her skin, her lips. His hand drifted down her neck, then behind, under her hair. He drew her close; her body moved, leaning toward him; he took a single step and kissed her. It was like Ollie had every step planned. Every move, every word. He'd probably done it a hundred times before, thought Deaver. No wonder the Aals were implicated in a lot of ugly stories.

She clung to him. Melted against him. It made

Deaver angry and wistful both at once, knowing what he was seeing wasn't right, that Ollie was fooling with a girl who believed all this stuff, that if he got caught he could cost his family their license to put on shows; yet at the same time wishing it was him, wishing to have such lips kissing him, such a sweet and fragile body clinging to him. It was enough to make a man crazy, watching that scene.

'Better go,' Ollie said. 'You first. You folks would just get mad and not let you see me again if they saw us come out of the orchard together.'

'I don't care, I'd see you anyway. I'd come to you at night, I'd climb right out my window and find you, right here in the orchard, I'd be waiting for you.'

'Just go on ahead, Nance.'

Far away: 'Ollie!'

'Hurry up, Nance, they're calling me.'

She backed away from him, slow, careful, like Ollie was holding her with invisible wires. Then she turned and ran, straight west, so she'd come up to the audience from the south.

Ollie watched her for a minute. Then he turned squarely toward Deaver and looked him in the eye. 'Got a cute little ass on her, don't you think, Deaver?' he asked.

Deaver felt sick with fear. He just couldn't think what he was afraid of. Like playing hide-and-seek, when somebody you hadn't heard coming suddenly says, I see Deaver!

'I can feel you condemning me, Deaver Teague,' said Ollie. 'But you've got to admit I'm good at it. You could never do it like that. And that's what Katie needs. Smooth. Gentle. Saying the right thing. You'd just make a fool of yourself trying. You aren't fine enough for Katie.'

Ollie said it so sad that Deaver couldn't help believing it, at least partly. Because Ollie *was* right. Katie could never really be happy with somebody like him. A scavenger, a range rider. For a moment Deaver felt anger flare inside him. But that was what Ollie wanted. If somebody lost his head here, it wouldn't be Deaver Teague.

'At least I know the difference between a woman and a cute little ass,' said Deaver.

'I've read all the science books, Deaver, and I know the facts. Women are just bellies waiting to get filled up with babies, and they pump our handles whenever they get to feeling empty. All that other stuff about true love and devotion and commitment and fatherhood, that's all a bunch of lies we tell each other, so we don't have to admit that we're no different from dogs – except our bitches are in heat all the time.'

Deaver was just angry enough to say the cruelest thing that came to mind. 'That's just a story, too, Ollie. Fact is the only way you ever get to pretend you're a real man is by telling lies to little girls. A real woman would see right through you.'

Ollie turned red. 'I know what you're trying to do, Deaver Teague. You're trying to take my place in this family. I'll kill you first!'

Deaver couldn't help it – he busted out laughing.

'I could do it!'

'Oh, sure, I wasn't laughing at the idea of you killing me. I was laughing at the idea of me taking your place.'

'You think I didn't notice how you tried to learn my whole job today? The way you had Katie hanging all over you? Well I *belong* in this family, and you don't!'

Ollie turned and started to walk away. Deaver dropped out of the tree and caught up to him in a few strides. He put his hand on Ollie's shoulder, just to stop him, but Ollie came around swinging. Deaver ducked inside the blow, so Ollie's arm caught him alongside the ear. It stung, but Deaver'd been in some good hard fights in his time, and he could take a half-assed blow like that without blinking. In a second he had Ollie pressed up against an apple tree, Deaver's right hand holding Ollie up by his shirt, his left hand clutching the crotch of Ollie's pants. The fear in Ollie's face was plain, but Deaver didn't plan to hurt him.

'Listen to me, fool,' said Deaver. 'I don't want to take your place. I got me a chance to apply to Royal's Riders, so what in hell makes you think I want to sit and run your damn fool dimmer switches? *You* were the one teaching *me*.'

'Hell I was.'

'Hell you *were*, Ollie, you're just too dumb to know what you're doing. Let me tell you something. I'm not taking your place. I don't *want* your stupid place. I don't want to marry Katie, I don't want to run the lights, and I don't want to stay with your family one second after we reach Moab.'

'Let me down.'

Deaver ground his left hand upward into Ollie's crotch. Ollie's eyes got wide, but he was listening. 'If you want to leave your family, that's fine by me, but don't do it by sneaking away and trying to stick me with your job. And don't do it by poking dumb little girls till their folks get your family's license pulled. However much you want to get away, you got no right to destroy your own people in order to do it. When you walk out, you walk out clean, you understand me?'

'You don't know me or anything about me, Deaver Teague!'

'Just remember, Ollie. For the next couple days till we get to Moab, I'm on you like flies on shit. Don't touch a girl, don't talk to a girl, don't even look at a girl here in Hatchville or I'll break more ribs on you than you thought you had, do you understand me?'

'What's it to you, Teague?'

'They're your family, you dumb little dickhead. Even dogs don't piss on their own family.'

He let Ollie slide down the tree till he was standing on the ground, then let go of his pants and his shirt and stepped back a safe distance. Ollie didn't try anything

202

though. Katie was still calling 'Ollie! Ollie!' He just stood there, looking at Deaver, and then got his little half-smile, turned around, and walked out of the orchard, straight toward the pageant wagon. Deaver stood there and watched him go.

Deaver felt all jumpy and tingly, like all his muscles had to move but he couldn't think what he should do with them. That was the closest Deaver'd come to really tearing into somebody since he was in his teens. He'd always kept his anger under control, but it felt good to have Ollie pressed up against that tree, and he wanted so bad to hit him, again and again, to pound some sense into his stupid selfish head. Only that wasn't it, after all, because he was already ashamed of letting himself go so far. I was being a stupid kid, making threats, pushing Ollie around. He was right – what's it to me? It's none of my business.

But now I've made it my business. Without even meaning to, I've got myself caught up in this family's problems.

Deaver looked over toward the pageant wagon, silhouetted in the last light of dusk in the western sky. Just then the generator kicked on, and bank by bank the fresnels and ellipsoidals lit up, making a dazzling halo around the pageant wagon, so it looked almost magical. He could hear the audience clapping at the sight of the stage, now brightly lit.

The backstage worklights had also come on, and now in that dimmer light he could make out people moving around, and seeing them, grey shadows moving back and forth on business he didn't understand, he felt a sweet pain in his chest, a hot pressure behind his eyes. A longing for something long ago, something he used to have. So long lost that he could never name it; so deeply rooted that it would always grow in him. They had it, those men and women and children moving in silent business behind the truck, hooded lights glowing in the dusk. It was there in the taut lines that connected them together, a web that wound tighter, binding them with every pass. Every blow they struck, every tender caress, every embrace, every backhanded shove as they ran from each other, all left still another fine invisible wire like a spider's thread, until the people could hardly be understood as individuals at all. There was no Katie, but Katie-with-Toolie and Katie-with-Scarlett; there was no Marshall, but Marshall-with-Scarlett and Marshall-with-Toolie and Marshall-with-Ollie and Marshall-with-Parley and above all Marshall-with-Roy. Roy who had hacked at those lines, cut them – he thought. Roy who went away never to return – he thought – but still the lines are there, still each move he makes causes tremors in his brother's life, and through him in all their lives, all the intersections of the web.

I've been caught in this net, too, and every tug and jiggle of their web vibrates in me.

A fanfare of music came over the loudspeakers. Deaver ducked under a branch and walked across the field toward the truck.

The music was loud, almost painful. An anthem – bugles, drums, Deaver came around the truck part-way, well back from the lights, till he could see that Katie was onstage, sewing with big movements, so even the farthest audience member could see her hand move. What was she sewing? A flag.

The music suddenly became quieter. From his angle, Deaver couldn't see, but he knew the voice. Dusty, saying, 'General Washington has to know – is the flag ready, Mrs. Ross?'

'Tell the general that my fingers are no faster than his soldiers,' Katie said.

Dusty stepped forward, facing the audience; now Deaver could see him, right up to the front of the truck. 'We must have the flag, Betsy Ross! So every man can see it waving high, so every man will know that his nation is not Pennsylvania, not Carolina, not New York or Massachusetts, but America!'

Suddenly Deaver realized that this speech was surely written for Washington – for Parley. It was only given to Dusty, as a young soldier, because of Parley's failing memory. A compromise; but did the audience know?

'A flag that will stand forever, and what we do in this dark war will decide what the flag means, and the acts of each new generation of Americans will add new stories to the flag, new honor and new glory. Betsy Ross, where is that flag!'

Katie rose to her feet in a smooth, swift motion, and in a single stride she stood at the front, the flag draped across her body in vivid red and white and blue. It was a thrilling movement, and for a moment Deaver was overcome with his feelings – not for Katie, but Betsy Ross, for Dusty's fervent young voice, for the situation, the words, and the bitter knowledge that America was, after all, gone.

Then he remembered that he was supposed to be backstage, ready to raise the flag when Katie was finished with the very speech she was beginning now. He was surely too late; he ran anyway.

Janie was at the lever; not far away, Parley, in his full George Washington regalia, was standing behind the pyramid, ready to enter and deliver his speech to the soldiers. Onstage, Katie was saying her last few words: 'If your men are brave enough, then this flag will ever wave – '

Deaver reached up and took the lever in his hand. Janie didn't even look at him; she immediately removed her hand, snatched up a script, and scrambled up the ladder to a position halfway up the back of the pyramid.

'O'er the land of the free!' cried Katie.

Deaver pulled the lever. It released the weight at the top of the flagpole; the weight plummeted, and the flag rose swiftly up the pole. Immediately Deaver grabbed the wire that was strung around the other side of the truck, invisibly attached to the outside top of the flag;

by pulling and releasing the wire, he made the flag seem to wave. The music reached a climax, then fell away again. Deaver couldn't see the flag from where he was, but he remembered the cue and assumed the lights were dimmed on the flag by now. He stopped the waving.

Janie wasn't helping Dusty with a costume change at all, though that was the original reason why they asked Deaver to run the flag effect. Dusty had run straight back to the tent, and Janie was half-way up the pyramid, prompting Parley in Washington's speech to the troops. She did a good job; Parley's fumbling for his lines probably seemed to the audience to be nothing but Washington searching for just the right word to say. Yet Deaver knew that Parley botched the speech, leaving out a whole section despite Janie's prompting.

The speech ended. Parley came down in the darkness. Onstage Toolie was playing Joseph Smith and Scarlett was playing his mother. Marshall moved through the darkness wearing brilliant white that caught every scrap of light that reached him; he was going to appear as the angel Moroni. Parley came down the steps and turned, a few steps toward Deaver, into the darkest shadow. He bent over, resting his head and hands against the edge of the stage, the edge of the flatbed truck. Deaver watched him for a while, fascinated, knowing that Parley was crying, unable to bear knowing it. A man shouldn't have to wait until he wasn't any good before he retired. He should be able to quit while he still has some fresh accomplishment in him. But this – to have to stay on and on, failing again every night.

Deaver didn't dare speak to him; had he and Parley even spoken yet? He couldn't remember. What was Parley to him? An old man, a stranger. Deaver took a step toward him, another, reached out his hand, rested it on Parley's shoulder. Parley didn't move, not to move away, not to show a sign that he felt the hand and accepted it. After a while, Deaver took his hand away and went back around the truck to watch the show from the side, where he'd been before.

It took a while to get back into the pageant, to follow what was happening. Dusty was onstage in blackface, to be the slave that Lincoln freed; Marshall made an imposing Lincoln, fine to look at. But Deaver also kept looking at the audience. He'd never watched a crowd like that before. The sun was long gone, the sky black, so all he could see was the people in front, where the light from the stage spilled back onto their faces. Mouths open, they watched the stage, unmoving, as if they were machines waiting for someone to switch them on. And now, onstage, Lincoln's hand reached out to the young slave and lifted him up out of bondage. 'O happy day!' cried Dusty. The music picked up the refrain. O happy day. The Tabernacle Choir singing it.

Then Lincoln reached out both his arms to embrace the boy, and Dusty impulsively jumped up and hugged Lincoln around the neck. The audience roared with laughter; Deaver saw how, almost with one movement, their heads rocked back, then forward again; they stirred in their seats, then settled. The comic moment had released the tension of their stillness. They relaxed again. Then burst into applause at something they saw; Deaver didn't even bother looking at the stage to see what it was. The audience itself was a performance. Moving, shifting, laughing, clapping, all as one, as if they were all part of the same soul.

Toolie played Brigham Young as he led the Saints across the plains to Utah. Deaver vaguely remembered that the settlement of Utah was before the Civil War, but it didn't seem to matter – it worked fine this way in the show. To Deaver it seemed a little strange that a show called *Glory of America* should have an equal mix of Mormon and American history. But to these people, he realized, it was all the same story. George Washington, Betsy Ross, Joseph Smith, Abraham Lincoln, Brigham Young, all part of the same unfolding tale. Their own past.

After a while, though, he lost interest in the audience. They only did the same things – hold still, rapt; laugh; clap; gasp in awe at some spectacle. Only a limited sort of entertainment for someone watching them. Deaver turned back and watched the stage again.

It was time for the rocket. Even though it actually looked like a missile, and nothing at all like the Apollo launches, it was still something to watch Marshall put the helmet over his head and climb into the missile. All wrong – one man, not three, and riding in the rocket itself. Every school in Deseret taught better than that. But everyone understood. There was no way to put a full-size Saturn rocket on the back of a pageant truck. What mattered was that it *was* a rocket with the letters NASA and USA on it, and the man getting in was supposed to be Neil Armstrong. A large puff of smoke represented the launch. Then the door opened again, Marshall came out; the music was soft, a high, thrilling violin. He opened the rigid American flag on its little stand and placed it on the ground in front of him. 'A small step for a man,' he said. 'A giant leap for mankind.'

The music reached a towering climax. Deaver's eyes filled with tears. This was the moment, America's climax, the supreme achievement, the high-water mark, and no one knew it at the time. Couldn't those people back in 1969 see the cracks, feel the crumbling all around them? Not thirty years later it was all gone. NASA, the USA itself, all gone, all broken up. Only the Indians to the south were making nations anymore, calling themselves Americans, saying that the white people of North America were Europeans, trespassers – and who could tell them no? America was over. It grew two hundred years, feeding and devouring the world, even reaching out to touch the moon, and now the name was up for grabs. Nothing left but scraps and fragments.

Yet we were there. That little flag was on the moon, the footprints unstirred by any wind.

208

Only gradually did Deaver realize that these things he was thinking were all being spoken; he heard the whispered words in the trembling voice of Scarlett Aal. 'The footprints still are there, and if we go back, we will recognize them as our own.'

Deaver glanced at the audience again. More than one hand was brushing a tear away. Just as Deaver's own hand went up to his cheek.

Now the collapse. Cacophonous music. Parley as the evil Soviet tyrant, Marshall as the bumbling fool of a President, together they mimed the blundering that led to war. Deaver couldn't believe at first that the Aals had chosen to show the end of the world as a comic dance. But it was irresistibly funny. The audience screamed with laughter as the Soviet tyrant kept stomping on the President's feet, and the President kept bowing and apologizing, picking up his own injured foot and hitting it himself, finally shaking hands with the Russian, as if making a formal agreement, and then stomping on his own foot. Every mimed cry of pain brought another roar of laughter from the crowd. This was their own destruction being acted out, and yet Deaver couldn't keep himself from laughing. Again he was wiping away tears, but this time so that he could see the stage at all through the blur of his own laughter.

The Russian knocked off the President's hat. When the President bent over to pick it up, the Russian kicked him hard in the behind and the President sprawled on the stage. Then Parley beckoned Dusty and Janie, dressed as Russian soldiers, to come over and finish him off.

Suddenly it wasn't funny anymore. They both held submachine guns, and jammed the butts again and again into the President's body. Even though Deaver knew that the blows were being faked, he still felt them like blows to his own body, terrible pain, brutal, unfair, and it went on and on, blow after blow after blow.

The crowd was silent now. Deaver felt what they all

felt. It has to stop. Stop it now. I can't bear any more.

At the moment when he was about to turn away, a drum roll began. Toolie entered, and to Deaver's astonishment he was dressed as Royal Aal. The plaid shirt, two pistols in his belt, the grizzly beard – there was no mistaking it. The audience recognized him at once, and immediately cheered. Cheered and leapt to their feet, clapping, waving their arms. 'Royal! Royal! Royal!' they shouted.

Toolie strode down to where the Russian soldiers were still pounding the corpse of the President. With both hands he thrust them apart, knocking them down. Then he reached down to the President's body – to lift him up? No. To draw out of his costume the gold and green beehive flag of Deseret. The cheers grew louder. He carried it to the flagpole, fastened it where the American flag had been. This time the flag rose slowly; the anthem of Deseret began to play. Anyone who wasn't standing stood now, and the crowd sang along with the music, more and more voices, spontaneously becoming part of the show.

As they sang, the flag of Deseret suddenly flowed outward, disappearing, as the American flag moved in behind it. Then the American flag flowed out and the flag of Deseret replaced it. Again and again, over and over, the flags changing. Even though Deaver had helped Katie set up the effect and knew exactly how it was done, he couldn't keep himself from being caught up in the emotion of the moment. He even sang with all the others as they reached the final chorus. 'We'll sing and we'll shout with the armies of heaven! Hosanna! Hosanna to God and the King! Let glory to them in the highest be given, henceforth and forever, amen and amen!'

The lights went out on the stage; only a single spot remained on the flag, which had come to rest as the old American flag. It could have been the end of the show right there. But no. A single spotlight now on stage.

Katie came out, dressed as Betsy Ross. 'Does it still wave?' she asked, looking around.

'Yes!' cried the audience.

'Where does it wave!' she cried. 'Where is it!'

Marshall, now dressed in a suit and tie, wearing a mask that made him look pretty much like Governor Monson, strode into the light.

'O'er the land of the free!' he cried.

The audience cheered.

Toolie, still dressed as Royal Aal, stepped into the light from the other side.

'And the home of the brave!'

The music immediately went into 'The Star-Spangled Banner' as the lights went out completely. The audience shouted and cheered. Deaver clapped until his palms stung and kept on beating his hands together until they finally ached and throbbed. His voice was lost in the crowd's shouting – no, rather the crowd's voice became his own, the loudest shout he had ever uttered in his life. It seemed to last forever, one great voice, one single cry of joy and pride, one soul, one great indivisible self.

Then the shouting faded, the clapping became more scattered. The faint audience lights came on. A few voices, talking, began among the crowd. The applause was over. The unity was broken. The audience was once again the thousand citizens of Hatchville. Little children were gathered up in their parents' arms. Families moved off together into the darkness, many of them lighting lanterns they had brought with them for the trek home in the night. Deaver saw one man he recognized, though he couldn't think why; the man was smiling, gathering his young daughter into his arms, putting his arm around his wife, a little boy chattering words that Deaver couldn't hear – but all of them smiling, happy, *full*. Then he realized who the man was. The secretary from the mayor's office. Deaver hadn't recognized him at first because of that smile. It was like he was someone else. Like the show had changed him.

Suddenly Deaver realized something. During the show, when Deaver felt himself to be part of that audience, like their laughter was his laughter, their tears his tears – the secretary was part of that audience, too. For a while tonight they saw and heard and felt the same things. And now they'd carry away the same memories, which meant that to some degree they were the same person. One.

The idea left Deaver breathless. It wasn't just him and the secretary, it was also the children, everybody there. All the same person, in some hidden corner of their memory.

Once again Deaver was alone on the boundary between the pageant wagon and the town, belonging to neither – yet now, because of the show, belonging a little bit to both.

Out in the crowd, Ollie stood up from behind the light and sound control panel. The girl from the orchard – Nance? – was standing by him. It made Deaver sad to see her, sad to think that she would translate all those powerful feelings of the pageant into a passion for Ollie. But there was nothing to worry about. The girl's father was right there with her, pulling her away. The town had been warned, and Ollie wasn't going to have his way tonight.

Deaver walked around behind the truck. He was still emotionally drained. Toolie had the door of the truck open and was peeling off his beard and putting it in its box by the light from the cab. 'Like it?' he asked Deaver.

'Yeah,' Deaver said. His voice was husky from yelling.

Toolie looked up, studied his face for a moment. 'Hey,' he said. 'I'm glad.'

'Where are the others?'

'In the tents, changing. I stay out here to make sure nothing walks away from the truck. Ollie watches out front.'

Deaver didn't believe anyone would steal from the people who brought them such a show as this. But he didn't say so. 'I can keep watch,' he said. 'Go in and change.'

'Thanks,' Toolie said. He immediately closed the box, shut the cab door, and jogged off to the tent.

Deaver walked out into the space between the tents and the truck. Because he was supposed to be keeping watch, he faced the truck, scanning across it. But his mind was on the people in the tents behind him. He could hear them talking, sometimes laughing. Did they know what they had done to him?

I was on both sides of this tonight, thought Deaver. I saw it, I was in the audience. But I also raised the flag the first time, made it wave. I was part of it. Part of every part. I'm one of you. For one hour tonight I'm one of you.

Katie came out of the girls' tent, looked around, walked over to Deaver. 'Silly, wasn't it?'

It took a second before Deaver realized that she was talking about the show.

'Of course the history in it is pure nonsense,' said Katie, 'and there isn't a genuine character in the whole thing. It isn't like real acting. Watching that show, you wouldn't think any of us had any talent at all.' She sounded angry, bitter. Hadn't she heard the crowd? Didn't she understand what the show had done to them? To *him*?

She was looking at him, and now she finally realized that his silence didn't mean he agreed with her at all. 'Why, you liked it, didn't you,' she said.

'Yes,' he answered.

She took a little step backward. 'I'm sorry. I forgot that you – I guess you haven't seen many shows.'

'It wasn't silly.'

'Well, it is, you know. When you've done it over and over again like we have. It's like saying the same word again and again until it doesn't mean anything anymore.'

'It meant something.'

213

'Not to me.'

'Yes it did. There at the end. When you said – '

'When I said my *lines*. They were memorized speeches. Father wrote them, and I said them, but it wasn't *me* saying it. It was Betsy Ross. Deaver, I'm glad you liked the show, and I'm sorry I disillusioned you. I'm not used to having audience backstage.' She turned away.

'No,' Deaver said.

She stopped, waited for him to say more. But he didn't know what to say. Just that she was wrong.

She turned around. 'Well?'

He thought of how she was this morning, coming so close to him, holding on to him. How she went back and forth between real and fake, so smooth he could hardly tell the difference. But there *was* a difference. Talking about Katherine Hepburn, saying how she loved that movie, that was real. Flirting with him, that was fake. And tonight, talking about the show being silly, that was phony, that was just an attitude she was putting on. But her anger, that was real.

'Why are you mad at me?'

'I'm not.'

'All I did was like the show,' said Deaver. 'What was so wrong about that?'

'Nothing.'

He just stood there, not taking the lie for an answer. His silence was too demanding a question for her to ignore.

'I guess I was the one who was disillusioned,' said Katie. 'I thought you were too smart to be taken in by the show. I thought you'd see it for what it really is.'

'I did.'

'You saw Betsy Ross and George Washington and Neil Armstrong and –'

'Didn't you?'

'I saw a stage and actors and makeup and set pieces and costumes and special effects. I saw lines getting

214

dropped and a flag that went up a little bit too late. And I heard speeches that no real human being would ever say, a bunch of high-flown words that mean nothing at all. In other words, Deaver, I saw the truth, and not the illusion.'

'Bullshit.'

The word stung her. Her face set hard, and she turned to go.

Deaver reached out and caught her arm, pulled her back. 'I said bullshit, Katie, and you know it.'

She tried to wrench her arm away.

'I saw all those things too, you know,' said Deaver. 'The screwed-up lines and the costumes and all that. I was backstage too. But I guess I saw something you didn't see.'

'It's the first show you ever watched, Deaver, and you saw something I didn't?'

'I saw you take an audience and turn them into one person, with one soul.'

'These townies are all alike anyway.'

'Me too? I'm just like them? Is that what you're saying? Then why've you been trying so hard to make me fall in love with you? If you think I'm one of them and you think this show isn't worth doing, then why have you been trying so hard to get me to stay?'

Her eyes widened in surprise, and then a grin spread across her face. 'Why, Deaver Teague, you're smarter than I thought. And dumber, too. I wasn't trying to get you to stay. I was trying to get you to take me with you when you left.'

Partly he was angry because she was laughing at him. Partly he was angry because he didn't want it to be true that she was just using him, that she wasn't attracted to him at all. Partly he was angry because the show had moved him and she despised him for it. Mostly, though, he was so full of emotion that it had to spill out somehow, and anger would do.

'Then what?' he demanded. He talked low, so that

215

the others wouldn't hear him in the tents. 'Suppose I fell in love with you and took you with me, then what? Did you plan to marry me and be a range rider's wife and have my babies? Not you, Katie. No, you were going to get me hooked on you and then you were going to find some theatre somewhere so you could play all those Shakespeare parts you wanted, and if that meant me giving up my dream of being an outrider, why, that was fine with you, wasn't it, because it doesn't matter to you what *I* sacrificed, as long as you got what you wanted.'

'Shut up,' she whispered.

'And what about your family? What kind of show can they do if you walk out? You think Janie can step in and do your parts? Is the old lady going to come back on stage so you can run away?'

To his surprise, she was crying. 'What about me, then? Doing these stupid little backwater shows all my life – am I supposed to be trapped here forever just because *they* need *me*? Don't I get to need anything? Can't I ever do anything with my life that's worth doing?'

'But *this* show is worth doing.'

'This show is worthless!'

'You know who goes to plays in Zarahemla? All the big shots, the people who work in clean shirts all day. Is that who you want to do plays for? What difference is your acting going to make in their lives? But these people here, what is their life except rain and mud and lousy little problems and jobs always needing to get done and not enough people to do them. And then they come here and see your show, and they think – hey, I'm part of something bigger than this place, bigger than Hatchville, bigger than the whole fringe. I know they're thinking that, because *I* was thinking that, do you understand me, Katie? Riding the range and checking the grass, all by myself out there, I thought I was worthless to everybody, but tonight it went through my head

– just for a minute, it came to my mind that I was part of something, and that whatever it was I was part of, it was pretty fine. Now maybe that's worthless to you, maybe that's *silly*. But I think it's worth a hell of a lot more than going to Zarahemla and play-acting the part of *Titanic*.'

'Titania,' she whispered. 'The Titanic was a boat that sank.'

He was shaking, he was so angry and frustrated. This was why he gave up years ago trying to talk about anything important to people – they never listened, never understood a thing he said. 'You don't know what's real and you don't know what matters.'

'And you do?'

'Better than you.'

She slapped his face. Good and sharp and hard, and it stung like hell. 'That was real,' she said.

He grabbed her shoulders, meaning to shake her, but instead his fingers got tangled up in her hair and he found himself holding onto her and pulling her close and then he did what he really wanted to do, what he'd been wanting to do ever since he woke up and found her sitting beside him in the cab of the truck. He kissed her, hard and long, holding her so close he could feel every part of her body pressed against his own. And then he was done kissing her. He relaxed his hold on her and she slipped down and away from him a little, so he could look down and see her face right there in front of him. '*That* was real,' he said.

'Everything always comes down to sex and violence,' she murmured.

She was making a joke about it. It made him feel sick. He let go of her, took his hands off her completely. 'It was real to *me*. It mattered to *me*. But you've been faking it all day, it didn't matter to you a bit, and I think that stinks. I think that makes you a liar. And you know what else? You don't deserve to be in this show. You aren't good enough.'

217

He didn't want to hear her answer. He didn't want anything more to do with her. He felt ashamed of having shown her how he felt about her, about the show, about anything. So many years he'd kept to himself, never getting close to anybody, never talking about anything he really cared about, and now when he finally blurted out something that mattered to him, it was to *her*.

He turned his back on her and walked away, heading around the truck. Now that he wasn't so close to her, paying so much attention, he realized that there were other people talking. Sound carried pretty good tonight in the clear dry air. Probably everybody in the tents heard their whole conversation. Probably they were all peeking out to watch. No humiliation was complete without witnesses.

Some of the talking, though, got louder as he rounded the back of the truck. It was Marshall and somebody else out by the light and sound control panel. Ollie? No, a stranger. Deaver walked on over, even though he didn't feel like talking to anybody, because he had a feeling that whatever was going on, it wasn't good.

'I can be back with a warrant in ten minutes and then I'll find out whether she's here or not,' said the man, 'but the judge won't like having to make one out this time of night, and he might not be so easy on you.'

It was the sheriff. It didn't take Deaver long to guess that Ollie'd got himself caught doing something stupid. But no, that couldn't be, or the sheriff wouldn't need a warrant. A warrant meant searching for something. Or somebody. Whatever was happening, it meant Deaver hadn't stayed on Ollie tight enough. Hadn't the girl said something about meeting him after the show, even if she had to sneak out of her window to do it? He should have remembered before. He shouldn't have let his eyes off Ollie. It was all Deaver's fault.

'Who you looking for, sheriff?' Deaver asked.

'None of your problem, Deaver,' said Marshall.

'This your son?' asked the sheriff.

'He's a range rider,' said Marshall. 'We gave him a ride and he's been helping out a little.'

'You seen a girl around here?' asked the sheriff. 'About this high, name of Nancy Pulley. She was seen talking to your light man after the show.'

'I saw a girl talking to Ollie,' said Deaver. 'Right after the show, but it looked to me like her father pulled her away.'

'Yeah, well, could be, but she isn't home right now and we're pretty sure she meant to come back here and meet somebody.'

Marshall stepped in between Deaver and the sheriff. 'All our people are here, and there aren't any outsiders.'

'Then why don't you just let me go in and check, if you got nothing to hide?'

Of course Deaver knew why. Ollie must be missing. It was too late to go find him before trouble started.

'We have a right to be protected against unreasonable searches, sir,' said Marshall. He would've gone on, no doubt, but Deaver cut him off by asking the sheriff a question.

'Sheriff, the show's only been over about fifteen minutes,' said Deaver. 'How do you know she isn't off with some girlfriend or something? Have you been checking their houses?'

'Look, smart boy,' said the sheriff, 'I don't need you telling me my business.'

'Well, I guess not. I think you know your business real good,' said Deaver. 'In fact, I think you know your business so good that you *know* this girl wouldn't be off with a girlfriend. I bet this girl has caused you a lot of trouble before.'

'That's none of your business, range rider.'

'I'm just saying that – '

But now Marshall had caught the drift of what Deaver was doing, and he took over. 'I am alarmed, sir, that there might be a chance that this girl from your town is corrupting one of my sons. My sons have little opportunity to associate with young people outside our family, and it may be that an *experienced* girl might lead one of them astray.'

'Real smart,' said the sheriff, glaring at Marshall and then at Deaver and then at Marshall again. 'But it isn't going to work.'

'I don't know what you mean,' said Marshall. 'I only know that you were aware that this girl was prone to illicit involvement with members of the opposite sex, and yet you made no effort to protect guests in your town from getting involved with her.'

'You can just forget that as a line of defense in court,' said the sheriff.

'And why is that?' asked Marshall.

'Because her father's the judge, Mr. Aal. You start talking like that, and you've lost your license in a hot second. You might get it back on appeal, but with Judge Pulley fighting you every step of the way, you aren't going to be working for months.'

Deaver couldn't think of anything to say. To Deaver's surprise, neither could Marshall.

'So I'm coming back in ten minutes with a warrant, and you better have all your boys here in camp, and no girls with them, or your days of spreading corruption through the fringe are over.'

The sheriff walked a few paces toward the road, then turned back and said, 'I'm going to call the judge on my radio, and then I'll be sitting right here in my car watching your camp till the judge gets here with the warrant. I don't want to miss a thing.'

'Of course not, you officious cretin,' said Marshall. But he said it real quiet, and Deaver was the only one who heard him.

It was plain what the sheriff planned. He was hoping to catch Nancy Pulley running away from the camp, or Ollie sneaking back.

'Marshall,' said Deaver, as quiet as he could, 'I saw Ollie with that girl in the orchard before the show.'

'I'm not surprised,' said Marshall.

'I take it Ollie isn't in camp.'

'I haven't checked,' said Marshall.

'But you figure he's gone.'

Marshall didn't say anything. Wasn't about to admit anything to an outsider, Deaver figured. Well, that was proper. When the family's in trouble, you got to be careful about trusting strangers.

'I'll do what I can,' said Deaver.

'Thanks,' said Marshall. I was more than Deaver expected him to say. Maybe Marshall understood that things were bigger than Marshall could handle just by telling people off.

Deaver walked along after the sheriff, and came up to him just as he was setting down his radio mouthpiece. The sheriff looked up at him, already looking for a quarrel. 'What is it, range rider?'

'My name's Deaver Teague, Sheriff, and I've only been with the Aals since this morning, when they picked me up. But that was long enough to get to know them a little, and I got to tell you, I think they're pretty good people.'

'They're all actors, son. That means they can *seem* to be anything they want.'

'Yeah, they're pretty good actors, aren't they. That was some show, wasn't it.'

The sheriff smiled. 'I never said they weren't *good* actors.'

Deaver smiled back. 'They *are* good. I helped them set up today. They work real hard to put on that show. Did you ever try to lift a generator? Or put up those lights? Getting from a loaded truck to a show tonight – they put in an honest day's work.'

'Are you getting somewhere with this?' asked the sheriff.

'I'm just telling you, they may not do farm work like

221

most folks here in town, but it's still real work. And it's a *good* kind of work, I think. Didn't you see the faces of those kids tonight, watching the show? You think they didn't go home proud?'

'Shoot, boy, I know they did. But these show people think they can come in here and screw around with the local girls and . . .' His voice trailed off. Deaver made sure not to interrupt him.

'That man you talked to, Sheriff, this isn't just his business, it's his family, too. He's got his wife and parents with him, and his sons and daughters. You got any children, Sheriff?'

'Yes I do, but I don't let them go off any which way like some people do.'

'But sometimes kids do things their parents taught them not to do. Sometimes kids do something really bad, and it breaks their parents' hearts. Not *your* kids, but maybe the Aals have a kid like that, and maybe Judge Pulley does too. And maybe when their kids are getting in trouble, people like the Aals and the Pulleys, they do anything they can to keep their kids out of trouble. Maybe they even pretend like anything their kid does, it was somebody else's fault.'

The sheriff nodded. 'I see what you're getting at, Mr. Teague. But that doesn't change my job.'

'Well, what *is* your job, Sheriff? Is it putting good people out of work because they got a grown-up son they can't handle? Is it causing Judge Pulley's daughter to get her name dragged through the mud?'

The sheriff sighed. 'I don't know why I started listening to you, Teague. I always heard you range riders never talked much.'

'We save it all up for times like this.'

'You got a plan, Teague? Cause I can't just drive off and forget about this.'

'You just go on and do what you got to do, Sheriff. But if it so happens that Nancy Pulley gets home safe and sound, then I hope you won't do anything to hurt

222

either one of these good families.'

'So why didn't that actor talk good sense like you instead of getting all hoity-toity with me?'

Deaver just grinned. No use saying what he was thinking – that Marshall wouldn't have gotten hoity-toity if the sheriff hadn't treated him like he was already guilty of a dozen filthy crimes. It was good enough that the sheriff was seeing them more like ordinary folks. So Deaver patted the door of the car and walked on up the road toward the orchard. Now all Deaver had to do was find Ollie.

It wasn't hard. It was like they wanted to be found. They were in tall grass on the far side of the orchard. She was laughing. They didn't hear Deaver coming, not till he was only about ten feet away. She was naked, lying on her dress spread out like a blanket under her. But Ollie still had his pants on, zipped tight. Deaver doubted the girl was a virgin, but at least it wasn't Ollie's fault. She was playing with his zipper when she happened to look up and see Deaver watching. She screeched and sat up, but she didn't even try to cover herself. Ollie, though, he picked up his shirt and tried to cover her.

'Your daddy's looking for you,' Deaver said.

She made her mouth into a pout. To her it was a game, and it didn't matter that much to lose a round.

'Do you think we care?' said Ollie.

'Her daddy is the judge of this district, Ollie. Did she tell you that?'

It was plain she hadn't.

'And I just got through talking to the sheriff. He's looking for *you*, Ollie. So I think it's time for Nancy to get her clothes back on.'

Still pouting, she got up and started pulling her dress on over her head.

'Better put on your underwear,' said Deaver. He didn't want any evidence lying around.

'She didn't wear any,' said Ollie. 'I wasn't exactly

223

corrupting the innocent.'

She had her arms through the sleeves, and now she poked her head through the neck of her bunched-up dress and flashed a smile at Deaver. Her hips moved just a little, just enough to draw Deaver's eyes there. Then she shimmied her dress down to cover her.

'Like I told you,' said Ollie. 'We men are just pumps with handles on them.'

Deaver ignored him. 'Get on home, Nancy. You need your rest – you've got a long career ahead of you.'

'Are you calling me a whore?' she demanded.

'Not while you're still giving it away free,' said Deaver. 'And if you have any idea about crying rape, remember that there's a witness who saw you taking down his zipper and laughing while you did it.'

'As if Papa would believe you and not me!' But she turned and walked off into the trees. No doubt she knew all the paths home from this place.

Ollie was standing there, making no move to put on his shirt or his shoes. 'This was none of your business, Deaver.' It was light enough to see that Ollie was making fists. 'You got no right to push me around.'

'Come on, Ollie, let's get back to the camp before the judge gets there with a warrant.'

'Maybe I don't want to.'

Deaver didn't want to argue about it. 'Let's go.'

'Try and make me.'

Deaver shook his head. Didn't Ollie realize his fighting words were straight out of third-grade recess?

'Come on, Deaver,' Ollie taunted. 'You said you were going to protect the family from nasty little Ollie, so do it. Break all my ribs. Cut me up in little pieces and carry me home. Don't you carry a knife in your big old ranger boots? Isn't that how big tough strong guys like you get other people to do whatever you say?'

Deaver was fed up. 'Act like a man, Ollie. Or don't you have enough of the family talent to fake decency?'

Ollie lost his cockiness and his swagger all at once.

He charged at Deaver, flailing both arms in blind rage. It was plain he meant to do a lot of damage. It was also plain he had no idea how to go about doing it. Deaver caught him by one arm and flung him aside. Ollie sprawled on the ground. Poor kid, thought Deaver. Traveling with this pageant wagon all his life, he never even learned how to land a punch.

But Ollie wasn't done. He got up and charged again, and this time a couple of his blows did connect. Nothing bad, but it hurt, and Deaver threw him down harder. Ollie landed wrong on his wrist and cried out with pain. But he was so angry he still got up again, this time striking out with only his right hand, and when he got in close he swung his head from side to side trying to butt Deaver in the face, and when Deaver got hold of his arms Ollie kicked him, tried to knee him in the groin, until finally Deaver had to let go of him and punch him hard in the stomach. Ollie collapsed to his knees and threw up.

The whole time, Deaver never got mad. He couldn't think why – rage had been close to the surface all day, and yet now, when he was really fighting somebody, there was nothing. Just a cold desire to get through with the fighting and get Ollie home.

Maybe it was because he'd already used up his anger on Katie. Maybe that was it.

Ollie was finished vomiting. He picked up his shirt and wiped off his mouth.

'Come on back to camp now,' said Deaver.

'No,' said Ollie.

'Ollie, I don't want to fight you anymore.'

'Then go away and leave me alone.'

Deaver bent over to help him to his feet. Ollie jabbed an elbow into Deaver's thigh. It hurt. Deaver was pretty sure Ollie meant to get him in the crotch. This boy didn't seem to know when he was beat.

'I'm not going *back*!' said Ollie. 'And even if you knock me out and carry me back, I'll tell the sheriff all about the judge's daughter, I'll tell him I balled her brains out!'

That was about the stupidest, meanest thing Deaver ever heard. For a second he wanted to kick Ollie in the head, just to bounce things around a little inside. But he was sick of hurting Ollie, so he just stood there and asked, 'Why?'

'Because you were right, Deaver, I thought about it and you were right, I *do* want to get away from my family. But I don't want you to take my place. I don't want anybody to take my place. I don't want anybody to *have* a place. I want the whole show closed down. I want Father to be a dirt farmer instead of bossing people around all the time. I want perfect little Toolie up to his armpits in pigshit. You understand me, Deaver?'

Deaver looked at him kneeling there, a puddle of puke in front of him in the grass, holding his hurt wrist like a little boy, telling Deaver that he wanted to destroy his own family. 'You're the kind of son who doesn't deserve to have parents.'

Ollie was crying now, his face twisted up and his voice high-pitched and breaking, but that didn't stop him from answering. 'That's right, Deaver, O great judge of the earth! I sure as hell don't deserve *these* parents. Mommy who keeps telling me I'm "just like Royal" till I want to reach down her throat and tear her heart out. And Daddy who decided I didn't have enough talent so *I* was the one who had to do all the technical work for the show while Toolie got to learn all the parts so someday he'd take Daddy's place and run the company and tell *me* what to do every day of my life until I die! Well, the joke's on Toolie, isn't it? Cause Daddy's never going to give up his place in the company, he's never going to take over the old man parts and let Grandpa retire, because then Toolie would be the leading actor and Toolie would run the company and poor Daddy wouldn't be boss of the universe anymore. So Toolie's going to keep on playing the juvenile parts until he's eighty and Daddy's a hundred and ten because Daddy won't ever step aside, he won't even die, he'll just keep on running everybody like puppets until finally somebody gets up the guts to kill him or quit. So don't give me any shit about what I deserve, Deaver.'

A lot of things were suddenly making sense now. Why Marshall wouldn't let Parley retire. Why Marshall came down so hard on Toolie, kept telling him that he wasn't ready to make decisions. Because Ollie was right. Their places in the show set the order of the family. Whoever had the leading role was head of the company and therefore head of the family. Marshall couldn't give it up.

'I never realized how bad I wanted to get out of this family till you said what you said tonight, Deaver, but then I knew that getting out isn't enough. Because they'd just find somebody to take my place. Maybe you. Or maybe Dusty. Somebody, anyway, and the pageant wagon would go on and on and I want it to *stop*. Take away Father's license, that's the only way to stop him. Or no, I've got a better way. I'll go shoot my Uncle Royal. I'll take a shotgun and blast his head off and *then* Daddy can retire. That's the only reason he can't let go of anything, because Royal's in charge of the outriders, Royal's the biggest hero in Deseret, so Daddy can't bear to let himself shrink even the teensiest bit, even if it wrecks everybody's life because my father is just as selfish and rotten as Uncle Royal ever was.'

Deaver didn't know what to say. It all sounded true, and yet at the core of it, it wasn't true at all. 'No he isn't,' Deaver said.

'How would you know! You've never had to live with him. You don't know what it's like being a *nothing* in this family while he's always sitting in judgment on you and you can never measure up, you're never good enough.'

'At least he didn't leave you,' said Deaver.

227

'I wish he had!'

'No you don't,' said Deaver.

'Yes I do!'

'I'm telling you, Ollie,' Deaver said softly. 'I've seen how your father is and how your mother is and they look pretty good to me, compared.'

'Compared to what,' said Ollie scornfully.

'Compared to nothing.'

The words hung there in the air, or so it felt to Deaver. Like he could see his own words, could hear them in his own ears as if somebody else said them. He wasn't talking to Ollie now, he was talking to himself. Ollie really did need to get free. His parents really were terrible for him, Ollie hated his place in the family and it wasn't right to force him to stay in it. But Deaver wasn't a son in this family. He never was, he never would be. So he could do Ollie's job and never feel the same kind of hurt at not being the chosen son. The bad things in the family would never touch him, not the way they touched Ollie – but the good things, Deaver could still have some of those. Being part of a company that needed him. Helping put on shows that changed people. Living with people that you knew would be there tomorrow and the next day, even if all the rest of the world changed around you.

What Deaver realized then was that he really did want Ollie to leave, not so Deaver could take Ollie's place, but so he could have a chance to make his own place among the Aals. Not so he could have Katie, he realized now, or at least not so he could have Katie in particular. He wanted to have them all. Father and mother, grandfather and grandmother, brothers and sisters. Someday children. To be part of that vast web reaching back into the past farther than anybody could remember and down into the future farther than anybody could dream. Ollie had grown up in it, so all he wanted to do was get away – but he'd find out soon enough that he could never get away, not really. Just like Royal, he'd find that the web held firm, for good or ill. Even if you try to hurt them, even if you cut them to the heart, your own people never stop being your own people. They still care about you more than anyone else, you still matter to them more, the web still holds you, so that Royal might have a million people adoring him, but none of them knew him as well, none of them cared about him as much as his brother Marshall, his sister-in-law Scarlett, his old parents Parley and Donna.

Deaver knew what he had to do. It was so plain he wondered why he never saw it before.

'Ollie, come back to camp tonight, and spend tomorrow teaching me everything you can about your job. Then when we get to Moab, I'll take you in and transfer my outrider application rights to you.'

Ollie laughed. 'I've never ridden a horse in my life.'

'Maybe not,' said Deaver. 'But Royal Aal is your uncle, and he owes the life of his wife and children to your father. Maybe there's too much bad blood between them for them ever to talk to each other again, but if Royal Aal is any kind of man at all, he'll feel a debt.'

'I don't want anybody taking me on because they owe my father something.'

'Hell, Ollie, do you think somebody's going to take you on cause you look so good? Try it out. See if you like being away from the pageant wagon. If you want to come back, fine. If you want to go on somewhere else, fine. I'm giving you a chance.'

'Why?'

'Because you're giving me a chance.'

'Do you think Father would ever let you be part of the company, if you helped me sneak away?'

'I'm not talking about sneaking away. I'm talking about walking away, standing up, no hard feelings. You doing no harm to the company cause I'm there to do your jobs. Them doing no harm to you because you're still family even if you aren't part of the show anymore.

229

That's what I think is wrong with all of you. You can't tell where the show leaves off and the family begins.'

Ollie stood up, slowly. 'You'd do that for me?'

'Sure,' said Deaver. 'Beat you up, give you application rights, whatever you want. Just come on back to camp, Ollie. We can talk it over with your father tomorrow.'

'No,' said Ollie. 'I want his answer tonight. Now.'

Only now, with Ollie standing up, could Deaver see his eyes clearly enough to realize that he wasn't looking at Deaver at all. He was looking past him, looking at something behind him. Deaver turned. Marshall Aal was standing there, maybe fifteen yards back, mostly in the shadow of the trees. Now that Deaver had seen him, Marshall stepped out into the moonlight. His face was terrible, a mix of grief and rage and love that about tore Deaver's heart out with pity even though it also made him afraid.

'I knew you were there, Father,' said Ollie. 'I knew it the whole time. I wanted you to hear it all.'

Well then what the hell was *I* doing here, thought Deaver. What difference did *I* make, if Ollie was really talking to his father all along? All I was good for was talking sense to the sheriff and punching Ollie in the belly so he'd puke his guts out. Well, glad to oblige.

They didn't pay any attention to him. They just stood there, looking at each other, till Deaver figured that it wasn't any of his business anymore. What was going on now wasn't about Deaver Teague, it was about Marshall and Ollie, and Deaver wasn't part of the family. Not yet, anyway.

Deaver walked on back into the orchard and kept walking till he got to the truck. The sheriff was standing there alone, leaning on the hood.

'Where you been, Teague?'

'Judge still coming?'

'He's come and gone. I've got the warrant.'

'I'm sorry to hear that,' said Deaver.

'The girl's home safe,' said the sheriff. 'But she's sure

230

pissed off at you.'

Deaver's heart sank. She told. Probably lies.

'She says she was just doing a little hugging and kissing, and along you come and make her go home.'

Well, she lied, all right, but it was a decent kind of lie, one that wouldn't get anybody in trouble. 'Yeah, that's it,' said Deaver. 'Ollie, though, he didn't appreciate any help. His father's out there now, talking him into coming home.'

'Right,' said the sheriff. 'Well, the way it looks to me, there's no harm done, and the judge isn't calling for blood either, since he believes whatever his sweet little girl tells him. So I don't plan to use this warrant tonight. And if everybody behaves themselves tomorrow then these show gypsies can do their pageant and move on down the road.'

'No bad report on them?' said Deaver.

'Nothing to report,' said the sheriff. Then he sort of smiled. 'Heck, you were right, Teague. They're just a family with the same kind of problems we got here in Hatchville. Sure talk funny, though, don't they?'

'Thanks, Sheriff.'

'Good night, Range Rider.' The sheriff walked away.

Moments later, Scarlett and Katie and Toolie were out of their tents, standing beside Deaver, watching the sheriff get in his car and drive off.

'Thank you,' whispered Scarlett.

'You were terrific,' said Toolie.

'Yeah,' said Deaver. 'Where do I sleep?'

'It's a warm night,' said Toolie. 'I'm sleeping on the truck, if that's all right with you.'

'Better than lying on the ground,' said Deaver.

As he was getting ready for bed, Marshall and Ollie came back to the camp. Scarlett came out of her tent and made a big to-do about his hurt wrist, putting a sling on his arm and all. Deaver just sort of stayed back out of the way, not even watching, just laying out his bedroll and then standing there leaning on the audience

231

side of the truck, listening to the scraps of conversation he could hear. Which actually was quite a lot, since Marshall and Scarlett hardly knew how to talk without making the sound carry across an open field. Nobody said much about how Ollie's wrist came to be hurt.

One thing, though, that maybe changed everything. It was when Marshall said, 'I think I'd better play Washington the next time we do *Glory of America*. You know how to do Toolie's parts, don't you, Ollie? As long as Deaver's with us, he can run lights and you can fill a spot on stage. Let Papa go home and retire.'

Deaver couldn't hear what Ollie said.

'There's no rush to decide these things,' said Marshall. 'But if you do decide to join the outriders, I don't think you need to use Deaver's right to apply. I think I could write a letter to Royal that would get you a fair chance.'

Again, Ollie's answer was too quiet to hear.

'I just don't think it's right to take away one of Deaver's choices if we don't have to. It's about time I wrote to Royal anyway.'

This time it was Scarlett who answered, so Deaver could hear just fine. 'You can write to Royal all you like, Marsh, but the only way Parley and Donna can retire is if Ollie comes on stage, and the only way he can do that is if Deaver runs the lights and sound.'

'Well, sometime before we get to Moab, I'll ask Deaver if he'd like to stay,' said Marshall. 'Since he can probably hear us talking right now, that'll give him plenty of time to decide on his answer.'

Deaver smiled and shook his head. Of course they knew he was listening – these show people always know when there's an audience. Right at the moment Deaver figured he'd probably say yes. Sure, it'd be sticky for a while with Ollie, partly because of beating him up tonight, but mostly because Ollie had some bad habits with local girls and he wasn't going to cure them over-night. Ollie still might end up needing to get away and join the outriders. Deaver could teach him to ride, just in case. And if Ollie left, then Dusty'd have to move up to doing some more grown-up parts. It wouldn't be long till his voice changed, judging from the height he was getting.

Or things might not work out between Deaver and Katie, in which case it was a good thing the right to apply was good for a year. All kinds of things might change. But it'd all work out. The most important change was the one Marshall made tonight, to take some of the old-man parts and give the leads to Toolie. It meant real change in the way the company ran, and changes like that wouldn't be undone no matter what else happened. No way to guess the future, but it was a sure thing the past would never come back again.

After a while things quieted down and Deaver stripped down to his underwear and crawled inside his bedroll. He tried closing his eyes, but that didn't take him any closer to sleep, so he opened them again and looked at the stars. That was when he heard footsteps coming around the front of the truck. He could tell without looking that it was Katie. She came on over to where Deaver was lying, his bedroll spread out on the pyramid curtain.

'Are you all right, Deaver?' Katie asked.

'Softest bed I've slept on in a year,' he said.

'I meant – Ollie was walking kind of doubled over, and it looked like he hurt his hand a little. I wondered if you were OK.'

'He just fell a couple of times.'

She looked at him steady for a while. 'All right, I guess if you wanted to tell what really happened, you would.'

'Guess so.'

Still she stood there, not going away, not saying anything.

'What's the show tomorrow?' he asked.

'The book of Mormon one,' she said. 'No decent parts for women. I spend half my time in drag.' She laughed lightly, but Deaver thought she sounded tired.

The moonlight was shining full on her face. She looked a little tired, too, eyes heavy-lidded, her hair straggling beside her face. Kind of soft-looking, that's how she was in the moonlight. He remembered being angry at her tonight. He remembered kissing her. Both memories were a little embarrassing now.

'Sorry I got so mad at you tonight,' said Deaver.

'I should only have people mad at me for that reason – because they liked my show better than I did.'

'I'm sorry, anyway.'

'Maybe you're right. Maybe pageants really are important. Maybe I just get tired of doing them over and over again. I think it's time we took a vacation, did a real play. We could get town people somewhere to take parts in the play. Maybe they'd like us better if they were part of a show.'

'Sure.' Deaver was tired, and it all sounded fine to him.

'Are you staying with us, Deaver?' she asked.

'I haven't been asked.'

'But if Daddy asks you.'

'I think maybe.'

'Will you miss it? Riding the range?'

He chuckled. 'No ma'am.' But he knew that if the question was a little different, if she'd asked, Will you miss your dream of riding out on the prairie with Royal Aal, then the answer would've been yes, I miss it already.

But I've got a new dream now, or maybe just the return of an old dream, a dream I gave up on years ago, and the hope of joining the outriders, that was just a substitute, just a make-do. So let's just see, let's find out over the next few weeks and months and maybe years just how much room there is in this family for one more person. Because I'm not signing on for a pageant wagon. I'm not signing on to be a hireling. I'm signing on to be family, and if I find out there's no place for me after all, then I'll have to go searching for another dream altogether.

He thought all that, but he didn't say anything about it. He'd already said too much tonight. No reason to risk getting in more trouble.

'Deaver,' she whispered. 'Are you asleep?'

'Nope.'

'I really do like you, and it wasn't all an act.'

That was pretty much an apology, and he accepted it. 'Thanks, Katie. I believe you.' He closed his eyes.

He heard a rustle of cloth, a slight movement of the truck as more of her weight leaned against it. She was going to kiss him, he knew it, and he waited for the brush of her lips against his. But it didn't come. Again the truck moved slightly and she was gone. He heard her feet moving across the dewy grass toward the tents.

The sky was clear and the night was cool. The moon was high now, as near to straight up as it was going to get. Tomorrow it might well rain – it had been four days since the last storm, and that was about as long as you got around here. So tomorrow there might be a storm, which meant tying little tents over all the lights, and if it got bad enough, putting off the show till the next night. Or canceling and moving on. It felt a little strange, thinking how he was now caught up in a new rhythm – tied to the weather, tied to the shows, and which towns had seen which ones within the last year, but above all tied to these people, their wishes and customs and habits and whims. It was kind of scary, too, that he'd be following along, not always doing things his own way.

But why should he be scared? There was going to be change anyway, no matter what. With Bette dead, even if he stayed with the range riders there'd be a new horse to get used to. And if he'd applied to the outriders, that'd all be new. So it wasn't as though his life wasn't going to get turned upside down anyway.

Sleep came sooner than he thought it would. He dreamed, a deep hard dream that seemed like the most important thing in his life. In his dream he remembered something he hadn't been able to think of in his whole life: what his real name was, the name his own parents gave him, back before the mobbers killed them. In his dream he saw his mother's face, and heard his father's voice. But as he woke in the morning, the dream fading, he tried to think of that voice, and all he could hear inside his head was an echo of his own voice; and the face of his mother faded into Katie's face. And when he shaped his true name with silent lips, he knew that it wasn't true anymore. It was the name of a little boy who got lost somewhere and was never found again. Instead he murmured the name he had spent his life earning.

'Deaver Teague.'

He smiled a little at the sound of it. It wasn't a bad name at all, and he kind of liked imagining what it could mean someday.

America

Sam Monson and Anamari Boagente had two encounters in their lives, forty years apart. The first encounter lasted for several weeks in the high Amazon jungle, the village of Agualinda. The second was for only an hour near the ruins of the Glen Canyon Dam, on the border between Navaho country and the State of Deseret.

When they met the first time, Sam was a scrawny teenager from Utah and Anamari was a middle-aged spinster Indian from Brazil. When they met the second time, he was governor of Deseret, the last European state in America, and she was, to some people's way of thinking, the mother of God. It never occurred to anyone that they had ever met before, except me. I saw it plain as day, and pestered Sam until he told me the whole story. Now Sam is dead, and she's long gone, and I'm the only one who knows the truth. I thought for a long time that I'd take this story untold to my grave, but I see now that I can't do that. The way I see it, I won't be allowed to die until I write this down. All my real work was done long since, so why else am I alive? I figure the land has kept me breathing so I can tell the story of its victory, and it has kept *you* alive so you can hear it. Gods are like that. It isn't enough for them to run everything. They want to be famous, too.

Agualinda, Amazonas

Passengers were nothing to her. Anamari only cared about helicopters when they brought medical supplies.

237

This chopper carried a precious packet of benaxidene; Anamari barely noticed the skinny, awkward boy who sat by the crates, looking hostile. Another Yanqui who doesn't want to be stuck out in the jungle. Nothing new about that. Norteamericanos were almost invisible to Anamari by now. They came and went.

It was the Brazilian government people she had to worry about, the petty bureaucrats suffering through years of virtual exile in Manaus, working out their frustrations by being petty tyrants over the helpless Indians. No I'm sorry we don't have any more penicillin, no more syringes, what did you do with the AIDS vaccine we gave you three years ago? Do you think we're made of money here? Let them come to town if they want to get well. There's a hospital in Šao Paulo de Olivença, send them there, we're not going to turn you into a second hospital out there in the middle of nowhere, not for a village of a hundred filthy Baniwas, it's not as if you're a doctor, you're just an old withered-up Indian woman yourself, you never graduated from the medical schools, we can't spare medicines for you. It made them feel so important, to decide whether or not an Indian child would live or die. As often as not they passed sentence of death by refusing to send supplies. It made them feel powerful as God.

Anamari knew better than to protest or argue – it would only make that bureaucrat likelier to kill again in the future. But sometimes, when the need was great and the medicine was common, Anamari would go to the Yanqui geologists and ask if they had this or that. Sometimes they did. What she knew about Yanquis was that if they had some extra, they would share, but if they didn't, they wouldn't lift a finger to get any. They were not tyrants like the Brazilian bureaucrats. They just didn't give a damn. They were there to make money.

That was what Anamari saw when she looked at the sullen light-haired boy in the helicopter – another

238

Norteamericano, just like all the other Norteamericanos, only younger.

She had the benaxidene, and so she immediately began spreading word that all the Baniwas should come for injections. It was a disease introduced during the war between Guyana and Venezuela two years ago; as usual, most of the victims were not citizens of either country, just the Indios of the jungle, waking up one morning with their joints stiffening, hardening until no movement was possible. Benaxidene was the antidote, but you had to have it every few months or your joints would stiffen up again. As usual, the bureaucrats had diverted a shipment and there were a dozen Baniwas bedridden in the village. As usual, one or two of the Indians would be too far gone for the cure; one or two of their joints would be stiff for the rest of their lives. As usual, Anamari said little as she gave the injections, and the Baniwas said less to her.

It was not until the next day that Anamari had time to notice the young Yanqui boy wandering around the village. He was wearing rumpled white clothing, already somewhat soiled with the greens and browns of life along the rivers of the Amazon jungle. He showed no sign of being interested in anything, but an hour into her rounds, checking on the results of yesterday's benaxidene treatments, she became aware that he was following her.

She turned around in the doorway of the government-built hovel and faced him. 'O que?' she demanded. What do you want?

To her surprise, he answered in halting Portuguese. Most of these Yanquis never bothered to learn the language at all, expecting her and everybody else to speak English. 'Posso ajudar?' he asked. Can I help?

'Não,' she said. 'Mas pode olhar.' You can watch.

He looked at her in bafflement.

She repeated her sentence slowly, enunciating clearly. 'Pode olhar.'

'Eu?' Me?

'Você, sim. And I can speak English.'

'I don't want to speak English.'

'Tanto faz,' she said. Makes no difference.

He followed her into the hut. It was a little girl, lying naked in her own feces. She had palsy from a bout with meningitis years ago, when she was an infant, and Anamari figured that the girl would probably be one of the ones for whom the benaxidene came too late. That's how things usually worked – the weak suffer most. But no, her joints were flexing again, and the girl smiled at them, that heartbreaking happy smile that made palsy victims so beautiful at times.

So. Some luck after all, the benaxidene had been in time for her. Anamari took the lid off the clay waterjar that stood on the one table in the room, and dipped one of her clean rags in it. She used it to wipe the girl, then lifted her frail, atrophied body and pulled the soiled sheet out from under her. On impulse, she handed the sheet to the boy.

'Leva fora,' she said. And, when he didn't understand, 'Take it outside.'

He did not hesitate to take it, which surprised her. 'Do you want me to wash it?'

'You could shake off the worst of it,' she said. 'Out over the garden in back. I'll wash it later.'

He came back in, carrying the wadded-up sheet, just as she was leaving. 'All done here,' she said. 'We'll stop by my house to start that soaking. I'll carry it now.'

He didn't hand it to her. 'I've got it,' he said. 'Aren't you going to give her a clean sheet?'

'There are only four sheets in the village,' she said. 'Two of them are on my bed. She won't mind lying on the mat. I'm the only one in the village who cares about linens. I'm also the only one who cares about this girl.'

'She likes you,' he said.

'She smiles like that at everybody.'

'So maybe she likes everybody.'

Anamari grunted and led the way to her house. It was two government hovels pushed together. The one served as her clinic, the other as her home. Out back she had two metal washtubs. She handed one of them to the Yanqui boy, pointed at the rainwater tank, and told him to fill it. He did. It made her furious.

'What do you want!' she demanded.

'Nothing,' he said.

'Why do you keep hanging around!'

'I thought I was helping.' His voice was full of injured pride.

'I don't need your help.' She forgot that she had meant to leave the sheet to soak. She began rubbing it on the washboard.

'Then why did you ask me to . . .'

She did not answer him, and he did not complete the question.

After a long time he said, 'You were trying to get rid of me, weren't you?'

'What do you want here?' she said. 'Don't I have enough to do, without a Norteamericano *boy* to look after?'

Anger flashed in his eyes, but he did not answer until the anger was gone. 'If you're tired of scrubbing, I can take over.'

She reached out and took his hand, examined it for a moment. 'Soft hands,' she said. 'Lady hands. You'd scrape your knuckles on the washboard and bleed all over the sheet.'

Ashamed, he put his hands in his pockets. A parrot flew past him, dazzling green and red; he turned in surprise to look at it. It landed on the rainwater tank. 'Those sell for a thousand dollars in the States,' he said.

Of course the Yanqui boy evaluates everything by price. 'Here they're free,' she said. 'The Baniwa eat them. And wear the feathers.'

He looked around at the other huts, the scraggly gardens. 'The people are very poor here,' he said. 'The jungle

241

life must be hard.'

'Do you think so?' she snapped. 'The jungle is very kind to these people. It has plenty for them to eat, all year. The Indians of the Amazon did not know they were poor until Europeans came and made them buy pants, which they couldn't afford, and build houses, which they couldn't keep up, and plant gardens. Plant gardens! In the midst of this magnificent Eden. The jungle life was good. The Europeans made them poor.'

'Europeans?' asked the boy.

'Brazilians. They're all Europeans. Even the black ones have turned European. Brazil is just another European country, speaking a European language. Just like you Norteamericanos. You're Europeans too.'

'I was born in America,' he said. 'So were my parents and grandparents and great-grandparents.'

'But your bis-bis-avós, they came on a boat.'

'That was a long time ago,' he said.

'A long time!' She laughed. 'I am a pure Indian. For ten thousand generations I belong to this land. You are a stranger here. A fourth-generation stranger.'

'But I'm a stranger who isn't afraid to touch a dirty sheet,' he said. He was grinning defiantly.

That was when she started to like him. 'How old are you?' she asked.

'Fifteen,' he said.

'Your father's a geologist?'

'No. He heads up the drilling team. They're going to sink a test well here. He doesn't think they'll find anything, though.'

'They will find plenty of oil,' she said.

'How do you know?'

'Because I dreamed it,' she said. 'Bulldozers cutting down the trees, making an airstrip, and planes coming and going. They'd never do that, unless they found oil. Lots of oil.'

She waited for him to make fun of the idea of dreaming true dreams. But he didn't. He just looked at her.

So she was the one who broke the silence. 'You came to this village to kill time while your father is away from you, on the job, right?'

'No,' he said. 'I came here because he hasn't started to work yet. The choppers start bringing in equipment tomorrow.'

'You would rather be away from your father?'

He looked away. 'I'd rather see him in hell.'

'This *is* hell,' she said, and the boy laughed. 'Why did you come here with him?'

'Because I'm only fifteen years old, and he has custody of me this summer.'

'Custody,' she said. 'Like a criminal.'

'He's the criminal,' he said bitterly.

'And his crime?'

He waited a moment, as if deciding whether to answer. When he spoke, he spoke quietly and looked away. Ashamed. Of his father's crime. 'Adultery,' he said. The word hung in the air. The boy turned back and looked her in the face again. His face was tinged with red.

Europeans have such transparent skin, she thought. All their emotions show through. She guessed a whole story from his word – a beloved mother betrayed, and now he had to spend the summer with her betrayer. 'Is that a *crime*?'

He shrugged. 'Maybe not to Catholics.'

'You're Protestant?'

He shook his head. 'Mormon. But I'm a heretic.'

She laughed. 'You're a heretic, and your father is an adulterer.'

He didn't like her laughter. 'And you're a virgin,' he said. His words seemed calculated to hurt her.

She stopped scrubbing, stood there looking at her hands. 'Also a crime?' she murmured.

'I had a dream last night,' he said. 'In my dream your name was Anna Marie, and when I tried to call you that, I couldn't. I could only call you by another name.'

'What name?' she asked.

'What does it matter? It was only a dream.' He was taunting her. He knew she trusted in dreams.

'You dreamed of me, and in the dream my name was Anamari?'

'It's true, isn't it? That *is* your name, isn't it?' He didn't have to add the other half of the question: You *are* a virgin, aren't you?

She lifted the sheet from the water, wrung it out and tossed it to him. He caught it, vile water spattering his face. He grimaced. She poured the washwater onto the dirt. It spattered mud all over his trousers. He did not step back. Then she carried the tub to the water tank and began to fill it with clean water. 'Time to rinse,' she said.

'You dreamed about an airstrip,' he said. 'And I dreamed about you.'

'In your dreams you better start to mind your own business,' she said.

'I didn't ask for it, you know,' he said. 'But I followed the dream out to this village, and you turned out to be a dreamer, too.'

'That doesn't mean you're going to end up with your pinto between my legs, so you can forget it,' she said.

He looked genuinely horrified. 'Geez, what are you talking about! That would be fornication! Plus you've got to be old enough to be my mother!'

'I'm forty-two,' she said. 'If it's any of your business.'

'You're *older* than my mother,' he said. 'I couldn't possibly think of you sexually. I'm sorry if I gave that impression.'

She giggled. 'You are a very funny boy, Yanqui. First you say I'm a virgin – '

'That was in the dream,' he said.

'And then you tell me I'm older than your mother and too ugly to think of me sexually.'

He looked ashen with shame. 'I'm sorry, I was just trying to make sure you knew that I would never – '

'You're trying to tell me that you're a good boy.'

'Yes,' he said.

She giggled again. 'You probably don't even play with yourself,' she said.

His face went red. He struggled to find something to say. Then he threw the wet sheet back at her and walked furiously away. She laughed and laughed. She liked this boy very much.

The next morning he came back and helped her in the clinic all day. His name was Sam Monson, and he was the first European she ever knew who dreamed true dreams. She had thought only Indios could do that. Whatever god it was that gave her dreams to her, perhaps it was the same god giving dreams to Sam. Perhaps that god brought them together here in the jungle. Perhaps it was that god who would lead the drill to oil, so that Sam's father would have to keep him here long enough to accomplish whatever the god had in mind.

It annoyed her that the god had mentioned she was a virgin. That was nobody's business but her own.

Life in the jungle was better than Sam ever expected. Back in Utah, when Mother first told him that he had to go to the Amazon with the old bastard, he had feared the worst. Hacking through thick viney jungles with a machete, crossing rivers of piranha in tick-infested dugouts, and always sweat and mosquitos and thick, heavy air. Instead the American oilmen lived in a pretty decent camp, with a generator for electric light. Even though it rained all the time and when it didn't it was so hot you wished it would, it wasn't constant danger as he had feared, and he never had to hack through jungle at all. There were paths, sometimes almost roads, and the thick, vivid green of the jungle was more beautiful than he had ever imagined. He had not realized that the American West was such a desert. Even California, where the old bastard lived when he wasn't traveling to drill wells, even those wooded hills and mountains were grey compared to the jungle green.

The Indians were quiet little people, not headhunters. Instead of avoiding them, like the adult Americans did, Sam found that he could be with them, come to know them, even help them by working with Anamari. The old bastard could sit around and drink his beer with the guys – adultery *and* beer, as if one contemptible sin of the flesh weren't enough – but Sam was actually doing some good here. If there was anything Sam could do to prove he was the opposite of his father, he would do it; and because his father was a weak, carnal, earthy man with no self-control, then Sam had to be a strong, spiritual, intellectual man who did not let any passions of the body rule him. Watching his father succumb to alcohol, remembering how his father could not even last a month away from Mother without having to get some whore into his bed, Sam was proud of his self-discipline. He ruled his body; his body did not rule him.

He was also proud to have passed Anamari's test on the first day. What did he care if human excrement touched his body? He was not afraid to breathe the hot stink of suffering, he was not afraid of the innocent dirt of a crippled child. Didn't Jesus touch lepers? Dirt of the body did not disgust him. Only dirt of the soul.

Which was why his dreams of Anamari troubled him. During the day they were friends. They talked about important ideas, and she told him stories of the Indians of the Amazon, and about her education as a teacher in São Paulo. She listened when he talked about history and religion and evolution and all the theories and ideas that danced in his head. Even Mother never had time for that, always taking care of the younger kids or doing her endless jobs for the Church. Anamari treated him like his ideas mattered.

But at night, when he dreamed, it was something else entirely. In those dreams he kept seeing her naked, and the voice kept calling her 'Virgem America.' What her virginity had to do with America he had no idea – even true dreams didn't always make sense – but he knew this much: when he dreamed of Anamari naked, she was always reaching out to him, and he was filled with such strong passions that more than once he awoke from the dream to find himself throbbing with imaginary pleasure, like Onan in the Bible, Judah's son, who spilled his seed upon the ground and was struck dead for it.

Sam lay awake for a long time each time this happened, trembling, fearful. Not because he thought God would strike him down – he knew that if God hadn't struck his father dead for adultery, Sam was certainly in no danger because of an erotic dream. He was afraid because he knew that in these dreams he revealed himself to be exactly as lustful and evil as his father. He did not want to feel any sexual desire for Anamari. She was old and lean and tough, and he was afraid of her, but most of all Sam didn't want to desire her because he was not like his father, he would never have sexual intercourse with a woman who was not his wife.

Yet when he walked into the village of Agualinda, he felt eager to see her again, and when he found her – the village was small, it never took long – he could not erase from his mind the vivid memory of how she looked in the dreams, reaching out to him, her breasts loose and jostling, her slim hips rolling toward him – and he would bite his cheek for the pain of it, to distract him from desire.

It was because he was living with Father; the old bastard's goatishness was rubbing off on him, that's all. So he spent as little time with his father as possible, going home only to sleep at night.

The harder he worked at the jobs Anamari gave him to do, the easier it was to keep himself from remembering his dream of her kneeling over him, touching him, sliding along his body. Hoe the weeds out of the corn until your back is on fire with pain! Wash the Baniwa hunter's

247

wound and replace the bandage! Sterilize the instruments in the alcohol! Above all, do not, even accidentally, let any part of your body brush against hers; pull away when she is near you, turn away so you don't feel her warm breath as she leans over your shoulder, start a bright conversation whenever there is a silence filled only with the sound of insects and the sight of a bead of sweat slowly etching its way from her neck down her chest to disappear between her breasts where she only tied her shirt instead of buttoning it.

How could she possibly be a virgin, after the way she acted in his dreams?

'Where do you think the dreams come from?' she asked.

He blushed, even though she could not have guessed what he was thinking. Could she?

'The dreams,' she said. 'Why do you think we have dreams that come true?'

It was nearly dark. 'I have to get home,' he said. She was holding his hand. When had she taken his hand like that, and why?

'I have the strangest dream,' she said. 'I dream of a huge snake, covered with bright green and red feathers.'

'Not all the dreams come true,' he said.

'I hope not,' she answered. 'Because this snake comes out of – I give birth to this snake.'

'Quetzal,' he said.

'What does that mean?'

'The feathered serpent god of the Aztecs. Or maybe the Mayas. Mexican, anyway. I have to go home.'

'But what does it mean?'

'It's almost dark,' he said.

'Stay and talk to me!' she demanded. 'I have room, you can stay the night.'

But Sam had to get back. Much as he hated staying with his father, he dared not spend a night in this place. Even her invitation aroused him. He would never last a night in the same house with her. The dream would be too strong for him. So he left her and headed back along the path through the jungle. All during the walk he couldn't get Anamari out of his mind. It was as if the plants were sending him the vision of her, so his desire was even stronger than when he was with her.

The leaves gradually turned from green to black in the seeping dark. The hot darkness did not frighten him; it seemed to invite him to step away from the path into the shadows, where he would find the moist relief, the cool release of all his tension. He stayed on the path, and hurried faster.

He came with relief to the oilmen's town. The generator was loud, but the insects were louder, swarming around the huge area light, casting shadows of their demonic dance. He and his father shared a large one-room house on the far edge of the compound. The oil company provided much nicer hovels than the Brazilian government.

A few men called out to greet him. He waved, even answered once or twice, but hurried on. His groin felt so hot and tight with desire that he was sure that only the shadows and his quick stride kept everyone from seeing. It was maddening: the more he thought of trying to calm himself, the more visions of Anamari slipped in and out of his waking mind, almost to the point of hallucination. His body would not relax. He was almost running when he burst into the house.

Inside, Father was washing his dinner plate. He glanced up, but Sam was already past him. 'I'll heat up your dinner.'

Sam flopped down on his bed. 'Not hungry.'

'Why are you so late?' asked his father.

'We got to talking.'

'It's dangerous in the jungle at night. You think it's safe because nothing bad ever happens to you in the daytime, but it's dangerous.'

'Sure Dad. I know.' Sam got up, turned his back to take off his pants. Maddeningly, he was still aroused; he didn't want his father to see.

But with the unerring instinct of prying parents, the old bastard must have sensed that Sam was hiding something. When Sam was buck naked, Father walked around and *looked*, just as if he never heard of privacy. Sam blushed in spite of himself. His father's eyes went small and hard. I hope I don't ever look like that, thought Sam. I hope my face doesn't get that ugly suspicious expression on it. I'd rather die than look like that.

'Well, put on your pajamas,' Father said. 'I don't want to look at that forever.'

Sam pulled on his sleeping shorts.

'What's going on over there?' asked Father.

'Nothing,' said Sam.

'You must do *something* all day.'

'I told you, I help her. She runs a clinic, and she also tends a garden. She's got no electricity, so it takes a lot of work.'

'I've done a lot of work in my time, Sam, but I don't come home like *that*.'

'No, you always stopped and got it off with some whore along the way.'

The old bastard whipped out his hand and slapped Sam across the face. It stung, and the surprise of it wrung tears from Sam before he had time to decide not to cry.

'I never slept with a whore in my life,' said the old bastard.

'You only slept with one woman who wasn't,' said Sam.

Father slapped him again, only this time Sam was ready, and he bore the slap stoically, almost without flinching.

'I had one affair,' said Father.

'You got caught once,' said Sam. 'There were dozens of women.'

Father laughed derisively. 'What did you do, hire a

detective? There was only the one.'

But Sam knew better. He had dreamed these women for years. Laughing, lascivious women. It wasn't until he was twelve years old that he found out enough about sex to know what it all meant. By then he had long since learned that any dream he had more than once was true. So when he had a dream of Father with one of the laughing women, he woke up, holding the dream in his memory. He thought through it from beginning to end, remembering all the details he could. The name of the motel. The room number. It was midnight, but Father was in California, so it was an hour earlier. Sam got out of bed and walked quietly into the kitchen and dialed directory assistance. There was such a motel. He wrote down the number. Then Mother was there, asking him what he was doing.

'This is the number of the Seaview Motor Inn,' he said. 'Call this number and ask for room twenty-one twelve and then ask for Dad.'

Mother looked at him strangely, like she was about to scream or cry or hit him or throw up. 'Your father is at the Hilton,' she said.

But he just looked right back at her and said, 'No matter who answers the phone, ask for Dad.'

So she did. A woman answered, and Mom asked for Dad by name, and he was there. 'I wonder how we can afford to pay for two motel rooms on the same night,' Mom said coldly. 'Or are you splitting the cost with your friend?' Then she hung up the phone and burst into tears.

She cried all night as she packed up everything the old bastard owned. By the time Dad got home two days later, all his things were in storage. Mom moved fast when she made up her mind. Dad found himself divorced and excommunicated all in the same week, not two months later.

Mother never asked Sam how he knew where Dad was that night. Never even hinted at wanting to know.

Dad never asked him how Mom knew to call that number, either. An amazing lack of curiosity, Sam thought sometimes. Perhaps they just took it as fate. For a while it was secret, then it stopped being secret, and it didn't matter how the change happened. But one thing Sam knew for sure – the woman at the Seaview Motor Inn was not the first woman, and the Seaview was not the first motel. Dad had been an adulterer for years, and it was ridiculous for him to lie about it now.

But there was no point in arguing with him, especially when he was in the mood to slap Sam around.

'I don't like the idea of you spending so much time with an older woman,' said Father.

'She's the closest thing to a doctor these people have. She needs my help and I'm going to keep helping her,' said Sam.

'Don't talk to me like that, little boy.'

'You don't know anything about this, so just mind your own business.'

Another slap. 'You're going to get tired of this before I do, Sammy.'

'I love it when you slap me, Dad. It confirms my moral superiorty.'

Another slap, this time so hard that Sam stumbled under the blow, and he tasted blood inside his mouth. 'How hard next time, Dad?' he said. 'You going to knock me down? Kick me around a little? Show me who's boss?'

'You've been asking for a beating ever since we got here.'

'I've been asking to be left alone.'

'I know women, Sam. You have no business getting involved with an older woman like that.'

'I help her wash a little girl who has bowel movements in bed, Father. I empty pails of vomit. I wash clothes and help patch leaking roofs and while I'm doing all these things we talk. Just talk. I don't imagine you have much experience with that, Dad. You probably never talk at all with the women *you* know, at least not after the price is set.'

It was going to be the biggest slap of all, enough to knock him down, enough to bruise his face and black his eye. But the old bastard held it in. Didn't hit him. Just stood there, breathing hard, his face red, his eyes tight and piggish.

'You're not as pure as you think,' the old bastard finally whispered. 'You've got every desire you despise in me.'

'I don't despise you for *desire*,' said Sam.

'The guys on the crew have been talking about you and this Indian bitch, Sammy. You may not like it, but I'm your father and it's my job to warn you. These Indian women are easy, and they'll give you a disease.'

'The guys on the crew,' said Sam. 'What do they know about Indian women? They're all fags or jerk-offs.'

'I hope someday you say that where they can hear you, Sam. And I hope when it happens I'm not there to stop what they do to you.'

'I would never *be* around men like that, Daddy, if the court hadn't given you shared custody. A no-fault divorce. What a joke.'

More than anything else, those words stung the old bastard. Hurt him enough to shut him up. He walked out of the house and didn't come back until Sam was long since asleep.

Asleep and dreaming.

Anamari knew what was on Sam's mind, and to her surprise she found it vaguely flattering. She had never known the shy affection of a boy. When she was a teenager, she was the one Indian girl in the schools in São Paulo. Indians were so rare in the Europeanized parts of Brazil that she might have seemed exotic, but in those days she was still so frightened. The city was sterile, all concrete and harsh light, not at all like the deep soft meadows and woods of Xingu Park. Her tribe, the Kuikuru, were much more Europeanized than the jungle Indians – she had seen cars all her life, and spoke Portuguese before she went to school. But the city made her hungry for the land, the cobblestones hurt her feet, and these intense, competitive children made her afraid. Worst of all, true dreams stopped in the city. She hardly knew who she was, if she was not a dreamer. So if any boy desired her then, she would not have known it. She would have rebuffed him inadvertently. And then the time for such things had passed. Until now.

'Last night I dreamed of a great bird, flying west, away from land. Only its right wing was twice as large as its left wing. It had great bleeding wounds along the edges of its wings, and the right wing was the sickest of all, rotting in the air, the feathers dropping off.'

'Very pretty dream,' said Sam. Then he translated, to keep in practice. 'Que sonho lindo.'

'Ah, but what does it mean?'

'What happened next?'

'I was riding on the bird. I was very small, and I held a small snake in my hands – '

'The feathered snake.'

'Yes. And I turned it loose, and it went and ate up all the corruption, and the bird was clean. And that's all. You've got a bubble in that syringe. The idea is to inject medicine, not air. What does the dream mean?'

'What, you think I'm a Joseph? A Daniel?'

'How about a Sam?'

'Actually, your dream is easy. Piece of cake.'

'What?'

'Piece of cake. Easy as pie. That's how the cookie crumbles. Man shall not live by bread alone. All I can think of are bakery sayings. I must be hungry.'

'Tell me the dream or I'll poke this needle into your eye.'

'That's what I like about you Indians. Always you have torture on your mind.'

She planted her foot against him and knocked him off his stool onto the packed dirt floor. A beetle skittered away. Sam held up the syringe he had been working with – it was undamaged. He got up, set it aside. 'The bird,' he said, 'is North and South America. Like wings, flying west. Only the right wing is bigger.' He sketched out a rough map with his toe on the floor.

'That's the shape, maybe,' she said. 'It could be.'

'And the corruption – show me where it was.'

With her toe, she smeared the map here, there.

'It's obvious,' said Sam.

'Yes,' she said. 'Once you think of it as a map. The corruption is all the Europeanized land. And the only healthy places are where the Indians still live.'

'Indians or half-Indians,' said Sam. 'All your dreams are about the same thing, Anamari. Removing the Europeans from North and South America. Let's face it. You're an Indian chauvinist. You give birth to the resurrection god of the Aztecs, and then you send it out to destroy the Europeans.'

'But why do I dream this?'

'Because you hate Europeans.'

'No,' she said. 'That isn't true.'

'Sure it is.'

'I don't hate *you*.'

'Because you know me. I'm not a European anymore, I'm a person. Obviously you've got to keep that from happening anymore, so you can keep your bigotry alive.'

'You're making fun of me, Sam.'

He shook his head. 'No, I'm not. These are true dreams, Anamari. They tell you your destiny.'

She giggled. 'If I give birth to a feathered snake, I'll know the dream was true.'

'To drive the Europeans out of America.'

'No,' she said. 'I don't care what the dream says. I won't do that. Besides, what about the dream of the flowering weed?'

255

'Little weed in the garden, almost dead, and then you water it and it grows larger and larger and more beautiful – '

'And something else,' she said. 'At the very end of the dream, all the other flowers in the garden have changed. To be just like the flowering weed.' She reached out and rested her hand on his arm. 'Tell me *that* dream.'

His arm became still, lifeless under her hand. 'Black is beautiful,' he said.

'What does *that* mean?'

'In America. The U.S., I mean. For the longest time, the blacks, the former slaves, they were ashamed to be black. The whiter you were, the more status you had – the more honor. But when they had their revolution in the sixties – '

'You don't remember the sixties, little boy.'

'Heck, I barely remember the seventies. But I read books. One of the big changes, and it made a huge difference, was that slogan. Black is beautiful. The blacker the better. They said it over and over. Be proud of blackness, not ashamed of it. And in just a few years, they turned the whole status system upside down.'

She nodded. 'The weed came into flower.'

'So. All through Latin America, Indians are very low status. If you want a Bolivian to pull a knife on you, just call him an Indian. Everybody who possibly can, pretends to be of pure Spanish blood. Pure-blooded Indians are slaughtered wherever there's the slightest excuse. Only in Mexico is it a little bit different.'

'What you tell me from my dreams, Sam, this is no small job to do. I'm one middle-aged Indian woman, living in the jungle. I'm supposed to tell all the Indians of America to be proud? When they're the poorest of the poor and the lowest of the low?'

'When you give them a name, you create them. Benjamin Franklin did it, when he coined the name *American* for the people of the English colonies. They weren't New Yorkers or Virginians, they were Americans.

Same thing for you. It isn't Latin Americans against Norteamericanos. It's Indians and Europeans. Somos todos indios. We're all Indians. Think that would work as a slogan?'

'Me. A revoluntionary.'

'Nós somos os americanos. Vai fora, Europa! America p'ra americanos! All kinds of slogans.'

'I'd have to translate them into Spanish.'

'Indios moram na India. Americanos moram na America. America nossa! No, better still: Nossa America! Nuestra America! It translates. Our America.'

'You're a very fine slogan maker.'

He shivered as she traced her finger along his shoulder and down the sensitive skin of his chest. She made a circle on his nipple and it shriveled and hardened, as if he were cold.

'Why are you silent now?' She laid her hand flat on his abdomen, just above his shorts, just below his navel. 'You never tell me your own dreams,' she said. 'But I know what they are.'

He blushed.

'See? Your skin tells me, even when your mouth says nothing. I have dreamed these dreams all my life, and they troubled me, all the time, but now you tell me what they mean, a white-skinned dream-teller, you tell me that I must go among the Indians and make them proud, make them strong, so that everyone with a drop of Indian blood will call himself an Indian, and Europeans will lie and claim native ancestors, until America is all Indian. You tell me that I will give birth to the new Quetzalcoatl, and he will unify and heal the land of its sickness. But what you never tell me is this: Who will be the father of my feathered snake?'

Abruptly he got up and walked stiffly away. To the door, keeping his back to her, so she couldn't see how alert his body was. But she knew.

'I'm fifteen,' said Sam, finally.

'And I'm very old. The land is older. Twenty million

years. What does it care of the quarter-century between us?'

'I should never have come to this place.'

'You never had a choice,' she said. 'My people have always known the god of the land. Once there was a perfect balance in this place. All the people loved the land and tended it. Like the garden of Eden. And the land fed them. It gave them maize and bananas. They took only what they needed to eat, and they did not kill animals for sport or humans for hate. But then the Incas turned away from the land and worshiped gold and the bright golden sun. The Aztecs soaked the ground in the blood of their human sacrifices. The Pueblos cut down the forests of Utah and Arizona and turned them into red-rock deserts. The Iroquois tortured their enemies and filled the forests with their screams of agony. We found tobacco and coca and peyote and coffee and forgot the dreams the land gave us in our sleep. And so the land rejected us. The land called to Columbus and told him lies and seduced him and he never had a chance, did he? Never had a choice. The land brought the Europeans to punish us. Disease and slavery and warfare killed most of us, and the rest of us tried to pretend we were Europeans rather than endure any more of the punishment. The land was our jealous lover, and it hated us for a while.'

'Some Catholic you are,' said Sam. 'I don't believe in your Indian gods.'

'Say *Deus* or *Cristo* instead of *the land* and the story is the same,' she said. 'But now the Europeans are worse than we Indians ever were. The land is suffering from a thousand different poisons, and you threaten to kill all of life with your weapons of war. We Indians have been punished enough, and now it's our turn to have the land again. The land chose Columbus exactly five centuries ago. Now you and I dream our dreams, the way he dreamed.'

'That's a good story,' Sam said, still looking out the

258

door. It sounded so close to what the old prophets in the Book of Mormon said would happen to America; close, but dangerously different. As if there was no hope for the Europeans anymore. As if their chance had already been lost, as if no repentance would be allowed. They would not be able to pass the land on to the next generation. Someone else would inherit. It made him sick at heart, to realize what the white man had lost, had thrown away, had torn up and destroyed.

'But what should I do with my story?' she asked. He could hear her coming closer, walking up behind him. He could almost feel her breath on his shoulder. 'How can I fulfill it?'

By yourself. Or at least without me. 'Tell it to the Indians. You can cross all these borders in a thousand different places, and you speak Portuguese and Spanish and Arawak and Carib, and you'll be able to tell your story in Quechua, too, no doubt, crossing back and forth between Brazil and Colombia and Bolivia and Peru and Venezuela, all close together here, until every Indian knows about you and calls you by the name you were given in my dream.'

'Tell me my name.'

'Virgem America. See? The land or God or whatever it is wants you to be a virgin.'

She giggled. 'Nossa senhora,' she said. 'Don't you see? I'm the new Virgin *Mother*. It wants me to be a *mother*; all the old legends of the Holy Mother will transfer to me; they'll call me virgin no matter what the truth is. How the priests will hate me. How they'll try to kill my son. But he will live and become Quetzalcoatl, and he will restore America to the true Americans. That is the meaning of my dreams. My dreams and yours.'

'Not me,' he said. 'Not for any dream or any god.' He turned to face her. His fist was pressed against his groin, as if to crush out all rebellion there. 'My body doesn't rule me,' he said. 'Nobody controls me but myself.'

'That's very sick,' she said cheerfully. 'All because you

hate your father. Forget that hate, and love me instead.'

His face became a mask of anguish, and then he turned and fled.

He even thought of castrating himself, that's the kind of madness that drove him through the jungle. He could hear the bulldozers carving out the airstrip, the screams of falling timber, the calls of birds and cries of animals displaced. It was the terror of the tortured land, and it maddened him even more as he ran between thick walls of green. The rig was sucking oil like heartblood from the forest floor. The ground was wan and trembling under his feet. And when he got home he was grateful to lift his feet off the ground and lie on his mattress, clutching his pillow, panting or perhaps sobbing from the exertion of his run.

He slept, soaking his pillow in afternoon sweat, and in his sleep the voice of the land came to him like whispered lullabies. I did not choose you, said the land. I cannot speak except to those who hear me, and because it is in your nature to hear and listen, I spoke to you and led you here to save me, save me, save me. Do you know the desert they will make of me? Encased in burning dust or layers of ice, either way I'll be dead. My whole purpose is to thrust life upward out of my soils, and feel the press of living feet, and hear the songs of birds and the low music of the animals, growling, lowing, chittering, whatever voice they choose. That's what I ask of you, the dance of life, just once to make the man whose mother will teach him to be Quetzalcoatl and save me, save me, save me.

He heard that whisper and he dreamed a dream. In his dream he got up and walked back to Agualinda, not along the path, but through the deep jungle itself. A longer way, but the leaves touched his face, the spiders climbed on him, the tree lizards tangled in his hair, the monkeys dunged him and pinched him and jabbered in his ear, the snakes entwined around his feet; he waded streams and fish caressed his naked ankles, and all the way they sang to him, songs that celebrants might sing at the wedding of a king. Somehow, in the way of dreams, he lost his clothing without removing it, so that he emerged from the jungle naked, and walked through Agualinda as the sun was setting, all the Baniwas peering at him from their doorways, making clicking noises with their teeth.

He awoke in darkness. He heard his father breathing. He must have slept through the afternoon. What a dream, what a dream. He was exhausted.

He moved, thinking of getting up to use the toilet. Only then did he realize that he was not alone on the bed, and it was not his bed. She stirred and nestled against him, and he cried out in fear and anger.

It startled her awake. 'What is it?' she asked.

'It was a dream,' he insisted. 'All a dream.'

'Ah yes,' she said, 'it was. But last night, Sam, we dreamed the same dream.' She giggled. 'All night long.'

In his sleep. It happened in his sleep. And it did not fade like common dreams, the memory was clear, pouring himself into her again and again, her fingers gripping him, her breath against his cheek, whispering the same thing, over and over: 'Aceito, aceito-te, aceito.' Not love, no, not when he came with the land controlling him, she did not love him, she merely accepted the burden he placed within her. Before tonight she had been a virgin, and so had he. Now she was even purer than before, Virgem America, but his purity was hopelessly, irredeemably gone, wasted, poured out into this old woman who had haunted his dreams. 'I hate you,' he said. 'What you stole from me.'

He got up, looking for his clothing, ashamed that she was watching him.

'No one can blame you,' she said. 'The land married us, gave us to each other. There's no sin in that.'

'Yeah,' he said.

'One time. Now I am whole. Now I can begin.'

And now I'm finished.

'I didn't mean to rob you,' she said. 'I didn't know you were dreaming.'

'I thought I was dreaming,' he said, 'but I loved the dream. I dreamed I was fornicating and it made me glad.' He spoke the words with all the poison in his heart. 'Where are my clothes?'

'You arrived without them,' she said. 'It was my first hint that you wanted me.'

There was a moon outside. Not yet dawn. 'I did what you wanted,' he said. 'Now can I go home?'

'Do what you want,' she said. 'I didn't plan this.'

'I know. I wasn't talking to you.' And when he spoke of home, he didn't mean the shack where his father would be snoring and the air would stink of beer.

'When you woke me, I was dreaming,' she said.

'I don't want to hear it.'

'I have him now,' she said, 'a boy inside me. A lovely boy. But you will never see him in all your life, I think.'

'Will you tell him? Who I am?'

She giggled. 'Tell Quetzalcoatl that his father is a European? A man who blushes? A man who burns in the sun? No, I won't tell him. Unless someday he becomes cruel, and wants to punish the Europeans even after they are defeated. Then I will tell him that the first European he must punish is himself. Here, write your name. On this paper write your name, and give me your fingerprint, and write the date.'

'I don't know what day it is.'

'October twelfth,' she said.

'It's August.'

'Write October twelfth,' she said. 'I'm in the legend business now.'

'August twenty-fourth,' he murmured, but he wrote the date she asked for.

'The helicopter comes this morning,' she said.

'Good-bye,' he said. He started for the door.

Her hands caught at him, held his arm, pulled him back. She embraced him, this time not in a dream, cool bodies together in the doorway of the house. The geis was off him now, or else he was worn out; her body had no power over his anymore.

'I did love you,' she murmured. 'It was not just the god that brought you.'

Suddenly he felt very young, even younger than fifteen, and he broke away from her and walked quickly away through the sleeping village. He did not try to retrace his wandering route through the jungle; he stayed on the moonlit path and soon was at his father's hut. The old bastard woke up as Sam came in.

'I knew it'd happen,' Father said.

Sam rummaged for underwear and pulled it on.

'There's no man born who can keep his zipper up when a woman wants it.' Father laughed. A laugh of malice and triumph. 'You're no better than I am, boy.'

Sam walked to where his father sat on the bed and imagined hitting him across the face. Once, twice, three times.

'Go ahead, boy, hit me. It won't make you a virgin again.'

'I'm not like you,' Sam whispered.

'No?' asked Father. 'For you it's a sacrament or something? As my daddy used to say, it don't matter who squeezes the toothpaste, boy, it all squirts out the same.'

'Then your daddy must have been as dumb a jackass as mine.' Sam went back to the chest they shared, began packing his clothes and books into one big suitcase. 'I'm going out with the chopper today. Mom will wire me the money to come home from Manaus.'

'She doesn't have to. I'll give you a check.'

'I don't want your money. I just want my passport.'

'It's in the top drawer.' Father laughed again. 'At least I always wore my clothes home.'

In a few minutes Sam had finished packing. He picked up the bag, started for the door.

'Son,' said Father, and because his voice was quiet, not derisive, Sam stopped and listened. 'Son,' he said, 'once is once. It doesn't mean you're evil, it doesn't even mean you're weak. It just means you're human.' He was breathing deeply. Sam hadn't heard him so emotional in a long time. 'You aren't a thing like me, son,' he said. 'That should make you glad.'

Years later Sam would think of all kinds of things he should have said. Forgiveness. Apology. Affection. Something. But he said nothing, just left and went out to the clearing and waited for the helicopter. Father didn't come to try to say good-bye. The chopper pilot came, unloaded, left the chopper to talk to some people. He must have talked to Father because when he came back he handed Sam a check. Plenty to fly home, and stay in good places during the layovers, and buy some new clothes that didn't have jungle stains on them. The check was the last thing Sam had from his father. Before he came home from that rig, the Venezuelans bought a hardy and virulent strain of syphilis on the black market, one that could be passed by casual contact, and released it in Guyana. Sam's father was one of the first million to die, so fast that he didn't even write.

Page, Arizona

The State of Deseret had only sixteen helicopters, all desperately needed for surveying, spraying, and medical emergencies. So Governor Sam Monson rarely risked them on government business. This time, though, he had no choice. He was only fifty-five, and in good shape, so maybe he could have made the climb down into Glen Canyon and back up the other side. But Carpenter wouldn't have made it, not in a wheelchair, and Carpenter had a right to be here. He had a right to see what the red-rock Navaho desert had become.

Deciduous forest, as far as the eye could see.

They stood on the bluff where the old town of Page had once been, before the dam was blown up. The Navahos hadn't tried to reforest here. It was their standard practice. They left all the old European towns unplanted, like pink scars in the green of the forest. Still, the Navahos weren't stupid. They had come to the last stronghold of European science, the University of Deseret at Zarahemla, to find out how to use the heavy rainfalls to give them something better than perpetual floods and erosion. It was Carpenter who gave them the plan for these forests, just as it was Carpenter whose program had turned the old Utah deserts into the richest farmland in America. The Navahos filled their forests with bison, deer, and bears. The Mormons raised crops enough to feed five times their population. That was the European mind-set, still in place: enough is never enough. Plant more, grow more, you'll need it tomorrow.

'They say he has two hundred thousand soldiers,' said Carpenter's computer voice. Carpenter *could* speak, Sam had heard, but he never did. Preferred the synthesized voice. 'They could all be right down there, and we'd never see them.'

'They're much farther south and east. Strung out from Phoenix to Santa Fe, so they aren't too much of a burden on the Navahos.'

'Do you think they'll buy supplies from us? Or send an army in to take them?'

'Neither,' said Sam. 'We'll give our surplus grain as a gift.'

'He rules all of Latin America, and he needs *gifts* from a little remnant of the U.S. in the Rockies?'

'We'll give it as a gift, and be grateful if he takes it that way.'

'How else might he take it?'

'As tribute. As taxes. As ransom. The land is his now, not ours.'

'We made the desert live, Sam. That makes it ours.'

'There they are.'

They watched in silence as four horses walked slowly from the edge of the woods, out onto the open ground of an ancient gas station. They bore a litter between them, and were led by two – not Indians – Americans. Sam had schooled himself long ago to use the word *American* to refer only to what had once been known as Indians, and to call himself and his own people Europeans. But in his heart he had never forgiven them for stealing his identity, even though he remembered very clearly where and when that change began.

It took fifteen minutes for the horses to bring the litter to him, but Sam made no move to meet them, no sign that he was in a hurry. That was also the American way now, to take time, never to hurry, never to rush. Let the Europeans wear their watches. Americans told time by the sun and stars.

Finally the litter stopped, and the men opened the litter door and helped her out. She was smaller than before, and her face was tightly wrinkled, her hair steel-white.

She gave no sign that she knew him, though he said his name. The Americans introduced her as Nuestra Señora. Our Lady. Never speaking her most sacred name: Virgem America.

The negotiations were delicate but simple. Sam had authority to speak for Deseret, and she obviously had authority to speak for her son. The grain was refused as a gift, but accepted as taxes from a federated state. Deseret would be allowed to keep its own government, and the borders negotiated between the Navahos and the Mormons eleven years before were allowed to stand.

Sam went further. He praised Quetzalcoatl for coming to pacify the chaotic lands that had been ruined by the Europeans. He gave her maps that his scouts had prepared, showing strongholds of the prairie raiders, decommissioned nuclear missiles, and the few places where stable governments had been formed. He

266

offered, and she accepted, a hundred experienced scouts to travel with Quetzalcoatl at Deseret's expense, and promised that when he chose the site of his North American capital, Deseret would provide architects and engineers and builders to teach his American workmen how to build the place themselves.

She was generous in return. She granted all citizens of Deseret conditional status as adopted Americans, and she promised that Quetzalcoatl's armies would stick to the roads through the northwest Texas panhandle, where the grasslands of the newest New Lands project were still so fragile that an army could destroy five years of labor just by marching through. Carpenter printed out two copies of the agreement in English and Spanish, and Sam and Virgem America signed both.

Only then, when their official work was done, did the old woman look up into Sam's eyes and smile. 'Are you still a heretic, Sam?'

'No,' he said. 'I grew up. Are you still a virgin?'

She giggled, and even though it was an old lady's broken voice, he remembered the laughter he had heard so often in the village of Agualinda, and his heart ached for the boy he was then, and the girl she was. He remembered thinking then that forty-two was old.

'Yes, I'm still a virgin,' she said. 'God gave me my child. God sent me an angel, to put the child in my womb. I thought you would have heard the story by now.'

'I heard it,' he said.

She leaned closer to him, her voice a whisper. 'Do you dream, these days?'

'Many dreams. But the only ones that come true are the ones I dream in daylight.'

'Ah,' she sighed. 'My sleep is also silent.'

She seemed distant, sad, distracted. Sam also; then, as if by conscious decision, he brightened, smiled, spoke cheerfully. 'I have grandchildren now.'

'And a wife you love,' she said, reflecting his brightening

mood. 'I have grandchildren, too.' Then she became wistful again. 'But no husband. Just memories of an angel.'

'Will I see Quetzalcoatl?'

'No,' she said, very quickly. A decision she had long since made and would not reconsider. 'It would not be good for you to meet face-to-face, or stand side by side. Quetzalcoatl also asks that in the next election, you refuse to be a candidate.'

'Have I displeased him?' asked Sam.

'He asks this at my advice,' she said. 'It is better, now that his face will be seen in this land, that your face stay behind closed doors.'

Sam nodded. 'Tell me,' he said. 'Does he look like the angel?'

'He is as beautiful,' she said. 'But not as pure.'

Then they embraced each other and wept. Only for a moment. Then her men lifted her back into her litter, and Sam returned with Carpenter to the helicopter. They never met again.

In retirement, I came to visit Sam, full of questions lingering from his meeting with Virgem America. 'You knew each other,' I insisted. 'You had met before.' He told me all this story then.

That was thirty years ago. She is dead now, he is dead, and I am old, my fingers slapping these keys with all the grace of wooden blocks. But I write this sitting in the shade of a tree on the brow of a hill, looking out across woodlands and orchards, fields and rivers and roads, where once the land was rock and grit and sagebrush. This is what America wanted, what it bent our lives to accomplish. Even if we took twisted roads and got lost or injured on the way, even if we came limping to this place, it is a good place, it is worth the journey, it is the promised, the promising land.

Author's Note

On Sycamore Hill

I never consciously made a decision to stop writing short fiction. I didn't even notice I had stopped until someone pointed it out. But then I wondered why.

It wasn't just because I was writing novels – I wrote some of my best stuff after finishing my first three books.

Maybe I stopped because I actually learned *how* to write novels. By the time I was through with *Hart's Hope*, *The Worthing Chronicle*, and all 1,000 manuscript pages of *Saints*, long treatments felt natural. I got used to having room to flesh things out. To linger a little. To build through lots of different scenes.

Even the few short stories I actually wrote in the last few years were really novel-length ideas struggling to get out. 'The Changed Man and the King of Words,' my last short story to see print, cost me tremendous effort just to cut it down to size. I left out a lot. And the story suffered from it. There were two stories before that, which were every bit as bad as the ones Ben Bova didn't buy when I was starting out. The story I wrote in the fall of 1983 was the first chapter of a novel. The editors noticed that fact and didn't buy the story.

You think I didn't worry? I'm the guy who had forty-plus stories published from 1977 to 1981. Four Hugo nominations, two Nebula nominations, an absurdly high paperback advance for my second novel. You know me – the one Ted White accused of indecent exposure.

And now I couldn't write short stories anymore.

I couldn't even *think* of short stories.

Now, that may not seem like much of a worry. As long as I'm selling novels for a fair price, it's not as if my kids will starve because I've got nothing to send Ed Ferman.

I wasn't even *reading* short fiction; ever since I burned out doing my *Science Fiction Review* short fiction review column, I hadn't opened a magazine more than a couple of times, just to read a story by a close friend. And I don't think I had read more than three sf novels I didn't write myself since 1982.

So when Mark Van Name and John Kessel invited me to the Sycamore Hill Writers Workshop near Raleigh, North Carolina, I wasn't sure. A workshop sounded good to me – I liked teaching at Clarion, and really enjoyed teaching science fiction writing at the University of Utah. Those were both workshops, and they were great. I said yes, definitely, count me in.

And then I realized that there was a key difference between those other workshops and Sycamore Hill. At Sycamore Hill, I was going to have to put my own stories at risk.

What stories?

I sent in my thirty-five bucks. I marked the days on the calendar. Then I buried myself in writing *Speaker for the Dead* and the script of *Space Pioneers* for the Hansen Planetarium in Salt Lake City. Halfway through *Speaker* I realized I had to throw away that draft – a minor character had taken over and it wasn't the book I wanted to write. That was November. I started doing a long overdue story for George Martin's Campbell Award Winners anthology. This will be the story I take to Sycamore Hill, I thought.

But it wasn't a short story. A third of the way through,

270

I knew it wasn't even a novella. If I told the whole story the way it needed to be told, it was a novel. I was doing it again. I still couldn't tell a short story if it killed me.

I left out chapters and kept it down to some 42,000 words and sent *Unwyrm* off to George. He told me he could tell where the chapters were missing and asked for changes. I made the changes, sent the new version, and then realized that I had half a novel sitting there and I knew what the other half was. Why not finish it? So I spent November and December turning *Unwyrm* into a novel, *Wyrms*. I finished it right after Christmas. Then I had to write a new version of the planetarium script and do my computer game programming column for *Ahoy!* magazine in a panic and here it was New Year's Day and I hadn't written anything short. I was committed to going to Sycamore Hill and I didn't have a story.

But all during the month of December, I had been thinking now and then about some stories I knew I wanted to write. They were set in Utah, the place I know best in all the world, in a future after a limited nuclear exchange and heavy biological warfare – enough to decimate the population, cool the climate, but leave plenty of hope for the future. The Great Salt Lake was filling up, covering the most heavily populated parts of Utah.

My stories focused around people surviving. Not just any people, *my* people. Mormons, and the non-Mormons who live among them and must adapt to this curiously secular religion. I had first worked on this milieu back in 1980, when I outlined a play about a small family of actors who traveled from town to town, putting on pageants on the back of their flatbed truck in exchange for gasoline and food and spare parts for the truck.

That story would be a novel, though, if I wrote it in prose, so I couldn't use it for the workshop. However, I had two more stories in that milieu vaguely plotted out. One was about a group of people who go to the half-submerged Salt Lake Temple to try to salvage some fabled gold that the Mormons were supposed to have hidden there. The other, set in a desert-edge community, was about a schoolteacher with cerebral palsy who uses a computer to synthesize his voice.

The only trouble was, it was already Wednesday afternoon. When Gregg Keizer got off work that day at Compute! Books, I would pick him up and drive us to Mark Van Name's house for the workshop. There was no time to write the story. There was barely time to finish up a couple of other things that absolutely had to be done so my family could eat while I was gone.

I was going to Sycamore Hill with nothing written, nothing at all. Oh, I could give them a fragment of *Wyrms*, but what a cheat that would be. I *knew* it was a good novel, of the kind I write, anyway, and what could they tell from a fragment? There was no way they'd want to read 300 pages, and no time to make eight copies even if they did.

So I packed up the PCjr – not the computer I usually work on, but the only one I owned that was small enough to carry and big enough to run a real word-processing program. Whatever I wrote at the workshop I could print out on Mark Van Name's PC, so I wouldn't have to worry about taking a printer with me. I loaded everything into the rust-corroded '76 Datsun B-210 so my wife could have the Renault, and drove up the road to get Gregg.

It was cold and rainy. Not surprising, for January in North Carolina. But we'd been spoiled lately, three weeks of summery weather – I'd taken walks in my shirt sleeves. I didn't even bring a heavy coat or a sweater, but I began to realize right away that this did nothing to prove my intelligence.

Gregg brought his Osborne and a suitcase; we stopped for gas and I bought six liters of Diet Coke. I had visions of maybe not eating anything but the Coke, to shed some of the forty-five pounds I'd picked up working at a desk the last two years. We drove I-85 and US 70 and then I managed to forget the name of the road we were supposed to turn on after that. We ended up driving right on into Raleigh, which I knew was wrong; we found a payphone, called, found out we were closer than I thought. Rain and darkness make it hard to find your way to a house you've only visited in daylight. But I also knew my mind wasn't working altogether right.

I was too nervous to see straight. I had to write a couple of stories in the next few days, and then listen to a bunch of writers tell me that I obviously must have had a ghostwriter on 'Unaccompanied Sonata'; these little drecklings couldn't possibly have come from the same mind. Not just writers, *published* writers, and the ones I knew, I had great respect for. John Kessel had pulled off the miracle and got a Nebula, Greg Frost had a novel that had actually earned out its royalties, Gregg Keizer and Mark Van Name had given me plenty of opportunities to know they were gifted writers and perceptive critics, and above all, every single person at the workshop had sold at least two short stories since I had last sold one.

It was dark and wet and the coldest night of the year. Everybody had already eaten spaghetti when we got there. There was some left, but true to my resolution to starve myself, I drank half a liter of Coke and dragged my stuff down into the basement. The temperature of the basement made me wonder if maybe it was heated with geothermal energy and the Earth was cooling faster than anybody thought. I went back upstairs.

There were a bunch of people sitting around the table laughing and enjoying themselves. Gregg Keizer, as usual, immediately fit in and was part of the conversation as if he'd been drinking beer with these guys every day for years. I, as usual, hadn't the faintest idea how to get into anything. I've long envied that quality in Gregg – without calling attention to himself, he can slide into any situation and within minutes it's as if he belonged there all his life. The only time I'm instantly comfortable, is when I'm expected to perform. Give me an audience of ten or ten thousand, and I know I can hold them as long as I want; I've never had stage fright in my life. I enjoy even more the kind of conversation where the idea is what matters and the level of thought is very high. But when I'm with ten people, many of them strangers, who are in party mode – banter, with no serious topic of conversation to attack – I don't belong. I've got no small talk. I always sound stupid to myself and the glazed look on other people's faces tells me they usually agree. So I did what I always do; I retreated, avoided the group at the table, busied myself with setting up the computer, putting my Cokes in the fridge, talking to Mark's wife Rana.

Finally things got structured for a minute and I could fit in. We all met together long enough to decide whose stories would be done which days. This was Wednesday night. Tomorrow we'd do only two stories, one from Jim Kelly and one from Greg Frost. We set up four a day for Friday, Saturday, Sunday, and Monday. Since I hadn't written a story yet – the only one who had come unprepared – they scheduled my first one for Saturday. I couldn't even tell them a title. Everyone was very polite about it. But I was sure that behind their smiles they were all calculating exactly how many pounds I was overweight. 'Enough extra flesh on this boy to create four small dogs, or perhaps a third-grader. *And* he has the gall not to bring a story.'

You're paranoid, I told myself. Get a grip on yourself, I said. Get me the hell out of here, I answered, get me back to where my wife and children cooperate to sustain the illusion that I'm a competent human being.

I took the stories for tomorrow – and the next day – and escaped into the basement.

As I lay there, my body providing the major source of heat for the room, it began to dawn on me that something was rotten in the atmosphere. Dear Teela Brown, the Van Names' most socially aloof cat, had a look of innocence and complacency that was not to be believed. Was it so? Yes, indeed, a little pile of kitty poo in my boudoir. It was going to be a long night.

Houses in North Carolina are designed for summer. Lots of air circulating through the walls, that sort of thing. This is not as comfortable during a real cold snap. By morning I felt like I had spent a night in the Gulag, stiff and cold. Ten people showering doesn't leave a lot of hot water, either, and I had stayed up so late reading stories that I was not exactly the first to shower.

So I was not feeling at my best when we gathered around a group of tables in the dining room at ten o'clock. John Kessel read a formal statement but couldn't keep a straight face through the whole thing. We had some pretty simple rules. Everybody got a turn to talk about the story except the author, who kept his mouth shut until it was all over. After everybody had spoken, the author could then answer, if he was capable of speech.

And I mean *he*. About as many women as men had been invited, but, each for her own reason, the female writers had all declined. So it was just us guys. The old locker room. I've never been half as comfortable with men as with women. Locker rooms always smelled like sweat and old spattered urine to me.

To my relief, this was no football team. Greg Frost, for instance, will be unable to keep a straight face in his coffin. Allen Wold has a pony tail down to here. Scott Sanders looks like a college professor among a bunch of freshmen who surprise him by being so young. Jim Kelly has a beatific grace and looks as sensitive as the young Peter O'Toole. Steve Carper looks like he's doing complex logarithms in his head, just for fun, and when he runs across an especially good one it's all he can do to keep from laughing. Not what you expect to find in the average locker room - nobody was taped up and slobbering; nobody was mumbling, 'Kill. Kill.'

The most forbidding-looking guys at the table I already felt pretty comfortable with: John Kessel, spectral and intense, with more than a hint of maniacal intelligence. Mark Van Name, the only person there who I knew felt as vulnerable as me, but who always seems confident enough to perform brain surgery with blinders. And Gregg Keizer, whom I had met in my writing class at the U of U (not that I had anything to teach *him*); even then, whenever I looked at him I had the vague feeling that I had just said something stupid but out of kindness he wasn't going to tell anybody. It took years, but I finally realized that this impression was absolutely right.

One thing I've always hated in bad workshop situations is when the critics vie with each other for the cleverest evisceration of the victim. The criticism of the first story made it clear that this group was not going to do that. Oh, there was some humor, but there was never any cruelty. I saw no evidence that anyone ever spoke without considering the feelings of the writer hearing the criticism.

And yet no one was ever sparing, either. If we hated a story, we said so. We also said why. And best of all, the comments were intelligent. When somebody pointed out something that I hadn't noticed, I always felt a little embarrassed that I hadn't noticed it. These guys knew how to *read*.

And I was going to give them a story?

There was only one bit of tension at that first criticism session. One of the writers did start making some comments that were on the level of, 'You said here, "Her eyes fell on the paper he held," and I thought, There they go, plop-plop.' I really hate that sort of criticism. In the first place, the metaphorical use of *eyes* for *gaze* is perfectly legitimate. In the second place, nobody ever notices those things if they're involved in the story; they are a symptom of a failure to engage the attention and belief of the reader, not a problem per se. So I broke in and said so. I thought I was saying it politely. Afterward I realized that I had been brusque and had, in effect, put down one of the most perceptive and experienced critics at the table. I had visions of being put out of the workshop with bell, book, and candle. Instead, because he was a perfect gentleman, he withered me with a forgiving look and went on. But the point was taken: never again in the workshop did anybody make that kind of criticism of the language of a story.

After the first story, everybody else attacked an incredible pile of cold cuts; I, still determined to be ascetic, retreated to the basement. It was too cold to type, but I did it anyway, every now and then pleading with Mr. Scrooge to buy more coal. Actually, the PCjunior put off enough heat to stave off frostbite.

A funny thing happened as I was writing the story. I had just finished listening to a bunch of highly intelligent and talented men criticize a story. It was exciting, it made me feel alert, awake to the possibility of the story. And as I wrote, I began to feel at ease in the story as I hadn't with a short story for years. It came fast.

By the time two o'clock rolled around, I had the story about a third done. I had worked out a heavily expository opening in such a way that the reader only realizes the teacher is speaking through a computer and has cerebral palsy in a few gradual steps. I was worried, though – to get some of the history and some of the social milieu across, I had included the teacher's lecture. Broken up with some tension between him and a student, but a lecture's a lecture no matter how you juice it up, and I was afraid it would be boring. Still, I couldn't see any other way. So I left it in.

We came back and did another story. This was a fairly artsy and ambitious one, interspersing lectures on Stonehenge with a cloning/incest/decadent-drug-society story. Just the kind of thing that makes me want to abolish the teaching of contemporary literature classes in universities. I mean, the writing was excellent, but the story took forever just to get from A to B. Like *New Yorker* stuff. But I couldn't help suspecting that part of the reason it put me off was because I have zero sympathy whatsoever with people who take drugs. I'm as compulsive as the next guy – you don't get overweight by ignoring candy bars and driving past Wendy's without stopping – but people who deliberately wipe out their brains get no tears of sympathy from me when they wake up and discover they've got no mind. That's part of why I hated *Neuromancer*. (I also loved *Neuromancer*, but ambivalence has always been my strong suit as a critic.)

Then, as the others commented on the story, I began to see virtues in it that I had been blind to, before. I also began to realize that they also saw the flaws I saw. That was when I really began to trust them to be good critics – they saw what wasn't working in the story, and yet they also saw the power in it that made the writer want to tell the story in the first place. That was both comforting and frightening. When I finished my story, I wouldn't be casting it among fools; but if they hated it, I'd be compelled to believe them.

They all went out to dinner that night. I had deliberately brought only about ten bucks with me, to avoid the temptation to do exactly that. I never did go out to dinner with them on the nights they went. And it wasn't just because I had to finish a story, or because I didn't have much money, or because I wanted to lose weight. It was because I still was afraid of situations where there was no subject matter to discuss.

When I said I had no small talk, that really wasn't true. I can slip right in and be comfortable with any group of my own community. But this wasn't my community. These guys were Americans, not Mormons; those of us who grew up in Mormon society and remain intensely involved are only nominally members

278

of the American community. We can fake it, but we're always speaking a foreign language. Only when we get with fellow Saints are we truly at home. If it had been a group of ten Mormons, I wouldn't have had any problem. We'd have a common fund of experience, speak the same language, share some of the same concerns. We could make jokes about Mormon culture, talk seriously about things that you can only discuss with someone who shares the same faith. With this group, though, relaxing would be much, much harder. I trusted their criticism, but once we were removed from the context of storytelling, they were gentiles and I would end up sitting and saying nothing or too much all night, feeling less and less comfortable. I know this from experience. So I was just as happy not to go.

Instead I stayed home and finished 'The Fringe.' The teacher betrayed the ring of smugglers and embezzlers; their sons left the teacher to die in a desert gully that would surely flood in the heavy rain that was coming. He struggled to climb only a few feet, and the pageant wagon people that I'll use later in the long story came and rescued him. There's more to it than that, but by the end I felt worn out but exhilarated. I had written a short story. I hadn't left anything out, and it was definitely under 7500 words. Best of all, it was *finished*.

At the same time, I was worried. This story, I thought, was probably OK; I wouldn't embarrass myself. But the second story – it depended completely on exactly that sense of belonging or not-belonging that had kept me away from the dinner that night. In fact, the comradeship, the *exclusiveness* of people who have the same faith and share the same culture was the *subject* of the story. I began to think I wouldn't try to write the second one. I wasn't sure I could bring it off, and if I failed, it would be excruciating, because it would be my own people who would be made to look ridiculous or unintelligible.

I wondered if anybody else there was feeling the

same level of anxiety. I saw a few signs of nervousness, but most seemed relaxed and comfortable.

We had a new face – Tim Sullivan had decided to drive down from D.C. and join the workshop at the last minute. He was a welcome addition, if only because he made Greg Frost seem solemn by contrast. The two of them sat together from then on during critique sessions, and the Greg & Tim comedy show kept us from getting too serious about Literature, for which we were mostly grateful.

Steve Carper had a story that morning that treated the void of space like a substance, which could randomly penetrate and turn things into obsidian; a weird and frightening concept. I had read Gregg Keizer's story in an earlier version; it was about a human in an alien concentration camp which consisted of a perfect but unpopulated reproduction of Paris; one of Gregg's best. Allen Wold had a fun ghoul-meets-vampire story, but it contained a sentence about heavy clouds releasing their load, which had struck some people as scatalogically hilarious the night before – including me. There were some cloud-dump jokes before the session began.

But the knockout was Scott Sanders's 'Ascension.' Funny, disturbing, literary without being dull for even a moment. We all wished we had written it. We even speculated that he was bound to sell it right away; unless he sent it to Ellen Datlow, I pointed out, who would reject it because of the punctuation.

That night they all went to have dinner and see a movie. I was tempted, but it was an old Hitchcock, one of the ones they've just re-released, and I wasn't in the mood for tension. So I stayed and worked for a while, writing the beginning of 'Salvage' but mostly reading the stories for Saturday. Then I took off and drove in to Raleigh and saw *Johnny Dangerously*. An unbelievably stupid movie – just what I needed.

Alas, when I came home, they were still gone, the

house was locked up, and I couldn't get in. When I left, Jim Kelly and John Kessel had still been there talking on the phone to Jim Frenkel of Blue Jay about their collaborative novel; but by now they had finished and gone to join the others.

I contemplated sitting in my car with the engine running for a while. Instead I broke all my resolutions, drove to Burger King, and ate more than God ever meant man to eat. That was it for my money supply, but by then I was *hungry*. I had a notebook with me, too, and all of a sudden things fell into place for me with *Speaker for the Dead*. I knew how to begin the thing – all my wonderful middles never worked because the beginning was totally wrong. And now it was right. I practically wrote the whole first chapter there with the smell of Cheeseburger Deluxe giving me an empty-calorie high. Who says Mormons can't have fun?

There was no doubt in my mind now. No matter what happened, this workshop had been worth it. I had written a story in about five hours, one that I thought had a decent chance of working; and now I had unknotted a novel that had been doing dirt to me for nearly three years.

On Saturday, I was last. Gregg Keizer's second story was a powerful fantasy about a woman who conjures the wind for a sailing ship by dripping her own blood into the sea. Mark Van Name had a story about a dream therapist working her way back to the painful secrets a nearly catatonic little girl was hiding from. John Kessel had a piece of his first solo novel, which was so beautifully written that it made me want to kill him, remembering the botch I made of *my* first novel. Even his synopsis was brilliant – we all suggested he ought to try to get it published as is? It was filled with the author's self-questioning – should I have this happen, or is the plot getting out of hand? There were some problems, of course, since it was a first draft, but it was plain that Kessel's debut as a novelist will be stunning.

I tried to be intelligent in my comments on their stories, but the truth is I could hardly keep my mind off my own. I kept trying to read Scott Sanders's notes on my story – it was on top of his stack – without letting anybody else notice that I was doing it.

When they got to my story, they were very kind; but it occurred to me for the first time that they thought my having written the story in a few hours right at the workshop was kind of a stunt. Actually, I always write quickly – when I know what to write. I couldn't *think up* a story and write it in five hours. I have to think about it – and *not* think about it – for weeks, months, or years; but when it's ready, it comes out in a burst. And this workshop had helped me more than they understood – that story had *not* been ready when I arrived, but by the time I wrote it, the intensity of the concentration on storytelling, the ambient talent and intelligence, all had had a profound effect on me. It's not that it reawakened my old understanding of how to write stories. 'The Fringe' was not like what I had written before. Most of my old stories, if I were writing them now, would have been novels this time. But 'The Fringe' *had* to be a story. It was not an accidental story, it was an inevitable one.

That night we went to John Kessel's and Sue Hall's place for a stuff-it-yourself baked potato dinner. I had no shame; I ate two, to celebrate the vast relief that my story had passed muster.

We also restrained ourselves from murdering Scott Sanders: the February *Asimov's* had just arrived, and there was the story we had critiqued only the day before – that we had been sure he would soon get published – and lo! it was a miracle. *Asimov's* had already fulfilled our prophecy. Not only that, but when he was directly questioned, he admitted that his other story, which we were going to critique the next morning, had also been sold – to the redoubtable Ellen Datlow. He was sheepish, and vowed that our criticism really *was* helpful; he still regarded the stories as works in progress. Besides, these were the only two sf stories he had written in recent years; most of his stories were mainstream. He was so sweet about it that we all agreed to forgive him, or at least pretend to. Truth was, his criticism of other stories was so perceptive and helpful that we should have paid him to come even if he didn't bring any stories at all. Still, it took some of the fun out of the criticism, to know that the stories had been sold. My only consolation was that he had sold the second one to *Omni*, so he still had no idea whether it was publishable or not.

That night I was feeling pretty good, now that my first story had been found acceptable. I began to realize that a lot of my feeling of awkwardness was because of my uncertainty about my stories. I didn't feel like hiding in the basement anymore. After reading the next day's stories, I wandered upstairs in my bathrobe. A lot of them were sitting around the tables while Mark Van Name read passages from Joe Bob's movie review column. The satire was bitter and delicious, and we laughed till we cried.

But on Sunday, I was burned out. Everything I said sounded stupid to me. Later, calm reflection assured me that my comments were indeed stupid. Fortunately, I noticed it in time and left most of the criticism to the people who were still making sense. We told Scott Sanders why his hunters-in-a-game-preserve-world story needed drastic revision, which it would never get unless the art department of *Omni* decided they needed thirty lines cut out to make it come even with the bottom of a page. (Actually, I loved the story, but I couldn't *tell* him that, could I? Not when he'd already spent the lousy two thousand bucks.)

Steve Carper had a comic story told as a series of articles in different magazines. Tim Sullivan's 'I Was a Teenage Dinosaur' was *not* comic; but a story that begins with a guy running over a dog, taking the bleeding animal home with him, putting it in his bed for the night, and waking up to find it dead beside him – my kind of story.

Poor Greg Frost made the mistake of calling his comic mystery story 'Oobidis,' which kept getting sung as 'Oo-be-doo-be-doo' in our best Frank Sinatra voices – but he did create the most engaging pair of aliens I have ever read in sf, two little furballs that copulate constantly in the messiest possible fashion.

That night I finished 'The Temple Salvage Expedition' and Gregg Keizer and I drove back to Greensboro. He had to work the next day, so he'd miss the last day of the workshop; Scott Sanders and Steve Carper also left early to meet Monday commitments.

I managed to make a wrong turn on the way through Durham. I never get lost unless Gregg's in the car. Another bad guess took us halfway to Chapel Hill. I'm not as mindless as this sounds – you have to have driven in North Carolina to understand. Signs are regularly posted just after the turn they warn you about. Lanes of traffic suddenly veer off and become highways going in the wrong direction. They put up highway number signs only if they feel like it. It's the locals' way of letting us Yankee carpetbaggers know that we aren't as smart as we all think we are.

We did get home. My kids were asleep; Kristine wasn't, but I was terrible company anyway. I spent an hour getting the story to print out and then xeroxing the copies I'd need. Finally we were able to talk. I woke the kids up enough to tell them I was home – Emily had been waking up with nightmares every night I was gone. Charlie did his normal midnight-is-really-morning routine, and seemed happy to see me. It was good to remember that the workshop wasn't the real world. It seemed hard to believe, though, that I had only been gone four nights and days. The experience had been so intense it seemed like much longer.

Bright and early I was back on the road to Sycamore Hill. Jim Kelly had finished his story only the night before, and I hadn't got a copy yet – I had to get there in time to read it before the eleven o'clock session. I got there and handed around my story, and then settled down to read Jim's 'Rat.' In five minutes I was in love. It was simply one of the most wonderful stories I've ever read. And he had written the last half of it on Mark's PC/XT upstairs – the other story that was written, in part, at Sycamore Hill. It's the story of a rat who is smuggling drugs; he swallowed several ampules of it and now is doing his best to defecate them until he can get safely back to his apartment – which ain't easy. Making a rat believable as the protagonist of an urban drug-smuggling story ain't easy, either, but Jim did it. You'll notice the story when it's published, believe me.

Allen Wold's story was an admitted item of juvenilia – he hasn't written very many short stories in his life, and all his published work is in novels. I thought of going back to my trunk and pulling out some of my earliest plays, and I decided that by contrast Allen's early stuff looked very, very good.

They were kind to 'Salvage.' The thing that had worried me most – that the intensity of the religious elements in it would put them off – turned out not to be a problem at all. Though few there had particularly strong religious impulses, the sense of holiness that the story depended on seemed to work.

I realized, then, that this milieu – of Mormon country underwater, the survivors struggling to keep civilization alive – was viable; more important, *I* was viable. I had written two presentable short stories for the first time in years. I felt as good as if I had actually lost all forty-five pounds while eating as much as I wanted.

We spent the afternoon cleaning up the mess we had made of Mark's house. The carpet was new enough that all our footscuffing had raised more fuzzballs on the carpet than a thousand cats. We vacuumed, moved beds out into the garage, and set up for a party for local fans that was scheduled for that evening – the formal ending of Sycamore Hill. The party was a party – I figured I wouldn't be good for anything until I found some people who wanted to talk about things they really cared about; I do know how to listen. But I was still cresting from the exhilaration of the workshop – I don't know if I seemed stoned to anybody else, but I was as close to manic as a good Mormon is allowed to get. The party ended up being a lot of fun.

And then I went home.

I spent the next several days doing the revisions that the workshop had suggested; then I sent the stories off to my agent. Ordinarily I would have sent them to the magazines myself, but at least one of them I figured had a fair shot at getting into a non-genre magazine, and Barbara Bova handles my non-genre short fiction sales. Besides, I wanted to show off to both Ben and Barbara that I was actually doing stories again. I even went crazy enough to make some more copies and send a few to other people – a college dean in Utah who has been following my fiction; a critic for a Mormon intellectual journal who had just done a thoughtful piece on science fiction; a few others. What they thought, getting a story out of the blue like that, I have no idea – but I was celebrating.

I don't much care who buys them, actually (though I care very much that someone does). The workshop's response to the story was better than a check. In five days I learned to trust their judgment and value their good opinion. I don't want to get maudlin about this, but they made a real difference in my writing – and my confidence about my writing – in those few days. We didn't become intimate friends; we're not going to sell our houses so we can live close together from now on, or anything like that (though, come to think of it, Mark's hot tub *might* be worth living closer to).

We exchanged gifts that to me, at least, came at a crucial moment. The burst of creative energy that it unleashed in me is still going. I know I'll coast back down to normal after a while, but by then maybe it'll be time for the second annual Sycamore Hill Writers' Workshop. With any luck I won't be a paranoid wreck coming into the workshop – but if that's what it takes to get the results I got, I'll be ready.

It has been nearly four years since I wrote the preceding account of the first Sycamore Hill Writers' Workshop; in a few weeks I'll be heading to the fourth. A lot of water has gone over the dam since then. A few months after Sycamore Hill, Gregg Keizer and I went to the Nebulas in New York, where he read my new opening to *Speaker for the Dead*, which had bogged down again; he provided the insights that allowed me to start over again – this time for the last time. I dedicated the book to him because it wouldn't have been any good without his help.

'The Fringe,' the first of my Sycamore Hill stories, was sold to Ed Ferman at *The Magazine of Fantasy and Science Fiction*. Ed rejected 'Salvage,' however; it ended up with Gardner Dozois, and with that I began a custom which lasted for several years, of sending every new story I wrote to *Asimov's*. I did write more short stories, too; though many of the tales that appeared in *Asimov's* were freestanding chunks out of my fantasy *The Tales of Alvin Maker*, others were independent stories – 'Dogwalker,' 'America.' Two older stories – among those referred to above as unpublishable – got resurrected; I revised them and 'Saving Grace' appeared in *Night Cry*; 'Eye for Eye,' after a rejection from Stan Schmidt at *Analog*, appeared in *Asimov's*.

'America' was a troubling story from the start. It began charged with sexual energy, as a story of an older woman falling in love with a boy. I couldn't write it, though, until I realized that the woman was an Indian who dreamed of the rebirth of Quetzalcoatl; and as I started writing, I suddenly discovered that the boy was a Mormon kid who was having trouble coping with his sexual desire within the bounds of what the doctrine of the Church permits. I am not comfortable writing about sex, especially when it is important to the story that the reader also experience something of the characters' sexual desire. Yet that is what the story required, and while I labored to make it tasteful, I also had to tell the tale truthfully. I was further surprised when I realized in the epilogue that the story had to be told by Carpenter, the palsied schoolteacher from 'The Fringe.' I went back and revised the story slightly so it would fit seamlessly into the future history of 'The Fringe' and 'Salvage.'

Thematically, 'America' is not fully about community in the way all the other stories in this collection are. The other stories are all science fiction; 'America' is unarguably fantasy. I debated whether or not to include it here; the book was certainly long enough without it. I finally decided that the mythic underpinnings, the sense that there was a purpose behind all the loss and suffering – that was vital to understanding the other tales. Though, except for the epilogue, 'America' takes place chronologically first, I put it last because it revises the meaning of all the other stories.

'West' was written in response to a request from Betsy Mitchell of Baen Books; she wanted a novella from me as part of the fourth volume of her *Alien Stars* series of triptych books. The idea was to write a story about a mercenary soldier. As I tried to develop a story for *Alien Stars*, though, I realized that everything I had ever wanted to say both for and against the military and soldiering and war was pretty well covered in my novel *Ender's Game*. I hadn't the faintest interest in telling soldier stories.

But I *did* have a long-time idea about the first story in my collection of 'Mormon Sea' stories. I wanted to write a story about a mixed-race group of Mormons leaving the eastern U.S. and making a difficult trek through chaotic, collapsing America to finally reach safety in the Rocky Mountains. It would deliberately echo the 19th-century trek of the handcart companies, with a new version of the murders and atrocities and other persecution that drove the Saints out of the United States in the 1840s; to Mormons, this is some of the most powerful material in our community epic. I also figured two of the characters would be named Deaver and Teague, and out on the prairie they would find the hero of 'Salvage' as a child. Still, this wasn't a story yet, just a milieu and a situation and some episodes. It didn't hang together.

When I thought of this story in the context of the 'mercenary soldier' theme, however, it finally began to open up for me. What if I continued the theme of an outsider looking in that was inherent in all the other stories? Why not have this party of Mormon refugees 'hire' a woodsman to serve as guide, leader, and defender – their mercenary soldier?

My first thought was to make this mercenary a Cherokee Indian, but as I tried to write the story it wasn't working. Then I came across a heartbreaking essay in *Harper's* about a family that kept two of their little children locked in a closet for years. The writer of the essay did a magnificent job of taking the large view – seeing that not only were the victims tragic figures, but so also was the mother who instigated this crime. Yet there was one person in this terrible story who was not fully explored: the next older child who took the victims their food and carried away their bodily wastes. This child held the key to their prison in his hand, and locked it; this child was the one who, accidentally or deliberately, let his imprisoned brother escape. And even though this story seemed utterly unrelated to my story about the trek west, I realized that my 'mercenary soldier' had to be the child who had held the key. He was the one who was equally victim and victimizer; he was the one who would hunger for the forgiveness and redemption that the community of Mormon survivors could provide.

At once the trek west became background instead of foreground; all my plans for having them pass through the empty ruins of Chattanooga, find some protection under the military government of Nashville, and only escape from black-ruled Memphis because of the pleadings of the black members of the party – those plans faded away. The story became something else, and something stronger. I wrote 'West' in one long draft. Betsy Mitchell made perceptive and helpful comments, and my rewrite became the story that begins this book.

Finally, 'Pageant Wagon.' It was the original story, the one at the root of all the others, and yet it was the hardest to write. The characters were drawn from my days as a theatre student at BYU and the years following, when I launched a community theatre on a shoestring. The intensity of theatre people, my love for my friends of that time, and my memory of my own passion and excitement and cliquishness and arrogance when I was in theatre were part of the reason for the story to exist; it was a tale of theatrical community, its intensity magnified by making the players a family, set against the equally intense but conflicting Mormon community of the desert fringe.

The plot first took form back in 1980. My long-time friend and collaborator, Robert Stoddard, came to visit me in my home in Orem, Utah, as we prepared new versions of our musical drama *Stone Tables*, for production at Brigham Young University, and our musical comedy *Father, Mother, Mother, and Mom*, for production at the Sundance Summer Theatre. We discussed *Pageant Wagon* then as an idea for a musical comedy, and the basic plotline emerged: the pageant wagon family, torn by internal conflict, picks up a stranger on the road who heals the family and stays with them forever; in that version of the story, the stranger was meant to function as, perhaps even *be* an angel, echoing the Mormon folklore of Godsent visitors met on the road. We also looked forward to writing a satirical yet powerful fifteen-minute pageant that would be commentary on the self-congratulatory pageants that Mormons are wont to put on.

The years passed, and other stories growing out of the same milieu got written. Robert got married and put down some roots in Los Angeles; we lost contact with each other, except through my cousin and dear friend Mark Park, a terrific pianist, who had also moved to L.A. Neither Mark nor Robert was working in music now, except for private pleasure. Yet I still treasured the memory of working with Robert on our shows in the past. I had worked with other composers and written many solo works, but nothing had ever been as satisfying as those hours standing by the piano, fitting my lyrics to his music, each of us serving as instant audience for the other's inventions. My skills were still primitive then, and I suppose his were, too, but we made each other better, and there was real joy in that. Not only did I want to make a play out of 'Pageant Wagon,' I wanted the story of it to include that feeling I had with Robert, the sense of making something beautiful together.

I signed a contract to produce this book with Alex Berman of Phantasia Press in November 1986. That winter I wrote 'West' and 'America.' All I had to do then was write 'Pageant Wagon,' and the contract would be fulfilled.

But I couldn't write it. I didn't know the people. I knew their 'type,' I even knew the family dynamics, but I didn't know *them*. Discovering that the man they pick up on the road was Deaver Teague from 'Salvage' – that helped. But I knew from the experience of writing *Speaker for the Dead* that creating an entire believable family was an enormous fictional task. And the story was so important to me personally that I retreated from it, backed away.

Ironically, after I signed the contract for the book that would contain 'Pageant Wagon,' I was asked to write the new script for the Mormon Church's Hill Cumorah Pageant, the oldest and best and most resonant of the Church's pageants. It was a mark of great trust in me, and I spent the winter of 1987 working on nothing else. The result was a script that I was proud of, given the institutional needs and pressures that must shape such a work. I also came to understand far more clearly just what such a pageant is for, how it feeds the hunger of a community; if I had not written *America's Witness for Christ*, the real Hill Cumorah Pageant, I could not have written *Glory of America*, the mini-pageant that is performed in 'Pageant Wagon.'

However, it was not until I got to the third Sycamore Hill in August 1987 – again without a story written! – that I actually started writing down the words of 'Pageant Wagon.' Even then I wrote five thousand words of another story, but it was so miserably bad that I determined that even if it killed me, I would write the tale that had to be written. I spent a couple of long and terrible nights hammering it out, forcing it into some kind of shape, just so a draft of the story would exist. I took it home and printed it out, xeroxed it, and brought it in for them to read. It was 111K on the computer – about 18,000 words, a novella – but they read it.

Sycamore Hill has only grown stronger and better over the years; the critique was intense and extremely helpful. In my first version, I had Deaver Teague violently expel Ollie from the family, with Scarlett's open consent. This seemed monstrous to the writers at Sycamore Hill, and it was; I had let the plotline control the characters, instead of the other way around. I emerged from the workshop with clear ideas of how to revise the story. They had taught me what the story ought to be, and again I felt like I had taken far more away from Sycamore Hill than I could ever repay. It is no accident that three of the five stories in this book were first written down while enmeshed in that powerful community experience.

Yet I *didn't* immediately revise 'Pageant Wagon.' The sheer effort of drafting it was so intense and exhausting that the thought of facing the story again daunted me. I went straight from Sycamore Hill to a semester of teaching full time in the Watauga College interdisciplinary studies program at Appalachian State University. That semester I lived in an apartment in Boone, North Carolina, during the week and commuted home on weekends. It was a wonderful experience, confirming me in my belief that I would be happier in a career as a teacher than I am as a writer, if only I could find a university English department able to overcome its bias against science fiction – and willing to let me teach whatever I want, from anthropological story theory to contemporary history, from Middle English romances to the writing of fiction, from Shakespeare to playwriting to game theory to hypertext. In other words, I realized that I will never find the teaching situation that I want, though the Watauga College environment comes close enough to have made that semester a season of joy.

It was also a season in which I did no writing of fiction. And when the semester ended, I got caught up in other projects. Some animated video scripts for Living Scriptures. Revising and finishing *Prentice Alvin*. Going to too many conventions. Teaching a writing class in the evenings in Greensboro. Alex Berman was patient, but he did wonder from time to time whether I would ever deliver the contracted book.

The temptation was strong just to put 'Pageant Wagon' into the book the way it was first drafted. It was certainly professional and publishable in that draft. I didn't have time or heart to go back to it and do the drastic revision that would make it the story I really wanted. Yet I couldn't turn in a book I didn't believe in. So I waited, and therefore Alex waited.

It wasn't until I was teaching the first week of Clarion West in June of 1988 that I finally had the fire and ambition to go back to 'Pageant Wagon.' I had brought

my critique notes from Sycamore Hill with me; the students at Clarion West were so fired up that I caught that spirit of creativity, and one afternoon I locked myself in my room for four hours and actually began to revise. I didn't finish that day, but I got a strong start, and when I got back to my family I was able to complete the new draft in several days. In the process, the story had grown from 18,000 words to 30,000, but I knew that the basic movement of the story was right.

I found myself in Ohio the next week, and many of my students at the Antioch Writers' Workshop were kind enough to give up mealtimes to hear me read the new draft and critique it. They helped me greatly in polishing and tightening; I ended up rewriting the beginning to make it less introspective, more eventful. Some weaknesses of the story, though, were inherent – before I could show the family changing, I had to show what the family was, and that takes time and pages. Finally, though, I knew the story was ready. The first story, the root story of this collection, was the hardest to write and the last to be completed.

Back when the story was a mere 18,000 words long, I had promised Gardner Dozois first look at it. When the story was finally finished, I sent it to him, confident that at 30,000 words there wasn't a hope in the world that *Asimov's* would publish it. But Gardner astonished me by accepting it – even though by his count it was 36,000 words long, and even though it could not appear in *Asimov's* until six months after the release of the Phantasia Press edition of this book. Dozois is either congenitally open-minded or pleasantly insane; either way, I'm grateful that he'll be offering it to his audience.

But I'm not through with 'Pageant Wagon.' Even after all this work, the narrative you have within these pages is still not final. For the story was conceived as a play with music, and I won't be satisfied until I have seen actors perform the roles, until I have seen the Aal family's flatbed truck on a turntable stage, with Katie

playing Betsy Ross and Toolie playing Royal Aal and Deaver finding his way into the family. Perhaps it will never come to be. But I'm sending the finished manuscript of 'Pageant Wagon' to Robert Stoddart.

Robert, it's in your hands now.

– Orson Scott Card
Greensboro
July 1988

Afterword:
The Folk of the Fringe

Michael Collings

In March 1982, I read a paper to a session of the International Conference on the Fantastic in the Arts, in which I argued that science fiction and Mormonism provide essentially opposing perspectives; since their expectations for the future and their modes of knowing that future are so opposite, it is difficult for one writer to incorporate both. The final version, published in *Dialogue: A Journal of Mormon Thought* (Autumn 1984), referred to Orson Scott Card's early novels as examples of writing that came close to blending the two, but I was still hesitant about the possibility of such a blending.

Then something changed my mind.

In January 1985, I received a letter from Card. It was entirely unexpected; we had never met, never corresponded – out of nowhere, a thick packet arrived from North Carolina containing a letter, a response to my article (later published as Card's 'SF and Religion' in the Summer of 1985 *Dialogue*), and a typescript of a short story.

The letter was enjoyable; the response, stimulating; but the story . . .

For me as science fiction reader and as Mormon,

'Salvage' was a revelation. The greater shock, however, was still to come.

A year later, 'Salvage' appeared in the February 1986 issue of *Isaac Asimov's Science Fiction Magazine*. I bought my copy and opened it eagerly – there is something exciting about seeing a story in print, even if you've already read it in manuscript. The story seems more finished, more final.

And there it was. The Salt Lake Temple half submerged in the floodwaters of a resurgent Lake Bonneville. One of the prime tenets of Mormon folk-belief is that the Temple was built to stand until the Second Coming, and here was a story that both validated and refuted that belief. Yes, the Temple was standing, but it was empty, a hollow shell bearing witness to the death of faith.

But not really. And that was the beauty of the story. The Temple became an external symbol for an internal truth. Outward faith might be dead in the world of the Mormon Sea, but the inward urge to belief is still as strong and powerful as ever. There *is* treasure buried in the Temple, but a treasure understandable and perceivable only to the few.

In a subsequent letter, Card noted that he had not been overtly aware of this level of the story – that it was 'threatening to a good many folk doctrines about the future of Salt Lake Valley.' The story was, he continued, intended as fiction, not as independent prophecy; the key to the tale is to understand that a science fiction writer may not literally *believe* the future he posits, but he *must* believe that that future communicates the fundamental assumptions of a story that must be told. 'On the matter of storytelling,' Card asserts, 'my vocation is as sound as anyone's, and I bow to no authority but the light I see by, which I will shine into every dark corner until somebody shows me a brighter one.'

'Salvage' and 'The Fringe,' written within a few days of each other, were ground-breaking stories for two reasons. First, they were Card's first short stories in several years. He had written and published much short fiction early in his career, but those were, as he notes in 'On Sycamore Hill,' actually 'novel-length ideas struggling to get out.' After publishing over forty stories between 1977 and 1981, his last science fiction story, 'The Changed Man and the King of Words,' had appeared in 1982. But the two stories he wrote during the Sycamore Hill Writers' Workshop in early 1985 were short stories by form and by design.

Second, they were *LDS* short stories. 'My stories focused around people surviving,' he wrote. 'Not just any people, *my* people, Mormons, and the non-Mormons who live among them and must adapt to this curiously secular religion.' For some time, he had been thinking about the plot lines for the stories that eventually appeared as 'Salvage' and 'The Fringe' (*Magazine of Fantasy and Science Fiction*, October 1985) – and one that appears in this volume for the first time, 'Pageant Wagon.' The stories, and the extended story of which they form a part, are uniquely science-fictional *and* Mormon in that they deal with the exclusivity of the community of faith and with the adjustments and adaptations that community must make to survive.

After the Sycamore Hill workshop, Card evaluated its effect on him, writing that he had 'realized then, that this milieu – of Mormon country under water, the survivors struggling to keep civilization alive – was viable; more important, *I* was viable. I had written two presentable short stories for the first time in years.'

Had the workshop just resulted in 'The Fringe' and 'Salvage,' it would have been a major achievement. Both stories were well received. 'The Fringe' garnered Hugo and Nebula nominations for Card and appeared in Gardner Dozois's *The Year's Best Science Fiction* collection in 1986; 'Salvage' appeared in the 1986 Nebula anthology, edited by George Zebrowski.

But there was more to the vision than these two

stories. In January 1987, *Asimov's* published the third story in the Mormon Sea series, 'America.' Here Card moved into a new and challenging direction. The first stories concentrated on Mormon backgrounds and folk beliefs. This one extrapolated from basic tenets of the Church. The Book of Mormon is the *sine qua non* of Mormonism, and its fundamental premise is the fulfillment of prophecy: America is the new Promised Land, and those who possess it do so with a responsibility for righteousness and worthiness. But in the world of the *The Folk of the Fringe*, European-Americans have abrogated that promise. The logical and inexorable corollary is that they have lost their right to the land itself. 'America' deals with the strict and literal fulfillment of prophecy as the Land itself raises up a new savior from among the Indians. It is legitimate as science fiction, understandable and moving, exploring possibilities and extrapolations. But it is even more powerful as LDS science fiction, based on assumptions central to what it is to be a Mormon, transcending rigid moralizing in its assertion of deeper truths.

Here is Card's greatest strength in *The Folk of the Fringe*, as it is in most of his works after the publication of his LDS historical novel, *Saints* (Tor, 1988; as *A Woman of Destiny*, Berkley, 1984). In his earlier works, he carefully excluded specific references to his own beliefs and religious heritage, although there are many allusions and stylistic connections in such novels as *Treason* and *The Worthing Chronicle*. Even *Ender's Game* and *Speaker for the Dead* – justly recognized as major achievements through their receiving the highest awards the science fiction community can bestow on its own – consciously avoid specifically LDS references, although the church is referred to in both, and in terms of style and symbolic content neither could have been written by a non-Mormon.

With 'Salvage' and 'The Fringe,' however, Card became more overt in incorporating his worldview into his fictions. His Alvin Maker series, beginning with *Seventh Son*, continues this direction as it builds on his LDS background to create a fantastic world that entertains while communicating specific values; a second series under contract, *Homecoming*, will transform the Book of Mormon history into science fiction, denying neither the truth of the former nor the artistic integrity of the latter. More and more, Card skillfully blends what has been called a uniquely American literary form, science fiction, with what has been called the only indigenous American religion, to create an entirely new perspective on speculation and extrapolation.

The Folk of the Fringe may be of greatest interest in that it includes the earliest manifestations of Card's combined vision. Throughout, the tales speak to science fiction readers as well as to Mormon readers, using a vocabulary appropriate to both.

Mormon readers unfamiliar with the conventions of science fiction may not understand at first what has happened prior to the opening paragraphs of 'West,' for example, but the post-holocaust setting resonates immediately for science fiction readers. The fact of nuclear exchange – if not the particulars of cause and extent – communicates readily through Card's control over the conventions of one branch of science fiction. Only later may such readers discover that this small band of survivors are in fact 'left-over Mormons.'

Non-Mormon readers, on the other hand, may initially have difficulties with references to Primary and bishoprics, to Lehi and the Liahona, or with the snatches of songs the children sing. But LDS readers will recognize the terms and, more importantly, the songs. We know at once that this story concerns our people, our history, our *epick* . . . no matter that it is disguised as future-oriented, speculative fiction. 'West' contains suffering, but is not about suffering; it is instead life-asserting, showing how faith unfolds even within a desperate struggle for survival. As did the

Mormon exodus in the nineteenth century, this story of expulsion and death ultimately affirms that there are things more important than death.

The Folk of the Fringe is not myopic, however. Not all Mormons are saints, not all are wise. In 'West,' the Christian Saints bear the burden of guilt for unjust acts; in 'America,' that burden is shared by all, including the Mormons, now caught between the mistakes of the past and the irrevocable, irresistible fulfillment of their own scriptures.

Here is the essence of science fiction – and of LDS science fiction: What if? *The Folk of the Fringe* speaks resoundingly to both audiences. The tales warn of human folly even as they affirm the value of human existence; they speculate about possible futures even as they refine and redefine our understanding of our past and of our present.